DEVIL IN BOOTS

STACEY MARIE BROWN

ALSO BY STACEY MARIE BROWN

Contemporary Romance

How the Heart Breaks

Buried Alive

Smug Bastard

The Unlucky Ones

Blinded Love Series
Shattered Love (#1)
Broken Love (#2)
Twisted Love (#3)

Royal Watch Series
Royal Watch (#1)
Royal Command (#2)

Paranormal Romance

A Winterland Tale
Descending into Madness (#1)
Ascending from Madness (#2)
Beauty in Her Madness (#3)
Beast in His Madness (#4)

Darkness Series
Darkness of Light (#1)
Fire in the Darkness (#2)
Beast in the Darkness (An Elighan Dragen Novelette)
Dwellers of Darkness (#3)
Blood Beyond Darkness (#4)
West (#5)

Collector Series
City in Embers (#1)
The Barrier Between (#2)
Across the Divide (#3)
From Burning Ashes (#4)

Lightness Saga
The Crown of Light (#1)
Lightness Falling (#2)
The Fall of the King (#3)
Rise from the Embers (#4)
Savage Lands Series
Savage Lands (#1)
Wild Lands (#2)
Dead Lands (#3)
Bad Lands (#4)
Blood Lands (#5)
Shadow Lands (#6)

Devil in the Deep Blue Sea
Silver Tongue Devil #1

See end of book for foreign translations

Timeline

Collector Series
Ends Here

FAE WAR
Darkness Series Ends here

Eastern Countries secede
from Unified Nations 1 year
after war.

Battle with Stavros/Stone of Fal
2 years after Fae War.

Croygen Leaves,
returning to piracy.
Lightness Series Ends here

The substance called nectar
is discovered 5 years after Fae War
and 15 years before Savage Lands.

Wars between Fae and
Humans in the Eastern
intensify.

Istvan finds Dr. Rapava's work.
Starts experiments.

Savage Lands starts 20 years
after Fae War.

CHAPTER 1
Croygen

Horse hooves pounded across the rocky ground, high above the fog, which still blanketed the valley below. Pinnacles of plant-covered rocks spiked high into the muggy air in dramatic formations, like blades turned in battle to the blue skies above. Dense green foliage trapped the humidity, and a buzz of insects hummed loudly in my ear.

Every sense was alive. Every nerve sparked under my skin, but nothing penetrated beyond the superficial. My thoughts, my drive, my goal were on one thing. I was a madman obsessed, and nothing would get in my way.

It felt more like I was possessed, a demon seizing me from the inside out, directing me as if I were its pet.

Anger kept the fear simmering underneath, or maybe it was fear that kept the anger checked. Both spurred me forward; my gut twisted at the task ahead.

Save Katrina and find this matter called *the nectar*.

This substance would change the world as we knew it, giving humans fae-like qualities. Equal power. And this wouldn't be used for all to come together for some kumbaya moment. No, it would be used for war. To annihilate the "others," no matter the costs. Humans had tried it before with fae, sending us to the Otherworld. Now no such place existed. Earth and the fae world were one, and humans were duking it out for supremacy, trying to find ways to once again be superior.

This would give them even footing to challenge us, annihilating us for good. *If* this substance was as real as it was said to be. A Dr. Novikov, an old associate of the demented Dr. Rapava, was alleged to have located it and was now on the run, hiding in the caves. But outside of this rumor being spread through the papers, no one else had seen it, held it, or had proof of it. We might find Novikov sitting in the corner of the cave, hugging a rock, whispering to it, calling it "Precious."

And Kat's life was on the line for an item that might not even exist.

Her face flashed in my mind, taking me back to the night before, recalling how her pussy locked on my cock, pumping me dry. Her purr wrapped around me, making me feel like nothing in the world could take me down. As if I finally found my place—the home I wanted to stay in forever.

It was the most intense, insane sex I had ever had. This coming from a man who'd had hundreds of thousands of partners over the centuries. Kinky, deviant, sweet, violent, slow, S&M, dom/sub, I'd had it all. This was different. It consumed me, drowned me, and had me so satisfied I think *I* was fucking purring, yet I craved her the moment I was no longer inside her.

Which had me feeling sick with guilt and crazed with need.

I still tasted her on my tongue. Her release still coated my cock, and her smell lingered on me. But there was more than that—a strange sensation, as if I could feel her pulling me forward, like I knew where she was, and she needed me.

But it was all in my head. It *had* to be. Because… no, it just had to be.

It was a one-time thing. A line I shouldn't have crossed in the first place. I never should have touched her. Katrina Roth, the daughter of Friedrich Roth, my old first mate, the man I stabbed through the heart.

The woman who was once my family was now my enemy.

"So, you plundered her treasure, huh? Pilfered the booty? Jolly'd your Roger? Did you scream out '*Thar she blows!*'" a voice jabbered in my ear, crunching my shoulders higher.

"Sprig." I choked out his name. Underwear fluttered against my cheek, his "cape" flapping in the breeze.

When he learned Kat was gone, he put it on, saying, "Super Sprig is on the case." He tucked his backpack with Pam in my side saddle, climbing on my shoulder, chanting his hero song.

"I can understand why *Bhean chait* ran off."

"She didn't run off." I clenched my teeth, guiding the horse over the terrain. "She was taken."

"Sure." He snorted. "So you say. Be honest, rum-licker, she was Dear John-ing your ass."

"What?"

"Dear John-ing." He sighed like I was an idiot. "She dumped you and ran. Probably so common you forget it's not what women do after you fire in their hole."

A rumble gurgled up the back of my throat. My patience and mood were on the cusp of annihilating everything in my anger.

"Sprig…" Annabeth's horse trotted closer to mine, its rider's tone full of warning. She could sense how thin the line was I walked. "Why don't you ride with me for a bit?"

"Oh, I couldn't leave the booty-humper alone in his time of need. When he has been so brutally and cruelly dumped like that? I mean, she even faked getting kidnapped to get away from him."

"She didn't fake—"

"I mean, that's *bad*, sooooo humiliating. Not sure how he is even able to function today and is not rocking in a corner. She must have been *desperate* to get away. Poor *Bhean chait*. What she must have gone through. I've thought about doing that when I'm around him too—"

"Oh, would you?" I replied through my teeth. "For real?"

"But I know you need me, cock-swan." He patted my cheek. "I'm here for you."

"Coxswain." My lids squeezed together, and a bellow threatened to roar from me, shaking the ground underfoot.

"I have honey," AB sang out.

"See ya, assbandit! Honeyhoneyhoneyhoneyhoney-honey!" Sprig leaped for AB, the black underwear sailing behind him as he jumped on Churro, patting the horse on the head and scrambling to the frail blonde. Every day AB seemed to get thinner, paler, and weaker. It was probably my imagination, but I was so hyperaware of Annabeth's sickness that it was like I could see her deteriorating before my eyes, which only drove me faster to the caves.

Getting this nectar wasn't just to save Katrina or fulfill Kat's vow; it was to save Annabeth's life. Our only chance.

The ghost of Lexie whispered in my ear, telling me to save Annabeth, to protect her at all costs. To do for AB what I couldn't do for her.

I pushed my horse into a full gallop, and Tootsie stayed right up next to Caramel. Kat's horse didn't even need to be tied to mine; she stayed right on my side, neighing and huffing, like she knew her rider was in trouble too, wanting to get to her. Katrina's boots and jacket were stuffed in the saddle bag, waiting for their owner to return and claim them.

Annabeth's horse, Churro, stayed close to me while Cooper remained a little behind us to make sure no one was following, sniffing the air, his senses on alert.

We spotted camping sites along the way, as groups of

treasure seekers clustered more and more frequently as we got to our location. It felt odd to see all the people who were going after the same thing still being civil to each other. Soon they would be rivals. Threats. How long until this politeness turned to bloodshed?

Following a gushing river, we came into a clearing, my head turning to the side. Tugging back on the reins, I urged Caramel to a stop as I took in the awe-inspiring view.

"Damn," I muttered. I didn't believe in many things, didn't care about much more, but nature, whether on sea or land, was where I saw true magic. A spirituality I felt and respected.

My head tipped back, my gaze going up high into the sky, the Tenglong Cave kissing the clouds. The width of it was so broad I felt like an ant, inconsequential to its mere existence. I understood why dragons chose this as their home. It was one of those places that dotted your flesh with goosebumps as you got lost in the grandeur.

Only years ago, hundreds of tourists milled around, touring, helicopters flying in and out of the massive caverns, a pebble compared to what used to reside in these caves centuries ago. Tour guides kept you on a certain path, telling you tales of "mythical dragons inhabiting these caves." Humans would walk along, imagining these Hollywood creations, as if it were some high fantasy story they could indulge in, *pretend*, when it was actually true.

The creatures were solitary animals who, only when threatened, would attack. But then humans turned them into killing monsters who were destroyed. They slaughtered them by the thousands, hunting them down in their caves when they were asleep and most vulnerable. And slowly the dragons and dragon-shifters went extinct.

Yet, even after generations, I still felt their magic humming from the cave, the crackle against my skin which told me to not enter, to turn around and run. Even now, humans would feel a little rush of anxiety, an overwhelming sensation of nervousness on entering the caves, a nip of warning at the back of their necks. When dragons were still around, their magic would keep most from even discovering the cave, magic that protected themselves and their treasure.

Slipping off Caramel, I slowly approached the entrance. A few groups were already making their way down the well-worn trail carved for the tours, their lanterns, axes, and shovels in their hands.

"Fuck." Cooper's voice startled me, whipping my head to the man standing beside me, a strange expression on his face.

"What?"

His eyes still moved over the entrance, a pool of water glinting from deeper in the fissure. "I've felt this magic before."

"Really? When?"

"In Greece. When we went hunting for the Sword of Nuada. It was hidden deep in a cave dragons also used to inhabit. The magic was *a lot* weaker there than here, so I didn't even think about why the sword was hidden there. Now it makes sense." He shifted his shoulders like the intensity bothered him. "The dragon magic had concealed it for millennia until it started to fade away."

The Sword of Nuada was one of the four treasures of Tuatha dé Danann. Sword, stone, cauldron, and spear. When gods and goddesses gave a select group of witches power that even fae could not challenge, Druids were created. They crafted such powerful objects they could destroy the world, their magic too much for even the strongest of fae.

They had a lot to do with why the Otherworld (Tuatha dé Danann) did not exist anymore and why Lexie and so many others had died when Stavros tried to take Lars's throne. The greed to obtain these objects, to rule, had been the downfall of the fae world and the reason they should never be found by fae or humans.

And here we were, trying to find one that might hold even *more* power and be even more critical if it fell into the wrong hands.

Cooper exhaled, his gaze darting back to where Annabeth was watering and feeding the horses, Sprig on her shoulder. I could feel his anxiety, his need to grab her and walk her right on out of here, keeping her clear of any danger.

"I know." I followed his line of sight. "But it's too late now. You know she will never let us go without her."

"For such a little thing, she is far more stubborn than people think." Cooper rubbed his brow.

"And it's why you love her." I smirked.

A hint of a smile played on Cooper's mouth, knowing I was right. He loved that about her. She challenged him, kept him in line. As sweet as AB was, she was also *fiercely* loyal and tenacious when it came to her family. I think because all she had gone through, losing her parents, her grandparents not really wanting her, she put her entire heart and soul into her "found" family. Into Cooper, Zoey, Ryker, Wyatt, Sprig, and me. And she put her heart into the orphanage she and Zoey ran.

"Speaking of stubborn women." Cooper smirked at me, slapping my shoulder. "Let's get this nectar so we can get yours back."

"She not mine," I snapped.

"Sure." He grinned, turning for the horses, his smile smug. "I said the same thing about Annabeth once." He looked over his shoulder. "Even I knew I was full of shit."

He strolled away, leaving me with a sick, sticky feeling in my gut—a sensation that I could feel her somewhere nearby, and if I pulled on the thread, it would lead me right to her.

Following behind Cooper, I shoved that thought deep back, because it would mean something I didn't want or couldn't have. Not with her.

Opportunists didn't hesitate, jumping on the chance to profit from those seeking the nectar. These were the true business people, providing shovels and carts, food, and gear. They were the ones who got wealthy, not the ones searching for gold.

Several people were already hocking "maps" of the cave and tools to dig it up like it really was gold. Another man had set up a corral for horses; his fee had the tradesman in me both offended and impressed. There were others providing food and water or their version of a "real" map, making far more than anyone here would.

Against everything in my being, I forked over money for boarding the horses, making sure the guy would be taking good care of them.

"I'll be back." I rubbed Caramel's nose, Tootsie nudging my arm. "And I will bring her back too." I scratched Tootsie's neck. I wasn't really a horse person, my life was on the sea, but these guys felt different. The voyage here had bonded me to them.

"Now behave, you guys." Sprig sprang onto my shoulder, talking to the horses. "No horsing around, okay?" He laughed, nudging my neck, wearing his pack with Pam sticking out on his back. "Get it? Horse-ing around!"

"Wonder how much that guy will take to watch you too?" I rubbed at my temple, the hot morning sun already dotting sweat down my spine.

"You need me, butt-neer." He shoved his hands in my face. "You need these… magic hands!"

"I'm about to shove those magic hands up your ass."

"What do you think I was doing last night with them?" Sprig's response had me groaning. "How I know they're magic."

"Once again, I walked right into that." I sighed to myself, grabbing my heavy pack and tossing it over the shoulder he was on, causing him to scurry. Sticking out his tongue, he jumped into AB's bag, flipping me off before disappearing.

My anxiety rose at seeing a steady stream of people heading into the cave. Some would give up and go home, but many may not come out again.

Greed and desperation did awful things to humanity. When everything else was stripped away, you discovered what kind of person you could be.

I already knew what kind of person I was. What I was capable of. I was capable of killing without remorse. I could slit someone's throat with a joke on my lips. And that was without AB's or Kat's life on the line. They thought the monster was the merciless Dark Dweller next to me… little did they know.

Cooper, Annabeth, and I stepped into the entrance, the temperature already lowering several degrees as my eyes adjusting to the dimness. The massive cavity consumed people and voices, all lost in the vastness between the ground and ceiling. The horde of people followed the designated tourist path, groups tailing each other like ants marching in line.

That route would be controlled, keeping the sightseers on a structured trail. It would lead them deeper into the cave, but not down to where we wanted to go. We needed to find a different way.

"Sense anything?" I asked Cooper.

He lifted his nose, his pupils going horizontal as he took in the scents, reminding me of last night with Kat and how her eyes glowed when she came. Her pupils also went horizontal, and her claws dug into my back, tearing at my skin, her mouth parting in a cry. I recalled how she felt coming around my cock, how it felt sinking even deeper in her, fucking her even harder before I exploded inside her.

Heat zinged down my limbs, straight to my dick, my teeth

grinding together. My lids slammed shut as I tried to calm the erection growing in my pants. *Fuck, I need to get a handle on this.*

"Come on," Cooper muttered, tearing my eyes back open. He took off around the large pond, his body low, blending into the shadows, moving opposite of everyone else.

Nudging AB before me, I took out my gun, following behind, keeping watch on anyone taking notice of us. Both Cooper and I could practically disappear in front of people's eyes. Our trio easily blended into the landscape, the lack of electricity in the caves making it easy to meld into the blackness.

Cooper found a set of hidden stone stairs leading down to what looked like a maintenance room, the darkness thickening the lower we went, absorbing any light above.

"I can't see," Annabeth whispered. I heard the panic she was trying to hide. It was getting harder and harder for me to see; only Cooper and Kat had night vision.

I yanked out a flashlight, hoping we were down far enough so no one would see the beam. Flicking the torch on, I guided AB down the rest of the stairs to Cooper.

"Locked." His eyes glinted similarly to both a wolf's and a panther's in the torchlight. "Magic-locked."

"What?" My brows shot up. "Really?"

"Is that odd?" AB glanced between us.

"Yeah." My forehead creased. "This was human-run before. A tourist destination. And since the fall of the wall, it was abandoned. So a regular lock, I can see, but magic-locked?" I tipped my head, and Cooper and I exchanged looks.

"Like someone's been through here who would know to do that." Cooper picked up on my own thoughts.

"Would have a *reason* to do it," I added, prickles of warning firing up the back of my neck, causing my skin to itch. Would the doctor have gone this way? Know to magic spell the door to stop people from following? "Do you smell anyone?"

Cooper shook his head. "Not strong enough. There are so many smells, too many people and fae magic around to get anything clear. I smell a mix of human and fae, but I can't pinpoint anyone. I just saw the passage coming down this way and had an instinct to follow it."

I would never second guess a Dark Dweller's instinct. It was in every cell of their makeup to hunt and track their prey.

"Hey, possum droppings." I tapped Annabeth's bag. "You're up."

Silence.

"Hey." I patted harder.

"I'm not talking to you." A muffled voice came through.

"Normally I would thank the sea goddesses for that, but right now we need you to unlock the door."

Nothing.

"Sprig," I gritted.

His head popped out of the bag. "What do you *say*, pirate hooker?" He blinked at me, feigning innocence.

I stared at him through lowered lids. "Just unlock the *fucking* door before you become monkey pie."

"That's not the way to ask nicely." He waved his finger at me. "Oh wait, did you say pie? I'm starving. It's lunchtime, right? Dinner? Second dinner? I'm craving churros, ohhhh... honey pie, honey cakes with honey drizzle... oh wait, is it supper? Honey chicken sandwich, or honey beef kabobs, honey fried—"

"Sprig, open the damn door," I growled. "Now!"

"Geeeeeez, someone's grumpy. You think you'd be nicer since you got your Jolly Rancher sucked." Sprig climbed out of the bag. "Can totally see why *Bhean chait* had people kidnap her. I mean, no one likes STD flavor."

"She didn't—" My fingers curled up with an aspirated noise from my throat. I gave up on trying to explain. "Just unlock the door."

Sprig hopped down AB's arm as she took him closer to the knob. He wiggled his fingers like he was warming them up, touching the handle. While he fiddled with the bolt, Cooper and I turned our attention behind us, making sure no one was sneaking up on us.

"Allllmooost got it." One eye twitched. Several moments went by. "Allllmoooosttt… there…"

Clink.

The door creaked open.

"See! Magic hands!" He waved his hands in the air. "What do you say, cockbuckler?"

"You're lucky I haven't stuffed you in a bottle and thrown you out to sea?" I grumbled, knocking past him, shining the torch in the room. The electrical room looked frozen in time, as it was five years before when it stopped working. The moment the wall between worlds disintegrated, magic funneled into Earth like a tsunami, fritzing out everything electrical, which was so much more than people imagined.

Nothing looked odd as we moved through the room, but I couldn't stop the uneasy sensation scraping down my back, warning me. It had nothing to do with the actual rooms, but what was ahead of us.

The first room was filled with all the generators and electrical stuff. The second was small and empty, but had a door. Opening it slowly, my gun drawn, my torch lighting up the darkness, I peered down a metal staircase, descending farther into the windowless caves.

The depth of the sea was as dark as night, with places at the bottom where not a sliver of light was able to penetrate. That's what this felt like—the darkness was the deep water wrapping around my lungs, suffocating me while I descended into its domain.

I couldn't even sleep with my door locked on my ship, afraid of being trapped with no escape. This was ten times worse because I understood the ocean, respected its power, its right to take life when it demanded it. There was a vivacity to the sea. She was a temperamental mistress. She spoke a language only true sailors could understand, as if all the sirens in the world sang the song beckoning us back to her.

This place was cold, empty, though I did feel life calling from the depth. It made me feel uneasy, like something was not right. A force I was not prepared for.

"There is a power, something I've never felt before ahead of us." Tsai's voice came back to me. *"I feel if we go, not all of us will return."*

Why did her words feel like a foreshadowing?

CHAPTER 2
Croygen

Our feet echoed, accompanied by the soft sound of water trailing down the cave walls, tapping on the rocks. The water bled into the cave from the river rushing close by, bubbling up underground streams through the cave. I timed my breaths to the drops of water, focusing on them like sand in an hourglass. Water soothed the anxiety, the nails clawing on the inside of my skin to get out and feel the wind on my face, taste the salty ocean on my lips.

Though something else pulled me forward, a restlessness I couldn't find the ultimate reason for. Anger, fear, and desperation strangled my lungs. Of course, finding the nectar for AB and Kat drove me forward, but there was something else. It unsettled me, made me feel violent and unhinged, the desire to plow through the rocks, tear them all down.

For her...

A voice nipped in the back of my brain.

No. I shook my head, trying to push away my own thought as it settled in my chest. *Fuck no.*

Although I couldn't deny the notion, I felt her. If I reached out, I would be able to find her. Like she was latched on to me, and no matter where I went in this world, I would know where she was in it.

No. No. No. No. That idea had acid swirling in my stomach, terror clamping down on my lungs.

"*Bebinn,* I'm *dy-ing!*" Chatter reached my ears from several feet in front of me, the back of Annabeth's head outlined by my torch. "I mean, I'm on the verge of no return. Look around, I'm already here. In the pits of despair. So don't I get a final meal? A last wish on a dying sprite's bed? Is there no compassion in this cruel, cruel world?"

"You had a granola bar ten minutes ago."

"Exactly!" Sprig's shape stood up on her shoulder. "And let me say that one was lacking the proper ratio of honey. I feel like I'm withering away."

"It was a trail mix *honey* granola bar."

"See, the trail mix took up all the room for more honey," he whimpered, sagging back on his heels. "I mean, it didn't even have honey drizzle on top."

"Hey, fur pelt." I pointed my beam directly at Sprig's face, highlighting the tiny monkey on her shoulder. "Shut the hell up."

"But… I'm gonna die!" He sniffed. "Does no one care?"

"No!" Both Cooper and I said in unison.

The Dark Dweller was directing us; his senses and ability to see in the dark put him as lead, taking us through the pitch-black caves with only our flashlights to guide us.

"*Bebinn…*" Sprig's bottom lip stuck out, whining. "I'm dy-ing! And you look like you need nutrients too."

My light caught AB's face. Pale, tired, she appeared ready to drop, yet she pushed on without one complaint. It had been hours without a break. Up and down huge boulders, squeezing through small fissures, crossing creeks, scaling rocks. It had to be draining for her.

"You're right. We should stop and take a break," I said.

"What?" Sprig's head darted to me in shock. "Did you say I'm right?"

"Don't let your pea size brain explode. You've been either sleeping, eating, or sitting there complaining." I motioned to the three of us. "*We* need a break."

"I got down a few times."

"To pee in the stream," I shot back.

"I pooed too!"

Shaking my head, I tugged off my pack, getting food and water out while Cooper started a fire. The massive cavern glowed under the flames, making it feel like a campfire at night. I had no idea what time it was, but Annabeth's fatigue and the fact she didn't fight us when we told her to sit while we set up told me we were done for the day.

The need to keep moving nipped at me, like I had restless body syndrome itching at my muscles, almost to the point I couldn't sit still. Taking out a bottle of whiskey, I downed a gulp, needing to take the edge off.

While cooking up some bean stew, Cooper rolled out the sleeping bags, getting AB comfy.

"Foodfoodfoodfood!" Sprig danced around the fire like he was part of some ancient ritual, his arms waving in the air, his cape dragging across the ground. "Does this have honey in it?"

"Oh, sorry, it's made with bananas." I shrugged one shoulder.

"What?" His arms sunk down, his eyes going wide.

"Yep, sorry. This bean stew is made purely of bananas and banana chips."

"Wha-wha-what?" Sprig's face crumbled.

"Croy-gen…" AB sighed heavily, gripping the blanket around her shoulders as if she was freezing.

It was cool, but not cold.

Her body was no longer able to keep her warm; it was too busy trying to fight off the cancer spreading through her.

I gulped down another pull of liquor.

"Why would they put bananas in it? Why? I knew this was

the pits of hell. My final meal is going to kill me. Death by a yellow dick." Sprig wailed from the other side of the fire. "Why? Why me?"

"Sprig." AB yanked out a honey packet. "To tide you over."

His eyes went wide, his tiny body starting to shake.

"Oh fuck," I muttered, knowing the signs of what was coming.

"Ahhhhhh!" He started going in circles, his excitement exploding out of him. "Honeyhoneyhoneyhoneyhoneyhoney!" He zoomed around the fire for Annabeth, his fingers already grabbing for the packet. "Givemegivemegivemegiveme… honeyhoneyhoney!" He danced around her like a puppy waiting for treats. "Ahhhh! Honey!" Leaping for it, he passed out midair, his fingers just clasping onto the plastic before he went headfirst onto her sleeping bag.

I chuckled at how his body curled around the honey packet like a lover, snores already sounding from him.

"He is entertaining." I snorted, swallowing back more whiskey. "I'll give him that."

"And you egg it on." Annabeth shook her head with a smile.

"He deserves it."

"You two really do act like siblings." She winked at me.

"Bite your tongue." I wrinkled my nose. "That thing is a circus act at best."

She started to laugh, but it switched quickly to a hacking violent cough, her lungs gasping and straining as she wheezed and grappled for air in between. Her eyes pooled with tears, her body almost jackknifing with each cough.

Cooper darted down to her, rubbing her back, whispering to her, soothing her muscles, like this was something he was used to doing. While I sat there like stone. Helpless. Useless. Terrified. Not knowing what to do, how to act, pretending it was nothing big because I wasn't supposed to know, but very aware I did.

In that moment, I really realized I was losing Annabeth. Sooner than any of us wanted, she would no longer be here. Another vacancy. Another hole in our hearts. A chasm nothing could ever fill.

And Cooper would probably go with her.

Another reason I never wanted a mate. To feel so much for someone that you no longer wanted to exist because they weren't there. No, thank you. I was far too selfish and in love with myself to do that.

The death of one's mate was basically a slow death for the other. They would keep living, but as such an empty shell of themselves, most didn't see the point. All species of fae were slightly different in how extreme their reaction to a mate's death was. To Dark Dwellers, their mate was life, so it pretty much equaled the end for them too. Either they'd wither away into a suit of bones, or they joined their mate.

There was no doubt what Cooper would choose.

So in AB's death, we would lose two people.

The moment he calmed her, laying her back on the rollout to rest, I rose, needing to get away and take a moment.

The fire gave me enough light to stroll down to the small stream running through the cavern. Splashing water on my face, I gazed up, sucking in a deep breath.

Everything felt so out of control, out of my hands, and I hated it. Even in the most extreme situations, I always felt like I had the upper hand. This time I felt like I was being played.

Your little kitty dies. I won't hesitate. But you already know that about me. The letter in my pocket burned through my mind, that last line tapping at something, nagging me to understand, to figure it out. A puzzle I didn't have all the pieces to.

"Gods dammit, Katrina." Her name whispered from my lips, and I rubbed my face with irritation.

A wisp of her scent, the feel of her sliding over me like a ghost, my name whispered back through my gut.

"Croygen."

My head jerked up, air halting in my lungs, my heart pounding. But the moment vanished faster than it came, leaving only the bubbling stream talking to me.

Groaning, I scoured my eyes, feeling like I was losing my mind. Being away from the sea was making me crazy. I missed my ship, my crew, and the open water. With Tsai and Scot in charge, I knew they'd be okay, but I longed to get back to where I belonged.

Walking back, I found Annabeth sound asleep in Cooper's arms. His gaze drifted to me as he stroked her hair. I sensed the grief and fear, the desperation and sliver of hope that this nectar might save her.

If we lost AB, it wouldn't only be Cooper who'd fall over the edge. She was my redemption, my salvation. It would be the only thing Lexie would ask of me—save her sister. There was nothing I wouldn't do; I just didn't know if it was in my power. Though with Cooper and I, if it was even a small possibility, we would find a way.

Whomever I had to kill, whatever I had to do. I would do it.

Taking the beans off the fire, I struggled down a few bites before wrapping them up for later. Rolling out of my bed, I muttered to Cooper to sleep. I'd be on watch.

Hours of staring at flames dancing across the cavern walls, listening to the soothing sound of the stream and my companions' heavy breathing lowered my lids, dropping me into slumber.

I knew I was dreaming. Grazing the surface between awareness and unconsciousness, like a specter. I peered down at Katrina, her body curled up, her eyes shut. Her arms and legs were tied, a metal goblin band wrapped around her wrist, keeping her from shifting.

A mix of fury at seeing her tied up and peace knowing she was okay fought for dominance. Though the longer I stared at her stunning face, my chest warmed, and I exhaled a happy sigh.

"Katrina…" I slid my fingers through her hair, feeling her silky strands on my skin. Her body stirred at my touch, but her eyes stayed closed.

This was a dream. I understood that, but she felt so real, like this was really happening.

Still wearing my shirt, she now had on ill-fitted black pants and worn shoes. Her face was bruised, her lip freshly cut, telling me these weren't wounds from the fight in the barn. They were new. They had beaten her.

Anger filled me like a cannon, ready to detonate. The need to protect her and kill whoever dared to touch her flowed through me. I tried to peer around, find the culprit, but I saw nothing except shadowy forms by a fire in the distance, hearing low murmurs I wasn't able to make out. But I knew they were in the same caves.

"*Katze*?" I whispered, my thumb sliding over her bleeding lip, feeling the cut and blood on my skin. How the hell could I feel it in a dream? This wasn't even real, right?

My gut was telling me differently.

"Kitty-Kat?" I rumbled in her ear.

She stirred again; her lids fluttered but stayed closed.

"Wake up." I brushed my thumb over her cheek again. "I need you to tell me where you are."

Her brows furrowed in pain, awareness pulling her from numbing slumber.

"Kitten. Wake up," I growled.

Her lids popped open, her head lifting. Her eyes met mine. Seeing me, seeing into my soul. She sat up, her mouth parting in surprise and fear.

"Where are you?" I asked, my voice feeling further away. I felt something pulling me back to my slumbering body. An awareness stirring me.

A warning.

Katrina's attention darted behind me, her eyes widening. I tried to turn to see who was coming. All I saw was a thin silhouette in the shape of a woman before Katrina's voice jerked me back to her.

"Croygen," she screamed.

As if my soul was sucked back into my body, adrenaline bolted me awake with a gasp, my body knifing up. I grabbed the gun next to me, already sensing the danger approaching.

The fire burned low, but I could see figures moving in on us.

Cooper jolted up, his instincts so finely tuned he didn't even hesitate, fear shifting him instantly into his dweller form. His clothes tore off him as a handful of men emerged from the darkness, their guns and swords drawn. They no longer cared about a sneak attack.

Cooper's roar rattled the cave, the blades down his back glinting from the fire, his enormous mass leaping for the group. Screams of death pierced the air, his claws shredding through the first two.

Bullets whizzed by my head, one slicing through my shirt.

"Annabeth! Go!" I waved her to get away from the fight. Instead, she yanked a gun from her bag, aiming it at our attackers, firing shot after shot as if she had been training with firearms for years.

I rushed toward the men, sword in one hand, a gun in the other. I flipped between the two, slicing through one as I shot another in the chest.

The dweller prowled through them, his flesh bleeding with bullet holes, but they had no chance once he got close, his claws and teeth cutting three more in half as I skewered the final one, my blade piercing through his stomach, pinning him to the ground. Keeping him alive on purpose, I towered over his body. His eyes were a blue-violet.

Low-bred, but a fairy. Seelie. Though those titles were starting not to hold as much weight as they once did now that the Otherworld was gone.

"Who are you?" I heaved for air, blood pumping in my ears. I peered around at the dozen bodies—light, brown, tall, short, though most seemed similar to each other in their features.

Eastern European.

Breathing heavily, he glared at me, not answering.

My gaze went down his form, taking in the dark clothes, a small crest on his arm—two circles with a sword cutting through the middle, the blade and handle engraved with Celtic symbols. It reminded me of the Sword of Nuada, but I didn't know anyone who would dare to have that as their insignia. Who took something that destroyed so many lives and wore it as a badge of honor?

What it did tell me was this wasn't a random war party moving through and killing people. They were trained soldiers. Had a purpose. "Why did you attack us?" I pushed my blade deeper. He grunted, snot falling from his nose, his lips pressing together in silence.

"He asked you a question," Cooper growled, his massive naked body stomping up, covered in blood, his eyes still flaming red. "Tell us or die." His words still struggled to come out clearly, his dweller barely under the surface.

"Baszd meg!" Fuck off. The man spat, hitting Cooper in the face.

Cooper's shoulders expanded, his spine spiking with blades, his hand forming claws. A snarl roared from Cooper as he swiped across the guy's neck. Blood sprayed over both of us, the man's body going limp as his head rolled off.

"Well, so much for questioning him." I wiped my face with my sleeve.

"He wasn't gonna answer anyway," Cooper grumbled, standing up, slowly returning to his human form.

"They were Hungarian. At least he was." I yanked my blade from his chest. "Like the group that was following us back on the road."

"They want to limit the competition." Cooper shrugged, strolling up to Annabeth, making sure she was okay, not caring that he was not only naked, but looked like he was ready to fuck her up against the wall, his muscles twitching with energy.

"Then why not just kill us back on the road? Doesn't make sense." Why did this feel like it wasn't an arbitrary attack? That it was personal?

My mouth opened to talk when what felt like a train drove through me, almost bending me over.

My skin zapped with energy, my soul twisting with sudden awareness… *of her*. I felt her.

My heart pounded in my chest with terror, knowing she needed me. I didn't know how, but I knew she did. I tasted her fear, felt her heartbeat, and heard her call my name.

My body reacted without pause. Grabbing a torch, I took off across the rocky terrain, not giving any thought but following the pull to her, like I could find her no matter where she was.

"Croygen!" Cooper bellowed my name, his calls growing fainter as I ran faster.

I had no control, no other thoughts than to get to her. Because through the darkness, the light leading me forward… was Katrina.

CHAPTER 3
Katrina

Pain sliced through my skull, bringing me out of unconsciousness. Flinching, I tried to reach up to soothe the ache in my head, but nothing worked, my arms not obeying, my lids still too heavy to fully open. Everything hurt, and I longed to slip back into the void where no pain or confusion existed.

As if sifting through mud, my brain struggled to recall my last memories. Glimpses of Croygen, a barn, an alleyway…

Voices murmured around me, pulling me further from peace, tugging my lids fully up. My blurry vision took in a fire shining in the gloom of heavy darkness a few feet away, and I inhaled the scent of stale, damp air and dirt. Cave walls towered above me, dripping with blackness. Even my cat eyes could barely penetrate the gloom.

Shifting on the cold ground, I groaned from deep within my chest, my muscles protesting, tight, sore, and stressed. Peering down, I noticed a shirt, pants, and shoes that weren't mine. A rope bound my wrists and ankles, and a goblin metal bracelet encircled my arm, keeping me lethargic and unable to shift.

Recollections formed in my thoughts—figures approaching me in a dark alley, someone knocking me over the head before everything went dark. An image of a woman leaning over me.

The same feeling tickled the back of my brain, like I knew her, recognized her face, but my mind was still too murky to put it together.

Then my brain rolled back to the barn and the fight with the assailants before. Heat burned through my body up to my cheeks, reminding me it wasn't only fighting that caused me to be so sore. My core pulsed, my thighs and ass burned with the memory of his hands. My skin thrummed with electricity, singling out every mark he put on me and how I had loved it.

Desire flushed through me as I tore my thoughts from him to what needed to take precedence.

Not important right now, Kat. Getting out of here is.

Twisting my head to slyly look around me, I counted a dozen silhouettes, all men, setting up camp, mainly talking in Mandarin. No one was paying me any notice, and I used that to take in more of my surroundings, searching for anything that might help me.

Noticing a sharp rock near my feet, I subtly wiggled down, tapping my shoe over it and slowly dragging it up. With every slight movement, I watched the men, hoping they wouldn't see what I was doing. I tried to pretend I was still asleep while moving the rock up far enough until I could reach it.

Ten minutes later, my fingers wrapped around the stone, pushing it between the ropes cuffing my wrists. The goblin metal would keep me from shifting, but if I could free myself of the ropes, I might have a chance of running.

Time seemed to stand still, sweat pooling down my back as I sawed at the rope. What felt like hours went by before I felt a break in the twine, loose enough so my hands could slip out. Bucking the need to escape, I kept the rope around my hands for appearances as I curled up tighter, starting on the rope between my ankles.

"Nǐ zài zuò!" What are you doing? a voice barked, freezing me in place. The air stalled in my lungs, and I waited for someone to stomp over and grab me. When no one came, I pried open my lashes, seeing the man marching over to another, the pair arguing. Air heaved through my lips, my throat swallowing back my fear.

Come on, Kat. You've been in worse situations than this, I berated myself. Since I was a kid on the streets, getting out of precarious circumstances was my thing. I learned young to never count on anyone else.

I saved myself.

Getting back to work, I rubbed at the rope, the goblin metal stealing more and more of my energy. I couldn't let it beat me. When I got loose, I had to run, because whatever reason I was taken was not a good one. My theory? I was being used as bait.

The men's voices suddenly stopped, their attitudes changing in a blink as they stood up straight. I knew their leader was coming.

A slim, lithe figure sauntered closer to the fire, and their heads bowed to this woman in sheer terror and respect. The shadows hid her face, but I saw she was taller than me with a model-thin figure. Her long, dark hair was up in a messy bun, and she wore designer cargo-style pants and a black shirt with clean boots. She appeared like she should be on a photo shoot for hiking and camping, not actually doing it.

She paid them no mind, her thin legs heading straight for me. The flames from the fire illuminated her features, causing a gasp to stick in my throat. I was no longer pretending to be asleep.

"You," I whispered, recalling the woman I met in the bathroom weeks ago in Shanghai.

A malicious smile curved her face, like I was the fool for not seeing through her facade.

"You believed I was some common whore trying to kindly warn you against Croygen's meandering ways?" She squatted down, her head tipping. She no longer bothered with the Chinese inflection, her phrasing now thicker and rougher, but I couldn't place where it was from. "How precious." Cruelty tightened her features. "If you *really* knew him, you'd know he doesn't sleep with prostitutes. He doesn't see the point." I sensed a familiarity there, a possessiveness, which women felt without a word being said. "Always an angle with him, looking out for himself. So if you thought you were more than a fuck of convenience, you are far more naive than I gave you credit for."

"Then why take me?" My mouth shot back before I even thought about responding, feeling the dig she was trying to make. "I mean, why bother kidnapping me if I am nothing to him?"

"Because he likes to play the part of a good man." Again, a malevolent smile played on her mouth. "You will see he is not."

"I already know he's not a good man." I glowered back. "And I do know him. I know him better than anyone. And I can pick out a woman he's left in his wake at a glance. Bitter, heartbroken, resentful, and angry they couldn't tame him. Still holding on because they hope he will give them another chance. I saw you women all the time." The stream of words dashed off my tongue; my hatred for this woman was not something I understood. "Hurts to find you're nothing special, huh?"

"Oh, you have no clue," she snarled back, her shoulders rising. "You're just another one of his little disciples who I'll have to put in their place." This felt personal. She didn't just take me for leverage. She wanted to make a point.

"Disciples?" I laughed. "I'm not the one following him like a stalker and kidnapping the woman he *fucked* last night because I'm jealous." Stopping my mouth was impossible. I wanted to hurt her, to let her know he was with me. It was so unlike me to feel possessive, to care enough, but with Croygen, something came over me I couldn't control.

Mine. The thought growled from the depths.

"Jealous? Of you?" She huffed, rage rolling her hands into fists. "Little girl, I already got that t-shirt… over and over and over. You know how many beds we broke?"

It took everything I had not to punch her, to take her to the ground. *Be smart. She still thinks you're tied up.*

"Oh, and after all that, he still walked away and won't go back," I volleyed.

The woman rose, her nose flaring. In a blink, her fist slammed down on my face, cutting my lip just before her boot heaved into my stomach. "You know he's probably going to take that nectar and run, leaving you behind. You are nothing to him."

The last thing I saw was her fist coming down for me again before everything blinked out, sucking me back into the darkness.

"Katrina…" My name whispered from the depths, the pull to it twisted in my chest. I thought I was happy in the nothing, floating in this blank void, but now I longed to get out. Swinging, clawing, I tried to find an escape. A way toward the voice that lured me like an addiction.

"*Katze*?" the man's voice called again, anxiety and desperation rushing through me.

"I'm here!" I tried to scream, but nothing came out. Fighting through the quicksand, I tried to climb out. To reach him.

A sensation dragged over my lips, making me finally feel my body, pulling me up from the blackness trying to keep me below. Awareness cracked through my mind, pressure beating like a heartbeat over my face, my lips stinging as I felt a thumb slide over the bottom one.

"Kitty-Kat?" He growled it in a taunt, knowing that name would pull me out of slumber. Though it was no longer because I hated it, and that's what scared me. He was still the man who killed my father, yet my heart pounded in my chest simply hearing his voice. "Wake up." Croygen's tone was controlled, but I knew him, sensed the fear and anxiety. "I need you to tell me where you are."

Pain fought against me, my body wanting to go back to sleep.

"Kitten. Wake up."

The demand caused my lashes to pop up, my gaze meeting his dark, sultry eyes. I was awake, but I couldn't have been, because Croygen was here, touching me. I noticed everything around me clearly, yet I knew he wasn't really there. As if we were caught in the in-between. A dream while being wide awake.

I have to be dreaming. But why does this feel so real?

What terrified me was it seemed normal. No big deal since I was able to see and feel him, knowing he wasn't near me.

This was anything but normal.

"Where are you?" he rushed out, his attention drifting, his form fading.

My captor took notice of me, her gaze going to the rope loose around my wrists, her feet rushing for me.

Fuck.

Croygen's head turned, like he was trying to see what was causing my panic. And I felt his panic rise like it was my own, warning bells trying to wake him up, but he was trying to stay with me, pushing against his instincts, ignoring them.

"Croygen!" I screamed, tearing my grip from his.

I blinked, and he was gone, my brain coming awake as the woman came for me. At his name, she halted, her head snapping around, searching for him, as if the man himself was going to leap out and save me.

It gave me a moment.

It was all I needed.

With everything I had, I yanked my wrists and ankles apart, slackening the ropes enough to pull them off. Gritting my teeth, I jumped up, pushing through the influence of the goblin metal. My legs wobbled as I struggled to take off, my feet slipping over the smooth stone surface.

"Get her! And find Croygen!" the woman ordered. The men flipped on a dime, some turning for me, guns already drawn, and some heading for the tunnels, looking for a nonexistent enemy.

I stuffed back an anguished cry. The metal weighed me down, ripping away the energy I needed. How much easier this would be if I could change into my cat and hide away in a corner, my fur blending in with the darkness.

Pure adrenaline and determination kept me going, my airways hissing with effort.

Bang! A shot bounded off the stone walls, causing me to duck as chips of rock rained down. Torch beams danced behind me, nipping at my heels. I needed to hide, to let the shadows swallow me up, so I could make a clean getaway. But her men were right on my ass, their bullets kissing the ground at my feet.

Pop! Pop! Pop!

Dust kicked up around me, clouding the air. The tunnel zigged and then split off in opposite directions. Turning down one, I instantly tucked myself into a cranny against the wall, holding still as footsteps thumped by me.

"Where did she go?" one asked in Mandarin.

"Half go this way, the other half go that way. We can't lose her!" another one barked. Their fear of the woman in charge was palpable. Whoever she was, she had men bowing at her feet, terrified of her.

Holding my breath, I waited in place, the beams of their flashlights consumed by the darkness as they got farther and farther away. Perking up my ears, I listened for any other movement before sliding out of my hiding spot. Twisting, I took off the opposite way, going down a smaller tunnel, my eyes seeing better than most with a torch.

My shoes hit the dirt, my attention drifting over my shoulder, making sure I wasn't being followed, when hands grabbed my arms. My spine rammed against the wall, a huge body pinning me against the stone. A palm clasped over my mouth, muffling the cry tearing up my throat.

"Shhh. Don't scream," he hissed in my ear. His voice poured down my body like lava, licking through me, causing me to shudder as his warm physique pressed hard into mine. Even in the dark, my body knew his, responded to it like he had me conditioned.

He held still another moment, waiting for anybody to come, before his hand slowly dropped away from my mouth.

"You're all right." He breathed out in relief, not really asking a question. I could make out his shape, his eyes somehow glowing, rolling down my figure.

"You hurt?" His thumb went to my lip, already knowing there was a cut there.

"I'm okay." I was too afraid to ask if that strange moment earlier was real. If he had experienced it too, it would make it valid. Something we had to face.

I'd rather not.

"Who had you? How did you get away?"

"Someone who clearly hasn't gotten over you." I huffed.

"What?" He leaned back.

"She knew you. *Intimately*. One of the many you left at the pier as you sailed away." I couldn't stop my derisive tone. I hated her, but her words stuck with me. And while I was telling her she was nothing special, I might have to add my own name to the list. Another one left by the Silver Tongue Devil.

"That makes no sense. Why would she threaten me to get the nectar, holding you captive, only because she is some scorned lover?"

"How do I know what you turn these women into? Crazy, clearly." I tried to push him back.

"Kat." He clutched my wrists, pushing me harder into the wall, his thigh parting my legs. "Are you jealous?"

"Fuck off," I gritted, trying to ignore the feel of him and the instinctive response to rub against him, stroke the erection I felt burning into me. "I'm about to turn you over to her myself."

He leaned over me, a smug tone coating his words. "*Definitely* sounds like jealousy."

"Croygen, I'm goin—"

His hand slapped over my mouth, cutting me off, his muscles locking up, immediately putting me on defense.

Footsteps sounded from down the tunnel, heading our way.

"Come on." Croygen grabbed my arm, pulling me to follow. We started to scurry down the passage when a glow flickered through the tunnel in front of us.

Her men coming back.

"Shit," Croygen hissed, his hand reaching for mine, pulling me in the opposite direction back where I came from. But flames danced in the distance, telling us the other half was returning as well.

"This way," he muttered.

"No." I yanked him back. "Her camp is down there."

"Fuck." Torchlight bounced off the walls in every direction as pounding steps came at us. There was no place to hide. I couldn't shift, nor did I have the energy to fight, and I knew Croygen wouldn't leave me.

Panic thickened my throat, and I darted from side to side, not knowing what to do.

"We can try to run, or we fight our way through." He gripped my face, giving me the choice of what to do. With either one, he would follow my lead.

Click. Click.

A gun barrel dug into the back of my head, another one in Croygen's.

"Don't even think about it," a man sneered in English, though his accent was thick. "Hands up."

Groups of her men flooded back out of the tunnels, their beams landing on us, guns lifted as they circled us, giving us no escape.

"I said, hands up," the man behind us barked.

Catching each other's eye, we both slowly lifted our hands, knowing there was no way out of this.

"Turn around," he snapped, the barrels shoved into our skulls, pushing us so we were now facing away from the tunnels.

A silhouette strolled up, her figure becoming clearer the closer she got to the lights, her saunter full of arrogance and utter confidence.

"Well done." Her voice matched her strut. "You captured the pirate and the puss."

Croygen went rigid next to me.

"No," he whispered.

The woman stepped up to us, her stunning face luminous under the torch lights.

"What's wrong, Croygen? Don't tell me you haven't missed me?"

He stepped back in shock, his gaze locked on her.

"Amara…"

CHAPTER 4
Croygen

Holy. Fuck.

Amara.

Watching her figure stroll up, my eyes recognized her before my brain did, the integral part of me which knew every curve, every nuance. I had touched it countless times, had watched it for decades, had been obsessed with everything about her, even when she was with someone else. Even the countless times she used me, sacrificed me, turned her back on me. In some sick way, I thought that was the love I deserved. After all I had done, I only merited a life that rotted me from the inside out.

She had me wrapped around her finger for decades and, at my darkest, only pulled me down deeper into the swamp. And I went willingly.

Shock went through my chest like a bullet, my mind struggling with who was before me, but my intuition was the opposite of surprised. Like it had known the entire time, but I just didn't want to accept it. See what was right in front of me. Identify the insignia she was putting everywhere.

Staring at the woman who had once been my lover and obsession, I only felt hate and disgust.

For myself.

I tensed momentarily, afraid of how my body would react to her. I was like a recovering addict being placed next to my most enticing vice, scared I might not be as done with it as I had hoped. Going back to her had become habitual, and I was terrified deep down nothing had changed.

Staring at her, her familiar pretty face, her eyes that seduced and chilled in a blink, I searched, picking at an old scab. The more I prodded, the more I realized—it was Kat who I felt. Aware of her burning gaze, her confusion, the sensation that I could touch her, talk to her without opening my mouth or moving.

The only thing I felt for Amara was annoyance. I was a moron for not placing her right in the middle of this from the beginning. This was exactly where she'd be. It was in her nature, her entire DNA.

"Croygen." Amara lowered her lashes seductively, a move I used to fall for every time. "It's been a while."

A laugh volleyed from my stomach, booming and bouncing off the walls. Heads whipped to me in surprise, Kat's gaze only burrowing deeper into me.

"Of course you're here." I wagged my head. "The one thing I can count on is you being predictable."

"Predictable?" Her voice went up, already unsettled that I wasn't reacting the way she was used to. "You were clueless that I'd been following you. I practically had to sign my name to the letter." She stepped up to me, her body lining up with mine. Without looking, I sensed Katrina bristle, imaginary claws digging into my skin.

"It was you I was thinking of when I sucked that guy off." Her voice went to a throaty timbre, peering up at me through her heavy lashes. How many times had I folded under that look, pushed her up against the wall, and forgotten whatever fucked up shit she had done to me? "I felt you under the bed, getting off. Made me so hot."

She used to use this trick on me with Ryker. When she was fucking or blowing him, she told me it was me she was thinking of. I used to get off on that, revel in how twisted it was. Like I was somehow winning over the Viking. Took me way too long to come to understand it was all bullshit. A lie to keep me hanging on, to keep me as her pet. Fuel for her ego.

"Thought I recognized that bad Russian accent," I recalled. Deep down, I had recognized her. My body reacted to the voice, but I brushed it off and shoved it far down before I even analyzed it. Plus, I had been preoccupied with who was underneath me at the time. "And thanks. I *did* get off." I peered down at her, not flinching at her nearness, my tone indicating it wasn't her I had gotten off to. My skin sizzled with the awareness of possessive need, but not for Amara.

Katrina hadn't moved, but I felt her everywhere, sinking into my bones. I recalled the other night with precise clarity—how my tongue stroked through her folds, how she tasted. How I spanked her pussy, hearing her cry out.

Katrina's breath hitched next to me, my gaze darting to her. It was as if she read my thoughts, felt everything I was doing to her in my mind.

And that scared the shit out of me. Far scarier than falling into Amara's shit again. Being with her was torture, but it was superficial. It would never break me.

Katrina felt different.

"I always could, if you remember." Amara ignored my implication, her hand sliding up my arm. "I know you've missed me. It's been a while."

"Not long enough." I kept my voice even, but every syllable rang with the truth. Amara had coveted the Stone of Fal, a treasure of Tuatha dé Danann. She'd been part of the fight with Stavros and had hitched her ride to the idea he might become King. That was who she was: a survivor at any cost. She used, charmed, tricked, killed, and slept her way into any bed she needed to stay on top.

Her being in the middle of this, going after the most dangerous and powerful object, was right on par for her.

Amara's brows lowered like lying dogs, and a tic flicked at her cheek before a smile curled her mouth. She patted my chest like I was teasing her. "Oh, I've missed you."

I knew every gesture, every manipulating, conniving trait she had. She wanted to get mad, confused by my pushback, but she was still trying to play the game. I had seen it time and time again. And sadly, most men—fae or human—were pretty simple, falling for her pretty smile, sultry eyes, and flattery, even as she robbed them blind. It was why we got along so well—she had no scruples and slept with whoever she needed to get ahead.

It took me a long time to realize I was just another one of her fools, not a partner in crime.

"Too bad I can't say the same."

Amara's dark eyes flickered with anger, her temper rising. She stepped back, her gaze turning hard on me. Her hair was knotted up, but in the torches, I could see a streak of purple reflecting in her dyed black locks, her true personality coming to the surface. Her eyes went over me as if she was coming up with a way to lash back, to cut me, but I should have known Amara would never go straight for my throat.

She'd go for my weakness.

Her gaze slid over to Katrina, cruelty tipping up her lips as she turned to face her.

Fuck.

"You know you're just a little substitute Zoey, right?" She tipped her head at Katrina. "A fill-in for the girl he really wants."

Kat stared at her, not responding.

"See, that is what Croygen does. Falls for the women Ryker has. First it was me, then he was bewitched by that stupid human."

"She's not human," I countered. Zoey had been at one

time, but after a strange fae storm, which transferred Ryker's powers to her, she became one of us.

"See?" Amara motioned to me. "Always so protective of her. Followed her like a puppy. Even became a lab experiment for her. So if you think you are special, that he cares for you…"

"Yet you kidnap me, fully knowing Croygen will come for me." Kat tipped her head like Amara's. She was smaller, but her power, the ruthless pirate, vibrated under her skin.

"Because he likes to think of himself as the *hero*." She chuckled. "When at worst he's the sidekick, at best the villain."

"I already know he's the villain," Kat spat back, sending a shiver down my veins. "And you can have him. I don't need a hero or a sidekick. I don't need saving."

It was a second, but I *knew* what she was about to do. Her thoughts streamed into me, notifying me of her actions. Like the girl who tried to take me down in my cabin, exhausted and weak, she fought me with all she had, never giving up.

Her elbow snapped back, cracking the nose of the man behind us. He stumbled back, his gun dropping from our heads.

Not hesitating, I spun, snapping his arm in the wrong direction. He howled and let go of the gun before I dropped him with a punch to his head. Other soldiers rushed for us, and as good as I was, I had no weapons, and they had many.

"Croygen!" a familiar voice rang out, freezing me in place. My head craned to the side, and I saw a slim girl being hauled into the room by a handful of men, a dozen behind her bringing in someone else.

Oh. Fuck. No.

It was like the earth under my feet fell away, my gaze landing on the girl shoved to the ground. Slumped over, she looked so frail. Her blonde hair hid her face, but I could see her chest heaving for air.

"Annabeth!" The need to run to her made me want to drag my boots across the gravel, but the soldiers held me back.

My attention went to more figures moving in after her. A dozen men huddled around Cooper, a metal collar around his neck keeping him from shifting. His eyes blazed red, his body puffed up and ready to kill, but he contained himself, letting these small men move him, his gaze locked on Annabeth. Seeing only her.

"How exciting." Amara smiled coyly. "It's like a reunion." Amara sauntered over to AB. Cooper's head jerked at seeing her, his nose flaring. His shock was brief before it turned into fury. He didn't have much interaction with her the last time she crossed our paths, but he knew her, knew all about her.

"I'm going to fuckin' kill you," he rumbled, leaning forward. It took all the men to hold him back. "This time I will make sure you don't escape. You'll stay dead for good."

"I don't understand all this hostility," she taunted, reaching down to AB. Amara cupped her chin, drawing her face up, the flashlights showing her features.

Arms grappled for me as I dragged men over the dirt. Several more held me back, and two punched me in the stomach, though I didn't feel it.

All I saw were the bruises and cuts on AB's face, and my vision went red.

"Stop, both of you." Amara pulled out her gun, pointing it at AB's head. "You know how trigger-happy I can get."

Ice solidified in my veins, halting me where I stood.

Annabeth glared up at her; not an ounce of fear showed, just pure hatred.

"Look how you've grown up," Amara said, lowering the gun slightly. "Such a beauty." She curved her head to me. "Maybe you went after the wrong little sister, Croygen?"

Bile burned in the back of my throat. Amara had a way of making everything ugly. She didn't understand anything pure, sweet, or kind, so she had to twist it, make it wrong.

Cooper let out a low growl.

Amara's gaze went to him, her thumb rolling over the trigger. It was a warning, a reminder to behave. She was holding all the cards.

Amara knew what the Dark Dwellers were capable of. They were the most feared beasts in the Otherworld at one time. Only a handful remained, but they were just as dangerous and vicious.

AB was a pawn because Cooper would do anything for his mate. Even submit to Amara.

"What do you want, Amara?" I was still trying to capture my breath.

"What I wanted before." She kept the gun up, turning more to me. "The nectar."

"We don't have it. We don't know where it is any more than you do."

"But you have more incentive to find it, don't you?" When she flicked her head, a guard near me shoved Kat forward, moving her away from me. My eyes caught with her yellow and green irises, reflecting in the light like a cat's. "Don't act like you wouldn't do the same." Amara moved up to me, purposely in front of Kat, cutting off our connection. "At one time, you were a man with no scruples." She lowered her voice, her hand tracing up my torso. "Who would do *anything* for me." She once again peered up at me through her lashes, her gaze heavy with meaning. "We used to have a lot of fun together, didn't we?"

"The manipulation, cheating, and scheming?" I huffed, trying to ignore how low her hand was venturing. "Yeah, great time."

"Don't act like you didn't love it." She moved in closer, fingers under my shirt, dragging her nails across my abs to my V-line.

At one time, I did. I couldn't deny that, but that guy was long gone.

"Someone's been working out." She bit down on her lip, giving me every indication she would let me fuck her right here, in front of everyone, if I wanted.

She liked that kind of thing. Power games. But that's what it was to her, control. Not only showing her hold over me, but wanting Katrina to know it too.

I don't know if it was Zoey who cracked the shell on my blinders before, or it was me finally having enough, but I stared down at the woman who would've had me back in her web just a handful of years ago and felt *absolutely* nothing.

"Amara?" I leaned in, my mouth almost brushing hers, feeling a slight shiver from her, a hum in her throat. "Get your fucking hands off me."

It took her a moment before she jerked back. This time nothing but rage was in her eyes, and her mouth twisted. "You're pathetic, Croygen. You always have been."

I scoffed, making her even angrier.

There was a reason she always came running back to me. I knew how many times I made her scream and had her passing out after. Far more than the Viking, but she wanted him because deep down Ryker didn't want her, and she enjoyed that. The challenge.

"Noooo, the lemurs can't hump the toilet. Only the ducks can…" A voice came from a bag one of her men was holding.

Annabeth's bag.

A head popped out, granola stuck to his fur. Sprig looked dazed and utterly confused.

"What? What's going on?"

Amara went still, her entire body locking up.

My gaze jumped from her to Sprig, watching them take each other in, registering who the other was. To say they hated each other was a vast understatement. He was team Zoey, through and through; he bled *bhean* colors.

"Oh, no! Nonononononono! Not you!" He shook his head.

"Oh, come on, why do bananas keep pooping in my Honey Nut Cheerios?"

"Oh gods," she hissed. "You're still alive? Haven't they gotten rid of you yet? Sold you off as dog food?"

"Listen here, purple-haired fungus!" Sprig crawled out of the bag, sitting on the rim. "You're the one past its selling date. You're like the Mexican honey-chili I ate that keeps revisiting me through my asshole. A thin substance that squeezes through and burns."

"And let me guess, you're still humping a stuffed goat?" she spat back. "You know it's not alive, right? That it's not *real*."

Oh fuck.

He jolted back, eyes widening. "How. Dare. You." He gripped the straps of his own backpack, Pam's head sticking out of the honey jar pack, his hand patting her head. "Don't listen to the anorexic Barney doll, baby. She's mad that she doesn't have a brain. Just an unemployed scarecrow."

"Fuck you, you little..." She went stomping for him, finally noticing the men's shock and fear, their eyes locked on the sprite.

It was easy to forget that even to the fae, he was a freak of nature. A fantasy character come to life.

One started to chant something under his breath, words like 'demon,' and 'monkey king.' *"Sun Wukong."* A legendary mythical figure, Sun Wukong was a monkey born from a stone who acquired supernatural powers.

His image was much different from Sprig, more a warrior than a tiny stuffed animal, but in their beliefs, he also has the power to transform, change his appearance. Sprig speaking spooked them enough. Had their myths come to life?

"No." Amara held up her hands, her men starting to retreat. She spoke to them in Mandarin, telling them it was not what they thought. But people's embedded beliefs and superstitions were stronger than her claims.

My gaze tracked them as they backed away from Sprig, their terror making them jumpy, ready to flee.

I glanced over at Cooper. His gaze said the same thing. I didn't even need to look at Katrina. I felt her voice strike through me like a match.

Now!

As if she really spoke, I reacted to Kat's order. Swinging around, my arm slammed into a nose, my other fist smashed into a throat. A roar from Cooper deafened the cave, sounding like an actual dragon had come back to life, tearing down the walls to get to his mate.

"Get them!" Amara ordered, though many of the spooked men ran, fear taking over any rational thought. The money she offered and the control she had were no longer enough to keep them here. Not when a demon monkey king had come to life before them.

I wanted to kiss that little furball and his flappy mouth.

Yanking a gun out of a man's hand, I turned and fired at another one, killing or knocking out every figure coming at me. I went into my zone, my training keeping me alert, and once again, Katrina and I made our way to each other. We fought back-to-back, our rhythm in sync, our movements smooth and precise. I felt energy firing between us, something I couldn't name, and I shoved it toward her, knowing the goblin metal around her wrist was draining her faster than she could kill.

"Cooper, get her!" I bellowed, spotting him barreling through a throng of men, his beast held back by the metal. His anger puffed him up, towering him over the men. Knocking through, he swept up Annabeth, his eyes flaming red.

"Kat, go!" I yelled at her to follow Cooper as I dove for Annabeth's bag left on the ground. I told myself it was because her medication was in it, not because I was saving the furball. Though I knew if anyone touched him, I would level them.

He was mine to annoy and piss off.

The fabric of the bag curled under my fingers.

"Croygen!" Katrina's scream sparked fear in my blood. It wasn't to hurry me up; it was a warning of death.

Flipping over, I saw a man with a *sai*, the devil's pitchfork, over me, heading right for my chest. Before I could move, Katrina whirled up, and I heard flesh being split open, the slicing of veins and tissue. The man's mouth fell open in a silent scream, and blood sprayed out, covering me. His head tipped to the side, his spine barely hanging onto it as he dropped to the ground.

Katrina stood over him, her chest heaving, holding a Yuanyang Tomahawk covered in blood.

"Fuck." I breathed out.

"Saved your ass again." She wiped the foreign blood from her mouth with her sleeve, not looking at me. "Let's go."

Scrambling to my feet, it took a moment to pluck myself out of my reverence at the badass pirate in front of me. The woman who had saved my life twice in the same number of days. And fuck if that didn't turn me on. I had never met anyone who could challenge me. Best me.

I had no doubt about how she got her title, how she became the best. Katrina Roth was a legend and a clear competitor for my title.

"Come on!" Cooper yelled, motioning us forward. I glanced around, the area strewn with bodies.

And as usual, Amara was gone. It's what she did best—vanishing into the chaos, a magician at escaping, at slipping away.

But like a magician, it was all a trick of the eye. She was somewhere close, conjuring up her next illusion to test us once again.

CHAPTER 5
Katrina

"I am a King! Bow down, my minions!" Sprig stood on Cooper's shoulder, his arms in the air, facing the rest of us trailing after the Dark Dweller, leading us further into the belly of the caves. "Did you see them run in fear? Shriek in terror? I am *all* powerful."

"You're full of something… though smells more like bullshit." Croygen exhaled behind me.

"Shush, subordinate. You are in the presence of greatness. Of a powerful deity!" Sprig froze, his eyes widening. "Oh… of a *god*!"

"There is no living with him now."

"There was before?" Croygen countered.

AB shook her head with a smile. The girl was barely keeping on her feet, but she refused help, spouting she was fine and to keep going. As fae, we might biologically be stronger, but this girl was tougher than all of us combined.

To subdue Cooper, those men had beaten her, which allowed them to get the goblin metal around his neck. She was injured and exhausted, and every day I picked up a more acute sour smell from her, the cancer claiming more of her.

Yet, she persevered.

"The King Monkey God!" Sprig declared with his hands waving in the air. "And as your god, I demand to be gifted an endless supply of honey."

"Sprig," Cooper growled. "Shut the fuck up before I gag you."

"Silence, underling!" Sprig touched his blond head. "These hands are bestowed with the magic of a god king! Released you from your bindings." He motioned to where the goblin metal collar used to be around Cooper's neck. He had taken off both mine and Cooper's bands after we got far enough away. "Cured you of your ails. Saved you all from the devil-horned, psycho, purple people eater."

Amara.

The same woman who had spoken to me in the toilet in Shanghai, taunting me about intimately knowing Croygen, which was truer than I thought. She was the same woman he thought himself in love with for so long. The one who twisted him up and kept him coming back for more, decade after decade.

A knot twisted in my gut, covered in something I hadn't felt in a long time, if ever.

Jealousy.

Not an emotion I liked or was familiar with. It made me feel wretched. Embarrassed. Weak.

This man, after this long, still evoked such a reaction from me. And his supermodel ex-girlfriend, with her confidence and poise, had a way of making sure I felt like a little girl playing dress up.

Many people took my small size to mean they could dominate me, only to find out they were sorely mistaken. Yet I couldn't stop feeling insignificant around her. Like she could wrap him around her finger again with a snap. The thought had my nails growing into my palms, my canine teeth digging into my lip. I was out of control, and that pissed me off. Made me annoyed at her, at myself, and most definitely at Croygen. I didn't even want to look at him. Though I sensed him behind me, sensed him everywhere. Buzzing at my brain, my skin… my soul.

I did everything to shut it out, to ignore what had to be only in my head, needing to rein myself back in. Take back control. Go back to hating my enemy. The man who killed my father.

"I am all-powerful Sprite-Monkey God!" Sprig snapped my attention back to him. "Who can strike fear into all who came before me."

Cooper wrenched his shoulder, tossing Sprig off.

"Ahhh!" The monkey fell to the ground, the underwear cape flapping after him as he hit the stone. "How dare you insult your Monkey King like that? You will be cursed!"

"Someone put him on mute before I use the rodent's tail as a noose," Croygen stated.

Annabeth scooped him up, opening a granola bar.

"Oh, honeyhoneyhoneyhoney!" He grappled for the treat. "Givemegivemegiveme!" Shoving a huge chunk in his mouth, he pointed at us. "I woll wurse you wall… waiter," Sprig garbled through his food, shoving in more until he looked like a chipmunk.

"Think it's time for the King's nappy-poo," Croygen grumbled, his deep voice making me tense up every time he spoke, as if he continued to break through the walls I was placing between us. I forbade myself to think of the other night, pretending it didn't happen. Nor would I even entertain all the strange moments since. I didn't know what was happening to me, and I wanted it all to go away.

Go back to before he fucked me over a saddle.

"Want my cock in your pussy, kitten?"

His heat instantly doused me in flames, my mind eager to revisit those memories, my body even more willing for a repeat.

The way he felt driving deeper in me, how frenzied I felt, how out of control.

"I need to fuck you deeper. To feel my cock inside you for decades to come. To know it's mine."

My thighs clenched and my core pulsed, disgust roiling through my head. Images of my father bombarded me with shame. Through the years, his face had become hazy and distant. It scared me that one day I might forget completely, unable to recall his laugh or voice. As if pardoning Croygen would make him disappear, like he wasn't important enough to fight for.

A strangled cry yanked me from my thoughts, and I saw Annabeth stumble, watching her feet tangle under her as she tumbled to the ground.

"Anna!" Croygen and Cooper both went for her, her mate getting to her first.

"Babe." His hands and eyes went over her, searching for any more injuries. "Are you okay?"

"Yeah. I'm fine." She flinched as she sat up. Her shoulder had hit the hardest, her body twisting, ensuring she kept Sprig safe. The monkey was fast asleep in her hands. "I just tripped over a rock."

She lied. We all knew it. She was getting weaker, but her stubborn side wanted to keep up with us. To not slow us down, though all it did was diminish her energy.

Squatting next to her, Croygen tried to hide his anguish, his grief, but I swear I felt it, thick and heavy in the air.

"Let's camp here." Croygen rubbed her back with one hand, using his flashlight to examine the area. "Get something to eat and rest before starting out again."

"I'm fine. We can keep going." Annabeth pulled from their grips, her brows furrowed, trying to get up.

"I'm not," Croygen huffed. "My ass is tired. Remember, I'm ancient." I knew what he was doing. We all did, including AB, but we pretended we didn't.

"Plus, I'm starving," Cooper added.

"You're always hungry." AB laughed.

"Yes, I am." Cooper's eyes heated, glowing a reddish color, his tongue sliding over his bottom lip as he stared at her meaningfully. The sexual chemistry and connection between them had me turning away, wanting some space from all of them—especially Croygen.

More embarrassment slipped over my cheeks now that I was aware Amara had been there when we were under the cot and knew what was happening between us. Though she probably assumed he was getting off to thoughts of her, using me only because I was there. And maybe he was. Somewhere in his reptilian brain did he know it was her too and was actually thinking of her?

Was he still in love with her?

You don't care, Kat. Once you get the nectar to Batara, get your crew and ship back, you get as far away from the Silver Tongue Devil as you can.

Revenge, the thing I pursued for so long with his head on a spike, felt like sand breaking away in my hands. Hunting him down and killing him was not something I sought anymore. I wanted space, distance, a sea between us. I needed to get back to my life of piracy, leaving him far behind in my wake.

The guys set up camp and got a fire going, eating some instant noodles and bundling AB in extra clothes as the air was getting slightly chillier the deeper we went.

Cooper had been able to run back, sniff out where they left their belongings and retrieve them—three mats, some food, water, and alcohol.

"Sooooo… are we gonna talk about the elephant in the room?" Cooper drank from a bottle of Baijiu, passing it to Croygen. The flames crackled, reflecting off the walls. AB was already asleep on one of the mats, Sprig curled up with her. "Amara." He said her name like it was a condition. "The bitch is back."

"Yeah." Croygen chugged down a huge portion. "Fuck, I'm an idiot. I should've seen this coming. I mean, I know her so well. What she does." He rubbed his head. "I don't know, maybe I did, just didn't want to think about the possibility."

Because he was scared he would fall for her again?

A worm of jealousy wriggled up my spine, making me grit my teeth at his claim of *knowing her*. Yeah, I bet he did. The years he spent with her, oblivious to me, while all I did was think about him. I had turned away from a man who actually loved me because I was so obsessed with Croygen. Even when I fucked other men, I thought of him, wanting to challenge him in every way. Like he would sense me riding someone, feel it in his gut like a stab, know I was coming for him.

In reality, he was living life without one thought for me. Not one time did he try to find me, see if I was okay, come rescue me from hell. He took my home and my friends, murdered my father, and left me to rot while he fucked Psychotic Barbie, drinking and pirating around the globe.

His arm went out, the white spirits bobbing in my face as he offered me the bottle. I glared at his arm at the intrusion into my space, feeling my stomach flutter, getting even madder at my reaction to him. How my body had *always* reacted to him, even when I was too young to really understand.

Croygen and I had become too friendly, and that wasn't even factoring in the sex. The unbelievable, light-the-world-on-fire-and-burn-it-to-the-ground kind of sex. This was something even more than that. A familiarity that took over every molecule of my body. The knowing where he was without looking, feeling him constantly around me, seeing him in my dreams which were so real it felt like he was actually there.

But he couldn't be. I wouldn't accept it because it meant something I would never allow myself. *Especially* with him.

My father spoke every once in a while about my mother. It hurt him too much because she had been his mate. And when she died, he threw everything into raising me. His love, his reason for getting up in the morning.

"She was my world, *Katze*, my light. My heart stopped the day she died," he would say. "But for you, she gave me her magic to keep it beating for you. To know you were loved so deeply. I am here until you no longer need me, *Schatz*." *Treasure*.

He wasn't even full fae, and he struggled to keep going after he lost her, his heart so broken it was me he lived for. He got us on a pirate ship, keeping me fed, happy, and healthy. But he never stopped loving her, talking to her, mourning her, waiting for the day they'd be reunited.

I didn't deserve to feel that kind of love. What I had done in my life, how many I had killed, all I had sacrificed on the altar of piracy. I gave my devotion to the sea and the sea only. I would never have more than a lover. And certainly *never* a mate.

"Hey?" Croygen wiggled the bottle at me, encouraging me to take it. "Drink?"

Jaw locked in ire, I moved away and leaned against the wall, tucking my arms into my chest. I didn't care how childish my response was.

His gaze rolled over me, and once again I felt like something was tapping at my skin, trying to peel back the layers to see beyond the thick barrier. My teeth ground together, shoving against the sensation stabbing me like daggers.

He pulled his arm back, his lids narrowed as if he had felt my rebuff, a strange emotion flicking in his eyes. Then it was gone faster than it came. He turned his back on me, taking another swig, his attention going back to Cooper.

"Amara will be back. We can't let our guard down."

"But all her men are gone or dead." The Dark Dweller's gaze still hopped between us, no doubt sensing the animosity.

"Doesn't matter. She will find a way. Whatever it takes.

The one thing about her, good or bad, is that she won't give up. Not until she gets what she wants."

"Is that *you* or the nectar?" Did my voice really sound that bitchy? I cleared my throat, forcing my vocals to relax, my face vacant of anything.

Croygen's dark eyes met mine, his tongue sliding on his lips as if he caught my possessiveness in his mouth and savored its bitter taste.

"Money. Power. In whatever means she has to get it." He smirked, his gaze almost challenging mine. Not denying she would go after him, and certainly not denying he'd like it.

"Well, just another to add to our list. *Everyone* is an enemy down here," I said poignantly back. We might pretend to be on the same side now, but once that nectar was found, it was everyone for themselves.

My vow and crew would be pitting me against Croygen and Cooper. They needed it for AB. I understood that and could sympathize, but it didn't take away what I had to do. I didn't have a choice.

"Don't underestimate her. Amara is a survivor. She is ruthless, cunning, and has no scruples."

"So you two really are alike," I countered.

Croygen watched me for a bit, though I wouldn't let myself try to figure out his look, guarding myself. Finally, his lip curled in a smirk. "Think it's time we get some rest. I'll take the first watch." Croygen stood up, motioning to the bedroll. "Go ahead. You *obviously* need to sleep." He winked, strolling past me, taunting me.

Exhaling, I dug my nails deep into my palms, restraining myself from smacking him across the head or stabbing him with the sword I acquired.

Fuck, that man drove me nuts.

Hearing a chuckle from across the fire, I saw Cooper shake his head. He moved his mat closer to AB with a knowing smile, his eyes dancing between me and the pirate.

"Shut up," I snapped, only making him laugh more.

I stayed where I was, slipping down farther against the rock and wrapping my arms tighter around me.

Maybe I could kill him after all.

Night or day didn't matter here; the same suffocating blackness stretched endlessly before us, the journey everlasting, just like the darkness. Up, down, squeezing through small fissures, to stepping in places that echoed our steps like a vast music hall. Numbly moving forward, I let my mind wander back to the open sea, the feeling of salt drying on my face, the rolling of the ocean under my feet, the familiar creaks of wood, my flag flapping in the wind.

My crew. Gage, Zuri, Typhoon, Hurricane, and Moses. They were still alive when I left. Did Batara kill them by now? While I was sleeping in a comfy crew room, were they being tortured? Dragged out into the square to be slowly and cruelly executed?

I still bore the shame and guilt for my mistake, the arrogance that led to Ruby, Dobbs, and Polly's deaths. Little did I know that night would set my life on a collision course, bringing me to the depths of a dragon cave with my longtime nemesis.

"Babe, grab my hand." Cooper's voice jarred me out of my looping thoughts. He reached back for AB, pulling her up a steep, smooth rock face leading into another tunnel. Annabeth scrambled up the boulder, her shoes slipping and sliding, Cooper easily yanking her up with him.

"Need a boost, Kitten?" Croygen's voice trailed down the back of my neck, forcing a shiver through me. The heat of his body pulsed against mine, and the need to step back into him, feel his lips graze my neck, his hands on my body, only had my muscles locking up.

"I can do it myself." I dug my elbow into his chest, trying to put space between us.

"By all means, *Kitty-Kat*." He stepped back, his hands up.

"Don't call me that." I hissed, the name firing up my ire once again, needling me.

He lifted his brow, motioning for me to go first. Cooper waited at the top to grab my hand.

Stepping back, I took a running start, leaping up with all my cat reflexes. My fingers clawed at the rock, trying to dig in. Cooper's hand was just out of reach, and I felt myself slip on the sleek surface, my body dropping. A gasp hitched up my throat as I felt myself fall, and I braced for impact.

Arms circled me, catching me before I hit the ground. Croygen yanked me hard against him, holding me tight. For a moment, I felt like I was suspended in air, my brain still ready for the blow while my body was tucked warmly into his. I felt every ripped ab, every muscle in his thighs, his cock pressing into my ass.

It was momentary, something I could almost pretend away, the sensation of him penetrating every barricade I had. Inside and outside. My body shuddered as something brushed through me, feeling like he was deep inside me, invoking so much pleasure, while at the same time touching every inch of my skin. So deep, so intrusive, yet so familiar and wanted.

Then it was gone. Threads of a dream. Something I imagined, not experienced.

Croygen let go and stepped back, his breath unsteady behind me, but every exhale I felt was like fingers trailing the curve of my neck. In and out. My hair tickled my skin, the sensation licking down my spine.

"Try again," Cooper yelled down, shattering the bubble and jolting us even further apart. Cooper wiggled himself lower, stretching out his hand to catch me. "Croygen, lift her up. I almost reached her last time."

Croygen muttered something I couldn't make out, turning to me. "Take a running start again, and I'll give you a boost," he told me. No feeling, no more flirty tone from earlier.

I nodded, receding before taking off at a sprint, my legs scrambling up the wall. Croygen's hands pushed at my ass, tossing me up where Cooper grabbed me, swinging me to the top of the boulder.

Croygen only took one try, Cooper helping him, his frame colliding with mine. His hands gripped my hips to keep us both upright, his body pressing into me. He hastily dropped his hands, stepping back. I ducked my head and twisted away, feeling shy and angry, like something had taken place that bared my soul, showing all my cards, leaving me exposed.

"Let's keep going." Croygen brushed by me, his tone tight, his demeanor aggressive as we continued into the next cave.

I kept toward the back, fighting between the urge to stay as far from him as I could and this need to be close. Like he was a drug I just got my first high from.

Cooper came to a stop, his nose lifting. Only a few seconds later, I picked up the same scent. My eyes caught a distant, hazy glow from a campfire flickering deeper in the cave. I knew Cooper saw it too, his senses even sharper than mine.

"What?" Croygen's head snapped between us.

"Someone's just ahead." Cooper flicked his chin.

I took a deeper pull of air, confusion creasing my brow. The fragrance of coffee, bean soup, and some kind of dumpling couldn't completely override the smell of humans.

Cooper's shoulders rose, nodding for AB to stay behind him as we moved in. The glimmer of the flame grew more and more pronounced, and we held our weapons at the ready as we snuck closer, finally spotting an outline hunched over the fire.

The lone man appeared to be around five foot six. He was an older gentleman, maybe in his sixties. He wore cargo pants and a button-down shirt, and he had a round face with a grayish-black beard, heavy eyebrows, and short hair with a receding hairline. I believed he was somewhere from the Eastern Bloc, but not sure exactly where. Since the wall dropped, places and cultures had been changing rapidly, everyone running to new countries, only to find it wasn't any better than what they left.

A kettle whistled softly as the man poked at the fire, seemingly oblivious to the threat coming upon him.

"Join me?" He finally looked up, his brown eyes peering right at us, noting the weapons we had pointed at him. His English was clear, but an accent lingered—one I couldn't place. "Coffee?"

"Coffee?" Croygen's forehead buckled with confusion, taken off guard.

"Yes," he stated firmly, waving us over. "Lower your weapons and come sit. I have plenty of food too."

None of us moved, suspicious of a lone man deep in the caves where this treasure was supposed to be, offering us food like we were in some Hansel and Gretel horror film.

"Ah." He bobbed his head, pouring coffee into his cup, looking anything but dangerous. "You are skeptical. I understand. Seems everyone is on the hunt… an article bringing in treasure seekers from all over the world. Ready to cut each other's throats for fortune."

"And are you one of those treasure seekers?" Croygen kept his gun on him, though the man didn't react to it.

"Me?" He indicated himself, head wagging. "No. I'm far more interested in how this place *protects* treasures and the ancient magic that is still here. I like to think of myself as a specialist, trying to preserve the species."

"Hate to tell you, but the dragons have been dead for thousands of years." Croygen scoffed.

"Oh, I don't know. I've seen things that make me believe it hasn't been as long as we think. But I am more a hunter of facts or truths of evidence."

"And you've found evidence of dragons?" Cooper's tone tipped over into mocking. "Like what?"

The man's bushy brows lifted like two caterpillars climbing a tree. "I've seen their nests."

"Nests?" Croygen halted, his arm lowering in surprise. "You have found an actual dragon nest?"

"I have." He nodded smugly.

Finding the nests meant you found the core of the magic, the most potent place to hide treasure—the dragon's lair. No matter how long ago they went extinct, that was where treasure would be concealed.

Maybe this was where the nectar was. Could we really find it? Would I end the curse that was placed on me? Could I save my family and somehow save AB before I gave it to Batara?

"Where?" Croygen demanded.

"A little journey from here, but most likely you will never find them on your own."

"How do we know you're not lying?"

"Guess you'll have to see for yourself with your own eyes," the man replied, still not reacting to the guns pointed at him, as if that was a common thing and a normal way to greet strangers.

"Take us there." Croygen's tone was even but still a clear threat, his weapon trained at the man's head.

The man only smiled. "First, come and break bread with me." He patted his hand on the ground next to him. "You look famished and tired. As you see, I'm not what I used to be. We can set out first thing tomorrow."

"Tomorrow?" Croygen inched closer. "How about we set out now?"

"Youth, always in a hurry to waste it."

"Now he sounds like Tsai," Croygen grumbled, only loud enough for me to hear him.

"I also have tea and some honey."

Oh. Shit.

From the depth of Sprig's slumber, wrapped up in Annabeth's bag, he heard his call, his siren song.

"What?" A furry head popped out. "Honey? Did someone say they have honey?" He scrambled out before AB could grab him. "It's breakfast, right? Did I miss it? Oh noooo, that would be awful. I didn't, right? Is it brunch, then? I am starving. I mean, really, really starving. Like on the verge of death kind of dying. There are pancakes, right? Oooo, I'm craving pancakes from Izel's. Oh, praise her honey tits, she made the best pancakes. Churros? Do you have churros?"

Croygen grabbed Sprig, covering the monkey's mouth and hiding him away in his hands. But it was too late; the man had already seen and heard him.

"That monkey…" He stood up, his eyes wide. "That monkey talked, didn't he?"

None of us responded, knowing we were past denying what he saw.

"Can I see him?" he asked. He showed no fear, only amazement and genuine curiosity.

I saw the hesitation, the flinch on Croygen's cheek, the need to keep Sprig protected and to keep this man on the other side of his gun.

A strange standoff—hostage or ally?

"Owww! Fuck!" Croygen bellowed, shaking his hand and glaring down. "You bit me, you little turtle fucker!"

"And I probably just got some crustacean disease by doing that." Sprig wiped at his tongue. "I don't even like crabs… or lobster." He sniffed, shoulders sagging. "I mean, I guess if it's drenched in butter and honey, it would be okay."

The man stood, muttering under his breath in a language I didn't know and couldn't decipher, staring at Sprig like he was a wonder of the world.

In a way, I guess he was.

"Please, I mean no harm. I just want to see him."

"You make one wrong move, and I will make sure this bullet hits you between the eyes. Got it?" Croygen's threat glided like a ship into the air. It was smooth and calm, but underneath, it was deadly.

"Yes. I understand." The man nodded.

Croygen sighed, opening up his hand to show the small sprite-monkey.

"This is Sprig." Croygen motioned to him.

"That's how you introduce me?" he squeaked, climbing to his shoulder. "How dare you. I am a *God*, a Monkey King! Feared and adored. I should have honey pouring down on me like that stripper girl in that movie." He bent back like it was cascading over him. "Naked."

"If you want a pole, I know where I can put it." Croygen eyed Sprig.

"Stop teasing me with a good time. I'm mad at you." He hmphed, crossing his arm. "I'm no longer talking to you."

"I have dreamed of this day." Croygen looked up blissfully to where the sky would be. "Thank you."

"I *can't* believe it." The man stepped closer, causing us all to bristle. My gun was still aimed at him, this man who was completely preoccupied with Sprig. "To see it firsthand."

"What?" Croygen tipped his head.

"No, I just can't believe something like this exists." The man shook his head, peering closer at Sprig. "This shouldn't be possible."

"Yeah, he shouldn't be. Yet, here he is." I noticed Croygen shift on his feet, moving Sprig farther out of this man's reach. No matter what he said, he was fiercely protective of his buddy.

The man must have picked up on Croygen's energy, stepping back.

"Sorry, I just find him so fascinating. A true marvel. The intelligence of a fae, put in an animal body."

"See? Intelligent." Sprig nudged Croygen. "I'm a *marvel.*"

"He meant your brain is a marble."

"Can I?" The man tentatively reached out, waiting for consent so we didn't shoot him.

"You have honey? You're not intercoursing with me, right?"

"What?" The man paused.

"He means you better not be fucking with him." Croygen slanted his head the opposite way, his expression deadly. "Are you?" His meaning went well beyond honey and Sprig.

"No. I am not." The man looked Croygen dead in the eyes.

"Then touch away, but keep it above the junk, please. Pam will get jealous." Sprig patted Pam's head peeking out of his backpack.

The man poked and touched his arms, peering close to the sprite, studying him.

"Truly exceptional." He leaned in closer, but Croygen stepped back. The gentleman cleared his throat. "Did… are there more of him?"

Croygen's lids slanted, watching the man. "No. He's one of a kind."

"Awww… buttaneer, I didn't know you felt that way." Sprig leaned into Croygen's neck, patting him.

"One of you is more than enough."

I could tell the guy wanted to say more, to hold Sprig, but he read Croygen's defensive stance and kept his distance.

"Come, please." The guy waved us over, traveling back to the fire. "Eat, rest, and then I can show you the nests."

"Thank you." Of course, Annabeth progressed to him

first, offering appreciation and manners while the rest of us moved warily to the campfire. My fingers still held the gun I had stolen from Amara's men, ready to act at a moment's notice.

This was the strangest hostage situation I had ever been in. It was clear we were in charge, our weapons still drawn on him, but he treated us like friends joining him at camp.

I had learned that kindness hardly ever came free. There was always a price, even if the price tag wasn't showing.

CHAPTER 6
Croygen

"Katrina." Her name was almost a growl. "I don't want to hear one more word from your mouth." I moved closer to her, trying to keep anyone else from hearing. "Get on my bed mat. Now." I pointed down at it.

"No." She scowled, her arms folding. "He's human. I think I can take him."

"Katrina…" I gritted my teeth, ready to gag and tie her up again. She was pushing all my buttons.

"I can take care of myself. I lived on the streets, remember?" She sounded like a brat. I didn't care if she actually threw a tantrum; I was going to get my way on this.

"I know you can, but I don't trust *him*," I muttered even lower, trying not to let the man hear me. Though he seemed harmless, something about him didn't sit right with me. We never put away our weapons, not that he was an actual threat. I mean, against us, what could he do?

Yet I still didn't want Kat out of my eyesight. I needed her right next to me.

The man had drifted off soon after eating, his back against the wall, his arms folded and head tucked down. Though with every exhale, my muscles locked up, ready to pounce.

"He's fast asleep." She motioned back to him. "He's old. He can't do anything. Cooper and I would hear him before he made a move."

Probably, but I didn't care.

We needed rest; all of us were running on fumes. Like the man, AB had crashed over an hour ago after we ate, her body giving out before her will did, which I feared might be a metaphor for what was to come. We needed to find this nectar; her life depended on it, and there was a good chance it might be hidden in the nests.

Every day I saw the regression in AB, her body losing its battle against the disease eating quickly at her. It made me wish I had pushed harder for her not to come on this journey. To keep her safe and bubble-wrapped until we brought it back to her. It was too late now, and like Kat, I don't think my strong stance on the matter would have stopped her.

I let out a huge, drawn-out breath, my lids closing for a moment as I tried to rein in my temper.

"Humor me tonight." I clenched through every word, my physique looming over her, our bodies almost touching. My mouth was only inches from hers. *"Please."*

She kept her attention to the side, her arms crossed, giving a little shrug of her shoulder.

I might have triumphed, but I wasn't sure I won. The energy had been bristling between us from the first moment on my ship when her naked body slammed into mine, and it has been tempestuous since.

That peculiar moment earlier when I caught her after she almost fell was like I had been stripped naked, my soul painfully exposed. At the same time, it felt like I was sinking inside her, engulfed by her, on the edge of the most consuming orgasm I could ever fathom. It was only a moment, the intensity so overpowering I felt like I was drowning in lava.

It scared the fuck out of me, made me want to run, get the

hell away from her. Yet I kept finding myself next to her instead.

Katrina Roth was forbidden—a line I crossed but should never cross again.

It was what I told myself as I lowered down on the mat, the padding at least easing the harshness of the ground a little.

"Aren't you going to be a gentleman and give me the mat?" She stood at the end, frowning. "And sleep on the ground?"

My eyes lifted to her, my voice deep, filled with implication. "When have I ever been a gentleman, Kitty-Kat?"

Her cheeks flamed, her eyes moving off me, and I knew her mind was going to that night. To the way I knotted my hands through her hair, tugging hard, driving deep into her over and over. How I made her cry out, her nail marks still carved into my back.

Clearing my throat, I tried to ignore my cock twitching awake. "Lay down and go to sleep." I grunted the order.

She glared at me for a moment, the refusal right on her lips, but she let out a noise and dropped down, curling up on a mat away from me.

My fingers twitched, wanting to run through her silky hair. My body sought to move in around hers, pulling her tight against me.

What the fuck was wrong with me?

I didn't "cuddle." I didn't stroke hair. As pathetic as Amara had me at one time, I never wanted to lie around in bed with her or spoon after sex. That was never me. That one night with Lexie before the battle was the closest I'd ever gotten to that kind of thing. Holding her was enough because I wasn't ready to go further. In time, that might have changed, but I did have boundaries. Restraint.

Where the hell was that with Kat? I wanted to fuck her and hold her, kiss her, and play with her hair. I couldn't count the number of times on this trip I almost grabbed her hand, cupped her face, kissed her, and even more when she was pissing me off.

Scrubbing my face, I tried to get myself in check. Annoyed and horny seemed to be my constant state around her.

Lying down, my back to hers, my eyes stayed on the slumbering man, my gun clutched in my palm. He *appeared* old and harmless, a lonely man hungry for company, but in this world, you learned to not take anything as it seemed.

Usually I could pick up on lies, especially from humans. He showed no sign of falsehood when speaking about the nests. If he led us to them, it was the most likely spot the nectar would be near or hidden in. We had to hitch our wagon to him for the moment, though I wouldn't let my guard down.

I had done that once. Trusted. Didn't see what was coming. And I lost everything.

Water cascaded down, and a scream stuck in my chest. I could hear the crashing of waves, the gunfire, and clanks of swords, but everything felt frozen in time. Someone hit the pause button on life.

Lowe sank the blade into Rotty's chest, his body stilling, his eyes widening with something beyond fear, like grief or regret.

"Noooo!" The cry bellowed from my chest, my legs already launching me forward in fury as Rotty's body tumbled to the ground.

Wood groaned from deep within the bowels, and the ship tipped further, sailing me away from my target. Landing hard on the deck, my body slid, knocking into the side, water crashing down on me.

Spitting and shaking the water off, I searched for Lowe, my blood boiling with the need to kill.

The wave had tossed him back onto the main deck, yards away from me. Getting to his feet, he swayed as the ship teetered. Sinking farther under, he looked back at me.

"It's fitting how the illustrious Silver Tongue Devil goes down into a watery grave." A malicious smile grew over his lips. "One thing about betrayal—it never comes from your

enemies. It's always those who are closest to you." With those words, he turned around and jumped on the railing, the ship groaning with its death throes. Lowe tipped his hat and leaped off the side. Below, his men were waiting in rowboats, ready to take their master back to the comforts of their sound ship. His men followed their leader overboard, knowing the fate of this dying vessel.

"Abandon ship!" I bellowed through the windy rain. There was no difference between the sea and sky, both engulfing us, taking us down to a watery grave.

"Captain?" I heard Scot shout, waving me to follow. "Hurry!"

We all knew any dinghy had to be well away from a sinking ship, or the power of it would tug everything down with it, like pulling a bath plug.

"Go! Go!" I motioned for the ones who were still alive to leave. The dead bodies of over half my crew were being washed back and forth on the deck like ping-pong balls. Out of my periphery, I saw Master Yukimura's smaller frame in his familiar haori jacket slide past me.

Agony bubbled under my skin, but numbness kept me from acknowledging the grief, not wanting to know who was dead. Who I failed.

"No!" Scot shook his head; a few other men were trying to get back to me. A loud crack of wood jutted through, water splashing over the side.

"That's an order!" I shouted. "From your captain."

Those words were binding, a law among pirates. One you could not question.

They hesitated but took it as law, grief flinching on their faces. Turning away, they jogged toward the back where the last rowboat was, understanding what my fate would be.

Did I want to die? No. I loved my life, but no man would be left behind.

Peering back up near the helm, I observed a body lying there, a blade sticking out of his chest.

"Rotty!" I ran to him, my knees sliding over the wet wood, kneeling beside him.

His eyes blinked up at me, his mouth opening and closing, gasping for air, the gold ornate handle sticking out between his ribs.

"It's probably just a nick of a lung. You'll be okay." I told him. He was half fae; he would heal from this. "Just hold on and let me get it out. You're going to be okay." I grabbed the handle.

"No." He croaked, his hand going over mine. "It's too late."

"No, it's not." I spit, wiping the stream of water splashing down on me. "Come on, I can get you to a boat."

His hand squeezed mine tighter. "I'm sorry."

"Don't be sorry. Get your ass up. The blade didn't hit your heart."

"Doesn't matter. This is the end for me."

"This is not the time to get all dramatic." I tried to get him to sit up, feeling his weight, the limpness in his muscles.

"I'm already dead."

"What are you talking about?"

"The blade…" He coughed, his face flinching in pain. "I dipped it in goblin extract."

I no longer felt the cold, the whipping rain, or the cuts and bruises covering my body. I went still, taking in what he had just said.

Goblin metal was painful and could kill a fae over time if exposed to it relentlessly, turning you mad first. Goblin extract was pure poison. Painful and merciless, it would make you tear at your skin with your fingernails, cut out your own heart, burn yourself alive just to relieve the pain.

We had pilfered it from a ship. I had Rotty lock it up, thinking it better in our hands than in someone else's.

"What?" I sat back on my heels, staring at the dagger in his chest.

"The blade was meant for Lowe…" He trailed off.

He had become the victim of it instead.

"No." I shook my head, not wanting to believe it.

"I am so sorry." His body jerked, his breathing becoming labored, his voice strangled as the poison found its way into his bloodstream. "For everything…"

"You have nothing to be sorry for." I still didn't want to believe it. He was the closest thing to a friend I'd ever had. "Don't give up," I demanded.

"Promise me you will keep Katrina safe."

"No need." I tried to keep the panic in my voice at bay. "You can do it yourself. I will get you off this ship. Just hold on, okay? Do it for Katrina."

"She is the reason for all of it…"

Her warm body brushed against mine, snapping me out of my memories. My chest was still heavy, like I was back in that moment, stuck in the past, filled with regret, pain, and grief.

Flipping over, I found Kat facing me, sound asleep, her body coiled up like she was ready to shift into her cat form.

My eyes tracked over her face, my fingers gently tracing her features. Fuck, she was beautiful. The face that launched a thousand ships. Or in my case, sunk it.

Little did I know that hiring a man who had an infant, with no place to go, would haunt me for hundreds of years after. A single choice altered the course of my life forever, weaving her in it, even when she wasn't there.

Little did I realize she would be my own downfall.

Pulling her to me, I wrapped my arms around her, my hand brushing her hair, my lips grazing her head.

"I swear, Rotty," I whispered into her hair. "I will keep her safe." I never made that vow to him then, but now I felt it bubble up, understanding the need to have her safe. To keep her protected.

A tingle of warning yanked my head over my shoulder, and I noticed the man was no longer in his spot, sleeping.

Dread shifted me away from Kat, bolting up, my eyes scanning the dark cavern.

Fuck. I berated myself. I took my eyes off him for a moment. Let my guard down.

Rising to my feet, gripping my gun, I crept quietly, my senses heightened. The flames from the fire dwindled the farther I snuck down the tunnel.

Did he decide to take off when I wasn't looking? Was this a setup? Ambush? Did he even know where these nests were? Or was he planning to attack us while we slept, limiting the playing field?

A noise stilled me in place. The back of my neck prickled, a screech so distant coming deep from the earth that I questioned its validity. Probably bats. The caves were home to many species. The alarm nipping at the back of my neck wouldn't ease: a feeling in my gut, a forbearing. Like something was waiting… something that dredged up fear I buried a long time ago.

"Hey." A hand smacked down on my shoulder.

"Shit!" I hissed. Spinning around, I cocked my gun, ready to fire.

"Whoa!" The old man stood there, overweight and inept compared to us; still, I couldn't shake something about him that unsettled me. None of us were stupid. This man was to be treated with caution. He was too friendly and welcoming, especially being partially our prisoner.

"Sorry to startle you." He held his hands up.

"Where did you go?" I snipped, taking a deep breath, taking my finger off the trigger but not lowering it.

"To urinate. Too much coffee." He chuckled, patting my arm, my paranoia rising in contradiction to his friendliness. "Better get some rest. We'll take off in a few hours." He went back to his place at the campfire.

I watched him, the gnawing feeling not going away, but I went back, lying next to Kat, keeping my eyes trained on him.

I sensed something was ahead.

I just didn't know if that was a good thing or a bad thing.

The darkness was oppressive, weighing down on you, pecking at your sanity. Days seemed like weeks down here, and every step we took magnified it.

Our footsteps marched in chorus; our torches danced across the rocky surfaces like a ballet while tension thrummed under the surface, keeping everyone silent. The old man led the charge, Kat and I keeping our weapons pointed at him. Annabeth stayed in the middle while Cooper tuned his senses to anything coming up behind us.

The first hour passed, taking us gradually down farther into the earth. Every once in a while, there would be markings on the walls—symbols, a forgotten language carved into the stone, demonstrating something had lived here before. Something ancient. Something powerful.

The magic was thicker than I was expecting, my ears nearly picking up the residual sounds of slumbering dragons. The farther we went, the more it threaded over me, sparking at my skin, tasting it on my tongue.

Maybe because, until now, no one had gone this far down. The intensity of it clung to the walls, a tomb of what was, a moment still trapped in time, not feeling thousands of years old, but just a few hundred. It made you want to leave, to turn the other way, to dismiss this place as a dreary cave. Nothing to see here; move along.

Druids had designed their hiding spells from dragon magic. The same type of enchantment, which had hidden King

Lars's property for decades, was how the dragons hid their treasure, but even better.

"You can really feel it, huh?" The old man turned around. He appeared oblivious to the guns pointing at him and the fact that he was a hostage, which unsettled me. "The nests are not too far now. Just around the corner there."

Anxiety rolled around in my gut as I twisted my head back to AB. She was having a bad day, exhaustion stripping away her light, stripping away the essence of the girl I knew. She was putting on a brave face, trying to pretend she didn't want to stop, curl into a ball, and let sleep take her. She was so stubborn in her need to protect others that it made me want to scream. The urge was nearly overwhelming to tell her I knew and to stop trying to be all right for everyone else. To just think of herself for a moment.

Her fingers absently stroked a sleeping Sprig, his head peeking out of her bag. Still in a honey coma, he woke up long enough to get a granola bar down his throat before he passed out again. He stuck close to AB as if he knew she needed him, needed his comfort.

Never in a billion years would I ever admit it to a living soul, but I was glad he was here. At least for Annabeth—one of those comfort animals for the sick. And I guess every once in a while, he was handy to have around.

But that was it.

Jumping from AB, my gaze met with Cooper's. His eyes were flickering red, a sign his beast was close to the surface. The magic down here had to affect his DNA, which was made to hunt and kill any threats.

His nose flared, sniffing the air, black fur growing on his arms before it receded.

"Croy—" I didn't even hear the rest of my name, my head snapping to Kat. Apprehension flooded me, raising my defenses up through my shoulders. But it was *her* unease, *her* feelings. I felt them broadcast through me like a radio, like I had my own private channel to her.

Given no time to even contemplate whatever the hell that was, my own instincts picked up on something as the old man veered us around the corner. Everything in my body rang with alarm, screaming something my brain had yet to understand, but my gut knew. A smell, an intuition, a recognition deep in my subconscious. It sucked the air from my lungs, locking up my muscles with a trauma I buried deep.

Before I could place my finger on the trigger, a horde of figures pulled away from the walls, their bodies almost invisible in the sheer darkness, coming at us in a blink. Guns went to our heads, halting us in place.

"Don't move." Sharp teeth snapped near my ear, his nasal voice turning my blood to ice. More things moved around, relieving me of my gun but not bothering to procure the blades attached to my hips. They were no threat to them. Behind, I heard Cooper roar, Kat trying to fight back while AB and I stood frozen. Shock held us prisoner, wrapping us in terror.

No. There's no way.

My eyes took in what my brain didn't want to compute, disbelief and fear spinning the room as less and less oxygen seemed to reach my lungs.

The old man stopped, turning slowly around, a strange smirk on his mouth as his gaze glided over the stocky, strange physiques around him. More of the forms moved up to him like they were his warriors.

"You were right to mistrust me." His friendly attitude and perfect English dropped away slightly, his shoulders pinning back, standing him up straight. "You thought I was your hostage when all along you were mine. Lambs to slaughter."

My lungs pumped, spots dotting my vision—I was close to passing out.

"I know who you are, who most of you are." He glanced from me to AB, to Cooper. "I've been waiting for you to finally make it down here. We all have." The man smiled, gesturing to his men. "They are eager to be reacquainted. One especially."

An enormous figure stepped forward from the shadows, his thick tail dragging along the dirt, almost dropping me to the ground.

It wasn't his barbed scorpion tail or his deformed human body that had terror flooding my veins; it was the piercing green eyes and the familiar heart-shaped face.

Zoey's eyes and face.

My body jolted back, vomit pooling in my stomach at seeing the scorpion tail.

Oh. Holy. Fuck.

I knew him.

Annabeth screamed beside me, a shrill, agonizing cry which cut through my heart. I tasted her pain, the nightmare she was experiencing right now, because I was in it too. We were both taken back to the underground labs and the castle where we fought against these things… lost loved ones.

My gaze moved around, taking in more creatures with Zoey's features, though some had dark hair and eyes, resembling their "mother," Sera. She was also part of DMG, another Seer like Zoey. They harvested eggs from her before she died.

The true originals.

The creatures that should never have existed.

Abominations.

I couldn't move as bile burned up the back of my throat, my head still trying to deny, to shake off what was in front of me.

This can't be happening. They were supposed to be dead. Killed after our battle with Stavros and the Stone.

But I couldn't deny Zoey was in a lot of these faces. Her DNA.

Dr. Rapava's experiments—his Frankenstein-like monsters were here.

Alive.

CHAPTER 7
Croygen

Alive.

My eyes locked on the misshapen creature, half scorpion, half man.

"Zander." His name grated off my tongue in repulsion. Fury started to clear my mind, my chest pumping up and down, my blood boiling under my skin.

His brother Zeke had been the one to kill Lexie during our battle with the Stone and Stavros.

Swallowing back the vomit, my gaze stumbled over more of the unnatural beings around me, my brain struggling to connect the dots and to understand how they were here in China.

"It's Z." He lifted his scaley lip. "And I'm flattered you remembered me." A grotesque smile carved his face. Zander had thick armor plating down his back like an arachnidan going into his thick, poisonous tail. The rest of him was man-like, but it was disproportionate, disturbing, and wrong.

They all were.

They went against nature, forced at the hands of a mad scientist whose ego made him think he was a god. He wanted to make an army of soldiers even stronger than the fae. He'd tried to turn Lexie and Annabeth into one of his monster creations. He had been successful with Sprig, but how many sprites were killed before or after? Sprig was the only one. And now he could no longer go back to his family, his home, or ever have a mate.

"I-I thought you were destroyed." They were supposed to be dead. Ryker told me he had their hideout bombed after the battle.

"Most were. But some of us knew we would be hunted down. So we escaped after Zeke was killed." His scratchy voice shredded my nerves.

Zoey had cut Zeke's head off after he stabbed Lexie, which I guess made Z next in line.

"Speaking of… how is dear ol' mom?" Z sneered, his tail curling, ready to sting. "Love to catch up with her again."

A chill ran down my spine, hating these disgusting things had any part of Zoey. That when she was unconscious, Rapava harvested her eggs and created these abominations.

"They had to go on the run." The old man nodded to the creatures. "Leave the US where they wouldn't be tracked down and slaughtered. They found me, hoping I would protect them from extermination."

"They need to be fucking annihilated," Cooper seethed. "They shouldn't exist… and I look forward to dissecting every single one."

"You should know not to underestimate them. Like cockroaches that will live far past anything else on this earth, they are not so easily eradicated." The old man clasped his hands. "Though *your* kind have been decimated over the centuries, haven't they? There are only a handful of Dark Dwellers left. How easily your entire species could be wiped off the earth for good." The threat was subtle, but I felt it, knowing this human wasn't all he seemed.

It was suddenly so very clear.

"You're…" I swallowed. More acid gurgled up my throat. "Dr. Jansug Novikov."

A smile arched the old man's mouth. "About time you figured that out."

I probably should have seen it, connected the dots faster, heard the Kartvelian accent hiding under his school-learned English. But the man before me was not who I had in my head as Rapava's villainous co-scientist. This heavyset, nonthreatening, friendly man.

"Dr. Novikov?" Annabeth whispered. "Isn't he… ?"

"Dr. Rapava's old partner," I replied and saw Rapava's name had AB flinching back, her lungs stuttering over each intake. "I guess when you said you were trying to preserve the species, you weren't talking about dragons," I spat.

Both men had been experimenting with how to advance the human species and make them more fae-like. Their studies had them parting ways. Dr. Rapava went to the United States, sinking deeper into his madness, building an army with spare body parts, while Dr. Novikov had gone after an ancient, more organic source, what the old fae called nectar.

And he found it.

"Boris was always impatient. Wanted results immediately. He didn't want to waste his time going after something he didn't know for certain existed. It eventually got him killed." Novikov's looks and attitude were vastly different from Rapava's. It made him seem more sympathetic, kinder, saner. But I had no illusions this was true. "We had our significant differences, but even *I* can't deny Boris's results, though they were never long term or sustainable. His little experiments were never going to alter mankind forever." He smiled. "I am." This was where I saw the resemblance, the egos of men who thought themselves above the fray. Their intelligence so advanced that they lost their grip on reality.

Novikov might be a lot more dangerous than Rapava ever

was. Because he was right. If this nectar could do what he said, it would change everything.

"And how nice you have built-in guards to hide the nectar." I swallowed, the guns digging into the back of my spine. I tried to see through the thick shadows. The large cavern could fit several dragons. The nests were long gone, but I saw the places still carved out for them, pits where they would hide their treasure under their beds. Symbols engraved on the walls of two large dragon shapes with smaller ones flying between them. Baby dragons.

"It was perfect—a place I could start testing my theories until my assistant let it slip where we were." Dr. Novikov's lips thinned.

"*My brother worked with a scientist in the Georgia Territory.*" The tiger shark's words came back to me from that night in Bulan's bar. "*They've disappeared. I last heard from him over three weeks ago when they were leaving Hong Kong to go up north, and I haven't received news from him since.*"

"I was forced to move around, create rumors to distract from our true location, but as you're aware, our hiding spot has been most *inconveniently* discovered by the press." Jansug stretched his arms to try and clasp them behind his back, starting to pace slowly. "Which has made things slightly problematic."

"But wasn't it *you* who spilled to the journalist?" Katrina asked, probably recalling the paper we read that night back in Nanxun, stating his name as the contributor.

"No. My *assistant* was the one to let it slip, his ego wanting the world to know what we had found." He scowled. "He became a *liability*." He peered at Z. "He had to be dealt with."

Meaning—he was dead.

"Is that what you're doing to us?" My lip curled. "Leading us down here to be dealt with?"

"Oh, no." His thick brow furrowed. "What a waste that would be. You are all such fascinating subjects." Dread dropped in my gut. *Subjects*. How many times I had been called that in Rapava's labs? "Especially you and the sprite." He faced Annabeth.

Her eyes widened, her hand going to the bag Sprig was in. "Why me?" Her voice was soft and even.

"Because, besides me, you are the only other human here, dear girl. And I need a test subject."

"What?" I belted.

"If you fucking touch her!" Cooper thrashed, almost slipping away from the group around him, but they were just as strong, and maybe even deadlier. Two of them appeared to have parts of a crocodile. Another had gorilla arms and legs, and another monster looked like a man and rhino-beetle, the black shell covering his chest and back like armor, his horn sharp and ready to gore someone.

"I'm doing you a favor, Dark Dweller. Isn't this why you are here, after all?" He tilted his head, shooting a look from Cooper to AB.

"Testing?" Kat gritted out. "What do you mean by that?"

"The nectar only really works on humans." The doctor answered. "I wanted to have more trial subjects and a lot more data, but I don't have many choices anymore. I must work with what I have." He motioned to Annabeth. "Bring her to me."

My head twisted, my eyes catching the monsters around Annabeth, their grips on her tightening as they dragged her forward.

"*Nooo!*" Cooper's roar ricocheted off the rock, cutting into my eardrum, his body lunging forward, claws sprouting from his hands.

Guns went to his forehead and heart. The gorilla monster slammed his fist into Cooper's stomach, folding him over as the rest beat on him too, one pistol-whipping him so hard he dropped to the ground.

"No! Stop!" Annabeth cried, trying to pull from her

captors' grips. "Please!" Tears filled her eyes, seeing Cooper try to rise, his eyes flashing red. "Cooper, no… please… stop… *for me.*"

Her pleas halted him in place, and a growl vibrated the ground in threat, his eyes locked on hers.

"Don't." She wagged her head at him, something passing between them, words and emotions no one else heard.

"I don't want to hurt her. That's not my plan, but I will if you can't control yourself." Novikov spoke directly to Cooper as Annabeth was placed next to him. "If anything, I'm *helping* her. I could tell last night that she's sick. The signs are obvious." He brushed hair away from her face, peering at her. "Cancer, am I right?"

Her nose flared, not looking at him.

"I am a doctor. I know the symptoms. And you are getting near the final stages."

It was exactly why we were here, what we wanted, but now I realized how naïve and single-minded we had been. So desperate to save her life, to do something, we didn't even consider any of the negatives, how it might affect her.

"With the right dosage, she should be good, which I think I have worked out."

"You *think?*" Cooper rose, his shoulders curving in a threat.

"She isn't my first test subject." Dr. Novikov tried to pretend Cooper's demeanor wasn't scaring the shit out of him, though his nervous swallow was giving him away. "It was how I found out what it could do. I'd never seen anything like it. So powerful, so magnified, but it was too much. They weren't able to handle it. They died a day later."

"Died?" Kat rolled her fingers up in balls. "How?"

"They basically melted from the inside out."

A bone-chilling noise came from Cooper.

"I am *certain* I have the perfect ratio now." Dr. Novikov held up his hand, thinking that would ease the Dark Dweller.

"You're testing on others before you take it," I stated, understanding his need for test subjects.

"It's what scientists do."

Cooper snapped his teeth. "You touch her, and I will rip your entrails out through your nose."

"I want to take it." Annabeth's voice came out strong and clear.

"What?" Cooper and I froze, our attention jerking to her.

Annabeth stood tall, her expression determined but oddly serene.

"Anna…" Cooper rasped.

"It's what we were coming here for anyway, right?" She swallowed. "I'm dying, Coop. There's no stopping it, and it's coming sooner than you want to believe. I feel it taking over. Winning." Her eyes filled with tears. "I love you more than anything, and if this gives me even the possibility of spending more of my life with you, then I want to take it."

"And if it doesn't?" he croaked.

"At least I went down fighting for the chance."

"I'm not ready." He shook his head. "I can't lose you… not now."

"You will never be ready." She tried to smile through her tears. "But time is not on our side. I have to take this chance. Now. I need you to be strong. Trust me to do this."

Emotion burned up my throat, grief hollowing out my chest at the idea we might lose AB today. Now. Everything was out on the table. There was no more hiding her disease, and without that barrier of pretense, I felt extremely helpless. Sacred and vulnerable.

Cooper's silence seemed to be the okay to proceed. Dr. Novikov nodded to Z, the original creation moving to the side, picking up a small box, looking dwarfed in his oversized hands.

That was it? All this death and sacrifice was over something which fit into my palm.

Z carefully handed him the box, and the doctor opened the lid, folding over some kind of cloth it must have been wrapped in. Its magic slammed into me as if it were freed from its prison. A whisper in my ear, the need to hold it, to take it from him, stole my breath.

Death, life, blood, earth, fire, air. I tasted it, felt it. A magic I couldn't describe buzzed down my spine, tightening my muscles, causing me to shiver violently.

It held a mix of extreme powers I had never felt before. I tasted blood and death, felt the heat of fire and air on my face.

The room reacted to its dominance, everyone stepping back with a jerk as if it spoke to all of us with the same intense command, needing someone to fall prey to it.

And it all came from a small brownish-yellow lump, a substance resembling honey or amber. It looked inconsequential, like something you forgot about in the back of your cabinet that was now dried up and expired. Not something that would give humans the power of fae, tipping the balance of nature and starting wars that would devastate this world. If it fell into the wrong hands, it could be internationally devastating. Where the hell did this even come from? How did it exist? Fae food was destroyed, so why and how did this survive?

Pulling on gloves, he grabbed shears from his gear, snipping off a piece the size of a raisin.

In the distance, commotion resonated, the monsters shifting their attention to the entrance, away from us to another threat. There was an awareness of something happening, but all I was focused on was the nectar.

The doctor turned to Annabeth, the piece in one of his gloved hands. Her throat bobbed, though her resolve did not waver.

Fear stomped up my throat, hazing my mind, and I felt myself push forward with the need to protect AB. What if we were all wrong? What if this killed her?

Voices and torch lights bounced in the space, twisting my head to the entrance. A handful of men dressed in dark clothes came creeping into the space, unaware of what they just walked into.

You could see it on their faces, the lights shining on those primordial manufactured creatures. Half human, half fae. Full monsters.

"What the fuck is that?" a man speaking in Hungarian shrieked at one of the crocodile monsters, his face stained in horror. I recognized the uniforms, the symbol on their arms from the group who attacked us the night before.

Crocodile-man lurched forward in a blink, his clawed hands slashing the man's throat so deeply his head almost fell off. Blood sprayed out, cascading down like a river, devastation and horror on his face while he dropped to the ground, knowing he was already dead.

Fear became a living thing that held its breath, taking a moment to comprehend what had just happened before it spewed out like a waterfall, devouring the room in a current of chaos. Unnatural screeches and sounds exploded as the monsters went for their new threat, abandoning Cooper, Kat, and me.

Cooper didn't hesitate to shift, his Dark Dweller roaring in a deafening pitch, the spikes on his back reflecting in the light. He leaped for the monstrosities, his teeth digging into the rhino-beetle's neck.

A barrage of bullets pummeled the walls and ground, zipping through the air. The doctor jolted with a cry. Snapping my head back to him, I watched a bullet hit the box in his hand, flinging the nectar from his grip. It tumbled to the ground, disappearing into the darkness.

I went still, my brain taking in what that meant. But I was too far away with too many barriers in my way. I wouldn't be able to reach it first.

"Katrina!" I bellowed her name, my gaze latching onto hers, shoving my idea toward her without another sound. I sensed the electricity, the buzzing, a connection going far beyond simple understanding. Deep and wordless, but just as clear. Just as loud.

Her head dipped in understanding, her body shifting as I flipped around, yanking my blade from the sheath, ready to put my body between her and any threat coming.

It was a game of catch the nectar.

A game we *had* to win.

CHAPTER 8
Katrina

My bones popped, my muscles twisting as I shifted into my cat form. My vision sliced through the darkness, my clothes landing beside me. I had known without even looking or hearing him what Croygen was telling me. It poured through my veins, whispered into my soul, etched every nuance into my muscles.

My sleek black fur blended into the shadows like I was part of them, my small frame racing across the cave without notice. I could clearly see Novikov scrambling to find the nectar, his hands frantically scraping the ground, landing on the small box.

Nooooo! My claws dug in more, zipping me to him as he started to stand. Lurching my body forward, I protracted my nails, sinking them into his face with a hiss.

"Ahhhhh!" A high-pitched scream emanated from him as he fell back. I dug in deeper, holding on, slicing and cutting trenches over his skin. His shrieks of pain yipped while he swatted and flailed to get me off, the box dropping from his hands.

Annabeth sprang toward us, reaching for it.

"No!" Novikov screeched, flinging me off. My body

smacked to the ground, rolling before I found my feet. He yanked out a gun from his pocket, trying to sit up.

Bang!

The shot rang in my ears, and everything went in slow motion. I watched the bullet discharge from the barrel, zipping only a few feet before it drove through the first obstacle in its way.

Annabeth! My mind screamed, a yowl coiling from my throat.

The force flung her down with a cry, her hand going to her arm, the contents of her bag scattering across the floor.

Fierce anger arched my back, a growl vibrating the back of my throat. This man needed to die. He scooted closer to the box, unfazed about shooting a young girl, his focus solely on the nectar.

Hissing, I pounced back for him, my nails clamping down on his arm. My teeth sank into his tendons, breaking his hold. The gun plunged to the stone, sliding a few feet away.

"Fucking bitch!" he spat, trying to shake me off, his movement only notching my claws in deeper. "Get off!" His free hand beat at my body, trying to pry me off.

Movement caught my eye as Annabeth tried to sit up, her hand on her bleeding shoulder, her mouth moving as a small shape darted for us.

Novikov snapped toward the small figure.

As commotion hurled around us, it felt like time had stopped. A standoff.

Sprig's tiny hands gripped the box, his eyes on the doctor. Sprig made a little nervous chirp sound, breaking the bubble. We all moved at the same time.

Novikov lunged for him, his hand wrapping around the monkey as Annabeth snatched up the fallen weapon, gripping it with both hands, her expression ready to rain down fire. Like this was personal. This was vengeance.

The gun fired, cracking the air like a whip.

Dr. Novikov's body jerked, his muscles locking up as his head snapped back, the bullet driving into his brain. It seemed to take a moment for his mind to register that it no longer functioned.

His eyes went down to where his hand gripped Sprig, the nectar that could have saved him within his grasp. But it was too late.

His eyes glassed over with understanding before they went blank. His hand loosened on Sprig, his muscles giving out, reducing him into a mere bag of bones.

I stared at the dead doctor for a moment, then slowly went to Annabeth. Heaving with pain and adrenaline, she kept her gaze lasered on him, the gun still pointed in his direction, ready to fire again. Bleeding and shaking, she looked like a badass fallen angel.

Gradually, she blinked, her gaze finding mine in the darkness, registering what just happened. She had killed a man.

Cooper's roar jerked her head, pulling us both out of the moment, the noise wailing back in my pointed ears, realizing violence and danger were moving in for us.

"Go!" Annabeth motioned to me and Sprig. "Get it out of here!" She flinched when she stood, her hand going to her bleeding shoulder, legs wobbling under her.

I didn't want to leave her, but she wouldn't be able to get out of here like I could.

"GO!" she demanded again, already heading toward her mate.

Gathering items up off the floor, Sprig shoved the small box in his backpack and leaped onto my back. *"Goooo! Bhean chait!"* With a whoop, his fingers gripped the fur at the base of my neck. "Ride on, kitty!"

I sprang forward, feeling his feathery weight, his heels digging into my sides to stay on, the knapsack filled with the nectar bouncing on his back. Keeping low, I darted for the exit, my heartbeat tripling as I veered away from people and through legs, our escape getting closer and closer. I saw the exit to the cavern; no one was aware the cat and monkey were stealing the treasure out from under them.

I could do it.

I *had* to.

What if I kept going? Took it back to Batara like I was supposed to. End the curse placed on me. Save my crew, my ship... myself. It was the pirate thing to do. Decency and honor were thrown to the wind. It was a weakness. A limitation. Being nice usually got you killed. I had to be cutthroat and ruthless.

Puss in Boots would take it without reservation, thinking only of herself, of the people depending on her back in Singapore.

You'd let Annabeth die? Leave all of them?

Darting out of the larger den, I curved around the corner.

Wham!

My frame ricocheted off what felt like cement, rolling back. The shock turned me back into my human-like body, and I skidded over the rough ground. I heard Sprig cry out, his body flying back, the honey bag falling off him as he hit the rocky floor. Pam and the nectar box tumbled out.

I shook my head, my brain spinning as I looked up.

Terror froze me for a moment, locked in the beam of the flashlights.

Violet-blue eyes peered down at me, and I took in his chiseled jaw and light brown hair. Two other men stood slightly behind him. I recognized them. The captains of the Hungarian men I saw following us that one night. The symbols of their prominent positions were embedded on their arm sleeves.

Sloane, Vale, and Conner.

"What do we have here?" Sloane pointed his light on the box, the lid slightly ajar, exposing the substance, which resembled a dried jumbo date.

"Is that what we were sent here for?" Conner tilted his head. "*That?*"

"Don't underestimate what it can do." A woman came from behind Sloane, her smug expression landing on me. Instant vile and hatred burned up my throat.

Amara.

My gaze snapped to the four of them, trying to understand the connection between them. Though with what I heard about Amara, I shouldn't be surprised.

She smiled hungrily at Sloane, touching his arm. "Didn't I tell you if you just waited here, it would come straight to you? I wouldn't lead you wrong."

He glanced at her dubiously while the other two appeared completely smitten, ready to answer her beck and call. That seemed to be one of her talents: seducing and conning men to get what she wanted.

Gunfire and loud yells from around the corner jerked their heads away for only a moment. I took advantage and scrambled for the box, my arm stretched out, my fingertips only inches from the nectar.

Crunch.

A boot pressed down on my hand, forcing a cry up my throat. Amara's heel dug in, snapping a few bones. "Not so fast, *pisică.*" Cat.

The sound of pounding feet headed our way put them on defense.

"We have to go," Sloane barked, looking at Conner. "Grab it!"

The fae bent over, his fingers about to touch the container, before he jerked back. I knew he sensed what I had. Something so powerful it sent shivers down your spine. The power thumped off it, a heartbeat under the skin, like it was declaring loudly what it was. Beckoning you to it, taunting you to touch. As if it was testing your willpower, your strength. Would you resist or fall victim?

"Now!" Sloane had his gun ready to fire at anything

coming around that corner, already backstepping, ready to take off.

Conner snatched up the box, shoving it in his bag.

"Nooo!" I thrashed against Amara's boot, pain pushing bile up my throat.

"Go!" Conner yelled, turning and running, Salone and Vale following suit, leaving the rest of their men to die for the cause.

"Thank you for making that so easy." Amara leaned down, her lips curling. "Getting it from them will be like taking candy from a baby." She drew out a gun. "And hurting Croygen will only make this day better." She pointed the barrel at me.

"Katrina!" Croygen's voice snapped both our heads in his direction as he barreled around the corner, terror wide in his dark eyes. "Amara, no!" He sprinted for me. Cooper was not far behind him, wearing only shredded pants, a barely conscious Annabeth in his arms.

Amara snarled, knowing she was no match for them. Lifting her boot from my hand, she took off running, catching up with the other three before vanishing quickly into the dark tunnel—along with the nectar.

"No!" I tried to get up, my eyes still focused on where they vanished.

"Kat?" Croygen dropped down next to me, his eyes searching my body, his hands moving over my bare skin. "Are you okay? Are you hurt?"

Cradling my hand, I shook my head. "I'm fine." Nothing I wouldn't heal from in a day. I peered up at him in utter failure. "They took it… those Hungarian soldiers have the nectar."

"Then we go after it." He tugged off his jacket, ripping off his shirt. He put my head through the hole, tugging it over my head and covering my naked frame.

More screams and cries came from the cave, some fleeing, running by us, while others were singing their death song.

If we stayed, we'd be next.

"We have to go. Now!" Cooper barked, adjusting AB in his arms, his feet already moving.

Croygen helped me up, pushing me to follow Cooper while he curved around, swiping up Sprig's sleeping form. He didn't pause before grabbing Pam too, putting the stuffed animal in Sprig's arms. He tugged on his long coat, looking even more like a sexy pirate with his bare chest and wounds. He placed his friend in his pocket, tucking him in deep to keep him safe. "Katrina?" he rumbled, his lashes lifting to mine. "Stop looking at me that way… and run."

Right. Run.

My bare feet hit the stone, my legs stretching as I trailed after Cooper, feeling Croygen right behind me.

Unearthly screeches and yells grew more and more distant as we headed for the surface. I hoped they would stay in the safety of their refuge. But with Dr. Novikov dead, would they remain there or venture out into the world?

I wagged my head, not wanting to think about the repercussions of that. What things like them could do in the world, especially if they reproduced.

They were a problem for another day. Right now I had to deal with the dilemma before us—getting the nectar back.

And knowing we were leaving this hellhole with even less than we came in with.

We rose from the depths, clawing and digging out of the tomb of darkness. The fresh air filled my nose, my face turning up to the rays of sun soaking into my skin. The sound of a rushing river was a balm to my soul as it drowned out the hustle of people streaming by me. It was stifling hot, but I lapped it up like cream, ready to curl up and absorb the heat.

It felt as if we had been underground for years. My throat tightened, and I swallowed back my emotion, shaking off the dread that haunted me the entire time—the fear that I would die there. Not on my ship or by the sea, but trapped in a crypt of darkness and death.

A shoulder slammed into me, causing me to stumble, and my eyes bolted open to the stream of treasure seekers making their way into the cave. The place was bustling and chaotic. Makeshift stands for supplies and food, corrals for horses, and peddlers with "authentic" cave maps packed the area in front of the cave entrance. Everyone thought they were the ones who would find it, had the right tools or strategy, and would come out of here the victor. And all were throwing their money away. The prize was already gone.

"Hungary," Croygen had said when we finally stopped for the night after running from those creatures, though I don't think the three of us slept. We stopped for Annabeth. Fatigue wore through her bones. "The men had some sort of insignia on their clothes. A legion. They must work for a fae ruler there. The only one is in Budapest."

"Do we know who reigns there?" Cooper rewrapped AB's wound with strips from his pants, his gaze locked on her. Her skin was pallid and clammy; she couldn't stay awake, her body too weak with blood loss and trauma. The bullet had gone straight through her shoulder, and her bleeding had slowed, but we all knew she was getting even weaker, unable to fight both cancer and a bullet wound.

The need for the nectar clanged in unsaid words. If we didn't get it soon, it would be too late. It might be already.

"No." Croygen shook his head. "Hungary being landlocked, I've not had any reason to know about it."

After the war, international news wasn't reported on like it had been. The countries that pulled from the Unified Nations were secretive and paranoid, cutting access to anything that might expose a weakness and becoming more totalitarian.

"So, do we head back to the ship or go over land?" I tied my dirty hair back in a ponytail, the knots in my shoulders pounding through my head, knowing either way would take too long.

"Land would be no less than four months, if not longer, on hard terrain. Dangerous." Croygen rubbed at his brow. "Going back to the ship and sailing will take at least two to three months."

"We don't have months." Cooper gnashed his teeth, trying to keep his voice down to not wake AB, his eyes flashing red. His anger streamed from what we all knew—Annabeth wouldn't make it.

She wouldn't even make the journey back to the ship.

"We're going to get it." He kept his gaze on Cooper. "We're not giving up." The problem was, Annabeth's body might decide to give up first.

"Kat?" Croygen stepped in front of me, breaking through my reverie and bringing me back to the present. The crowd bustling around us, the smell of food, horse manure, and dense, sweaty air collided with my senses. "Come on." He flicked his head for me to follow.

We had barely spoken the entire journey back, keeping our distance, neither wanting to talk about anything other than our plan to get the nectar. Ignoring our issues seemed to suit us.

Even a month ago, I would never have imagined the only thing I wanted to do besides kill him would be to run… to save myself from him. Or to fuck him.

Wearing his shirt, his smell wrapping around me twenty-four-seven, it felt like the latter was winning out. Awake, and especially trying to sleep, my thoughts wouldn't stop from slipping back to the time in the barn. The memories of him pushing deep in me, making me come so hard I blacked out. The way he felt over me, coming inside me. How nothing in the world could match it.

Tugging his shirt to stretch it further down my thighs, I

weaved through the throng of people, the smell of rice and chicken causing my stomach to growl. Food was high on the wish list, along with a bath and a proper bed to sleep in.

"I'll get the horses. You get AB anything to help with the pain." Croygen spoke to Cooper. "There has to be some kind of healer here." He glanced around at the stalls. "And maybe get some supplies." He started to turn. "Oh shit, I don't have money."

"What?" I recalled he had quite a bit of money. "What happened to it?"

Cooper snorted, digging into his pocket and slapping a few bills in his hands. "No porn and hookers this time, okay?"

"Funny." Croygen stuffed the notes in his pocket.

Cooper and AB shuffled away, his steps trying to match her small ones. She was barely functioning. She was moving, but her mind was far away. She held onto his arm, using him as a crutch, disappearing into the crowd.

"Hopefully they can find something to ease her pain." I tried to sound hopeful.

Croygen swung around, not responding, his jaw tight.

"So, what happened to all your money?" I caught up with him.

"I lost it."

"Lost it?" Pirates didn't *lose* money. We pilfered it. "What happened?"

"It's gone, okay?" He stopped, turning to me with a furrowed brow. "Taken."

"Taken?" My eyes widened. "As in stolen? From *you*?"

He huffed out, looking to the side. "Amara." He shifted on his feet. "She robbed me the night…" He drifted off. "You know, the night you and I…"

The night in the barn.

Blood rushed faster through my veins, heating me up and dripping sweat down my back.

It was the night that seemed to live on repeat in my head, which made me feel defenseless and vulnerable.

"Oh." My arms crossed, walling myself up from emotion.

Croygen sucked in through his nose, his mouth opening like he was going to say something. Instead he shook his head, stomping off to the rudimentary horse enclosure.

I felt a vital need to go after him, shake him, challenge him to say something about how he felt. At the same time, I had the same desire to run from him, to protect myself, make sure he didn't hurt me first.

Nothing good can come from this. I scolded myself. *You slept with a man who admitted to murdering your father. That makes you more despicable than him.*

Nails embedding into my palm and vowing to keep my distance to get through this ordeal, I tracked him inside the corral, finding him rubbing the head of his horse, Caramel. Emotion fluttered behind my lids when I saw Tootsie right next to them.

"Tootsie!" I wasn't an animal person really, but I missed that damn horse more than I thought. The horse neighed, flickering her head, strolling up to me as if she was excited to see me too.

"Hey, girl." I scratched her nose, blinking back the tears. "I missed you too."

A teenage boy dragged the saddles to us, dropping them at Croygen's feet with lethargy.

"Those two also." He nodded at Chocolate and Churro while he started to resaddle our horses.

"Oh, Caramel!" Sprig sang, crawling out of Croygen's pocket, where he stayed almost the whole return journey, sleeping a lot after his trauma. "Oh, now I'm sooooo hungry. Caramel and Chocolate on a Churro and lick it like a Tootsie Pop."

"Sprig. Be quiet." Croygen held up his finger to his lips, glancing around.

"They'll think they're high from all the fumes from the horse shit. Wow." He fanned his nose. "Thought the inside of your pocket smelled bad."

"Maybe if you didn't throw up in it."

"That was one time… okay, maybe twice. No more than five times, though… I think."

"And you pooped in it too."

"Yeah." Sprig grinned with pride. "I did do that." He leaped onto Caramel's head. "Well, maybe if you fed me proper food. I know you hate me, swattlebucket, but you want me to die a slow, cruel death?"

"Yes."

I heard Sprig and Croygen rattle on as I saddled Tootsie, but a squeak of metal drew my head to the side. On the other side of the overcrowded corral, I noticed a young boy opening a section, letting out a few riders.

Four horses trotted out of the stall, following an older man and his son riding behind on a smaller Mongolian horse. Three men dressed in dark colors and a woman with long dark hair rode behind one of the men. The sun glinted off her strands, making them look more purple as they galloped away. My stomach lurched with recognition.

"Croygen!" I shouted, pointing at the group. "That's them!"

His jaw locked down, a twitch jumping his cheek, determination set on his brow. He moved fast, his leg swinging up on the horse, settling in his saddle like he was made to ride.

"Get Cooper and AB!" He picked Sprig off Caramel, tossing him to me before he tapped his heels into the horse's side, galloping toward the exit. The boy who was closing the gate saw Croygen racing for him. With a yell, he yanked it back open just as Croygen barreled through, galloping after the group.

"He just tossed my ass like a football," Sprig twittered angrily. "I'm definitely going to poop in his shoes now!"

"Sprig." I climbed on Tootsie, placing him up on my shoulder. "Shut up." Spotting the top of the Dark Dweller's blond head, his size still casting a shadow on most people, I shouted at him, tugging on Tootsie's reins. "Cooper! We have to go now!"

Clicking my tongue, my heels nudging Tootsie, I took off after Croygen, not wanting to think about the fact I was wearing nothing but a t-shirt with no underwear, my bare ass rocking against the saddle.

But there was no way I would let Croygen do this alone.

We had the nectar within our grasp again.

They had no path back to Budapest that wouldn't take months. We would track them down and take it from them long before they reached the Hungarian border.

This time we would not leave empty-handed.

CHAPTER 9
Croygen

The heavy, sticky air clung to my skin, making me miss the coolness of the cave—slightly. Caramel's huffs grew more pronounced, pushing faster and farther, his hooves tearing through the terrain. It was a difficult dance. I needed to stay back far enough that they didn't catch me, but near enough I didn't lose them.

They were so close, the nectar still within reach. I couldn't let it slip through my fingers again. Annabeth's life was on the line. I would not fail her like I did Lexie.

A pinch of anxiety flared in my chest. The sun was lowering toward the horizon, notifying me we were heading north. Away from Shanghai, away from any port along the coast, and from the easiest route across land through India. Heading up toward Mongolia was asking for death. It may have been beautiful, but it was a harsh, unforgiving land, where only natives survived. And that was *before* the barrier fell. Now it was suicide.

We cut around a bend with vegetation so thick the trail was harder to see. I slowed Caramel to a trot, and a shiver went down my spine, countering the sweat beading at my temple. Magic pulsed and weaved through the trees.

I knew this type of magic…

Sliding off my horse, I snuck forward on foot, hearing a distant neigh of a horse. I tugged out a gun from my sheath, one of the many weapons I took off a victim in the dragon cave, and crept quietly, ready to fire.

My heart slammed in my chest, my muscles tense as I moved through the brush. Alarm pounded in the base of my neck like a drum. I could hear the horses and sensed they had stopped. Trepidation clogged my throat, my intuition already knowing, but hope kept the idea from fully materializing.

Slinking up behind some brush, I saw the five horses through the foliage nibbling on hay while the young boy brushed them down. Their fur was still sweaty from where the saddles used to be. He was the only one there, his pack on the ground with a bedroll suggesting he would be staying here tonight.

Waiting.

With my finger on the trigger, I searched for any kind of trap before I stepped out, my gun pointed at the boy. He let out a cry, his eyes widening, his body going still.

"Where are they?" I spoke in Mandarin, my head still jerking around, ready for Amara to step out with her new playthings.

The boy didn't move or speak.

"I asked you, where are they?" I barked, moving in closer, my voice seething. "The people riding these horses. Where did they go?"

The boy swallowed, his hands trembling as he pointed a few yards away through the brush.

"They went through there." His voice shook.

My gaze followed, dread swallowing me whole. My worst fear, the one I already knew deep down, was right before me.

Thick air rolled like an ocean wave, a glitch in the earth, a tear in the atmosphere.

A door to another place.

"*No.*" I heard a strangled cry whisper from me, my feet taking me closer like I was hoping it was a mirage. "No!" I bellowed, feeling everything not just slip through my fingers, but wash away in a tsunami.

When the Otherworld existed, fae doors were how fae entered and exited Earth's realm. When the barrier between our worlds fell, the doors we used like airport terminals deteriorated into illogical rabbit holes. They could trap you inside, letting you out in desolate places across the world, only to vanish from that spot, leaving you stranded. They were harder to see now because of the magic in the air, and there were a lot more of them since the worlds blended. They had no rhyme or reason, like a computer system with an internal glitch. There were only two people I knew, Ember and Lorcan, who were able to make their way through them, and I had no understanding of how they did.

Most would walk through and never be heard from again. It was similar to getting in a car with someone so drunk they weren't capable of even standing and hoping for the best.

And my chance at saving Annabeth's life just walked into one.

The nectar was gone.

I stared at the ripple in the atmosphere in disbelief, my shoulders sagging with despondency. Energy hummed at my skin; just through this wave of magic was Annabeth's life and probably Kat's life too. If the vow didn't kill Katrina, Batara would.

A thought nibbled at the back of my brain. Why was the boy still here? Where was his father?

Whirling around, I strode up to him, my intensity forcing his feet back in terror.

"Where is your father?" I growled, looming over him. "Did he take them through?"

He tried to open his mouth, but only a squeak came out.

"Tell me!" I fisted his worn shirt, not caring he was

probably only about fourteen. My entire world was on the precipice. This was life and death.

A sensation slunk over me, an awareness, a rudimentary part of my DNA recognizing and responding. It was peace, excitement, strength, and aggravation all in one.

"Croygen." Her figure slipped soundlessly through the brush, strolling up to me. My teeth clamped together, spiking fear into my pulse. Because I had felt her, knew she was here. I seemed to always fucking know. Every sense tuned to her like a radar.

"Croygen, stop." Her hand touched mine, sparking desire down my arm to my cock.

Snarling, I shook her hand off, gripping the kid's shirt tighter. "Not before he tells me where his father is. Did he take them through the door?" Mandarin hissed through my teeth.

"Ye-ye-yes," he stuttered out his reply.

"He knows the fae doors? How to go through them?" I leaned my face close. "If you lie to me…" I glanced back at the ripple. "I will be tossing you in there after him. Want to see how many decades it takes to find your way out?"

The boy gulped, fear streaking his face. He understood that was a real threat. If he went in, he probably wouldn't see his family again.

"Talk."

"My fa-father knows how to get through the doors." Sincerity blinked back at me. "People pay him to lead them through."

"Bullshit. No one knows how to work them now." Katrina crossed her arms. "This is a complete scam."

"No. No." The boy held up his hands. "He really knows."

"He can't—"

"Actually, I do know people who have figured them out." I loosened my grip on his shirt.

"Really?" Kat's brow wrinkled. "How?"

"I have no idea, but they do. Must be some genetic thing, like how some people eat cilantro and taste soap." I shrugged. Zoey and Annabeth were both ones who hated it.

Katrina scoffed, shaking her head at the comparison.

"Your father will come back through here, then?" I turned back to the boy.

"Yes." He nodded. "I wait with the horses for him, and we go back."

"How long?" My intensity drove back up. "When does he return?"

"Depends." The boy lifted one shoulder, his body still trembling. "Might be hours, could be a day, maybe two."

I let out a frustrated growl. I didn't want to wait. I wanted to go now.

"Do you know where they went?" I figured Hungary, but I wanted to hear it for certain.

He shook his head.

"No hint on a destination?" The boy continued to wag his head. "Can you tell me anything else?" Aggravation had me shaking him.

"Croygen." Kat once again touched my arm, trying to ease me back. "He's just a boy. He doesn't know anything more."

I breathed out, slowly uncurling my fingers from his shirt.

"And here I thought the Silver Tongue Devil used honey, not vinegar." The moment the word came out of her mouth, her eyes went wide, knowing what she just did.

"Honey? Did you say you had honey?" Sprig parted through her long, thick, tangled hair, peeking his head out from her shoulder. "Is it lunchtime? Oh wait, it's getting dark. That must mean I need to get a fast lunch in before dinner... then supper. Oh, and need dessert after both. Can we get Izel's pancakes? I've really been craving them. Swimming in honey... they just melt on my tongue. Oh... or crispy honey chicken and double honey waffles, with a side of honey?"

The boy's eyeballs practically popped out of his head at seeing Sprig, his panic slamming into me like a bomb. A piercing scream exploded through the air, terror flaying his arms, slapping me away from him. He darted for the Mongol horse, muttering something under his breath frantically, which sounded like Sun Wukong. He leaped on the horse, striking his heels into the animal's ribcage, jolting the horse forward and tearing out of there.

"Does he not like chicken and waffles?" Sprig sniffed. "How can you not like waffles? They're like tasty clouds of heaven."

"Think it was you." Katrina wiggled her shoulder. "He couldn't be in the presence of a god."

Groaning, I palmed my face. "Why? Why did you have to do that?"

"That's right!" Sprig puffed up. "I am a Monkey God!" He peeked out toward where the boy departed. "You should fear me, peon! I am the all-powerful, supreme, invisible…"

"You mean invincible."

"King of all kings…"

"He can't hear you anymore."

"Packed with extra glory! Don't let this tiny, super cute body fool you. I make grown men weep."

"That you do." I nodded, rubbing my hand over my face.

"I make them bow! I make them tremble. I am the God of all gods!"

"He really needs an off switch."

"Shush, lesser one…" He held up his hand to me. "Your god is speaking."

"When will that narcolepsy kick in again?" Kat sighed.

"Shhh." Sprig put his hand over her mouth. "Subordinates do not speak in my presence."

Kat wrenched her shoulder.

"Ahhhh!" Sprig flew off, hitting the ground.

"How the mighty have fallen." I smirked.

"Curse on you! And you!" He pointed at us. "Poop on both your shoes!"

The sound of hooves hitting the earth pulled my attention, and I moved in front of Kat and Sprig.

"It's Cooper and AB." Kat's senses picked up on them way before I could see them.

The horses came up the trail, Cooper and Annabeth on one horse, with Churro tied to Chocolate, carrying some supplies on her back. The Dark Dweller held AB tight to his chest, keeping her secure to him. Only an hour's journey, and it had clearly taken its toll on her. She appeared fatigued and pallid.

"Oh good! I am saved!" Sprig chirped, scaling up Chocolate as they trotted up. "Thank gods you arrived when you did. I almost died!"

Cooper ignored him and glanced around, his eyes taking in all the other horses, his jaw straining when it landed on the fae door. "What's going on?" He swung off the horse, gripping AB's sides and helping her down. "We saw a young kid on a horse barreling down the hill like a bat out of hell. You guys have anything to do with that?"

"That one did." I pointed at the furball sitting on Chocolate's head.

"Fae and human cower at my name! I really need my cape on for this, don't I?" He paused for a moment, like he was debating going to find it in his backpack. It was the one thing that hadn't fallen out in his tumble, the fabric stuffed tightly inside. "Next time." Sprig stood up, his arms reaching for the sky. "He couldn't handle my power, my ultimate-cy…"

"That's not a word."

"It is now. I decree it so."

"Have anything to shut him up?" I tipped my head at Cooper, nodding at the supplies, ready to lose it.

"Come on, Sprig." Annabeth motioned to him. "I found

some granola bars at a stall." She shuffled unsteadily toward Churro.

"Honeyhoneyhoneyhoneyhoneyhoney." Chatter splintered in my ear, his high-pitched sounds of excitement, his tiny frame racing down the horse's back and leaping to the other one.

The moment AB was out of ear range, Cooper inched in closer, his expression deadly, his tone tense. "If you tell me they went through the fae door. That the nectar is gone…" His gaze took in Kat and me, realizing that was exactly what happened.

"Okay, I won't tell you that is exactly what happened."

"Trasna ort féin!" Go fuck yourself! Cooper rubbed the back of his neck, anger and frustration strangling his vocals, his Gaelic coming through strong, like he no longer comprehended English.

"It's not totally hopeless." Kat touched his arm.

"How?" His head jerked up, his eyes feral, swimming in deep crimson. "Once you go through, you might never come out." His arms flung around, his pitch high and wild. "And the only two people I know who can work them are on the other side of the world. And if you can't tell, we have no way of contacting them." Cooper was losing it, the threads of his sanity starting to unravel, the idea of losing his mate for real chipping away at him. If she died, he would ultimately go all beast—an unstable one at that—if he didn't kill himself first.

"Cooper." I peered over at AB, trying to keep my voice low.

"Why would they even do that? They could be lost in there for centuries."

"Cooper—"

"Fuck!" he bellowed, blackish fur starting to pop out of his skin, his Dark Dweller clawing at the surface, ready to destroy everything, to make the world feel his pain and anger.

"Cooper!" My forearm went into his chest, slamming him

up against a tree. Fire flamed in his eyes, his teeth becoming deadly, sharp fangs. "Get your shit together. I know you're mad, and I know you want to tear this world apart." My voice was low and threatening. "But losing it won't help her. She needs us to be strong, not to fall apart on her." I nodded back at AB. He took a deep breath, tendons in his jaw still twitching, but he didn't push back. "She's my family too. And you know I will do *anything* for her."

Cooper sucked in through his nose, his eyes lowering.

"The boy told us his father knows how to work the doors."

"What?" Cooper's head jerked up, hope flooding his eyes back a light brown. "He can work the doors?"

"That's what the kid told me, and I believe him. I almost made him piss himself." I eased off Cooper, stepping back. "All we can do is wait for him to return." I motioned to the magic wrinkling the air. "And make him take us *exactly* where he took them."

The crickets hummed loudly through the dense forest. The sultry humidity clung to me like another layer of dirt. I heard the owls and bats hunting for their meals, skittering small rodents through the brush.

An abundance of stars peeked through the canopy of trees, bright and twinkling, having no care or thought for those who suffered below. Lucky damn stars.

It was deep into the night, and Annabeth and Sprig were fast asleep, though I knew the rest of us were awake. Cooper couldn't sit still, his energy needing an outlet. He disappeared into the forest an hour ago, his Dark Dweller hunting the night.

Katrina was curled away from me, but I knew she wasn't asleep by the way her chest moved up and down, the way her muscles didn't relax. I seemed to be aware of every single molecule in her, her nearness giving me a strange calmness. Like her being safe and close was all that truly mattered. It fucking unnerved me, had me stirring like I needed to run away from that feeling as well.

And seeing her in my shirt, knowing she was bare underneath…

Running my hand over my face and through my hair, I sighed, wishing for a bottle of alcohol, maybe a case, to drown my thoughts. I preferred dealing with my problems that way. It was easy. Simple. And I longed for easy—because with Kat, everything felt so complicated.

More and more, I was seeing how everything since the day I forced her off my ship led back to her. She was the root cause of my ruin, my slide into darkness. Yes, I made those decisions, but it was Katrina that led me there. And she didn't even know how she had caused my demise. How she plagued me. I had been destroyed from her departure on.

What's that stupid superstition? Crossing paths with a black cat is bad luck? Yeah, this time it was true.

Kat huffed, sitting up, irritation curling her spine.

"What?"

She glared over her shoulder at me, standing up, her bare feet padding across the forest bed.

"Where the fuck are you going?" I shot at her. Why was she pissed at me?

She ignored me, slipping quickly into the night, out of sight.

"Katrina?" Annoyed, I stood up, not liking her out of my eyeline, my feet already following her. "You shouldn't venture off."

Yes, I sounded like a masochistic prick. She could take care of herself; I knew that. The girl had a reputation for being a ruthless killer in the pirate world.

Yet, she was still *Katze* to me.

"You know, there are a lot of things in these mountains that eat kitties for an appetizer." Saying that made my mind go to a very different place. I wanted to be the hunter, the stalker of my prey, to feast on her.

I stopped, feeling her near, a hum in my body, a certainty in my gut.

"Kitty-Kat?" Her silence made me laugh. "Think you're hiding from me?" I scoffed. "That I don't know exactly where you are? That I can't find you like before? You can't run or hide from me, Katrina. Not anymore."

Her energy buzzed my skin, hardening my cock.

Motion came from behind. My blade was yanked from my belt, digging into the side of my neck. I didn't resist, a smile curving my mouth, filled with cruelty. With malice. For all the hell her existence had put me through.

"How many times do I have to remind you?" Adrenaline pulsed in my ears, the tip of the blade breaking my skin. "You had your chance." I started to twist at the same time she shoved me back. My feet stumbled, catching my balance, my spine cracking against a tree, her father's blade kissing my neck.

"This is getting kind of old." My lashes lowered to the weapon.

"It is," she hissed, her green and yellow eyes glowing bright. Angry. Scared. Frantic. I could feel it all coming off her. "*This* needs to stop."

"What does?" I knew what she was talking about, but I wanted her to say it. To confirm it first.

"This!" She wagged her head between us. "You. Me. *This feeling...*" Her free hand rolled into her stomach. "This sensation..." Her shoulders wiggled. "Like you're everywhere. All the time. Crawling over my skin, burrowing into my bones. I want it gone. I want to cut it out of me. I don't want to feel this!" She pushed the blade in deeper, my dick rock hard, my need to take my own anger out on her making me dizzy. The need to fuck her until I didn't feel anymore, to free myself of her.

"You don't think I feel the same?" I snarled back, tapping into my anger, turning to anything which kept me from touching her. "I don't want this either!" I gestured between us.

"Then make it stop!" she demanded of me, like it was all my doing.

"You make it stop!" I yelled back. "You're the one who cursed me… afflicted my life."

"Me?" Her mouth parted. "You blame me for your own failings? You were the one who destroyed *my* life."

Rage surged up my spine, burning away any decency, any guard rails. Adrenaline pushed me forward, and I went into survival mode, the actions embedded in my muscle memory. When I hit her elbow, the hand with the knife dipped. I knocked the blade from her hand, dropping it to the ground. Clutching her neck, I twisted her around, shoving her up against the same trunk.

The shirt she was wearing of mine caught on the wood, tugging up as she slid back down to her feet, showing me her pussy, letting me feel the warmth of her need.

Rage and desire came to a pinpoint, a knife's edge. The one drop that would burst the dam.

I wanted her to feel my pain, to experience my loss, to go through everything from that day.

My free hand moved between her thighs, parting her folds.

"My ship sank… *because of you*." I slipped my fingers through her wetness, my thumb grazing her clit.

"What?" A gasp hitched from her throat. Confusion furrowed her brow as her hips widened for me, feeling the same contradictory emotions I was.

Good.

"My crew died… *because of you*." I sunk two fingers inside her, slowly pumping them in and out.

"Oh gods…" A deep moan arched her back while her head shook against my claim.

"I lost my money, my livelihood, and my reputation… *because of you.*" I added another finger, thrusting in harder, the sound of her desire overtaking the crickets.

"No." She dared to defy me. "You did that yourself."

I huffed, leaning over her until I was a breath away from her lips, my tongue sliding over my bottom lip as my thumb pressed down on her clit, causing her to gasp again. "I fucked my first mate's daughter like a fiend… *because of you.*" I was so close to undoing my trousers, sinking into her again, my dick craving her more than I needed air.

"Well, guess what?" She kept her face right at mine, her lips brushing mine. "I *fucked* my father's best friend, the one he trusted with his life… *because of you.*"

Her words, her raspy voice, almost undid me, my balls so tight and heavy they became cement, my pre-cum soaking my pants. I knew she wanted me to fuck her. I could feel her need wrap around my cock, her moans slipping from her throat, begging me to thrust into her, seeking more. Seeking release.

Seeking peace.

Which she would not get from me.

I felt her pussy start to squeeze around my fingers before I slipped out of her. Her cry of desperation, a plea to make her come, took everything in me to ignore, going against my nature. But it felt more than that with her, like it went against my soul. I knew if I allowed myself to sink under, be consumed by her one more time, I would never find the surface again. I would let myself drown in it.

I stepped back, needing to suck her taste off my fingers, but knowing I would fold, the line I was trying to hold was almost nonexistent.

Her lids narrowed, fury brightening her eyes, realizing what I was doing.

My cruelty wasn't done.

"Your father?" I gritted my teeth, already wanting to stop the words from coming out. "He's dead… *because of you.*" I turned, stomping off back to the camp, feeling like my malicious words only drove that dagger into my own heart.

CHAPTER 10
Katrina

Croygen's silhouette slipped back into the darkness, leaving me staring after him, unable to move. My body heaved, aching for release, wondering what had just happened. I tasted his cruelty like a bitter pill sticking in the back of my throat. The pleasure he inflicted was turning to pain, cold shivering through my body.

Disbelief, confusion, hurt, disappointment, and anger collided, a battle playing out between them with no winner.

I had wanted him to feel my rage, to drop to his knees under my brutality. Yet in seconds, he flipped my emotions about like a dying fish, staring wide-eyed and gasping for air, relinquishing me to perish.

At the camp, I had felt his irritation and ire stronger than if he actually spoke words. It billowed off him, was in every breath, spearing into me like a thousand razors. It wasn't normal. This shouldn't be something I could feel. Not like this. Not like he somehow embedded himself in me like bacteria, growing and spreading into my soul.

Laying there, a dozen ways to kill him went through my mind, yet all ended with me sliding down his shaft, riding him until we both expelled our demons. My core squeezed with desperate need, and I forced the imagery from my mind. My thoughts only seemed to gain his wrath, like somewhere inside him, he was battling back without even realizing why.

The need was there to turn my father's blade on myself and cut out whatever disease blackened my soul, whatever weakness Croygen was making me feel.

I wanted it to stop. Because somehow I knew—one time with him, and there was a chance of escape. The second time, there would be no way out for me, and I'm not sure I would even fight it. Just let myself sink into my ruin. I couldn't let myself do that. I made a vow to myself and to my father…

"Your father? He's dead… because of you." Croygen's malicious words rang through my head, finally breaking through the fog, and finding their place front and center in my mind.

What the fuck did he mean?

He killed my father. His ship sank and his crew died because of *his* failings, not mine. He ruined his reputation and put himself on Amara's leash because *he* was weak.

I had nothing to do with any of that; he had affected my whole life. I was beaten and abused in boarding school, orphaned, and then lived on the streets, hungry and scared. I became a pirate because of him, lost my best friend because he was all I could think of.

It all led back to *him*.

Pricks of rage tingled the back of my neck, my gaze going down to where his t-shirt still hitched up, exposing my traitorous body, still throbbing with need, not caring what it had to sacrifice or do to feel him inside me again.

A hiss gurgled up my throat, my gums aching as my canines grew longer, my focus locked on where he left. How dare he turn this on me. Getting the last word in. Walking away as if it were nothing.

Yanking my shirt down, I pushed off the tree, stomping

for the camp. Fur danced down my vertebrae, my cat ready to attack.

As I stepped out into the clearing, magic sizzled at my skin. A slight crackle of energy popped in my ears, whipping me around as a small, older human man in thin cotton pants and a threadbare robe-style jacket came out of the fae door.

The moment he exited, his feet came to a halt, his gaze darting between me and Croygen. His slight frame locked up, his shoulders going back defensively, his gaze searching over the space like he was looking for someone.

"Your son is not here," Croygen spoke in Mandarin.

The man's eyes still jerked around in pursuit of finding him, taking in Annabeth's sleeping body near the fire, evaluating and analyzing everything before his dark, sharp eyes went to the pirate.

"Where is he?" he replied in English, already assessing our first language. "Who are you?"

Closer to my height and weight than Croygen's, the man didn't wear pride and strength as a badge; it was embedded in his DNA. He knew we were fae and had no fear of us. His shoulders back, he was ready to battle us if he needed to.

"Your next customers." Croygen eased closer, his charisma oozing from him. "Take us to the exact same place you took the last group, and we pay you a nice sum. Simple as that."

The man's lids narrowed. He was guarded. Suspicious. "How much?"

"One thousand yuan."

"Seven thousand."

Croygen choked out a laugh. "You're joking." He shook his head.

"You want to go to the *same* place?" The man tilted his head, a challenge in his tone.

"You want to know where your son is?" Croygen countered, his expression hard, giving away nothing.

"You don't have him."

"You want to take that chance on your son's life?" Croygen lifted a brow. "That I wouldn't hold him as collateral?"

The man's nose flared, calculating Croygen was exactly the type of man who would do that.

"Six thousand. And I take you exactly where I took them," he said firmly.

"Two thousand, and I won't gut you and feed your entrails to him." Croygen flicked his head to the side. From the darkness, a low growl shuddered the air. Two red eyes glowed from the bushes as the enormous outline of Cooper's beast stepped forward, the razors lining his back glinting in the firelight.

If I didn't know him, I would have shit myself.

The man watched the beast, his face emotionless, but the bob of his throat signaled his anxiety. His jaw clenched down. "Three thousand. No less."

Croygen slanted his head as if he was pondering it, letting the man stew while Cooper let out another low vibration.

"Okay." Croygen nodded, though I had no idea where he was going to get three thousand yuan from. "But you tell us every single thing you know. Everything you heard. And you take us to the exact spot."

The man dipped his head, having no allegiance to them.

"My son?"

"He's probably back home." Croygen shrugged, a cocky grin showing he was deceiving the man the whole time. "Though he might have nightmares of mythical monkey gods now."

The older man's lids lowered in confusion.

Croygen strolled closer, his own puzzlement wrinkling his forehead. "You are human." Croygen stopped right before him. "How do you know the doors? How is it possible a human can access the doors when most fae cannot? It shouldn't be possible."

"The person who says it cannot be done should not interrupt the person doing it." The man spoke an old proverb, staring at Croygen cooly.

Croygen peered down at him, huffing as his lips twisted in a ghost smile. Respect for the old man danced in the pirate's eyes.

"You better be right, old man." He turned, picking up Cooper's clothes and tossing them toward the beast shifting back in the bushes. "Let's go."

It took us barely ten minutes to get our minimal stuff together and get Annabeth up.

The man's only reaction to Sprig was to stare at the sprite, not moving from his spot, showing no outright panic over a talking monkey, which made me curious about was going on in his head.

"But I don't want to say goodbye." Sprig darted to the horses, climbing up on Cooper's horse.

Honestly, I was having a tough time too. Rubbing Tootsie's nose, I leaned my head into hers, thanking her for being such a wonderful companion. I was going to miss her a lot.

The man promised when he returned, on Sprig's claim that he would smite his whole family, to take the horses back and give them a good home.

The man seemed to take his promises very seriously. I guess when a monkey king demands you to do something, you do it, not willing to chance your luck or his wrath.

"Chocolate, oh Chocolate… you know how I love you." He hugged his ear. "How you melt in my mouth… and sometimes I pour you over my body and Pam's." He leaped from Cooper's horse to mine. "And Tootsie… I could suck on your tasty goodness for hours."

I heard Croygen make a noise behind me.

Sprig leaped to AB's horse. "Churro. You are the dough beneath my wings… your scrumptious center, drizzled in cinnamon, sugar, and pure goodness. The ways I can consume you. How many times I fell asleep with you in my arms, mouth, and up my—"

"Sprig," Croygen warned, hitching a bag of supplies up on his shoulder.

"But it is you…" Sprig bounced over to Croygen's horse. "Caramel… I will miss the most. The closest to honey. The golden goddess of my heart." He draped himself between Caramel's ears. "Praise Saint Honey Tits… wait…" Sprig perked up his head. "Do horses have tits? Udders of caramel honey I can suckle from?"

"It's a *male* horse." Croygen snorted, grabbing his pack. "But sure, go ahead and try, fuzzball… think whatever you suck down there will come out yellow… or maybe a cream—"

"Stop." I held up my hand, my lids closing, needing to bar all thoughts going forward. "Just stop there." I shook my head, causing Croygen to snicker to himself.

"Is he intercoursing with me again?" Sprig sniffed, his lids blinking. "He knows not to intercourse with me about honey."

"Sprig, come on." I patted Tootsie one last time, stepping away. The sprite bounded from Caramel to me, climbing on my shoulder and tucking under my hair.

Cooper helped Annabeth to the door, her wound redressed, her legs steadier thanks to the magic herbs the healer gave her back at the caves. But we all understood that any resurgence was only temporary.

AB would not get better. Not unless we found the nectar.

"Rule One." The man stood right before the rippling magic. "Do not let go of each other. There are many doors. Many times we must run to catch one before it is gone. If you get lost? You are on your own. Rule two." He opened his palm. "Half up front."

"No." Croygen struck back. "That was not our deal. You will get paid when we get there."

"No. That is impossible. Half now."

Croygen stepped up to him, not needing anyone else, his demeanor enough of a threat.

"Your son may be afraid of a superstition, but I think you're wise enough to fear *me* out of everyone." Croygen's voice was low, scraping the ground, his authority clear. Dominant.

And fuck did my body respond.

"Pirates tend to hold very long grudges. Your great-great-great grandchildren's lives aren't even a blink compared to mine. I won't kill you. I will rain hell on your family for generations to come." Croygen's silvery tongue spun around his threat like silk. "Do you understand me?"

For the first time, I saw trepidation in the man's eyes. He swallowed, his head dipping.

"Good! Let's go." Croygen slapped him on his shoulder, hitching his bag higher, a smile widening his features like they were old friends. The sudden switch made him even more dangerous and scary because he couldn't be predicted. Something Croygen was good at. I had seen him do this to captives and sometimes troublesome crew on the ship many times when I was a young girl.

"Sprig?" Croygen glanced back at Sprig on my shoulder. "Come on." He tapped at his coat pocket, where I knew Pam was. "You know you're gonna pass out."

Sprig chirped, hopping from my shoulder, using all the others to get to Croygen. Climbing down, he slipped into his pocket.

"If you pee or poop in there, Pam is not going to get a facelift again, but an entire head lift." He grumbled at the monkey, then faced our guide.

The man blinked, still in shock at the monkey-sprite.

"Lead the way," Croygen ordered.

The man shifted around, facing the door, nodding for Croygen to take hold of his loose robe-style jacket.

Croygen took the lead, grabbing the fabric. I shuffled back, nodding for AB to go next, that I would take the rear. "She needs to be between you two." I motioned for Cooper to go next. It was better to keep AB with them, in a protected bubble, but in truth, I needed to be as far from Croygen as possible. My mind was pissed, and my feelings were hurt, but my body was even more of a defector.

I seemed to have no morals when it came to him. No ethics or principles either.

The tour guide stepped into the door with us trailing behind like a gaggle of waddling geese.

Before the wall fell, fae doors weren't as prominent or as plentiful as they were now. When the barrier broke, it ripped thousands of tears through the atmosphere, making these glitches.

Before that, they were a lot harder to find, and most didn't even use them. I had no memory of using one, though my father said I did a few times when my mother was still alive. There was no reason for me to. I enjoyed the journey, the wind in my hair, sailing across the sea.

My knuckles turned white, my grip on Cooper's shirt strangling my fingers as we stepped through.

A gasp punched my chest. Magic batted at my skin, slipping over and charging the hair on my arms, feeling like I was walking through jelly. Magic pummeled my senses, everything shifting in color, humming at my ears. The man zigzagged us down a hall. Then through a door, which looked like a vast desert, before going in another door. Doors would multiply and disappear, alter locations mid-step. Everything sped up, slowed down, tilted, and spun until I no longer knew which way was up or down. Nausea burned in my stomach, confusion distorting my mind. It took everything I had to keep holding on to Cooper.

I could see how easy it would be to get lost in here forever, giving up and wandering aimlessly around, tangled in the magic, lost in the contents of your mind.

I had to be going mad because I kept hearing Croygen, not so much in words, but I sensed him right in my ear.

Don't you dare let go, Kitten.

For what could have been minutes, hours, or days, our guide hurried us through another door, spitting us out into a small space. My bare feet hit cement floor, my eyes taking in a river in the distance, night heavily blanketing the city with only a few lights dotting the landscape.

Arms came around my figure, grabbing me before I hit the wall at my running speed. Croygen pulled me into him, cushioning my landing. His warmth circled me, my skin instantly feeling the change in weather, prickling with goosebumps.

"You okay?" he muttered in my ear. It felt too easy to stay here, to not move from his arms. To let myself sink into his embrace.

"Yeah." I pulled away. "Fine."

"Fuck." Cooper leaned on the railing, his hand on AB's back as she threw up over the side. We looked to be in some kind of bell tower, the dome of a church below us. "That was… fucked up." He brushed her hair away. "You okay, babe?"

She nodded, wiping her mouth.

"That was no joke." Croygen rubbed his head. "How the hell do you know how to get through those?"

"Strength of mind." The man stared at Croygen, his underlying jab very clear.

"Getting sassy for a guy who hasn't been paid yet."

The man held out his hand.

"Tell us everything you know first. Like where the hell we are?" Croygen inched around the space, trying to stay clear of the fae door.

"Budapest," he replied dryly. "A boarded-up church. That is all I know."

Croygen stood over him, his shoulders eclipsing the small man.

"They said they wanted to go to Budapest. I brought them. They paid me, and I left."

"You have no idea which direction they went?"

"They motioned over that way, across the river. That is all."

My head poked through the open arches, taking in the view across the river. On the other side of the Danube sat what looked like a palace up on the hill. Firebulbs made the pristine baroque-style building glow like a cake topper, showing off its glory with arrogance. The beautiful structure stretched out over its perch above the city like a white, fluffy, spoiled cat, giving no heed to the darkness that suffocated the other side.

"Look." Cooper pointed to a flag flapping in the wind above the building. The same insignia that crested the men's clothes was on the flag. That was the fae ruler's home.

"I know no more." The man held out his hand again. None of us had money except Cooper, and I doubted he had enough to cover the fee.

Croygen's hand slid down, stopping on the pure gold handle of my father's blade. My muscles locked up, air leaking from my lungs. Melted down, a chunk like that would be worth hundreds of thousands of dollars in the market today.

Croygen's eyes flicked up to me before his hand slid down farther, gripping the handle of his own sword. The one he got when I was just a baby. A gift from Blackbeard. It had a skull and two cutlass swords designed on both sides of the hilt carved out of gold, hidden gems in the skull's eyes. It was subtle, but you felt its power, its history. I used to ask to hold it so I could gain the magic from the lineage of buccaneers, to feel the pirate blood running through it. To hear their tales whispered in my ears and feel their kills. I wanted so badly to be part of the history of those legends.

As children, Killian and I used to "borrow" it from Croygen, pretending we were sea captains, battling for sovereignty.

Yanking it from his sheath, Croygen inhaled. "You'll have to melt it down, but the gems in the handle are worth *far* more than our price. For this, I ask another favor. See that my crew on the ship, *The Silver Devil,* in Shanghai knows where we are. I assume you can find your way there through the doors." Croygen waited for the man to nod, then started to place his sword in the other man's hands.

"No." I stepped up, pushing the sword back to Croygen. "You can't."

"We don't have a choice." His eyes searched mine. I knew how painful this was to him, but he was doing it anyway. He wouldn't offer my father's because he knew that meant something to me.

"Croy-gen," I whispered, my voice breaking off, our gazes locking. My father's blade was the last real thing I had, but Croygen's sword was like cutting out my chest. A sword was personal. Like our ship, it became part of us, soaking in our blood, thirsting off our kills, giving us strength.

"It's only a sword, *Katze.* Just an object." He shrugged one shoulder. He was lying; it was more than an object, but he was willing to sacrifice it.

For me.

The guide started to reach for it again, his hands wrapping around the handle. My entire body jerked like he was ripping out my soul. Soon the legacy and history of it would be gone, vanishing from the world like most of the Golden Era pirates.

I recalled a hazy memory of sitting on Blackbeard's lap as a little girl, the captain letting me tug on his long beard. A brutal pirate to many others, this man would make silly faces and bounce me around on his knee to get me to laugh. I would giggle until my cheeks hurt and my belly ached, and he'd do it all again, for hours, entertaining me. His booming laugh would fill the room. I remember looking over at my father one time, sitting back, a smile so genuine and warm on his face as he watched us, like we had finally found our family. Our place. Our home.

The sword represented that time. Happiness. Contentment. A peace for my father he hadn't had since losing my mother.

My gaze snapped to my father's blade on Croygen's hip. That dagger only made me feel grief and heartbreak. Death.

My hand moved before I fully understood what I was doing. Yanking it from Croygen's waist, I flipped the handle out toward the man, pushing Croygen's sword out of the way.

"Take this one."

"Kat, no." Croygen tried to wiggle back in front of me. "I can't let you do that."

"Take this one." I offered the dagger to the man. "The handle is made of pure gold. That would be a fortune for you."

"No," Croygen barked. "You are not giving it away."

"I'm telling you I am," I shot back, nodding for the man to take it. "Your family will be set for life."

"Gods dammit, Katrina!" Croygen tried to snatch the blade from me. "I said no! He's taking mine."

"You *said?*" I whipped to face the pirate, my jaw straining. "Well, I say he's taking this one. And that is final."

"I won't let you trade *your father's* blade." He moved in closer to me, his intensity sparking off his gaze. "He'd want you to have it. It's *your* blade. You are not handing it over to anyone. And *that* is final!"

"I don't want something that only knows his death," I hissed, getting in his face. "It doesn't hold my father's memory. It holds his murder."

Croygen's nose flared, his eyes burning, ready to fight me, to challenge me. But before he could, I spun back, handing it over to the guide. "Here. It will bring your family prosperity."

The man hesitated, probably nervous about what karma came along with this weapon. Still, as the weight settled in his palms—and the realization of the money he might get from it—he bowed his head, accepting the payment.

He should. He made about three hundred times what was negotiated.

"Promise you will see his crew knows where we are." I stared the man down. He was human, but a promise was still heavy with those with honor.

"You have my word." He bowed.

"Katrina…" Croygen growled.

I nodded for the guide to leave before my mind could be changed. The man dipped his head at all of us before he went for the fae door.

"No!" Croygen lunged forward, but the man slipped through, disappearing into the wobbly air, lost to us for good. "Fuck!" Croygen knotted his fingers through his hair, tugging on it, turning to me. "What did you do?" He flung out his arms as I stood blinking at the empty space, my actions sinking in. "Do you understand what you just did? You can't get it back, Katrina. It's gone!"

"I know." I felt shock mixed with sadness in my disbelief, but it didn't feel wrong.

"Why?" Croygen grabbed my arms, lightly shaking me with frustration. "Why did you do that? I was willing to give him mine."

I knew he was, and maybe that was why. Shaking my head, I pulled away from him, my brain too scrambled to contemplate the whys or any future regrets.

"It's done." I tucked my dirty hair behind my ear, progressing to the spiral stairs leading down into the basilica. "Let's move."

"*Katrina…*" I ignored Croygen's deep rumble following me down the steps into the church.

As we made our way into the cathedral, I noticed every window had been boarded up at one time, but you saw the money in every detail: the gold leaf paint, high arched ceilings, painted images, and ostentatious architecture. It was in extreme contrast to the garbage, blankets, and small possessions of the people living inside the vacated church. For once, it was being used for what it was actually for—helping the poor.

The smell of urine and body odor watered my eyes as we made our way through, finding a side door with the lock broken off. We slipped out into the night.

Deep in the witching hours, silence prickled at my skin—tense and filled with danger. No firebulbs lit the street, the moonlight casting a gruesome glow on the pedestrian lane. The arcade filled with gutted-out old tourist shops and cafes, signs hanging like ghosts above doorways, left hollow and tagged. Most were being used for people to sleep in.

Five years after the Fae War, after the Eastern Bloc pulled away from the West, you could feel the decline, the decay of the society they once knew. I had no idea about the politics here or who was in charge, but it was clear the people were being left out on their own.

Making our way to the river, it felt like a snapshot in time, taken on the day the barrier fell, leaving everything frozen in place. Post lamps still with flyers, bus stands with dated ads, cars abandoned on the streets, their tires stripped away and glass broken, sitting along lanes like carcasses left out to rot.

The breeze from the river had me wrapping my arms around myself. It was a balmy night, but compared to the stifling heat we came from, it was a big difference.

"Wow." Annabeth's voice caught on the wind when we stepped up to the river's edge, her head turned to the side.

Following her attention, my mouth parted. "Wow..." I echoed her wonder, staring at the building across a square from us, looming high in the sky. Its spires dramatically spiked the air like the top of a crown. The structure rose above with grandeur, capping its white stone façade with a red dome cap. We gaped in awe at the architecture, feeling tiny in its presence.

Croygen gripped my hand, tugging me further into the shadows. "Look," he whispered in my ear. My gaze lowered to a group of human soldiers marching around the front of the building, disappearing behind a half-built wall.

The splendor of the building had pulled my focus from noticing the small details and the set of guards securing the doors. A thick wall was being erected in front of this building, like it was trying to divide itself from the rest of the civilization. Carts, wagons, and old-fashioned pulleys were left, ready to be picked up tomorrow and start working again. Only a few lampposts burned through the section I could see, but the rest were dark, as if trying to conserve energy.

The atmosphere was odd, as if everything there was repurposed for something different, not fitting, and everything slightly off… as if time would rewind at any moment and everything would go back to the way it was.

Five years wasn't enough for anything to feel normal yet, to feel like it had always been this way. Change was slow, but it crept on you until one day you almost forgot it had been different.

Survivors accepted and adapted to the times; the unwilling perished.

"Humans," Cooper muttered to us.

"Still think I'll try to avoid the automatic rifles," Croygen mumbled in reply, his hand still on my lower back, his head darting around. "We need to figure out a plan. I don't think marching into the fae leader's palace and demanding the nectar is going to work."

"You sure?" Cooper tipped an eyebrow. "I can be persuasive."

Croygen snorted. "That's my line."

"What, you gonna sleep with the fae leader to get the nectar?" I cocked my head at him.

"Whatever I have to do." He smiled smugly, needling me. "Jealous, Kitten?"

"Of you sleeping with a rich, successful, probably extremely good-looking fae man? Yes."

Croygen's top lip pulled up, his body moving closer to mine. "You're just describing me, Kitty-Kat."

"I said, rich and successful. Sorry."

"So you think I'm extremely good-looking then?"

"I think *you* think you're extremely good-looking."

"And everyone I slept with—"

"Which is probably most of the population by now."

"And you have the other half, Kitt—"

"Sprite spit, will you just put cream in her soda again?" Sprig poked out from Croygen's pocket, climbing up to his shoulder. "Bury your treasure in her because I can't sleep when I keep getting smacked in the head by your very long and girthy pirate plank." Sprig motioned with his arms. "You're making us all *bananas*… and you know how I feel about those. Ohhhh, but now I'm hungry. Can we get honey soufflé? Or maybe honey saffron rice?"

"Yeah, I'm sure they have those to take away down the street," Croygen huffed.

"Really?" Sprig clasped his hands together with excitement.

"Yep."

Sprig's face slowly scrunched up. "Why don't I trust you, pirate?"

"Because you are smarter than you look." Cooper patted him on the head. "Come on, we need to find shelter for the night." His attention flickered to AB, making us remember we had real issues and problems. Her energy was already back down to zero. Between cancer, being shot, and the fae doors, the girl was barely standing.

"Yeah." Croygen cleared his throat, stomping ahead, getting farther from me.

We had no idea where we were going or if there were any places here, but we knew we needed to get off the streets.

The deeper we went in, the more my skin shivered. Everything about this city felt off, like it was on the precipice of falling. There were a handful of stores, businesses, restaurants, bars, and even a theater still operating, the outside glowing with a handful of firebulbs, the names of the actors scrolled on the marque. As if they were still pretending life was normal, and if they ignored the slow decline, the hundreds gathering in homeless camps around them by the day, they could get through unscathed. Not wanting to confront the fact it was harder and harder to get food and supplies. Living in wait, holding out hope that life would resume. But I sensed the shine of hope coming off and reality sinking in. Soon their last bits of optimism would snap.

And darkness would devour this city whole.

CHAPTER 11
Croygen

My head swung left and right, my teeth on edge as we made our way through the city. When despair set in, things turned to violence. Desperation made people feral, cutthroat, and cruel.

In my time, I had seen empires fall and fascism rise. The words 'rise and fall' made it seem as if it happened fast. It just ended or changed in one day. That's not how it worked. It was a slow process, a gradual one that people let happen by staying silent and accepting the small changes with little fight. It wasn't until later you found out you had gradually been boiled alive, never jumping out to save yourself. To fight back.

That's what Budapest felt like. Being slowly cooked alive, sinking further into despair, too busy trying to survive to see how bad it was getting, especially if it still hadn't quite affected you yet. One by one, the businesses that didn't offer necessities or an escape from life would disappear.

Drugs, drink, sex, and food were always the things that persevered. That never changed.

And I could see it happening. Handfuls of women and a few young men were strolling the corners at this late hour, some seemingly comfortable doing it and some looking terrified and ready to bolt, like they had no choice but to turn to prostitution.

Another thing that never changed: prostitutes were the most knowledgeable about everything going on.

"Give me some cash," I muttered to Cooper.

He followed my gaze, his forehead lifting.

"I'm not trying to get laid." I rolled my eyes.

"Good thing, because I think you'd have claw marks from a cat carving your dick into shreds."

"For information."

Cooper scoffed, slamming a few bills in my hand. "We don't have much left."

Cueing up a roughish smile, I sauntered over to one, her eyes raking down my frame, desire blushing a smile over her face as she stood up straighter. "What can I *do* for you tonight?"

"Not here for sex." Disappointment shrunk her shoulders instantly, her smile dropping away. "Though you are lovely." I winked. "I'm here for information."

Her defenses went up, along with her attitude. Information was harder to get than sex on the streets. People didn't like talking to strangers. Snitches didn't get stitches. They got murdered.

"Just need to find some lodging." I moved in closer, letting her take in my flirty smile and cheeky wink. She was a young, cute, dark-haired, dark-eyed human, who sadly looked like the oldest one here at only twenty-five or so.

Yet all I sensed was the person behind me, a petite figure with a huge presence, which seemed to consume me all the time now. I could feel Katrina rubbing against my skin, her nails dragging down my back.

I shivered, peering back, about to tell her to knock it off, like she was actually doing those things. Fuck, I was losing it.

"And you look like someone who *knows* this city, knows every nook and cranny of it. Like the fae leader."

She tipped her head, studying me for a moment. "What do you want to know about him?" She spoke English, but her Hungarian accent was thick.

"Anything."

"He just appeared one day." She shrugged. "Like the last guy, he lives in his ivory tower and ignores everything on this side. Too pure fae and rich for the likes of us humans. Or half fae, like Lotti there." She nodded her head at a woman down the way. "Human Elite are no different. They think of anyone who's poor or has mixed blood as savages." She sneered, waving me off. "If you're not here for a good time, I'm done talking to you."

As I pulled out one of the notes, she stopped, the desperation in her eyes zeroing in on the cash.

"Then tell me who can." I waved the bill. "I know you know of a person. You girls are the smartest and most savvy here. You have to be to survive."

She tipped her head back, a sadness in her eyes, like she forgot what it felt like to be seen.

"There's a place called the Lantern." Her eyes darted to the side, making sure no one was in earshot. "It has no sign. It's…" I got it. It was the underbelly of society. The ones doing illegal, shady shit. "Ask for Dzsinn."

"Dzsinn?" I folded my arms, knowing it basically meant genie.

She nodded, her attention going back to the money.

"Place to stay?"

She flicked her chin down the street. "There is a pub with rooms above down that street."

"Thanks." I handed her both bills. "Get yourself some food and a safe place to sleep tonight."

I turned, gesturing for my group to follow.

"Umm…" The girl suddenly appeared a tad edgy. "Be careful. I've heard things about Dzsinn."

"Sweetheart, he needs to worry about us." I winked, strolling off.

What could a genie possibly do against a beast who was a hired assassin and two cutthroat pirates?

Laying my head back in the bathtub, I let my eyes close for a minute, relishing the barely lukewarm water. The boarding house above the pub was bare-bones, with no running water or electricity. The old-school oil lamps we had to carry from our room to the bathroom disguised the peeling paint, mold, and wear the place had. Five years with no maintenance and constant people coming through quickly eroded the building, which had been old to begin with.

It was only a matter of time before someone tipped one of these lamps over and the whole place went up, probably catching the rest of the block on fire. The man and wife who owned this place, just trying to feed their family, would lose everything.

But today wasn't that day, and soaking the thick crust of dirt off my body after weeks of being on the road felt incredible.

We were lucky to get baths at all, costing extra for us to take up our own buckets from the pub, filled with warm water each time one of us took a bath.

I purposely chose to be last, not wanting to rush, taking a moment to get my shit together. To feel my feet under me again, which had nothing to do with this crazy adventure and everything to do with a cat-shifter down the hall.

I still felt her on my fingers, heard her groaning in my ear, felt the desperation to drive into her, to fuck her hard against the tree. It physically hurt to step away, like it was ripping open my guts. But I had to. Without understanding how, I knew if I crossed that line, I wouldn't come back from it.

And I hated her for it.

Then she screwed with my head again by trading her father's dagger instead of my sword for payment. What the fuck was that? I was ready to give mine up, wanting her to have her father's weapon, something I should've given her long ago. I didn't, either because I was afraid she'd use it on me or I didn't want to let it go. I wore it every day on purpose; it was my lashing, my punishment, to carry the burden of what happened. To be reminded of sacrifice, to see how love destroyed.

Then she *sacrificed* it for me. Gave up that last connection to her father. Why? She hated me, blamed me. Why would she make such a stupid decision? One she was going to regret. To penalize me? Make me suffer more?

"Fuck," I snarled. Irrational anger rocketed down my spine into my cock. My fingers dug against the tub. I struggled against the need to pull myself out of this tub and march to her, demanding why she did such an asinine thing. To reprimand her. To make her cry out. I wanted her to feel the burden I had been carrying, to mark her with my weight.

My lids squeezed, my rational part trying to keep me in check, but it barely held on. For so long, I shoved everything back, even Lexie's death, living life in my blasé existence, never too fussed about anything.

It was hiding, lying in wait, lingering under the surface until something triggered it. Little did I know that thing would be Katrina Roth.

Gripping my length, I squeezed down until I felt pain, my dick so hard it pulsed under my palm. Every emotion rode on my shoulders: shame, confusion, sadness, fear. It all knotted into pure rage. Pointing at her, wanting to be released on her.

Fuck her for even being on my ship in the first place.

My hand pumped down my shaft, a noise huffing my nose.

Fuck her for the curse she left behind.

I stroked even harder, craving the pain.

And fuck her for everything that's happened since, for showing back up on my ship and obliterating my world again.

My molars gritted, the water slapping as I fisted myself

harder, my balls starting to tingle with release, my mind giving over to the pleasure.

Something shifted the moment I let go. It was so natural and almost expected that it took me a moment to understand the change, to recognize the buzzing in the back of my brain, digging in deeper to not break the fantasy.

I could feel her in the room, crawling into the tub, her hands slipping up my thighs as she lowered herself into the tub with me. A gasp hitched my throat, feeling her tongue slide up my cock.

Fuck. It. felt. So. Gods damn. Real.

My knuckles curled into the lip of the tub, my hips rolling forward, sensing her mouth wrap around me, sucking at my dick. My eyes rolled back in my head with a loud groan at the sensation of her fingers digging into my ass, taking me further down her throat.

"Fuck!" I hissed, my mind even feeling her hair between my fingers as I grasped the back of her head, fucking her mouth with punishing thrusts. I could feel her tonsils, every tendon and muscle gripping my swollen cock. A strangled roar came from me, the water splashing all over the floor as my hips bucked. "Take it deeper, kitten," I gritted, my hand feeling the back of her head as I pushed my dick deeper into her throat.

Her tongue and lips sucked me until every vessel popped behind my lids, her throat retracting as I released with a bellow. She swallowed my cum as my hips drove twice more into her before my body went limp, sagging back into the tub, my brain scrambled, and my lungs gasping for air.

What the fuck?

I blinked, my head shooting up, my eyes going straight down, like I would actually see her in the bath with me. But nothing was there besides the few inches of water remaining around my frame. Yet my cock still tingled with the imprint of her tongue and the warmth of her mouth—and not a drop of my release was anywhere on me or in the water.

Darting out of the tub, I grabbed the small, threadbare towel and wrapped it around me, feeling anxious and edgy. My hands rubbed at my forehead and through my wet hair. *It was just in my mind. Completely my imagination.* Except my imagination had never been *that* good.

What was happening to me? This no longer felt like something I could ignore or pretend away, but that was all I wanted to do. Run. Deny. Hide. Imagine it never happened.

Striding into the room we all shared, my gaze drifted over the space. One lamp flickered on a side table, allowing me to make out the shapes in the room.

Cooper and AB were curled up on one bed. Sprig, holding Pam, slept on a pillow by Annabeth's head near the door. Katrina, with her back to me, was on the bed near the window. Somehow I knew she was awake, but like her, I feigned she was slumbering along with everyone else, quietly pulling on a pair of torn cotton pants.

The owner's wife let us dig through the lost and found, getting a few cleaner items to wear until the market down the way opened in the morning.

Without thinking, my body herded me to the bed with her, yearning to curl around her, but my brain twisted me back for the chair in the corner. Sitting in the creaky old wooden seat, I puffed out a long exhale, staring out the soot-covered window, noticing the contradiction of pricey abandoned cars next to now valuable wooden wagons and horses. Singapore, Shanghai, and here were all the same. People were trying to change, adapt to the environment, but the instinctual dictatorship mindset was making them fall into ruin, more being taken from the citizens who were barely surviving as it was. When the top was too heavy, it toppled over and destroyed everyone.

My gaze went over the crowns of the buildings, seeing just a glimpse of the fae palace on the other side, glowing brightly.

The nectar was there somewhere, and this newly oriented

leader would become the most powerful in the world, even over Lars, the moment he made everyone aware he had it.

My gaze slid over Annabeth to Katrina, then back to the flag waving in the distance.

Whomever he was, he wasn't ready for me.

CHAPTER 12
Katrina

Following the group to the market, I stayed far behind, my mood already sour, my tight muscles needing to stretch and work out. Every morning up till a month ago, I worked out on the deck. A routine Master Yukimura had shown me when I was a girl, training my mind to center itself to control my emotions. Which I couldn't seem to do anymore.

My lids compressed against the morning sun streaming down the street, my muscles aching from being locked in a tight ball all night. I had barely let myself breathe when Croygen stepped back in the room, ordering myself not to think, not feel his every move and breath across the room.

The morning hadn't diminished the "dream," the taste of him still lingering on my tongue.

Digging the heel of my palm into my eye, I scrubbed at the vision that had claimed me after my bath the night before. I had been drifting off to sleep, and my mind drifted as well, following him down the hall into the bathroom. It had been so clear, every detail of the surroundings and him, as if I were really there. I had stared unabashedly at his naked, muscular physique leaning back in the tub, his eyes closed, his cock hard, sticking far up out of the waterline, his hand sliding down his shaft. My mouth watered, my pussy dripping for him, and the "dream me" had no qualms about doing what she wanted. Climbing in, I had taken him in my mouth… it had felt so real. I heard his moans, felt his fingers digging into my scalp, pushing my head down until my eyes streamed with tears. I jolted awake, my eyes watering and throat sore. I was painfully horny, his cum sliding down my throat.

Throbbing at the memory, ire jolted my spine, and I peered around the street as if my dirty thoughts had been seen. I was on the cusp of losing it, and on top of that, I needed food, coffee, and a fucking pair of pants.

The skirt I found in the lost and found box was annoying the hell out of me. The cheap static material clung to my thighs, feeling worse than just wearing Croygen's shirt with no underwear for the last couple of days.

Smells of cooking food made my stomach growl the moment we stepped into the market hall. Most of the booths were full of trinkets people pulled from their own homes to sell, some with very limited essentials like toilet paper or salt, but most tables were empty. The market was more shoppers than goods. Not many countries outside the Unified Nations were producing products, making it harder for people to get items, driving the costs of simple items far out of range.

Finding the used clothes, which were probably stolen out of homes or off dead people, I grabbed some pants, boots, underwear, and a few shirts. Changing out of my skirt behind a rack, I left it for someone else, though I couldn't imagine why anyone would wear it now. That was for a time when you went on dates or out to dinner with friends, when life was carefree and you didn't think about how you'd get through the day, focusing on mere survival.

Not that I ever lived a life where I went on dates or even had friends. The pirate's life was always set on survival every day.

"Here." Croygen placed a paper cup in my hand filled with watered-down coffee, sticking a plate of stuffed cabbage rolls near my face. "They only had a few left. And don't ask what they're stuffed with." He glanced back at the stall. "Though I'm pretty sure it's either sheep brains or duck intestines."

"I've swallowed down worse." I reached for one, my body freezing when I realized what I had said. My mind jumped back to the night before, recalling it with such clarity it didn't feel like a dream.

His head snapped to me, his dark eyes locking on mine as if he were searching for an answer, a deeper meaning. It had me feeling even more vulnerable, like he had been in my head and seen what I had done to him in my fantasy.

His throat bobbed, a nerve in his jaw jumping before his gaze darted to the side. "We need to get moving. Find this Lantern place." He shoved the plate into my hands, stalking off, leaving me blinking after him.

He didn't even reply with an innuendo or tease me about my insinuation, which had me unsettled, like he was trying to shove me back into the "little girl" section of his brain. The one where he didn't think of me past the growing nuisance on his ship. The one who followed him everywhere. Even when I shouldn't have.

I tiptoed closer through the dark, my ears picking up hushed voices. I tuned into my developing senses, seeing if I could hunt down his exact location, wanting to impress him with how keen my skills were getting at eleven. My eyes were adjusting quicker in the dark, but it was my nose where I felt the strongest change. I had already picked up his scent, pulling me down the shadowy, gloomy, dirty alley. It was something I knew by heart—rich and deep, like the rum or whiskey he drank, with a hint of the sea. Sweet, salty, and spicy all at once. It was ingrained in me, like I was able to track it anywhere, to the ends of the earth if I had to.

My ears twitched when I heard a breathy female voice pitching, "Oh god! More!"

A warning ticked in the base of my skull, the noises I had heard coming from the crew's rooms tapping at my subconscious, but I snuck closer, still denying what I was hearing. Or maybe I knew, and curiosity was a weakness to my cat as well.

I had seen hundreds, if not a thousand, women try to sail away with us, begging my captain to take them along. They declared their love, the need to escape their horrible husband or restrictive life. I had seen him kiss many of those ladies, but I had never seen him bring a woman into his cabin. When he left for the night, I only imagined the adventures he was pursuing, the swashbuckler escaping death and pilfering treasure troves.

The woman's cries grew louder, along with the wails of his name.

It was a balmy night, the Caribbean breeze grazing my body, but I felt heat start to prickle from inside, a queasy feeling dampening my skin. Darting to the entrance of the alley, I tucked my tiny frame behind a wooden house, peeking around. A gasp stuck in my throat. I froze, not able to move or breathe, trying to make out what I was seeing through the dark.

The woman was painted up like the wealthy ladies I had seen around town. Her hair was in perfect ringlets, and they bounced as she tipped her head back in a loud cry, her petticoats and layered full skirt hitched up around her waist, her legs wrapped around him, her pantaloons at her thighs.

But it was my captain's bare butt that held my focus, his pants at his ankles, his hips pitching forward in carnal thrusts into the woman, each one making her cry louder, completely wild and abandoned, screaming things that were almost unintelligible.

"You can have every coin of my husband's savings, just never stop," she bayed like a hyena.

The longer I stood there, the more my stomach tied up into knots, and I felt like I was going to throw up. I flushed hot and cold. I wanted to run, to stop watching, but at the same time, my feet wouldn't move, my eyes greedily watching him violently hitch her up and down the wall.

Tears started to fill my eyes, vomit pooling in the back of my throat, my mind and heart feeling betrayed for some reason, while something in my body heated with an emotion I wasn't able to pinpoint. I had heard the crew and their lovers before, but I had never actually seen more than kissing. And to watch my captain, the man I adored more than anything, doing that…

His head suddenly snapped over his shoulder, his piercing eyes locking right on mine, somehow knowing I was there.

I jerked back with a gasp, my face burning with humiliation at being caught.

"Gods dammit," I heard him snarl.

"What are you doing? Don't stop," the woman pleaded as I turned and fled, running full speed back for the ship. "Croygen, come back here, you coxcomb!"

"Katrina!" I heard him bark at me, his long legs catching up faster to me than I thought possible. "Stop!" His hand clasped my shoulder, turning me to face him. "What were you doing? Why were you following me?" he demanded, his expression twisted with anger. "Tell me! Why did you follow me?"

"Because…" I burst into tears. I wanted to impress you. I wanted you to smile and be proud I'm becoming such a good pirate and cat-shifter. I couldn't get any of my reasons out because suddenly I didn't know if those were the reasons I followed him. It was instinct, a need to be near him. An understanding that wherever he went, I would go too.

"Fuck." He sighed up at the sky. "Your father is going to kill me." After buttoning up the pants he was clenching around his waist, he gripped both my shoulders, lowering his face close to mine. "You shouldn't be out here, Katrina. It's dangerous."

No intelligible words came through my blubbering, and I cried more because I was unable to stop, hating I was showing weakness. But lately I couldn't seem to prevent it—emotions were coming out of nowhere, knocking me over like rogue waves.

"Hey..." He lowered himself down to my eyeline. "Calm down. Deep breaths, like Master Yukimura taught you." He waited patiently for my tears to ebb, taking the slow inhales Master Yukimura had me practicing every morning on the deck. When I'd had another flare of temper after losing to Killian, Master started these lessons. He had Killian do them too, but I knew it was for me. I was the one out of control.

"Did you see anything?"

I wanted to lie and say I saw nothing, but all I did was stare at my feet.

He took another inhale, like he needed to calm himself too.

"You are never to follow me again. Do you understand?" He grasped my shoulder firmly. "You are much too young to be out on these streets, to see things like that."

I clenched my jaw, my entire body still burning up with humiliation.

"You are becoming a pain in my ass, Katrina." He stood fully up, pinching his nose. "Come on, let's go home." He led us back to the ship, forgetting about his rich lover left in the alley.

But I never got the vision of what he had been doing to her out of my head. Later, at boarding school, wrapped in the jacket I stole from him, I imagined myself in her place.

"Are you going to eat that?" Sprig's voice jolted me out of my thoughts, his little body crawling down my arm to the plate of cabbage rolls. "Do they have honey in them?" He poked at the roll. "Why does it look like an uncircumcised wet penis? Not that I would know what that looks *or* tastes like. I mean, if it had honey on it... or even a little squirting out of it—"

"Sprig." I shoved one in his mouth. "Shut up."

Frowning down at the one left, I sighed, my hunger evaporating, my mind still on the past.

For a while after that night, we both pretended nothing had changed, that I hadn't seen his bare ass thrusting into that woman.

But everything had changed for me; the innocence in my admiration was tainted. I felt different around him, my hormones not only shifting how I viewed him, but how I reacted when he strolled up on deck, how I felt about him. My body flared with awareness, and instead of being disgusted about what I saw, I was curious. I continued to follow him, getting better at staying hidden, wanting more and more for the woman to be me.

I was no longer the young, innocent girl who wrote his name in my diary. Nor the woman he could screw in an alley and leave. I became the woman who fucked *him* and left and would not become one of his whores.

I mean, I was fuckin' Puss in Boots! Though without my boots or jacket, I felt defanged and clawless. Maybe that was the problem. I just needed to get back to my ship, sail the high seas—kill, pillage, and screw every handsome, rich guy in port.

Get back to what I knew. What I loved.

Though, watching Croygen stroll away, his firm ass straining his new cargo pants, I ignored the hollowness of being with anyone else, as if what I loved before was a mirage, an empty vessel. I had seen through it, gone to the other side. Something in me once again had changed, and as much as I wanted to go back to how it was, I knew I never would.

Just like that night. Croygen ruined me.

I thought I cursed him when I left his ship, but in reality, he cursed me.

It took us most of the afternoon to find someone willing to tell us where this place was. People kept clamping their jaws shut, looking around before dashing off. We were outsiders, and most weren't willing to talk to us. Finally, some teenage kid who got a good chunk of change brought us down an ordinary-looking lane. It held a handful of shops, with wagons and people weaving down the tight passage, the sun low enough to cast deep shadows. The boy's head tipped purposely as we passed a nondescript building.

"Look," Cooper muttered to us, his chin flicking to an iron door. A small, freshly painted symbol of a Lantern tattooed the wall near the door, almost unnoticeable unless you were really looking for it.

"Think we found our place." Croygen glanced over at Cooper, lowering his voice. "Take AB home. Kat and I will handle this."

"No." Cooper shook his head. "What if you need backup?"

Croygen snorted, his gaze landing on me for a moment as if to say *I got backup right here*, then went back to Cooper. "We'll be fine."

"Croy—"

"She's exhausted." Croygen nodded at AB, speaking for only him to hear. "We don't know what we're walking into. Take her back. Be with your girl." *While you can.* "Kat and I got this."

Was it sick somewhere deep inside I felt pride he considered me an equal? Not as man or woman, but as a pirate. With any trouble, he knew I could take care of myself and probably him too.

Cooper scanned the door, his feet shifting, not wanting to leave, but taking AB into a situation where things might go bad… he wouldn't do that to her if he didn't have to.

"Okay." Cooper nodded. "But if you aren't back in a few hours…"

"What, you'll huff and puff and blow the house down?" Croygen grinned wickedly.

"Fuck off." Cooper rolled his eyes, taking AB's hand. "I'm serious."

Croygen nodded in understanding, watching them stroll away before he turned to me.

"Ready to follow me into the abyss where we might be attacked and killed, Kitten?" Half his mouth inched up in a grin.

"Always." I grinned back before both of us realized we couldn't stand the other and stepped back.

"Let's go." He cleared his throat, strolling across the lane, his gaze scanning everything around us, looking for anything odd before hauling the heavy door open. "After you."

"So you can use me as a shield if someone attacks."

"Fuck, yeah. I'm too pretty to die." He slipped in behind me, shutting the door and cutting out almost all the light. My sight instantly adjusted. A firebulb flickered at the steep stairs we descended. The air changed as we went below ground, the cool temperature pimpling my flesh.

Stepping around a corner, we came out into what looked like an old, cramped pub. The dark place appeared to have been part of an underground tunnel system at one point with curved brickwork ceilings, ducts, and pipes running along the ceilings and walls. The missing bricks in the ceiling suggested this place hadn't cared about health and safety codes long before the wall fell.

A dozen patrons filled the place. Their low voices bounced off the brick in a steady murmur, making it hard to pick up on anything anyone was saying. I felt their eyes crawling over my skin, a few fully turning to check out the strangers daring to step into this place.

Croygen's hand slid along my back, pointing me toward

the stools at the bar, neither of us showing any sort of nervousness. You gave one inch in these types of places and they pounced, smelling blood in the water. It was in your confidence, your right to be there, and if they fucked with you, they would come to regret it. Most picked up on it, but some, mainly the chauvinist human males, looked at me like prey.

I loved showing them how wrong they were.

"Hey." Croygen greeted the barkeep, a man who had to be at least half fae. His burly size and larger head and nose hinted at troll heritage. He was good-looking enough, with curly black hair and a sharp, dimpled chin—definitely not full troll.

Cautiously, he watched us, his dark eyes taking us in.

"Two whiskeys," Croygen ordered, his confidence and ease seeming to work on the barkeep. He nodded, pouring two drinks for us while I turned my body toward Croygen, gazing out into the dark, windowless room and taking a sip.

My cat eyes pierced the veil, able to see every face with clarity. Fat, skinny, fae, human, men, and a few women sprinkled in. They all seemed poor because of the shabby clothing they wore. Most paid no attention to us anymore, and no one stood out as being dangerous or suspect. Though I understood looks could be deceiving.

"Two more." Croygen downed his last swallow, placing more cash on the counter, far more than what these watered-down drinks were worth, nodding at the bartender.

The man eyed the money, a spark of greed in his eyes.

"We're looking for someone." Croygen slid them closer, keeping his hand firmly on them. "And we were told this was the place to find him."

The man's lids narrowed, but his focus on the money gave his greed away.

"We're looking for someone by the name of Dzsinn."

His chin jerked up at the name, and his gaze leveled on us, jumping between me and Croygen guardedly.

"We just need information," Croygen spoke smoothly, his countenance like the rolling sea, easing the man's shoulders down. He watched Croygen push one of the bills toward him. "Get the other half after you help us out."

The barkeep hesitated for a moment before reaching over and taking the single bill, probably more than he earned in a week or two here. "Come back around eleven," he muttered low, making sure it was only us who heard. Croygen dipped his head in acknowledgment before the guy walked away, serving another guest down at the end.

"Guess we're coming back." Croygen turned to me, taking a huge gulp of his drink and draining the cup, his eyes landing on me with a sexy half grin.

I slammed mine back, and with no food in my stomach, the booze went straight into my bloodstream.

"Want to go get a drink?" His husky voice covered my skin with electricity.

"We've already had one."

"Somewhere less…" He peered around. "Hostile." Leaning in closer to me. "Get something to eat? I can hear your stomach growling from here, *Kitty-Kat*."

My blood boiled instantly at the pet name, but not the way it used to.

My lids narrowed, and I jerked away from him. "Don't call me that."

He grinned, seeing right through me.

"Come on, let's get this pussy fed," he rumbled in my ear, grabbing my hand and pulling me up the stairs and out the door into the twilight. A bell rang out the hour in the distance, a sign they were still trying to hold to tradition here, signaling the end of the day, which probably meant nothing anymore.

Not far from the Lantern, we found an area that was busier than the rest, with a few pubs dotting the lane. Outside, a man played a piano for tips, a violinist on another corner, while prostitutes walked up and down the lane trying to find patrons inside the taverns drunk enough to fork over money for sex.

Where the rest of the city was winding down, this place was coming alive, ready to take the money you had worked all day for to provide just a little escape, a little diversion.

Croygen took us into a tavern, everyone stuffed into the community tables, which were jammed together. The place had no menu or choice; it was the same for everyone.

A bottle of alcohol was slammed down in front of us with two glasses, the server dropping two dishes of what smelled like tripe stew and a stale roll in front of us, barking off the price in Hungarian.

Croygen handed her some coins before she moved on to the next customers.

"What is that?"

"*Palinka.*" Croygen dispensed a heavy pour in each glass. "A fruit brandy." He picked up the glass. "Cheers."

I clicked my glass into his, taking a drink.

Coughing, it burned all the way down to my gut, my eyes watering like I had been slapped in the face. The drink tasted like rubbing alcohol with a hint of a fruit I couldn't pick out. Too minimal to really tell.

Croygen's head tipped back in a laugh, enjoying my pain far too much.

"Not funny," I croaked, tears spilling from my eyes. "I wasn't ready for that."

"Then let's try again." He touched his glass to mine. "Cheers." Croygen sipped his slower, his darkly intense eyes not leaving me. This time, I took a smaller swallow, though I still flinched as it burned down.

This was purely to get people drunk, fast and cheap.

Croygen, not even reacting to it, poured more into our glasses before looking down at his food. "Probably more sheep brains and duck intestines." He spooned up some of the hot stew. "But you've *swallowed* down worse before, right?"

There it was. The teasing that was missing earlier, except it hit differently, the alcohol sending his implication straight between my legs. My mind recalled what I did to him in my dream while evoking every detail of us in the barn. The liquor was knocking down my walls, allowing desire to steamroll me.

Crossing my legs, I looked away from him, needing to cut the charge that always seemed like a hot wire between us, trying to find distraction in anything. Men played cards and dice at one table in the corner, betting their meager wages, hoping to walk home with a little more.

Everyone here wanted an escape, to find pleasure or peace for just a moment, to not face the truth. That life here was not going to get better; they were nowhere near rock bottom yet, and life would *never* be the same.

"Eat." Croygen's order drew me back to my bowl, scooping up a chunk of potato into my mouth, the bland, watery soup doing nothing to satisfy my hunger.

"Then what would satisfy your *hunger*, kitten?"

My head jerked up, my eyes widening, desire and fear constricting my lungs. I knew I hadn't said that out loud.

"Wh-what?" I croaked out.

He went still, blinking, before his attention darted to the side.

"What did you say?"

"Nothing." He shook his head. "I didn't say anything." He picked up his glass, not bothering to sip, downing it like a shot.

I did the same, the almost pure alcohol relaxing my muscles, my brain glazing with a hazy film, convincing myself I must have imagined it. All of it.

But truth was a funny thing, and with every drink, it grew louder, hovering around us. An acknowledgment neither of us wanted to face but could no longer ignore.

"Croygen..." I set my empty glass down, no longer hungry. "What is going o—?"

Slamming his cup down, he cut me off, standing up from the table, his head shaking like he couldn't face the question I was about to ask. Needing to run from it. "Let's go."

"Where are we going?"

"To a bar that has whiskey." He turned for the door.

Getting up, I trailed him out, leaving my hardly touched soup. The alcohol raced through my veins, making all the lights go blurry, taking away my hunger and numbing my emotions.

When we stepped outside, a fire burned in a pit, a dancer rolling her body to the music from the violinist and piano player. This place had the power to seduce, offering an invitation to let go and just experience your basic desires.

Croygen took my hand, pulling me into another pub. And I let the devil take me…

Willingly.

CHAPTER 13
Katrina

The tavern held a reckless type of hopelessness. Some were sitting at a table silently staring off in grave contemplation, a drink away from stumbling home drunk or pulling out their gun to end it all. Others were boisterous and loud, drinking away the weight of the world and pretending all was okay, but their anger walked a high-wire act the more they consumed. Prostitutes threaded through, finding their mark among the drunk and willing.

"Two whiskeys," Croygen ordered at the bar, his gaze moving over the room, assessing everyone in the place the same way I was. We didn't get to be where we were without knowing every player, threat, or potential target in the room.

The barkeep slid our drinks to us from a non-labeled bottle, the harsh scent already telling me the so-called whiskey was barely that.

Croygen tapped his glass against mine, downing a gulp, his brows flinching at the taste. "Fuck." He coughed. "I miss the Scotsman's stash. This is shit."

Trying not to cringe, I swallowed mine down.

"I miss Moses's rum. He made his own, and it could knock you on your ass without even knowing it." Grief arrowed through my chest speaking of him. I tried to keep my mind off what my crew was going through, to not imagine how they were suffering. It did me no good right now, but they snuck in more than I let on.

Croygen watched me, his body turning to me. "Tell me how you met them. How you became captain."

Staring out, I watched the people in the bar, unable to look at Croygen.

"Gage, I met on the streets after I ran away from school," I said. "Part of a street gang which got rounded up by the constable. They were all sentenced to die because of their crimes, though I think it was because, deep down, people knew they were different. Feared them. They were put in holding stocks until their execution. I picked the locks, getting a few of them out before they were hung." I sipped more of the alcohol, my tongue spilling out the story. "He stayed by my side from there on out. I saved Typhoon and Hurricane from a slave-trading ship heading to the Caribbean. Dobbs and Polly I got when I claimed a trading ship, and they chose to stay on after. Zuri and Moses found me. And little Ruby." I swallowed. "Well, I spotted her trying to steal some food, and she reminded me so much of Kill and me…" I tapered off, Killian's name sticking in my throat.

"Of you and *Killian*," Croygen finished for me, his gaze steady on me. "I'm gonna ask once again, where is he now? Why did he leave you?"

"I told you why." I shifted against the bar, my head turning away like everything else was much more interesting.

"And I think there's more to it."

"I think you want there to be more to it."

A rumble coiled into my ear, my skin prickling at the vibration. "Look at me, Kitten."

I huffed, not giving in to his demand.

"I said look at me." His fingers clasped my chin, tugging

my face to him, his body looming over mine, his gaze searching. "He loved you, wanted you more than anything, and *all* you thought about was *me*, isn't that right? You let him walk right out of your life."

"Because I vowed to *kill* you," I snarled. His fingers burned into my skin, sparking down through my legs.

"If you *vowed* to kill me?" He smirked. "I'd already be dead. But not only am I not…" He moved in closer, his body heat covering mine like a blanket, his voice low. "Against all your so-called values and promises, you've ridden my cock like it was your only obsession in this world. Your pussy gripped me so tight I could feel you fuckin' *branding* me. And you want more. Admit it, Kitten."

Fire licked up my muscles, my breath puffing out. I felt seen. Vulnerable. Defenseless.

"Fuck you." I jerked away from his hold, fury blazing from every syllable. "There is nothing to admit except I made a *huge* mistake," I spat. "And you don't know me. How I feel. I loved Killian. He's ten times the man you are. At least he's honest and faithful."

"Like a fucking dog." He gripped the back of my head, yanking me back into his frame, his fingers digging into my hair, pointing my face to him, his eyes darkening. "Killian never stood a chance because I'm all you've wanted," he growled against my ear. My body lost all fight when his thick cock pushed into my stomach. "All you've *ever* wanted."

There was truth in his statement. Since I was a teenager, Croygen had been the only man I wanted. To kill or fuck, sometimes all at once. I thought of no one else but him.

"And you are my curse, Katrina." His mouth brushed my ear. "But fuck… When I was inside you, you felt like my savior."

His words evaporated the last of my rationality, and I let the devil take me down.

I gripped his shirt, yanking him to me, my mouth crashing into his with a vengeance. The moment our lips touched, every wall between us shattered like glass.

A noise rattled in his throat, and his grip on the back of my head tightened, flattening my body completely against his, allowing me to feel every inch of him. My brain was already hazy from drink, but kissing him made everything melt away, as if I reached inside, touched his mind, and invaded his soul.

"Katrina." His tongue wrapped around mine, deepening the kiss and lighting my entire body on fire. I felt feral, not caring that we were in a room full of people, craving his dick inside me so badly a whimper bubbled up. "Fuck," he swore, walking me back into the bar with his body. One hand left my hair and curled at the top of my pants button, flicking it open.

"Croygen?" Desperation almost drowned out my alarm, my gaze going around us, to all the customers. We were at the end of the bar, near the corner, and the place was very dark, but still, people milled around and could look over and see us.

"Let them watch." His voice dragged down my spine. "Feel their envy and need while my fingers fuck you."

My mouth opened, though no refutation was voiced when his hand slipped inside my pants, fingers parting my folds and rubbing over my clit before sinking into me.

A gasp shook my body.

"Keep your eyes on the room. I want you aware of what I do to your body in front of a roomful of people. And how much you like it, Katrina." He pumped his fingers in deeper, his thumb rolling my clit.

"Oh god." Sweat coated my skin, my gaze dragging over the space, knowing anyone might glance over and catch us. It only stimulated me, rattled at every nerve, my nipples hard against my shirt, my breath catching, reveling in the high this gave me.

A man strolled up to the bar near us. Croygen finished his

drink, nodding at him as his hand fucked me harder below the bar table, pinching my clit.

A low moan slipped out, my nails digging into the wood, my hips widened, no longer in my control, bucking against him. My orgasm prickled up my back.

The man's eyes widened, meeting mine for a moment. I saw the desire and surprise in the man's gaze, but it was Croygen's possessiveness I felt in every bone in my body. It sunk into me like ownership, submerging me in its power. A growl came from Croygen, the man scampering off in terror.

Croygen's head snapped to me, his jaw tight, his eyes almost black. The charming Silver Tongue pirate was nowhere in sight; he was all devil. Slipping out of me, he clutched my hand, towing me with him through the bar and out the back. Once outside the door, he slammed me against the brick alley wall. His jaw rolled, his gaze intently on mine, searching for something.

"Katrina..." Gravel ground up my name, shredding down my skin and peeling everything away. I heard it in his tone, saw it in his eyes, felt it in my chest. It was a warning. An advisement to stop him. Though we were both too late. We were past redemption, past saving.

The anger I had earlier was gone; the warnings in my head and the reasons I despised him floated away with the alcohol. I watched Croygen boldly. He appraised me; his gaze was like a caress. Desire and need hummed between us with power that felt like it wasn't meant for this Earth. And we no longer could control it.

Gripping his shirt again, I ripped it over his head, tipping us into a frenzy of hands and lips, tearing at each other's clothes. My tank and sports bra hit the floor next to his tee as his teeth sank into my bottom lip. He yanked off my pants and boots, leaving me in only a slip of underwear. Clutching my waist, he lifted me up, my legs hugging his hips. My heels shoved down his pants, and I pushed down his briefs. When I wrapped my hand, rubbing against him, Croygen pulsed and hardened against me.

"Fuck, Katrina… I'm not going anywhere near gentle. I need to own your fucking pussy. Now." His teeth scraped over my neck, arching me back into the brick, his mouth taking in my nipple, sucking on it, his tongue flicking it.

"Croygen." My nails grew into claws, raking through his hair and pulling him closer. I needed him so badly that my mind and tongue no longer had any filters. We were both drunk, tearing at the feeble wall we tried to keep up. "Fuck me so hard my back feels these bricks for centuries." I bit his ear, his hands tightening on my ass at my breathy words. "Fuck me harder than you did that woman I watched you in the alley with when I was younger."

His chest shuddered, his nose flaring because he knew exactly which night I was talking about.

"Katrina." A hand tangled in my long, dark hair as he wrapped his fingers around my throat. He leaned in, his thumb pressing down on my pulse, and I felt it pound in my pussy. I was so hungry for him I let out a cry. "You aren't some pussy I'd fuck in an alley." He hitched me up higher, his hand tearing at my cheap underwear, making me gasp. "You're the *only* pussy I want to fuck. Anywhere." He positioned his tip at my opening, squeezing my neck until I saw spots as he thrust into me.

A cascade of pleasure and pain took me over like a waterfall, summoning a deep cry from my lips, my eyes rolling back as he filled me, my body jerking with sensations.

"Fucking hell!" he moaned, both of us ready as it took over, ripping the air from our lungs, drawing us out of our bodies and back in. I could feel him, experience his emotions on top of mine, exploding so much through me that tears burned behind my lids. It was even more than the first time, blocking out all the alarms, all the reasons I should be scared. I bathed in the raw desire consuming me.

Croygen pulled out, pushing back in even deeper, dragging me up against the rough wall. My nerves rubbed against the harsh brick, purring at the abrasive texture.

"Oh gods." My hips bucked up and down his shaft, my core desperate for more.

His warm mouth took mine as he pumped long, deep strokes, cries gurgling in the back of my throat.

Simply kissing him felt better than the best sex I ever had before. Just his touch made me orgasm; his sounds made me lose my sanity. He weaved in every bone, intensifying every thrust inside me, bursting fireworks behind my lids.

"I could fuck you relentlessly, Kitten." He went harder, pulling deep, loud moans from me. My claws raked down his skin, my sharp teeth biting into his neck.

"Fuck." The last bits of his restraint broke as my rough tongue lapped at my bite mark.

He pulled out of me, dropping me to my feet, turning me before I could even think, and bending me over an abandoned police car in the lane. "Spread your legs wide," he demanded, his fingers parting me, playing with me.

"Croygen…" I opened my legs, stretching over the hood like a cat, hearing the purr in my throat.

"Such a bad girl," he rumbled in my ear, kissing me deeply before dropping to the ground, yanking my ass to him. My nails dug into the hood as his tongue licked through me.

A choking cry hitched my lungs, a shiver quaking me violently.

"You taste so fucking good. I've been craving your pussy like a damn fiend." His tongue pushed into me, his lips sucking and lapping me up until my nails shredded through paint, my wails piercing the air, my hips rocking back into him, my orgasm burning at the base of my spine. "Croy-gen."

He eased back, his body coming over mine.

"No," I whined.

"I need to come inside you." He nipped at my ear and rubbed his cock through me. "I told you. This pussy is completely *mine*." He flipped me over onto my back. Taking my hands, he wrapped them around the windshield wipers. "Hold on." He grabbed my thighs, pulling me half over the hood, his cock pushing at my entrance. He took a moment, his hungry gaze rolling over me, and an emotion I couldn't decipher flickered through his dark eyes, his lips curling with a possessive need.

"You were always mine, weren't you?" He gripped my neck firmly as he drove in, the angle hitting so deep my scream rattled off the brick.

I moved against him, hating he was able to cut to the truth so easily. I tried to pretend differently, but feeling him sink inside me, I couldn't hide from the certainty. I had always been his. Waiting to grow up, waiting to become the best pirate, waiting to be able to challenge him in every way.

"Yes." I stared boldly at him, my thighs squeezing him closer, matching his intensity with my own. "And you have been waiting for me."

His jaw clenched, his thumb pushing harder on my throat, my pussy clenching on his cock. He sucked in. There was a moment when our eyes met, and then everything broke.

A growl rose from his chest. His free hand seized my hip, holding me down, then he lost all control.

His hips snapped so hard, fucking me so deep, I could no longer do anything but hold on. I yowled as he took me with punishing strokes, splitting me open. Then I pleaded for more, required his blood, needed him to shatter everything inside and out. I felt him consume me, tearing into my soul, demanding his right to it, and all I could do was retaliate, burrow in even deeper, demand even louder, consume even more.

"Fuuuuuuuuuuuuuccckk!" Croygen roared, only thrusting into me harder, our sounds smacking loudly off the walls. His eyes were wild as they found mine.

He was all I heard, felt, and saw… *mine.*

The electricity we had been ignoring, that connection we pretended wasn't there, locked around us as I felt myself fall over the edge, my back jackknifing as the orgasm hit me like a train, blinding me as light burst behind my lids. My pussy clamped around him, and I moaned with abandon.

Magic sang around us, cracking the air and vibrating the car under my back. The tension around us burst almost like a sonic bomb, tearing me from my body, feeling like I sunk into his.

"KAT!" he bellowed, plunging into me three more times, his hips bruising mine before I felt his hot cum blister through me, burning his mark deep into my bones. "Fuck!" He continued to fill me, to the point his cum gushed down my leg, my pussy orgasming again as it greedily milked more from him, not wanting him to ever stop fucking me, being inside me, filling me with his seed.

His mark settled into my body like a brand, a claim, making itself at home. And what terrified me was how familiar and natural it seemed.

He roared again before he slumped over me, his breath trailing down my neck, his forearms on either side of my head.

"Fuck," he heaved, his dick still throbbing inside me, his eyes going back and forth between mine as our lungs gasped together. My body shook violently, understanding in one drunken decision, we crossed that line of no return. Changing *everything.* It was even stronger than before, a connection sinking in with every breath, evoking confusion and terror.

We stayed like that for a while, unable to move or think.

"You're purring again, Kitty." His hoarse voice snapped me back into myself, pulling my attention to him. I took in his face. Every detail was sharp—his dark eyes, his sensual mouth, how his hair fell around him, tangled from my hands.

I sensed his bewilderment like it was my own. He had the same questions—and the clarity that in fucking, we might have completely fucked ourselves.

We weren't ones to be held down or beholden to another, but we also knew whatever had just happened, there was no walking away.

"*Katze*—" His thumb stroked my cheek, his eyes searching mine in the same way.

No words found their way out. Nothing seemed like it could explain or understand any explanation—except one.

One I still didn't want to utter, even to myself. I couldn't. I wouldn't accept it. My father's ghost still clung to me, his memory. I proved I was an awful person, but that… that would make me reprehensible. Wholly unforgivable.

In the distance, the bell tolled the late hour, marking the time we had to be back at the pub, clanging us back to reality.

"Shit." He pulled out of me, his cum streaming down my leg, causing us both to suck in sharply. The magic sparked so intently between us that I was incapable of finding my bearings. I already missed him, needing him inside me again.

Grabbing our clothes strewn around the lane, he stepped back to me, helping me sit up. He used his shirt, wiping his seed from my thighs, his burning gaze catching mine.

"Your shirt is ruined now."

He shrugged, raising my arms and putting my bra and top back on. "Think I kind of like the shirtless jacket look." His fingers glided down my ribs, tugging my shirt into place. "I mean, who wouldn't want to see this body?"

I snorted, my head wagging. The man wasn't wrong. He was perfection. I wanted to lick every inch of his toned, tattooed physique.

We finished dressing and he took my hand, sliding me off

the car hood, my legs wobbling under me. He pulled me into his arms, holding me up. "At least you didn't run this time."

"I would if I could." I wasn't completely sure if that was a lie or not.

The side of his mouth pulled up in self-satisfaction.

"We need to deal with business right now." His mouth brushed my head. "But we *will* be talking about this later." He slapped my ass and turned for the exit. "Come on, Kitty-Kat, it's time to rub a genie bottle and make a wish."

CHAPTER 14
Croygen

Holy. Fuck.

My muscles shook with each stride, straddling the line between I could take on the world and unable to take another step, needing to stretch out like a cat in pure ecstasy. If I thought the first time with her was a fluke, this just smashed that theory to smithereens.

I hadn't meant for it to happen. I hadn't gone into that bar thinking I would fuck her behind it. We were drunk. Stupid. Though looking back, I couldn't have stopped it if I tried. Katrina was a force I was incapable of fighting. And now I was terrified that I didn't want to.

With every step, I felt her sinking deeper into me, wrapping around my cock and burrowing into my soul. Her purr was an aphrodisiac; it had me so fucking hot and content I wanted to curl around her and fall asleep. Then wake up and fuck her all over again, set on repeat… forever.

Forever. What the fuck? I didn't *do* forever. I barely stayed more than a week with a woman. Amara might have been the exception, but only because, deep down, I knew I was safe. She would never love me, nor I her. Let alone something deeper.

Like…

Mate.

The term nipped at the base of my brain, squeezing down my lungs. Panic and serenity both pounded at my chest and head.

Shoving out the thought, I crossed the road to the pub, my dick still throbbing, already craving her so badly I was going cross-eyed.

Touching her lower back, I steered her through the pub door into the dark entry, my fingers zapping at the touch. The impulse to press into her, grip her hips, and slide my mouth down the curve of her neck was nearly overwhelming. To tug her pants down enough to enter her, slowly fucking her in the dark, with the sounds of the bar only feet away, hearing her moan.

Her frame went still, and a small gasp fluttered her lungs, as if she could hear, feel, and see what I was thinking, tapping into every part of my soul, taking up space there. Owning it.

My hand jerked back, scrambling to put up walls, feeling exposed and vulnerable. I was aware I should hate myself for crossing that line again because of who she was supposed to be to me, and what I was hiding from her.

Barricading myself against her, I rolled my shoulders back, putting my concentration on the mission. I had no idea what was ahead with this man we were meeting. I had to be focused and alert.

So much was riding on this.

Strolling back into the underground tavern, my lungs filled with the smoky haze of cheap cigarettes. The dim firebulbs barely cast enough glow to see any details. I sensed a different energy than even a few hours ago. Distrust, violence, and greed had a sour taste, a prickling energy of every eye being upon you. Shifty and crooked.

The bartender glanced up, his head nodding us toward the

back. My attention followed his to an outline of a single person sitting at the far table against the wall.

Dipping my head in acknowledgment, I kept Kat behind me, my hand ready to grab my sword, my muscles locked tight, ready to act.

Interested gazes followed our figures through the tables, assessing us, trying to figure out if we were villain or victim. And most eyes, when they landed on Kat, turned hungry. For sex, for power, for someone they perceived as "weaker."

A man licked his lips, lust running over her, the smell of sex still pumping off her like pheromones. He reached out to touch her, whispering something to her.

A growl came up my throat, and I whipped around, ready to rip him to shreds, when she yanked out my sword from my belt. Grabbing his arm, she twisted it behind him, slamming his head into the table with a crack, placing the blade near his crotch.

Blood gushed from his nose, and she held his head to the table, stabbing the tip of the blade through his pants and pinning him to the seat.

"You touch me again, and I'm gonna use your balls as garnish." She leaned in close to his ear. "You even look in my direction or touch anyone without their say, I will slit your throat and use your skin as my next jacket and your dick as my necklace."

She shoved his face in his own blood again before yanking out the sword from between his legs, sauntering up to me, handing it back. "Thanks."

A noise worked up from my gut. I stared down at her in awe, noting the rest of the pub was too. My cock was rock hard. "Fuck, Kitten." I swallowed roughly. "Not sure if I was turned on or scared shitless."

She lifted a brow, pushing by me.

Both… most definitely both. And that only made me harder.

I never had any doubt Katrina was capable and could handle herself, but it didn't make it any less hot when she did. And by the silence, the room tuned into her. I knew many had the same thought.

They would die happy as long as they were between her legs.

And I was no different.

My woman is badass.

I stopped cold. The thought ran down my spine, robbing me of breath.

What. The. Fuck.

Blowing out, I shook my head, pushing the thought away before catching up with her.

The man's dark eyes watched us intensely as we approached the table. There were absolutely no qualities that would pin any notice on him. Sitting, I couldn't tell his height, but I guessed around five foot ten. His face would be forgotten if you looked away. Dark eyes and light brown, close-cropped hair. He so easily blended in with a crowd.

My first instinct was to think, *This is the one they're afraid of?* But something about him gave me pause; he held a heavy presence, a weight that tipped the room. Though part of me felt that was something he was putting on for the world, dressing for the job he wanted, not what he actually was. Yet.

"So it really is the notorious Silver Tongue Devil." The man had a blank expression. "And the infamous Puss in Boots."

"You know who we are." There wasn't a question, but certainly a worry about how he knew our identities so easily.

"I know everything that happens here, who steps into this hellscape, especially if they are looking for me." Dzsinn motioned at the chairs. "Sit."

Kat's eyes met mine for a moment, and I swear I sensed an entire conversation in a single blink. A decision for us to stay guarded and alert.

We sunk into seats across from him.

"You might be gifted to slip away unnoticed, but you two don't exactly blend into a room." His brow curved up, gesturing to the eyes still on us. "You can't help but attract, charm, and seduce. Have willing victims in every port."

"Doesn't explain how you know our names, though." I eased back in the chair, claiming even more dominance than him.

"I have known about you for a *long* time." He stared at me. "But let's get to why you're looking for me."

I watched him for a moment as we calculated and gauged each other.

"We're here to find information about the new fae leader." My tongue moved skillfully around every word, precisely without giving much away.

"And why would two seafaring pirates need to know about a fae lord in Budapest?" he challenged, playing the game of information. Something fae took very seriously.

"The more you know, right?" I lifted my eyebrow, folding my ankle over my knee. "Also ways *into* the palace."

"Now we're getting somewhere." Dzsinn leaned back, eyeing me with contemplation. "You want to rob the palace of treasures."

"Of one," I corrected. "Which was not his to take in the first place."

"So you want to know secret passages or ways into the palace to steal back said item."

A grin plucked the side of my face in the affirmative.

"That's not a simple or small task." Dzsinn folded his hands on the table.

"But not impossible," Kat pressed, drawing his focus.

"No, but the cost will be very high."

"Name it," I bade, knowing perfectly well we didn't have it now. But pirates always found a way.

Dzsinn exhaled, leaning on his elbows; a glint sparked in his eyes.

"I don't want money, pirate."

A stone sunk into my gut.

"What do you want?" Kat asked.

Dzsinn's gaze darted from her to me, the hint of a smile on his lips. "A deal."

"What kind of deal?" I stayed calm on the outside but felt my muscles strain against the lining of my jacket, not liking where this was going.

Dzsinn sat back as if he was fully in charge of this meeting. "I know who you are, pirate, who you work for."

Anger balled up at the base of my spine, sitting me up.

"I don't work for anyone," I snarled. "I am the captain."

"Except when you're at the *King's* call."

Lava flooded my veins. I went still, my nose flaring, my teeth gritting. Few even knew I had a connection to Lars, that I took his products and sold them all over the world. Some were certified by him, and some—okay, a large number—were not.

"I know you traffic Western fae-made products."

My anger rose, my limbs twitching with fury, wanting to strangle this man to death right here. He shouldn't know any of this.

A hand gripped my knee under the table, and a rush of calmness washed through me. Kat's touch vibrated through me like a purr, instantly bringing me back down.

Struggling to swallow, I exhaled, not able to look at Kat, though fuck, I couldn't deny I felt her everywhere. Inside and out.

"And you want to become one of my contacts." I sat back again, the tension in my body reducing.

"I think you and I could have a very lucrative relationship." Dzsinn took a sip from his glass. "Every day, this place falls deeper into poverty and desperation, yet the rich build their high walls and fight their petty little battles with each other while we remain mired in destitution and despair. It's getting worse and worse out there." Anger pinched his forehead. "You know what the elite call us here?" He frowned. "Savages… when it was them who made us so."

"And parting the poor with what little they have for these items is really sticking it to the man, huh?" I scoffed.

"They will get them from somewhere. Might as well be me," he stated bluntly. A true opportunistic response.

And I was no different. We saw a void and made sure *we* were the ones to fill it. Fuck, I think I liked this guy.

"You provide me with items I ask for, and I will ensure you are well compensated."

I pretended to mull over his offer, wanting him to squirm for a few minutes.

"Fine." I nodded. "We have a deal. But I want everything you have on the fae leader and the palace, all access in and out. And weapons."

"Tomorrow night. Same time. At the docks." Dzsinn stood up, pulling up his hood. He gave us both a nod before leaving.

"You know, to a genie, a deal is pretty much a vow," Kat said. "You can't get out of it."

"I know." I exhaled, my head tipping back, realizing what I had just got myself into, though no anxiety crept up.

My eyes dropped to my widened legs. I noticed my hand was cupped over Katrina's, holding it against my inner thigh, my thumb rubbing absently at her skin like a security blanket. I hadn't even known I was doing it. It felt so natural, so instinctive to touch her. To be "boyfriend-like" with her.

Standing up, I cleared my throat, trying to cover up the intimacy of that small interaction. She stepped back as if she too just became aware of what we were doing.

"Katrina…"

"We need to get back before Cooper comes looking for us." She took off, her head held high, with every wall locked back in place.

"You smell like a pirate hooker."

I blinked awake to an eyeball peering into mine.

"Gods dammit." I jerked, batting at the fuzzy thing on my chest. "Sprig. Go away." I slumped back onto the bag I used for a pillow, my bones aching from sleeping on the floor. Well, at least some soreness was from that. Most of it was from the girl sleeping in the bed across the room.

We had wordlessly returned to the room after our meeting with Dzsinn. Cooper bolted awake the moment we stepped in. He took one look at us, smelled us, and laughed.

"Shut the fuck up," I muttered, making a place on the floor to sleep. He snickered louder, his head shaking.

"So?" he crooned. "What have you two been up to?"

"For that, I'm not telling you shit," I muttered, watching Katrina take some of her items and head down the hallway to the restroom.

The moment she stepped out, Cooper chuckled again. "You two." He rubbed his head. "You're screwed. You know that, right?"

"No." I gritted my teeth. "Just drunk and needed an outlet."

"Yeah. Okay. Sure." Cooper folded his arms. "Deny all you want, but you know the truth. We all know. Hell, we all *feel* it."

"I said shut up," I growled.

"Fine." He grinned, knowing he was needling me. "What did you find out?"

I told him about meeting Dzsinn, leaving out the deal we

made. No one needed to know my side hustle, especially one who also worked for the king.

"Now leave me alone. I'm passing the fuck out," I grumbled, taking up space on the floor. Pretending not to notice Kat when she returned and that I wasn't craving to be near her so badly, it took me over an hour to settle down. Everything in me wanted to crawl in next to her, to fall asleep with my cock snuggled against her ass and my arm wrapped around her.

I was assaulted by memories of us in the alley, how I still felt her, even when she was guarded.

I didn't want to think about what Cooper said, but to have someone call it out and put it front and center…

Mate.

Did fate hate me that much?

Scouring my face, I forced all thoughts from my head, ready to fall asleep.

"You normally smell like alcohol and pussy." Sprig sniffed me again, white underwear around his neck as a cape and Pam in his arms. "But this time it's a real pussy."

"Sprig," I growled, sitting up.

"*Oh pussycat, pussycat, I woooove youuuu…*" he sang out, leaping out of the way of my hand. "*Yes, I dooooo!*"

Disregarding my morals, I stood, but I was too slow to catch him as he darted out of the way, leaping on the end of Kat's bed.

"*You and pussycat nose—*"

"Sprig." I rolled my fists up. "If you don't shut up, I will use Pam to wipe my ass this morning."

"She's not *really* into ass stuff. Though I've persuaded her a few times."

"Oh, come on," Cooper groaned, covering his face. "You know better, pirate."

"Yeah." I pinched my mouth. "I should've seen that coming."

"Speaking of coming…" Sprig snickered, nodding at Katrina and me.

Kat's foot kicked out, flinging him off the bed.

"Ahhh!" He flopped on the floor.

Laughing, my gaze met Kat's with approved collaboration, and I went still. The intensity punched through my gut, leaving me breathless. The connection webbed thickly, wrapping me in a cocoon. She was everywhere, purring through me, rubbing herself over my soul.

"Hey, *Bhean chait!* Thought you were on my side." Sprig's yelp snapped me away from her. "Ohhh, speaking of sides. I'm so craving those potato poops."

"Potato poops?" AB sat up in bed, brushing her hair out of her face. Her wound was healing, but the wear on her body fighting for its life was streaked across her face. "You mean potato puffs?"

"Puffs? Why are they called that when they are in the shape of deer poops? Not that I would know that. I mean, that was a very dark time for us sprites. We never, ever talk about those few hours we went through. It's so painful to relive that day without honey. It was survival…" He sniffed, covering Pam's ears. "See, now you've gotten her all upset. And when she's upset, I want pancakes… ohhh drizzled in honey." His eyes went big. "Ohhhhh, crepes and pancakes layered together in a sugar honey syrup." A chirp of excitement came out of him. "With honey fried cakes dunked in sugar and honey." He licked his lips, his legs bouncing with frantic energy. "And honey-baked fritters on top. Ooooooohhhhhh… caramel and molasses crème on a honey cheesecake."

"Oh, boy." Annabeth peered at me with a weak smile, both of us knowing what was coming.

"I demand all the honey in all the land!" He zoomed off her bed, leaving Pam behind. "For I am the Monkey God! Do my bidding, minions!" He zipped around the room. "Honeyhoney…

sugar… honeyhoneyhoneyhoneyhoney!" He bounced off the table and rebounded on the bed, his cape fluttering behind him.

I grabbed a honey packet we got at the market from AB's bag and opened it.

"Ahhhhhhhhhhhhhh! Hon-ey!" He ran in a circle as I tossed the package to AB, where she darted her hand fast enough to smear some honey over his mouth.

"SAINT HONEY TITS!" he bellowed, grabbing the packet and getting a few gulps down before he fell over, passing out. Silence ticked at the room, his legs still twitching with energy.

"Wow." Kat shook her head. "You guys have that down."

"Have to with him." I scoffed. "Survival in the Daniels' house, right?" I winked playfully at AB, her smile warming my heart.

How many times did that happen when I lived with them? Too many times to count. I remembered one time with Lexie, tossing the honey bear like a baby bottle back and forth to each other, getting him fed before he flipped out.

Thinking of Lexie still hurt, but this time I felt myself smiling at the recollection instead of the raw, guttural agony.

And I didn't know how I felt about that. I didn't want to feel so at ease with her memory. It felt like I was letting her go… forgetting her.

My gaze swung to the woman rising from the bed wearing only a tank and knickers. My chest clenched at the sight of her, filling with something I didn't want to feel. As if I were going over a cliff kicking and screaming, but gravity was pulling me down whether I wanted to or not.

The demented part of me seemed eager for the fall. It made me want to resent Kat, to hate her, because remembering Lexie should ache every bone in my body. I needed to feel the punishment in every breath for letting her down.

For not loving her enough.

The palace reflected off the dark water; the glow of lights from the building glistened and blurred over the river like an impressionist painting. A breeze lapped off the Danube, skating over my face. I could feel the slight shift in the air, the drop of autumn on the horizon. These were the last months when living on the streets would be bearable.

The area where we were was silent and dark, the late hour keeping most tucked away somewhere safe. The construction of the wall down toward the old parliament building stopped only a few hours ago, workers waiting for morning light to finish the last parts. Guards milled around, making sure no one got in who shouldn't be there.

They weren't even trying to be subtle with this wall. Just like everywhere else in the Eastern Bloc, the middle class no longer existed. It was between the haves and have-nots.

Cooper paced behind me, his shoulders curled in defense. He wanted Annabeth to stay back in the room, safe, but he also didn't want to leave her alone. Her determination to be part of this had won out, and Cooper now prowled the ground like a lion, circling her and sniffing out any danger that might show itself.

"Stop," she whispered to him. "You're making me crazy."

"You always make me crazy," he murmured in her ear, kissing her temple.

After watching her throw up twice today after eating, the pressure to get this nectar, to find a cure for her, was immeasurable. The weight I felt ramming down on my shoulders was bad enough. I couldn't imagine what Cooper was experiencing.

Imagine it was Katrina dying right now? What would you do? A voice niggled at the back of my head. My reaction was instant. A growl hummed deep in my chest, and the need to drive my sword into the world and slice it into pieces until I found the answer swarmed violently through me.

Grunting, I moved farther toward the pier, my answer in every fiber of my being. There wasn't anything I wouldn't do.

My gaze slid subtly to her. She was in what I tore from her body the night before, her hair in a ponytail. My jaw popped, and I tried not to think about how my hand could wrap around those strands while railing her from behind.

Fuck.

I hissed through my teeth, turning my attention back out to the water. We had done well with ignoring each other all day, staying in our corners, but my mind did not behave with the same restraint now.

There were a few times I pushed out, sensing her barrier between us, poking and prodding at it. Testing what I was afraid to give voice to. She was busy doing something, her back to me, when her head snapped over her shoulder at me as if she felt what I was doing, sensed me peeling at the wall. I had no doubt I would be able to push through, force myself past every layer, but I didn't. Because for once in my life, I was afraid to. Afraid of what I would find on the other side.

The sound of water slapping at the dock yanked my focus to the river. Through the shimmering lights from the palace, I saw a boat with three men heading to the pier.

I observed Dzsinn sitting at the back, and the two others were beefy, their solid forms rowing with quick strokes to us.

Katrina came up to my side, both of us watching the men climb out of the boat.

"I see you brought backup?" Dzsinn took in Cooper. He tried to not show fear, but the man was smart enough to understand what Cooper was. He was meant to be feared.

"As you brought yours." I nodded at the two fae bodyguards he had.

"It's a dangerous world. No one can be too careful."

"I agree." I dipped my head. "Do you have what we need?"

Dzsinn motioned for the two men to grab a trunk from the rowboat.

"I was only able to get a few weapons. The black market is struggling to get even these items now." He watched his men open the lid, displaying a sword, two daggers, and three handguns.

Kat and I progressed to the box, checking out the items. She immediately snatched up the sword, feeling the balance and weight in her hands. She gave a slight nod of acceptance, approving the trade.

"These will work." I tucked one of the guns in my belt. "And the information we seek?"

His attention briefly went to the palace across the river, a frown lining his forehead.

"There is not much I found on him." I could tell he didn't like not having answers. Power was in information. Being the one in the know. "He came out of nowhere about a year ago. Built up a strong following and then challenged and killed the old fae lord. And no one is upset by this. Lord Orbán was not only lazy and apathetic about ruling, but the rumor among the household was he was… depraved… sexually speaking." Dzsinn shifted on his feet. "We fae are far more open about sex than humans, so when we do have lines, it is even more vile to cross them."

Katrina's fingers rolled into balls, disgust and rage painting her expression. I felt it barrel through her, her muscles locking up. And without thought, my hand reached for hers, lacing through her knotted fingers, trying to calm her. She took a deep breath, her shoulders sinking back down.

"As much as we are glad Orbán is dead, no one knows much about this man. Who he is or where he came from. Other than he fights like he has been trained by the best, and because of his looks and violet eyes, he must come from some noble line." Dzsinn shrugged. "Though not all are happy about the change in the status quo. Some were fine with ignoring what was happening behind closed doors with Orbán, enjoying the money, privilege, and power. All that ended when he died."

Casting my attention across the river, I stared at the palace as if it would give me answers. "So not all are faithful to this new leader?"

Dzsinn's smile was hardly noticeable, but it somehow still glinted in his eyes. "No. It's how I was able to find where the secret entrances and exits are located."

"Where?" Katrina's fingers squeezed down, reminding me I was still holding her hand. As if she too became aware, she pulled her hand from mine, running it down her long hair.

"Across the river is an old boarded-up church built into the base of the mountain." He pointed over. In the dark, it was hard to see, but I could make out a turret almost blending in with the rocky landscape, the crumbling stone buildings blending in so well with the mountain and foliage, you might possibly overlook it.

"There are tunnels he has constructed to connect his palace to his new project up there at Citadel Hill."

"What's up there?" Kat's pupils went horizontal, her cat eyes trying to make out clear details. "Looks like an old run-down fortress."

"It's not what's on top but what's being built below the fortress."

"And what is that?" she asked. "A secret hideout?"

"No." Dzsinn paused. "A fae prison."

"Fae prison?" My head snapped up, my eyes gliding over the land on top of the hill. A statue of a woman holding a feather was outlined in the moonlight. It was a symbol to the fae, no matter what the humans thought it meant to them. It was when we had to hide among them, live life like we didn't exist. A secret signal that fae were here and one day we would be free again.

How ironic to build a fae prison below that symbol.

Fae prisons were no ordinary human penitentiaries. They were able to contain the most magical and ruthless beings to ever exist. The jail had to be powerful and secure enough to keep the most cold-blooded beasts locked up for good, cutting off their magic and abilities.

Humans had no chance there.

A shiver ran down my spine, thinking of being locked underground for eternity. It went against everything in me. Pirates needed to be free, to feel the air and taste the sea. I couldn't imagine a worse fate than getting put in there.

"The church is now another secret access in and out. A way to move people through without anyone seeing."

"And these tunnels connect to the palace?" Putting my hands on my hips, my attention returned to the bright beacon on the hill.

"As far as my contacts stated. Yes. There is a connection." Dzsinn nodded. "But I don't know how or where. That is up to you to figure out. But my end of the deal has been fulfilled." A heavy connotation hung in the air.

I dipped my head in acknowledgment. "Yes. And a deal is a deal."

Something told me he would be a great person to have on my side. Getting him products from the West to sell would only profit us both, especially the more this place slid into this land of savages.

"Then I look forward to our business relationship, pirate. I think it will be very prosperous. If you survive."

His two men grabbed the empty trunk, putting it back in the rowboat. Dzsinn stepped into it, taking a seat.

"I think we'll be fine." I smirked.

"Don't underestimate him. I've heard he is cutthroat and

ruthless when he needs to be. He slaughtered all twenty of Orbán's personal guards single-handedly like a samurai warrior before he gutted and beheaded the fae lord." Dzsinn wrapped his coat around him as his men started rowing the boat. "I'm just saying, be careful of Lord Killian."

Everything in my body went still, a pitch ringing in my ears.

"What?" I uttered slowly. "What did you call him?"

"Lord Killian," Dzsinn said, his boat gliding away into the night.

Like a samurai warrior.

No. It's just a coincidence. There was no way.

Except I didn't believe in coincidences.

CHAPTER 15
Katrina

Killian.

"No." The word barely made it off my tongue, so low it felt like a breath. The tightening of my ribs strangled the air from my lungs.

It wasn't possible. It was just a name.

My gaze went up to the flag flying high on the palace. Nothing in it gave me an answer, except somewhere in my gut, I just knew. As if my tie to my old friend was still there, still a thread that linked me to him.

"Killian?" I whispered, a hand covering my mouth.

"We don't know it's him." Croygen turned to me, his head wagging like he was trying to deny it. "Many people have that name."

"It's him," I croaked, my gaze on the palace, emotion clotting my throat.

"You don't know that." He stepped in front of me, blocking my view. "I mean, come on, what the fuck would Killian be doing here? And a *lord*?" He scoffed. "It's just a coincidence, Kat. Just a name."

"And this *Lord Killian* just happens to fight like a samurai warrior?" My voice pitched. We both were there. We knew how well Killian could fight and how seriously he took Master Yukimura's teachings. Pushing Croygen away, I stomped over to one of the many row boats tied up at the dock, my brain analyzing if it would be faster than going to the bridge to cross over.

"What are you doing?" Croygen bellowed as I climbed in, set on my mission. "Where are you going?"

"I need to see if it's him." I reached for the docking line, panic clawing at me.

"Kat, stop. You're being ridiculous."

"I need to go."

"And what, Kat?" Croygen grabbed the rope, stopping me from untying it. "What if it is? Are you going to knock on the door and ask if he can come out and play with you?" Croygen leaned over, getting in my face. "You think you can even get that far? And what if it's not him? You want to end up in that prison they're building over there? You know how fae prisons work, Kitten. You go in and you don't come out," he seethed, though all I sensed was his fear, the need to keep me safe. "Take a breath and think for a moment."

I didn't want to. I just wanted to act. To see if it was Killian. *My* Killian.

"The guards will shoot you before you touch the gate." Croygen continued, feeling my hesitation. "They know who we are. Know what we're after. You can't just walk up there."

I knew that, but it didn't change my desperation to confirm what my gut was telling me.

"It's not him, Katrina." Croygen held out his hand for me to take. "I know you miss him, but don't do something foolish in the heat of the moment."

I stared at the lights, the large windows adorning the great palace, teasing me with the possibility of peeking inside.

A hacking cough came from Annabeth, snapping my head to her. Cooper rubbed her back and brushed the hair off her face. She was getting sicker. I could smell the bitter stench consuming her.

Without the nectar, she would die very soon.

"Katrina?" Croygen wiggled his hand for me to take.

Exhaling, I sat a few more moments before I took it, letting him lift me back onto the pier.

"We will be going there soon enough." Croygen tossed one of the guns to me. "We need a plan first, all right?"

Nodding, I tucked a blade and gun into my waistband, following the group back toward our lodging. At the last moment, I peered over my shoulder at the glowing throne on the hill, my heart twisting in my chest before we disappeared into the heart of the city.

I didn't know if I wanted it to be him or not.

"What is our plan?" Cooper carried AB up the steep stairs to our floor. "We know where to get in, but what after that?"

"Yeah." Croygen sighed, getting to our door and pushing it open. "Be helpful if we knew where the nectar was being held."

"I might be able to help with that," a voice spoke, I caught a woman's silhouette on my bed.

Croygen yanked out his gun, pointing it at the figure.

"Oh, I think that's unnecessary, but you know how I like it." Her eyes slid to me briefly, returning to him with a knowing smile. "Don't you, Croygen?"

Fuck my life.

Amara.

"What the hell are you doing here, Amara?" Croygen stepped in closer, his finger pressing firmer down on the trigger.

"I'm here as friend, not foe." She put up her hands like they were playing some kinky game. "I swear."

"Like I believe a word that comes out of your lying mouth." Croygen sneered, letting Cooper move into the room with him. Amara sat up, finally snapping out of her sultry tone.

"I'm here to help." She sounded more honest.

"Funny, 'cause the last time we saw you, you broke my hand and stole the nectar," I snarled, moving past the boys, my gun pointed at her, anger growing my nails out long. "*Helping* the Hungarian soldiers."

"Yeah, well…" Her lip lifted. "That didn't work out."

"They saw past your bullshit, huh?" I tipped my head. "Cut you out."

She glowered at me, telling me I hit it on the nose.

"Or this could be a trap." Croygen inched to the end of the bed. "I know your backhanded deals too well. Come crawling back, pretending to be betrayed while you are actually betraying both parties."

"This time, I'm being truthful." She stood, turning to Croygen, ignoring our weapons on her. "The moment we got through the fae door, they took the nectar and ran." Fury flashed over her features. "I've been watching them for the last few days. I know where they are keeping it."

"Where?" Cooper growled.

She shot him a dirty look. "You know that's not how it works. You help me, I help you."

"Help?" Croygen laughed bitterly. "All you know is how to help yourself."

"You didn't say that when we were in bed."

Like a thousand birds taking off at once, fury swooped down on me, burning through my limbs, flying me toward her in a hum of wrath.

He was mine.

"Whoa. Whoa." Croygen stepped in my path, hustling me back. "Calm down, Kitty-Kat."

Her smirk over his shoulder spurred me forward, and I tried to push through Croygen.

"Hey." He cupped my face, blocking out everything else except him. "She's not worth it," he muttered to me, the truth hitting every nuance in his claim, pulling my attention completely to him. "It's what she wants. Don't let her get to you." His thumb grazed my bottom lip, his mouth so close it looked like he was going to kiss me. "Okay?"

He didn't move until I nodded.

"Aren't you guys so cute," Amara taunted, swinging us back at her. "You two are a thing now? The Puss and the Pirate finally banging each other?"

"Amara, if you don't tell me what the fuck you are doing here," Croygen spoke, his timbre dragging the floor, filled with the barest of truth. "I will *fucking* kill you."

Amara blinked, her mocking expression falling from her face as if, for the first time, she knew he might do it.

Something had changed. Her power over him was gone.

Swallowing, she tucked her purple-black hair behind her ear.

"I really am here to help."

"You don't help. So what do you want from us?"

"I can't get into the palace alone," she confessed.

"You want us to provide cover and assistance to get in so you can grab the nectar and take off?" Croygen snorted. "I don't think so."

"We know it can be divided." She signaled to Annabeth. "I was watching when the doctor cut it up. So I propose we divide it up. Half for me and half for you guys."

"Giving you half of the most powerful substance on Earth?" Cooper's laugh boomed through the room. "You've got to be joking."

"Why?"

"Because you are the last person who should *ever* have it." Cooper shook his head. "No. No way."

"Then I guess you're not getting it either. Since you don't know where it is."

"And how do we know you do?" I came up between the boys. "That you aren't lying to us. Leading us into a trap."

"I guess you'll have to take my word."

"Then I also say no." I moved closer to Cooper, both of us glancing over at Croygen.

"Wait, you aren't actually going to trust her?" Cooper watched him, his brows crinkling.

Croygen continued to study her, probably knowing all her tells after so many years together.

"How do you know where it is, Mar?" Croygen stepped closer to her.

I cringed at his nickname for her, hating their years of history.

Her lips pinched together.

"O-kay, I didn't tell the whole truth." *Shocker*. "I mean, they took the nectar and left me, but later that night, in a pub near the palace, I tracked one named Vale down there, and…"

"You pulled an Amara." Croygen snorted. "Which means you got him very drunk. Then once he took you back to his room, you drugged him, getting answers. And probably robbed him too."

My throat tightened.

That sounded very close to what I used to do. I couldn't stand this woman—I hated her—but I was no different. I screwed, stole, and "drugged" men with my pussy. I didn't judge her for that part. I hated her because she fucked Croygen for the pleasure, not because he was a "job."

The thought of him being with anyone else, especially her, twisted me up and itched my skin. My cat skimmed the surface, ready to attack and kill.

Mine.

"Don't act like that's not exactly what you do," she snarled at him.

"I don't have to drug them. They gave their money and secrets to me willingly," Croygen jabbed back.

"He told you where it is?" I cut into their conversation, fur bristling down my back.

Croygen's head shot to me, his mouth twitching with smugness, and I knew he somehow detected my anger… my jealousy.

"It's being temporarily held in this new prison he is building right now. The walls are thick, and it is guarded around the clock."

"The prison." Croygen clicked his tongue. "The one with tunnels connected right to that church."

"Yes. And I know where." She looked at all of us. If she knew about this prison, she might be telling the truth. "Do we have a deal?"

A thump came from somewhere, twisting us around in search.

"Wait." Annabeth finally spoke, her attention darting over the room. "Where is Sprig?"

"Oh… that thing?" Amara tapped her lips as another thud came from the dresser. "He needed a little time out."

"Shit." Croygen darted for the bureau, yanking the drawer out. Inside, tied up and muzzled with his new white underwear cape, Sprig wrestled around, noises muttering from him.

Croygen picked him up, pulling the fabric from his mouth.

"Purple-Medusa!" he shrieked. "I will poop in your mouth as you sleep! I will piss in your ears, you anorexic Muppet! Curse you, purple cabbage head!"

"Uh-oh." Croygen unwound him from his bindings, looking at Amara. "You've pissed off the Monkey King."

Moonlight streamed through the thin curtains, accompanied by muttering from the homeless below the open window or those fae enjoying the night. The room was hot with so many supernatural bodies inside it. My ears twitched at every sound, every heavy breath in the room, especially from the one sleeping on the floor.

None of us wanted her here, but we trusted her less to not be in our sight. Amara threw a fit about being on the floor, but Croygen put his foot down.

"Remember Peru?" He got in her face. "I slept on that floor for weeks. Ryker was way too considerate of you. But you see, I've learned that lesson. You don't get to be the evil backstabbing bitch from hell and still demand privileges. Not how it works here." He tossed down a hard pillow from the chair with a thump. "Enjoy the nice comfy floor, Mar." He turned away, strolling to the bed I was in. "We'll review our plan tomorrow morning. Think we could all use some sleep." He addressed the room before crawling in next to me, his back to me, his walls up and prickly.

So here I lay wide awake hours later, dawn approaching, next to the captain who ruined my life, the same man who turned my body to liquid with a look.

But for once, my issues with Croygen took a back seat. Killian was all I thought of. My memory was full of the boy I grew up with, who became not just my best friend, but my family. One of the only people I truly trusted in this world. And when he left, I pretended it didn't break my heart, yet it had.

All those feelings of guilt, hurt, anger, and love simmered in my limbs, twitching and moving my body relentlessly.

I couldn't sit here not knowing the truth. Not knowing if he was only a few kilometers from me.

Lifting my head, I scanned the room, my senses picking up that everyone was sleeping. With a command, my muscles retracted, my bones popping, and in a blink, my four paws landed softly on the wood floor, leaving my tank and undies in a pool at my feet. Leaping up on the windowsill, I glanced back, watching for any movement before I jumped out the window to the ground below.

My paws padded over the cobblestone, my slick black fur slipping into the darkness like it was part of it. It felt good to be in my cat form, to become almost invisible to people, easily winding through the city with no one noticing me. It was freeing, reminding me of how often the stresses of trying to get money and keep my crew together would send me on nightly escapades. I would walk the whole city, letting myself just be in the moment.

Trotting over the bridge, crossing from the Pest to Buda side, my whiskers twitched at the magic thickened by the cluster of fae in one area. The air also held a different weight— a command, power. Confidence that humans and even fae would find daunting. A dominance that didn't need to be said because it just was.

Guards were positioned at every gate leading up to the palace, and I had no doubt there were more hidden around, unseen. I sensed magic laced around fences, alarms that would set off if things like me tried to slither through. Hopping up on a high wall at the border of his royal grounds, I was able to see what most couldn't: a clear view of the palace.

The front arched with high windows and doors, a balcony waiting for speeches to be made to the masses. The old royal castle was a mix of neo-baroque, medieval, and modernism. Beautiful, but it felt somber, with fewer embellishments compared to the Parliament building across the Danube.

Soft light glowed from inside the upstairs room of the main building, the chandeliers dimmed low as if someone was awake but wasn't ready for the harshness of the day to begin. Enjoying the time when it was quiet and still, most of the world asleep, and the demands of the day were still a few hours off.

A silhouette moved by a window like a ghost, causing my heart to ball up in my throat, as if something in me recognized him before my brain did. The figure pushed out the glass doors with what looked like a drink in his hand, sleeves rolled up on his white dress shirt, the top buttons open, letting me see a hint of the tattoo on his chest. One I knew. He ran his hands through his hair with frustration as he stepped out to the railing, the light from the palace igniting his features.

A gasp stuck in my throat, sounding like a yowl, emotion slamming into me with force. Shock shifted my body from cat to human and back again before I reined in control, digging my claws into the stone wall to keep steady.

Oh gods.

I heaved in oxygen, black dots hindering my vision. Deep down, I knew, but I still wasn't prepared.

It was Killian… my Killian.

Every memory, every tiny detail of my youth, was connected to him, from the moment they found him hiding on our ship to the night he walked away from me for good. It felt like I had locked everything that had to do with him away, and now that box had been torn open, dumping it all out at once, overloading my senses.

"Killian." His name came out a choked cat cry of emotion, drowning me in memories, sending me into the past.

"Kitty-Kat?" Killian climbed the ratlines up to me, his voice slightly croaking out my name. Every day, I swore he grew another inch just to spite me. The crew teased him all the time now about his deepening voice, what a ladies' man he was going to be, and the fact soon they'd be bringing him to "shore." I knew what that meant, and it made me feel ill that my friend would do things with those types of ladies. Another one who would choose those women over me, leaving me alone.

"Hey?" He plunked down next to me in the crow's nest, knowing exactly where to find me.

I kept my knees pulled into my chest and sniffed.

"Don't cry." He tried to wipe a tear away.

"I'm not." Brushing away the evidence, I scowled at him, though I was angry at myself.

"Are you upset about training?" He spoke softly, like he didn't want to unleash the wild animal in me.

I was told many times I had a temper, but lately it seemed to be out of control.

"You almost beat me. I swear," he soothed, like I needed to be lied to.

I glared at him over my shoulder, keeping my head tucked against my knees.

"Then what's wrong, Kitty-Kat?" He rubbed at his chest, the new tattoo healing. Captain had placed his brand, the tattoo of a pirate, near his heart, declaring Killian as a full crew member.

Even I hadn't gotten that yet. It made me sick with jealousy. I wanted Croygen to brand me. To claim I was his too.

"Kitty-Kat?"

I exhaled, not knowing what exactly was wrong. My feelings were all over the place, and I felt something was changing with Killian. We were best friends. I couldn't imagine doing anything without him. I liked how things were, but even in myself, I felt different when he looked at me. An awareness in his touch that bugged me.

"Maybe this will cheer you up." A smile pulled his mouth, his hand digging into his pocket. "I got you something when Captain took me to the market with him today."

And there was the sticker in my paw. The straw that turned my day completely sour.

It wasn't just Killian who had changed, but Captain. After that night I watched him with that woman, my interest and need to be around him had tripled, while he avoided me like a rocky shore, veering far around me. I was invisible unless it was to scowl at or make a comment to my father that I should be at a proper girls' school.

And my awareness of him was taking away all my concentration. I lost to Killian today in a sword fight because I wouldn't stop watching Captain, wondering what he was thinking, wondering what he was doing when he left the ship.

He used to take me to the market, letting me pick out a treat; now he was choosing Killian to join him on outings. Treating him like he was his apprentice.

"Here." Killian dropped a polished stone about the size of a marble into my hand. The rich green jade was laced with bright yellow flares. "I saw it and thought of you."

My chest clenched, my gaze darting up to Killian's violet eyes, intently going back and forth between mine. "It reminded me of your eyes."

I held my breath, a wave of fear and confusion prickling at my skin. I didn't understand why he was looking at me like that. He never had before.

"Kitty-Kat." His hand touched my arm, his tone wanting something. I think I knew, but I didn't want to acknowledge it. If I did, it would change everything.

He leaned forward, like he was going to kiss me, and my body locked up.

Boots clumped across the deck, jerking my head away from Killian. Croygen sauntered to the railing, his spot when the world got too chaotic. I had spied on him a thousand times at his spot, and it never got old. Watching him give his thoughts over to the sea like it was his confession. It fascinated me, pulled me in, had me on pins and needles, though he never spoke out loud. It was like I heard him and the sea talking anyway because the sea spoke to me in the same language.

Staring at him now, I wanted even more to crawl into his mind and hear what problems weighed on his shoulders. Was I one of those problems? Had he ever spoken to the sea about me?

"Kat?" My name barely registered, my attention completely absorbed on the pirate in communion with the ocean, his stunning features tingling every bone in my body.

"Kat!" Killian nudged me hard, jerking my head back to him. His mouth parted, his eyes widening while his head went back and forth between me and Croygen. "Shiver me timbers… you like our captain?"

"No." My defenses went up, my head shaking, my expression contorting into overexaggerated disgust. "I don't!"

"He's our captain!" He ignored my pathetic denial. "He's like your father's age. That's so gross, Kat." Killian's bewilderment was filled with anger. "You love him." Hurt filled his eyes as he scooted toward the rope. "I-I can't believe you."

"No, wait… Kill, I don't like him that way." I reached out for him, feeling the marble heat in my palm. "I swear."

"Don't lie to me," he spat. "It's so obvious."

Was it? Was I totally transparent? Was that why Croygen avoided me? He felt disgusted by me too?

"Killian, don't…" I scrambled to the ratline, grabbing his arm. A surge of desperation and fear opened my mouth. "Don't tell anyone, please."

It was a confirmation, a truth he was hoping to be wrong about, and I only gave it validation.

His lids narrowed, his mouth pinching in a thin line. He shook his head before disappearing below the crow's nest, swinging down the rope like a monkey and dropping to the deck below.

My chest felt hollow, and my heart and brain were even more confused. I sat there with the jade stone in my hand, feeling like I lost my best friend. Once again, a single moment had changed everything, and there was no going back.

My eyes took in the man now, his hair slightly longer, his body taut, filling out his expensive clothes, radiating power. Money gave people an air, the security and confidence of someone who never had to be without. This man had the demeanor of a lord, someone you'd never know came from nothing. Abuse, abandonment, starvation, knowing cold so deep in your bones it felt like it would never leave. The exhaustion and trauma of survival. The boy who stowed away had been filled with so much anger and hate that I thought Captain was going to leave him ashore, letting him be someone else's problem. Instead, he turned Killian's wrath into a weapon, training him to release his energy in other ways. Fighting, stealing, and probably whoring later.

When Master started training us, the crew made a dummy from rice bags and straw to practice our blades on. Killian had named it Hazem, his supposed best friend at the orphanage, who tried to kill him. The day after that incident with Killian in the crow's nest, the dummy's name changed. A big C was drawn on the bag of rice instead.

No doubt for Captain or Croygen.

Killian became disrespectful and angry toward Captain. And when he found me later, after my father died, it had turned into pure abhorrence.

But by then, he had an ally in his animosity. A partner in despising our old captain and fantasizing about his death. Though Killian didn't plan on my fury turning into an obsession. I didn't want it to be just a fantasy. I wanted it to be real. So, once again, Croygen consumed my thoughts and had more power than Killian's feelings for me.

I remembered the night he left me so clearly.

"One day you'll come crawling to me, when I'm the one swimming in riches and power."

Was that what this was about? Did he become lord to prove something?

Killian slammed back his drink, his hands running through his hair again. I sensed his frustration, a burden hanging on his shoulders. I knew all his ticks. We had been together so much, there was nothing either of us could do without the other one picking up on it. It's why we had made such a great team in starting my crew. He was supposed to be my right-hand man. My first mate.

Dragging his hand over his face, he turned for the door. It was instinct to want to go to him, comfort him. Like we always did with each other.

My paw took a step to jump down.

A hand gripped the back of my neck, yanking me down off the wall. Terror flooded my veins. Spitting and hissing, I shifted back into my human form. Then I was twisted around and pushed against the stone wall, piercing dark eyes glowering down at me.

"Dammit, Katrina," Croygen snarled, leaning over me, his nose flaring, his hand gripping my throat. "You really want to use up all your nine lives in one night?"

"You know that's not really a thing, right?"

He rolled his jaw, his chest knocking into mine. "Shut. Up." He ground through his teeth in a demand, a vein popping on his neck. His thumb pushed up my chin. "I'm saving your ass so I can kill you myself."

We glared at each other, his anger infectious, triggering my own against him.

"How are you even here?" I hissed.

He slanted his head, his thumb sliding up over my mouth.

"You don't think I can find you?" He pressed his clothed body into my naked one, his tone lowering. "Know *exactly* where you are? I can find you *anywhere*, Kitten. Even from the dead of sleep, I can feel you *wherever* you go." It was a challenge, a dare to counter his claim. "Besides, I know how your fucking mind works. I *know* you. There was no way you would let this go. Not when it comes to *him*."

"You sound jealous," I shot back, trying to ignore how his clothes rubbed at my nipples, how his leg pushed slightly between my thighs. His thumb pressed between my lips, and the desire to wrap my tongue around it and suck clamped my teeth together.

He moved his leg, parting my legs more. "Did you sleep with him?"

"I slept with him all the time." I smiled cruelly.

"You fuck him?" He tugged down on my bottom lip, his gaze dropping to my mouth, tension riding his vocals.

Part of me wanted to lie, to say yes, just to inflict my anger on Croygen, but looking into his eyes, I could feel him slipping under my skin, bubbling the truth from my lips.

"No."

Exhaling, his shoulders went down.

"This was stupid, Kat. There are guards everywhere." He dropped his hand from my face, gripping my hip. "What were you thinking?"

"I wanted to see him." I swallowed. "To know for sure."

"And were you just going to slip past all the magic guarding this place and walk right up to the front door, where he would greet you like an old friend?"

"I don't know… But…" I looked away. "It's *Killian*."

"In name, but you don't know who he is now. It's been a long time since you've seen him. That man up there is not the same Killian you knew." Croygen pressed me harder into the wall with his body, his cock hard against me. "Though I'll bet one thing hasn't changed." He arched his eyebrow. "His hatred for me. How do you think he'll react to find you not only didn't kill me, but you've been riding my cock, coming in my mouth? I've tasted the one thing he has *always* wanted and couldn't have." He adjusted his leg, the fabric of his clothes parting my folds, rubbing through me.

I bit back my moan, my desire devouring any sense and reason in my brain.

"It will not be the happy reunion you are hoping for."

"So, what? I sneak behind his back and rob him instead?"

"Technically, he robbed us first."

My lids tapered.

"His men knew to follow us specifically. What if he already knows about us? This might be revenge, a trap. The point is… we don't know. And you can't just waltz in there, naked, I might add, and act like Killian is the boy who worshipped the ground you walked on." Croygen ran his hands through my loose hair, tugging on the end. "I don't trust him. And I'm sorry, but you can't either."

There was valid truth in Croygen's words, none of it I wanted to hear, but I hadn't gotten where I was by being foolish. I wasn't about to start now.

"Yeah, I know." I sighed.

"Wait." He pulled back. "I think that sounded an awful lot like, 'Croygen, you are soooo right—*as usual*—how are you so smart and also the most amazing, dirty, fucking god in bed? A truly magnificent virile beast.'"

"You meant *venereal* beast, right?" I snorted.

A cheeky smile took over his face as he yanked a bag off his back, tossing it to me. "Here."

My hands grasped the sack he threw. Opening it, I stared down in stunned silence at the contents. Laying inside were my boots and jacket. His old jacket.

"Oh my gods…" I whispered. My throat tightened when I yanked out the long leather coat and my unique boots. "You had them the whole time?" I could barely talk, my voice raspy and emotional.

"Wanted to make sure you wouldn't use those blades on me first."

"And how do you know I won't now?"

Naughty cheekiness curved his mouth, and he gave me a knowing glance.

Even while angry with me, Croygen had the forethought to bring me clothes, aware I would be naked. In giving me the jacket and my bladed boots, he was handing over his trust, his respect. The coat was officially mine. I was more than just an equal.

The gesture hit me deeper than I expected, flooding me with emotion I couldn't handle.

"No pants?" I squeaked out, pretending to not be affected, pulling on the worn, soft jacket.

"Easier to spank you this way." Walking backward, his arms open, he winked playfully at me.

I stood there immobile for a moment, watching the swashbuckler slip into the shadows, my heart thumping with emotion.

"Come on, Kitty-Kat." His voice pulled me like I had no choice, no debate, no question about who I would follow.

It felt like some bizarro world where I was running to the villain, the man who killed my father and destroyed my life, instead of the supposed hero, my best friend, the one who had always claimed to love me.

CHAPTER 16
Croygen

Creeping back over the bridge to the Buda side for the second time in twenty-four hours felt quite different. This time I wasn't tracking down a cat-shifter I wanted to strangle.

My gut had pinpointed Katrina like a tracking device, knowing where she was without hesitation. And all day I waited for my brain to acknowledge the truth, to understand what that meant, and totally lose it.

What freaked me the fuck out was I *wasn't* freaking out. And that bothered me. I vowed never to let a woman take hold of me again, the sea my only mistress. But when Katrina caught up with me on our way back, her boots clicking on the pavement, my old pirate jacket flapping in the light breeze behind her with *nothing* else under, I almost went down on my knees, ready to declare my allegiance and worship every inch of her. It took all I had not to, to keep my eyes forward and not take her against an alley wall like I had before. Her claws had already sunk into me. A prisoner of my own making.

I was pretty sure I cuffed myself freely to her.

Her presence next to me as we snuck toward the church caused my teeth to grind together, and the instinct to touch her, be near her, be *inside* her, was making me crazy.

"Unless you're going to put a white flag, waving in defeat on that enormous flagpole of yours, can you aim it away from me?" a voice huffed, climbing out of my jacket pocket. "I swear, butt bandit, you could float on it in the ocean. Use it as a harpoon!"

My teeth clenched down more, ignoring the tiny monkey-sprite clambering up to my shoulder.

"Oh, what's wrong? Someone go cat-a-tonic?" He chuckled. "Get it? *Cat*atonic."

"Hilarious, sand puppy," I grumbled. "Now zip it, or I'll see if *you* can float out on the ocean."

"You can't, poor-man's-version-of-a-Viking. You need these too much." He jiggled his hands in my face.

"Annabeth, you want to take your stuffed toy back?" I glanced back at the blonde, who would not sit home even when we threatened to tie her down. AB was so sweet and kind, but fuck, that girl was stubborn. She held her chin high, her hands on her hips, defying me and Cooper to the end. Kat stood behind her, telling us she had just as much right to go. This was her fight too.

One glance at Cooper and I knew we had lost.

As much as I wanted to protect her, I wouldn't take her choice away. We also didn't know what was ahead or how this night would go. If we found the nectar, we had no time to go back and get her. We had to run and not stop until we got to a country that was part of the Unified Nations, giving us a slight umbrella of safety.

A chime rang, declaring the late hour, the shadows covering the five (and a quarter) of us as we moved across the city.

Amara waved for us to follow her up the path, keeping low and quiet as we snuck to the old monastery built into the mountain. The stone structure appeared to have been in a state of decline for a while now, the neo-Gothic structure chipping away like the rocky terrain around it. It blended in so perfectly, as if it'd been born from the earth and grew among the stone. A fortress where ancient Druid magic crusted in the rock—weak, a voice from long ago, with only whispers of it remaining.

Two guards patrolled the gated arch doorway, the emblem on their outfit stating who they belonged to.

Killian.

Half of me was shocked at how the little boy I provided a home to so long ago turned out. The other half wasn't at all. Killian always had this dire need to prove himself, to be better than everyone else. To rise from his poverty-stricken life like it was a reckoning for anyone who doubted him. Who hurt him.

Retribution for the cruelty of his father. And I was the face he hung that vengeance on. The father he despised, the pirate he envied, and the man he felt took the woman he was destined for.

Ducking behind a wall, we watched the guards stroll around the front. A heavy chain locked the gate opening to the cave/church. Chatting in Hungarian back and forth, they hardly glanced around, too busy with whatever gossip they were talking about to notice intruders. They probably never had to deal with any before. If the prison was just being built, there would be no one inside or outside to guard against. They stood in mind-numbing boredom for hours with nothing to do. After a while, their attention would wane, responses dulling, not believing they had to be vigilant right now.

I automatically glanced at Katrina as if I needed to check in, to contrive a plan between us. Though I didn't have to look at her to know we were on the same page, our movements being one.

There was a thrill and fear in that. The overwhelming sensation of wanting to run from it, at the same time knowing I'd scorch the earth if anyone hurt her.

Her green and yellow eyes reflected in the night back at

mine, her pupils vertical, ready to attack. I felt her slip under my skin, buried so deep I couldn't recall how she wasn't always there. Though I think she had been. Waiting. Hibernating.

In that single moment, I realized we never had a chance to fight what was between us, nor would I want to. She was part of me. My possessiveness of her swelled, desire tightening my muscles, needing to claim her, mark her in every way as mine.

Cooper's low growl drew me back into the moment.

"You're distracted," he muttered to me. "I need your head in the game. You can fuck her later."

I couldn't even try to deny his claim. I was horny all the time now. "Yeah." I cleared my throat, dipping my head. "I'm here."

"Get their attention." Cooper's eyes flashed red, his hands growing into claws. "I'll come from behind." He slipped silently away, his body staying mainly in his man form.

My gaze once again found Kat's, though I felt Amara's burn into my profile. She was used to being the one with me on missions, the one who had my focus.

"Let's do this, pirate," Kat's eyes said to mine.

"Tradesman."

Her lips quirked up, her eyes rolling as her thumb clicked off the safety.

It was so natural, so innate, to communicate with her like this. Like we always had been this way.

Dipping my head, I pushed off the wall, moving around the barrier. The two fae men froze, instantly feeling a shift in the air, my boots crackling the loose stone underfoot.

"Did someone here order a sexy-as-fuck pirate?" I winked at them, their shock turning into defense, their hands yanking out their guns.

"Állj!" one of them barked, his finger about to press down on the trigger. "Stop!"

Through the darkness, an enormous figure snuck up

behind him. A vibration rattled from Cooper's throat as his claw sliced the fae's throat, blood sputtering out, the body dropping to the ground before he could cry out. The other man screamed, whipping around to Cooper, his gun pointed at the beast.

"No…" I rushed forward.

Bang!

The single shot ricocheted off the stone, echoing like a bomb, spearing the air like a warning bell.

With a roar, Cooper grabbed the man's weapon, ripping it from his hand while yanking him closer. His claws wrapped around the man's neck, picking him off the ground.

Crack.

Cooper twisted the guard's head almost clean off, snapping his spine with a loud pop. He tossed him down, the body twisted like a pretzel.

"Someone's a little cranky." I nodded at the dead man, pulling Sprig out of my pocket.

"He shot me," Cooper snarled, his long teeth making him lisp over his words, his features slipping back to normal, his claws retracting. He patted the bleeding wound in his shoulder, already starting to heal. "Fucker."

In the distance, yells permeated the darkness, coming from the top of the hill, alerted to the commotion here.

"Fuck." I shoved Sprig toward the lock on the doors. "You've got to hurry."

"You can't rush the magic hands of a Monkey God King," Sprig huffed, stretching his fingers like he was warming up.

"Want to bet?" I snapped, my shoulders rising with each tick of the clock, ready to see Killian's soldiers invade this area at any moment.

Sprig's forehead creased, his fingers digging into the lock.

More ruckus came from the palace, tying my muscles into knots.

"Hurry the fuck up, gopher."

"Keep your sword sheathed, pussy-raider." Sprig's face twisted up. "I almost… got… it."

Tick. Tick. The sound of time clicked loudly in my ear.

"I hear horses coming," Katrina hissed at us.

"Sprig," Cooper growled in warning, his feet bouncing, his eyes tainting red again. "Open it now!"

"This takes skill and stamina, murder-cat. Something *neither* of you would understand."

My fingers itched to strangle him, my jaw locking down until it popped.

Finally, the chains fell away from the lock, clanking loudly to the ground.

"Happy now?"

"Ecstatic." I shoved him in my pocket and ripped open the gate. The glass entrance, which used to be behind the gate, was long gone. "Come on." I waved everyone in as the sound of horses could be heard along the paved road.

Slipping inside the pitch-black space built inside the mountain, we moved deeper into the cavern. Pulling out my torch, I took in the rough arched ceilings and empty rooms. Rooms that housed religious prayer and sacrifice long before any human religion or history book, when fae ruled Earth.

The place was small, directing us to a connecting tunnel off the side of the main room. The passages were as ancient as the monastery but had firebulbs flicking every twenty feet or so, lighting the way as we zigzagged deeper into Gellért Hill. Sweat dripped down my back, and I tried to rush us through. If Killian's men had found their dead comrades and saw where we went, they would cut us off at the top.

At the end of a steady incline, we finally came up to a leveled area, the floor recently cemented. The base for stairs had been set in to dry, but the actual stairs were missing, leaving our exit out of reach.

"Fuck!" Cooper yelled, staring up at a door at least two stories above our heads. "What the hell do we do now? There is no way we can get up there."

Out of the corner of my eye, I saw Katrina travel to the wall, her hand moving over the stone.

"What?" I followed her.

"That is freshly poured." She nodded at the cement. "And there are no stairs to get in or out."

"Yeah, so?"

"That means they had to get heavy cement and builders in here." She moved to another section of the wall, the dim lights making it hard to see anything. "There's got to be a door. Somewhere they could get all the material and people in this room, right?"

"Fuck." Cooper nodded, realizing Kat understood something neither of us probably would have.

My girl was smart, sexy, funny, and badass.

Emotion gathered under my ribs. I stared at her in awe and lust, my gaze practically peeling away her clothes.

"What?" She peered at me as her finger glided over the walls.

"Nothing." I shook my head with a smirk, overwhelmed by what I was feeling for her.

"Ugh. Get a room." Amara sneered, moving to the other side of the chamber.

The five of us scoured the walls, searching for a break in the surface, the clock ticking over us like a bomb. At any moment, Killian's guards could come from the tunnel or from above to capture us.

"Guys? I think I found something." AB's voice shot us to her, her long, thin fingers digging into a crevasse in the wall.

"Move, babe." Cooper slid around her, his fingers wrapping around and pulling, tugging it enough to show a seam in the door.

"Holy shit." I jumped in next to Cooper, helping him yank it open, while Kat moved in close, her gun primed, ready to shoot anything on the other side.

We let out a final grunt, and the opening finally gave way, releasing the smell of dank earth. Distant sounds of pounding metal, voices, and buzz saws filled the air from below.

Gun in hand, I stepped out onto a floating metal walkway, noticing we were all the way up at the top. The ground was so far below I had to grip the railing to stay steady. My mouth parted, my mind unable to fully understand what I was seeing.

I had been in many brigs and jails in my time, but nothing would have prepared me for this.

This place was immense, much bigger than I ever imagined. Twenty-plus floors of various-sized cells were stacked on each other, all facing each other on four sides. Every level had a floating catwalk going around it, with some having tunnels leading you to places deeper in the prison. Two cages hung from the ceiling, ready for that inmate to be left, starving, and forgotten.

My throat tightened, sweat dripping down my back. I already felt the agitated oppression, the deep claustrophobia, the need to get out or I'd lose my mind. I couldn't image what it would be like when it was full. The relentless piercing noises. It would be a constant abuse and attack on your senses. This place would be pure hell.

"Hurry up. Lord Killian wants this finished up now." A man's nasal voice tugged my attention down to the workers at the bottom, putting on the last of the doors to the cells. "You need to complete the stairs and seal off any exits in the next few hours. He has someone coming to put on the protection spells tonight."

Our time was running out; we needed to get to the nectar before they put the spells into place.

"Where do we go, Amara?" I gritted through my teeth, talking low.

She peered around, not looking at me.

"Amara," I repeated her name in warning.

"What?" she hissed. "I don't know. It's not like he drew me a map. I mean, I barely got it out of him that it was somewhere in the prison."

"Wait." My spine straightened. "Somewhere? I thought you knew *exactly* where it was."

Her eyes fluttered to the side in annoyance. It was her sign when I caught her in a fib.

"You don't fucking know?" Twisting, my body vibrating with anger, I moved to her. Any sound we made was eaten up by the bangs down below. She treaded back, a muscle in her eye twitching.

"I knew it was in the prison." Her tone reeked with attitude. "Did you? You wouldn't even be here if it wasn't for me."

Fuck, she was a conniving liar.

You had to hand it to her—she was a survivor, no matter what she had to do. Betrayal, murder, deceit, fuck, lie, seduce. There wasn't a line she wouldn't cross to get what she wanted. And that was her power. To be the victor and hold all the cards.

"He said it was guarded, so find a door that's being guarded," she said, like she made any kind of contribution to the mission.

"Wow. Thanks. Would've never thought about that." Dry as toast, my response parched the air between us.

"You're welcome," she replied with a coy shrug.

Huffing, I stared at this piece of work, wondering how I ever let myself follow her around. How I ever liked her.

Truth was, I never *liked* her. But I loved how awful and deceitful she was because I wanted to be the same. With her, I didn't feel any pain or guilt. No conscience or moral ground. I could be my worst to escape what had happened.

Shaking my head, I turned away with a disgusted grunt. She no longer had any hold on me.

She was nothing to me.

To Amara, that was worse than me hating her.

I had seen how she reacted when Zoey came into Ryker's life. Amara sensed the connection between them. The great warrior Viking had not only met his match in Zoey, but she was his mate. Amara hated that. She lost her power, her control over him.

"Croygen..." she called softly after me, a thread of anguish hinting, as if she felt the tie break for good. She would never curl her finger and have me running back to her *ever* again.

CHAPTER 17
Katrina

The empty prison, not even layered with spells yet, had acid burning holes in my stomach, dread pitching like rogue waves.

This place was built to intimidate, petrify, and mentally brutalize you. So overwhelming, your own senses would feel like torture.

My mind couldn't fathom that this idea came from Killian. The boy who snuck into the galley with me as children, playing pranks on the cook so we could nick extra sweets. Who sat next to me and watched the sea when I was feeling sad. The man who stood by me through the tough times when we were older, scraping every coin so we could buy a ship. Who proved his worth and kept me sane. That person was kind and had such a loving heart.

Not that I didn't see the other side of Killian. Angry, resentful, short-tempered, and vengeful. He had been hurt so many times by people that he built up a high, thick wall, scarcely letting anyone in. But he let me in and then felt I turned on him because I didn't love him the way he wanted me to.

Was all this a result of the pain he felt? Not just me, but his father, Hazem, Croygen, and countless others? Needing to prove something, needing to be above all those he felt betrayed him?

"Move, Kitty-Kat," a deep voice rumbled in my ear, scattering tingles down my spine like a startled bird.

Croygen's hand touched my lower back, his fingers imprinting on me, pushing me toward the stairs to the next level. His body was close to mine, moving in tandem.

The treachery Killian would feel if he saw me with Croygen, the anger and hurt, would be the ultimate betrayal. And I would understand. It was for me as well. Everything I said I stood for, had dedicated my life to… yet I wasn't able to stay away from this man. I couldn't deny or explain the ties I had always felt to the pirate. Where Killian had followed me wherever I went, I had followed Croygen.

Focusing back on our mission, we went down several levels before one led off into a hallway, the noise and action below creating a great cover for our movements.

"Maybe I should shift, scout out, and come back and get you guys," I whispered to the group.

"So you can take it all for yourself?" Amara stepped up to me. "I don't think so, cat thief. I know you'll backstab us all to save your own crew and ship in a moment."

"Me?" I pointed at myself in a quiet, mocking guffaw. "*I'm* the one who will backstab?" Though there was truth to her words, which had my hackles raised. I had once devised taking it for myself to save my crew. Somewhere along the way, I had stopped thinking about it so I wouldn't have to pick a side. Did I even know who I would choose anymore? Did I know? Deep down, I think I did, and that made me feel worse. "And how do you know about my crew?"

A squeak came from Croygen's pocket.

"I didn't mean to!" Sprig poked out. "Ursula, the sea witch, drugged me. I couldn't stop myself."

"Please. It took one packet of honey," she scoffed.

"See?" He motioned to her. "I'm innocent! Honey is my Achilles' heel, a truth serum."

"Sprig." Croygen's jaw ticked. "Now is a wise time to stop talking."

"Just saying. Evil Raggedy Ann doll here drugged me. I'm not to blame."

"Your brain isn't smart enough to be drugged." Croygen shoved him back in his pocket.

"We're staying together." Amara made her stance clear, though I didn't care what she wanted, my gaze going to Croygen's.

"Let's just stay together for now," he muttered low. It irritated me that he chose her side. Did he still bow to whatever she wanted? Did he not trust me?

Did I really trust him?

Even with all these feelings, could I completely trust he wouldn't cut me out if he had to?

Lips pinching together, I circled around, giving my back to him, heading down the tunnel.

"Kitten." I swear I heard his cheeky voice slide over my skin and through me, but I shoved it back, putting up every fortification.

Sneaking down another couple of levels, voices buzzed in my ears, drawing me to the end of the hallway. Cooper and I glanced at each other, giving caution to everyone behind us. Slowly, we crept forward, hiding behind a wall and peering into a room. A cafeteria. Along the far wall was where they'd serve food, swinging doors behind, probably leading to the kitchen. Hundreds of bench-style seats and tables were bolted to the floor, filling the massive room.

A handful of fae gathered at one of the tables near the door, drinking and snacking, all wearing clothes with Killian's crest on it.

"He wants this place fully running by next week. Our first group of inmates will be transferring here from the temporary location," one spoke. He was tall and lean, his head and wide-set eyes reminding me of an insect. "So everyone here needs to step it up. Have the pit and the workrooms fully functioning."

"Shut the hell up, Mantis," another man sneered, his nasal voice sounding like the one yelling at the workers earlier. "Stop acting like you're in charge. You're not."

"And you are?"

"Like I give a shit what this new leader says. He's just one holding the seat warm until another privileged asshole comes along." He stood up, his frame thick and strong, his brown hair short, but I could see nothing notable about him past that.

"That's heresy," Mantis hissed.

"No, it's the truth. The only thing we should be loyal to is ourselves."

"Funny," a tall blonde woman spoke. "Because every time he comes around, all I see is your nose going farther up his ass, Boyd."

"Fuck you." He sneered at her, his shoulders rising, leaning toward her. "I know how to play the long game, while you worship the ground he walks on."

"Back off, Boyd." Mantis pointed at him to move away from her. "It's time for your guard shift anyway."

"Guard," Boyd huffed. "What the hell are we protecting, anyway?"

Mantis shrugged. "Something very important that many of our brethren died for. That is all we need to know."

Very important. It had to be the nectar.

My attention snapped to Croygen next to me, his head bobbing, coming to the same conclusion.

"Go, Boyd," Mantis ordered. "Learn your place, or you won't last long here."

"You're wrong." Boyd glared at him, condescension dripping in his tone. "You will be the one who doesn't last long here. I'll be the one *ruling* this place." He curved for the doorway, scrambling us back into the dark corners, staying motionless as he stomped out of the cafeteria, heading down another passage.

Keeping our distance, we tracked slowly behind him, venturing once again deeper and deeper into the Earth's core after this substance.

Chills prickled at my skin when we reached the last level, far below the prison. The dark passage was lined with metal doors, a brick-sized opening at eye level, only accessible to someone on the outside. One was open, and I spied chains hanging from the ceiling, collars with sharp rods, and whips with razors on them.

Dungeons.

Holes they would put prisoners into torture or die a horrible, painful death.

My past was shady; I had no real moral ground to stand on, but this had vomit pooling in the back of my throat.

Only a few pirates I knew had gotten off on torture and cruelty; most of us killed with efficiency. My boot blade in your gut, my dagger in your throat. Revenge was swift and humane.

This was designed to break every mental and physical fiber in a person.

"About time, Boyd." A man's voice coming from around the corner slowed us down. "I'm bored as fuck down here. Plus, this place creeps me out."

"Really?" Boyd mused. "I like it down here."

"You would, you sick fuck."

"Give me the walkie-talkie," Boyd grumbled.

Walkie-talkie? Shit. That meant he could notify people if we came up on him.

"The new lord must have deep connections; this thing is right off the black market," the other guy noted. "What the hell is he hiding in here that we have to guard a magic-locked prison door with no one here?"

"We should find out. Break in and take it for ourselves."

"No way. I saw the carnage he did to Lord Orbán and his men."

"Coward."

"Screw you, Boyd."

Boyd let out a low laugh like he got off taunting people.

Boots clipped the floor, coming around the corner, heading directly for us.

Croygen's arms circled me, yanking me into one of the dungeons, tucking me against his body against the wall. Cooper, AB, and Amara slipped in beside us.

The guard's footsteps got closer. There was a chance he had vision like Cooper and me, able to see us in here. Terror raced in my veins, my breath held in my lungs as he started to pass.

Croygen's grip tightened on me, his hand gently skating over my chest, pressing his palm against my racing heart. It instantly slowed as if he commanded it. How easily he could have my heart racing or soothing with just a touch. Whichever intention he had was felt through every fiber of my being. My muscles relaxed against him, his mouth against the back of my neck, centering me back in place.

The soldier muttered under his breath, passing the room, none of us moving until only silence rebounded back from where he departed.

There might be only one guard on the door, but with a click of his finger and a single word, Killian's entire army would know we were here. Any plan we had before of approaching wasn't going to work. But I had an idea that might.

I turned to Croygen, my eyes set on him as I yanked off my jacket, lowering any barrier between us, expressing my plan without a word spoken.

His gaze went back and forth between my eyes, understanding every nuance, his head shaking no.

I tilted my head, feeling the buzz between us, the webs we

tried to shear and cut through every day binding even stronger. Becoming unbreakable.

"*No.*"

"*Yes,*" I countered, pulling off my boots and inching up to the door.

"*Katrina.*" My name blasted through me right before I commanded my body to shift. My clothes fell around me in a puddle, my sleek black form about to slip out into the passage when I felt something drop down on my back.

"Giddy up, *Bhean chait.* Let's go grab some smelly pirate booty." Sprig gripped my fur.

I heard Croygen and AB make a noise, reaching after him, but it was too late to stop. Already out the door, I debated going back, but then I realized he might be beneficial. While I distracted Boyd, Sprig could be starting on the lock.

Staying close to the wall, I peered through the dim light the single firebulb on the wall provided, taking in every detail.

Boyd stood in front of a heavy goblin metal door, a rifle in one hand, a walkie-talkie in the other, his attention on affixing it to his belt.

Darting up, I threaded through his legs. His head jerked, his gaze landing on me. He blinked at the monkey on my back with white underwear for a cape.

"What the fuck?"

"Is that how you address a divine Monkey God King riding his pussy-steed, underling?"

His eyes widened, his mouth parting, his hand diving for the walkie-talkie.

It was now or never.

Stretching up, my claws sunk deep into the hand with the device, a yowl pitching from him. The gadget dropped, skidding across the ground as Sprig leaped off my back for the door.

Footfalls drummed for us as Croygen and the rest moved in with speed.

Grunting, Boyd tossed me off, reaching for his gun.

One shot from it, and we'd have all the prison guards down here.

Croygen darted in, his sword going to Boyd's throat, ramming him back into the wall, forcing the gun from his grip.

"Whoa! Wait!" Boyd held up his hands, a little panic showing in his eyes. "I don't want to die over this." He swallowed against the blade. "How about we make a deal?"

"We don't make deals with venal traitors." Croygen bared his teeth.

"Oh, this is a gummy, sticky, thick one…" Sprig worked the knob, his forehead creasing. "Though these magic fingers can get in the tightest, most gooey places."

The man's eyes sprang to Sprig, his throat bobbing. "That thing fucking talks."

"And I recommend addressing him as Monkey King if *you* want to continue to speak." Croygen pinned his sword at his voice box as Amara picked up his discarded gun from the ground.

Croygen's sensual gaze drifted over to me. "You okay, Kitten?"

I padded up to him with a tiny cry of yes, rubbing my body against his leg to reassure him.

"Here." Annabeth dropped my clothes, boots, and bag down beside me, her hands shaking from fatigue. As a cat, I could smell her insides rotting with cancer, the stench pungent. If we didn't get the nectar, she was going to die *soon*. It wasn't weeks. It was days.

Pushing my furry head through my tank, I commanded my body back into my human form, getting dressed quickly while Boyd tried to make a deal.

"I'll make sure you get out of here," he propositioned. "Just get me in on it, and I'll show you the exit myself."

"Think we'll take our chances," Cooper responded.

"I think I got it… wait… no." Sprig *hmphed*, his mouth pinching, fingers moving around.

"You get that open, furball, and I will bathe you in honey," Croygen encouraged.

"Oh, like that time when you squeezed honey all over me, then strapped me to a bug zapper?" Sprig's eyes brightened. "Or the time you dunked my head in honey until I couldn't breathe?"

"Good times. Now open the door," Croygen ordered Sprig.

"First say, *please, my Monkey God King.*"

"Sprig, I'm gonna stuff bananas so deep in your ears and nose, they will be all you smell, taste, and poop for the rest of your life."

Clank.

The lock snapped, the door squeaking open.

We were about to move for the entrance when a crackle hummed in the air, followed by a voice that stilled me in place.

"Lord Killian, checking in," the familiar voice spoke over the walkie-talkie laying on the cement. Hearing him scooped out my insides and dumped them on the floor. It sent me back in time—comfort, love, friendship. It hurt more than I expected, like I had been blocking him out, never allowing myself to mourn his loss in my life.

The distraction was enough. The focus on the device created a moment, and Boyd took it. Gripping Croygen's sword, he rammed it back into the pirate, slamming his boot in his gut, and shoving him back.

I saw Boyd's gaze drop to the walkie-talkie, his muscles twitching.

"No!" I bellowed as he leaped for it at the same time I did. Clawing the ground, we both scrambled for it, my hands trying to reach out. His elbow rammed into my eye, knocking me back, getting to it first as Cooper and Amara came down on him.

"Code red!" he barked into it. "We're bei—"

Cooper kicked the walkie-talkie from his hand, his boot hitting Boyd's nose with a crack as Amara stomped on it, Killian's response beeping out.

It was too late.

He heard the distress call. Troops would be coming for us.

"Shit!" Croygen barked, grabbing Sprig and putting him in his pocket for safety. "Go!" He waved, motioning for Cooper, AB, and Amara to head for the exit while I vaulted inside the tiny windowless room. There were no chains or any kind of torture devices, though I still could feel the evil in this room, designed to break your sanity.

A small box sat on a table up against the wall. It looked so unassuming. A single item in this empty room. The last layer of defense, behind prison walls, a guard, goblin door, and Druid spells.

"Katrina! We've got to go!"

Snatching it up, I twisted, running out of the exit. Hopping over Boyd's body, I felt a hand wrap around my calf, yanking me down. "Ahhh!" I hit the floor with a painful thud, the box rolling out of my hands across the passage.

Kicking and punching me, Boyd tried to get around me to get it. A blade jabbed between his eyes, pushing in enough to trail blood down his face.

"You move and I skewer your brain." Rage burned from Croygen's eyes while he reached down, helping me up. "This is for daring to touch her…" He seethed, flicking his sword down in a sharp movement.

A scream pierced the air, blood squirting from Boyd's mouth, his entire upper lip cut up to his nose, showing his bloody teeth in a grotesque image. Wailing in pain, he thrashed on the floor, Croygen's gaze still locked on him, wanting to end his life. I felt his anger, his vengeance like my own.

"Croygen, we have to go!" I yanked on his arm, pulling him with me.

He didn't budge for another moment, sounds far in the distance reaching us.

"Croygen?" I pleaded.

Snarling, he slammed his boot into Boyd's skull, knocking him out cold before he relented.

"Hurry up!" Cooper belted from far down the passage, sounding like they were already heading up.

Turning to retrieve the container off the ground, panic froze me in place, my stomach sinking.

The box was gone.

Slowly, my gaze lifted to see Amara standing a few yards away with it in her hands, along with Boyd's gun.

"What are you doing, Amara?" I swallowed, anxiety rising.

"Nothing more than what you guys would do to me." She sneered righteously, pointing the gun at me. "I'm just making sure I come out the winner in this." She clicked the safety off, ready to shoot.

"Wait." Croygen stepped slightly in front of me. "Don't shoot."

"Why not? It would make me so much happier." She smiled at me. "Plus, I'm only helping you out."

"How is that?" Croygen gritted through his teeth.

"Stopping you from becoming Ryker." Wrath billowed off her. "Becoming a pathetic, lovesick puppy. Come on, Croygen, look at what you've become. Have you forgotten what you used to be like, how much fun we had? Deep down, you know you liked what you were with me. It was the most real you've ever felt."

Croygen didn't respond, not fighting back, plunging my stomach even further into the floor. Did he think that too? I couldn't gauge his emotions, his walls locked tight around him, but hurt and shock bubbled up in my lungs.

"You'll thank me." She started to push down on the trigger, the barrel pointed at my head.

"No." He stepped more in front of me, his cheek flinching in agony. "Fine, Mar. You win."

What?

"Take it and go. Just don't shoot her."

She shook her head in disappointment at him.

"I should, just to watch you grieve," she mocked. "Just another sentimental fool. What a waste."

"You have what you want. Just go," Croygen repeated.

What the fuck was he doing? Was he willing to give up the cure for Annabeth? Take away my only leverage to get my ship and crew back?

"Croy—"

"Go, Amara." Croygen cut me off with his order. "Before it's too late and you can't get out of here."

Amara paused for a moment, suspicion lowering her brow, but sounds from above getting closer whipped her around, running up the stairs and out.

My lips parted in disbelief. "What the fuck, Croygen?"

He turned his head, a bad-boy smirk lifting his mouth. With a wink, he went to the opposite wall where the nectar box fell, yanking out a handkerchief from his pocket. Deep in the murky darkness, my sight caught him wrapping up an item before he stood back up.

"It fell out of the box when you hit the ground," he muttered. Yanking my bag strap, he pulled me to him, sliding the nectar into my bag. "She didn't notice."

Relief washed over me.

"So she has a box of nothing?" My lips started to curve, realizing how devious this man was. He had completely played Amara. And I fucking loved it.

"Matches her heart." His mouth was only about an inch from mine, his eyes sparking with energy. We both loved this kind of adventure, got high on close calls. "It will take her a while to notice. I do regret not being there to see her face when she realizes she shafted herself, which makes this a good fucking day."

"Be better if we get out of here."

He dipped his head, taking my hand. We both ran, knowing until we got out of this hellscape, away from Killian's men, this adventure could turn deadly.

CHAPTER 18
Katrina

"Where the hell have you guys been?" Cooper whispered sharply at us when we caught up with him and AB a few levels up, hiding in a tunnel. The sounds of guards yelling echoed up, heading toward the dungeons below. "And why the fuck did Amara just take off past us with something in her hands?"

"Well, she does have the nectar box," Croygen replied.

"Whaaaat?" Cooper's eyes flamed red, his shoulders curling.

"Too bad the nectar isn't in there." He smirked. "That's gonna be so disappointing for her."

Cooper's dubious gaze narrowed on Croygen. "She doesn't have it?"

"No." Croygen patted my bag with a grin. "It's safe."

Cooper's body eased, running a hand through his blond locks, his gaze darting to his mate. In that one look, I could see his whole world flash in his eyes. The chance to save her, the thought of losing her. His emotions rode the edges, the Dark Dweller wanting to come out.

A loud boom of a metal, like a gate slamming, directed us all back to our biggest concern. Getting out of here.

Creeping to the end of the tunnel, I poked my head out.

About midway through the tunnel, a flood of soldiers ran in from what had to be the main entrance. Orders and shouts from the prison guards already came from above us, bouncing and banging off the metal cages, filling the prison with chaos and confusion.

They were all heading down, while we had to sneak up. And some would be coming straight past us.

Voices and footsteps pounded toward the tunnel we were in. "Shit!" Croygen grabbed me, yanking me into a tiny cell, Cooper and AB taking the one next to us. We barely made it inside before boots stomped around the corner.

Croygen pushed me into the corner, his body hiding mine, flattening himself into me until there wasn't one inch of him I didn't feel. His breath stroked against my ear, shivering my skin, his protection wrapping around me and cradling me in a bubble. I knew he would keep me safe, and I would do the same for him.

"Hurry! Hurry!" Fae guards stomped by the cells, no one bothering to look inside, their focus on the emergency they thought was down below.

But it wouldn't be long before the first guards saw Boyd, saw the nectar was gone, and ordered everyone else to hunt the prison for us.

I listened for the last guard to go by, my hearing traveling out to pick up movement.

Feeling Croygen's eyes on me, I peered up at him. His expression was intense, his chest pumping hard against mine. The barriers between us were as thin as parchment. Practically an invitation when it came to us. It would be so easy to push through, to see and feel everything, to sink inside him, to feel myself submerge in him. Experience and see the connection we both knew was there, yet still thought we could deny.

But neither of us pushed through, too scared of what that invitation meant. How in doing so, everything would alter, crossing the line and solidifying the very thing we claimed to not want.

My soul barely rubbed up against the thin wall, the erotic sensation just a whisper of what was behind, what might be. Croygen jerked, sucking in sharply like he felt it. My entire body trembled with the sensation, the pleasure beyond.

"Come. On." Cooper's voice cut through, waving us on from the cell door. Croygen stepped back, his throat bobbing. He turned away from me and jogged out, not daring to look back, leaving me slightly dizzy.

Get it together, Kat. I bade myself, angry for my moment of vulnerability. The only important thing was getting out of here, healing AB, and saving my crew and ship so I could go on my merry way.

Quietly, we snuck the opposite way everyone was going, heading up the many levels, back to the tunnel out.

"Search everywhere! They must still be here!" The order belted through the prison, dancing off the cages like a tambourine.

"Fuck. Fuck." Croygen pushed me to go faster. Cooper picked up Annabeth, urging her to cling to his back, her body not physically able to go as fast as we needed.

Sweat trickled down my back, my thighs burning when we finally reached the top level. My heart pounded in my ears, my lungs pumping for air.

We darted through the room without the stairs, but I stopped, turning back for the door.

"Kat? Come on!" Croygen glanced back, skidding to a stop. "What are you doing?"

"Closing it," I grunted, trying to push the heavy door back with very little success. "If they see it open, they'll know exactly where we went. Have someone waiting at the end."

The logic of my theory blinked Croygen's eyes. "Right."

"Croygen!" Cooper yelled from the passage.

"You go ahead. We'll catch up!" Croygen vocalized, running back over to me and putting his weight against the door. The voices of the guards were filling the prison, some getting very close.

A strangled cry broke from my lips as we pushed it closed, heaving and shaking with exhaustion.

"I need a fucking drink." Croygen wiped at his brow, taking just a second to catch his breath.

"Me too. A nice whiskey, maybe tequila."

"Rum."

"So stereotypical."

A naughty smile twitched his cheek. "Yo ho," he muttered close to my ear, causing my body to shiver. "Come on, Kitten." He yanked me with him, rushing us toward the tunnel.

We were so close I could taste it; with every step, freedom rang louder, beckoning like a siren, pulling us deeper into the mountain. Twisting and turning, we headed back for the old church, where I hoped Cooper and AB were already out.

A feeling crept over me, slowing me down, my stomach twisting with awareness, though I couldn't pinpoint what it was.

"What?" Croygen glanced back at me, taking in my expression.

"I don't know…" But it was there. My intuition clawed at the back of my neck, telling me something I couldn't quite hear.

"Come on. We have to get out of here."

My nose picked up a scent, so light it blended in with others, slipping through my fingers before I fully identified it. Though I felt it in my bones. Taking another breath, it sunk into my chest like a knife.

Oh gods.

"This way." Croygen veered around a bend, my mouth not able to open, not able to tell him before it was too late.

He was waiting for us.

He was here…

I couldn't stop the gasp as Killian stepped out of the shadows, moving into the middle of the passage, blocking our way.

A freak wave came out of nowhere and crashed down, spinning me around like a clothes dryer. I wasn't capable of moving or breathing.

His piercing violet eyes shone brightly, narrowed on us. He was strong, built, in a crisp suit and styled back hair.

He was beautiful. Lord of Fairies and the Master of Death.

Under his fancy clothes was my friend, the boy I grew up with, the man I thought would be by my side for the rest of our lives. My first mate, my companion. At one time, he had nothing but awe and love in his eyes when he looked at me; now I saw only coldness and hate staring back.

If he was shocked to see us, he didn't show it.

"Once a thief, always a thief." His silky voice almost dropped me to the ground with emotion and memories. Killian had always been handsome, the women taking notice of him at a very young age. He got a lot of attention when he was part of my crew, and he could've used it to his advantage, many throwing themselves at his feet without him even trying. But he never did, nor did he like the interest, always coming to me to "save him."

Now I realized he embraced it and had grown in his power and confidence. Everything about him was refined, commanding, and controlled. He now wore a fancy suit and shiny shoes, his hair shorter than it used to be when he was on the ship. He was a leader, a lord. Not the gritty pirate I used to know.

"You would know," Croygen replied evenly, though I tasted the bitterness in it. He stepped closer, his gaze rolling over the boy he had saved from starvation. "Wow, look at you. All fancy now, aren't we?"

Killian's nose flared, his glower moving over Croygen

with deep disgust. "Looks like nothing has changed with you. Still a second-rate thief…"

"Tradesman." Croygen tipped his shoulders back. They were about the same height, but Croygen still had an edge Killian never did. "And you think because you wear an expensive suit and have a title before your name, you are above the rest of us now?"

"I am the *Lord* of Budapest." Killian's eyes twitched, a sign of his anger. "I rule everyone here now. This is my kingdom."

"You *don't* rule me." Croygen inched forward. It was a taunt. A challenge. I knew every single one of Killian's tells, but I recognized Croygen's emotions threading through my veins, inching me up to them. "You forget, Killian, I know the *real* you. I was the one to put the brand on your chest. I know where you come from. If your minions only knew how you really got this role—who you were before—would they still worship you?" Croygen scoffed at his finely tailored suit. "Play dress up all you want. I know the real street rat underneath."

Oh. Shit.

Killian's stoic resolve vanished in a blink.

"Fuck you!" He lunged for him.

It happened fast, my mind not even allowing me to think. *Mine…*

Possessive instinct took over, my hand pulling a dagger I got from Dzsinn out of my boot. I slipped between them in a blink, overcome with the need to guard, to fight and kill anything coming for Croygen.

"Step back, Kill," I gritted, pressing the blade against Killian's throat.

Killian's eyes widened, darting from me to Croygen, noticing how I pressed against the pirate, how I defended him. Shock turned to blistering hurt, which cut into my soul. His gaze pleaded with me to tell him what he saw was wrong.

"Kitty-Kat," Killian whispered, full of agony. The

arrogance and control he had earlier dropped away, allowing me to see the man I hurt on that rooftop, the one who kissed me and walked out of my life.

But I was hurt too. Because his love was conditional. If I wasn't going to be his lover, then he was no longer going to be my friend.

My nickname coming from him was a blade to my heart. He had given up rights to that intimacy. "Don't call me that." My bottom lip trembled, liquid filling my eyes, pushing the blade harder against his jugular.

His gaze briefly went over my shoulder, then back to me, his head wagging.

"So you're with him now?" He stared at me, wanting so badly to hear the lie. I did too. A big part of me wanted to take his hand and fall back into what we had before. Live out my life with the man who found me after my father's death, not the villain who caused it, who never came for me. But I couldn't speak, couldn't tell him the words he wanted to hear.

My expression must have told him the truth. Killian shut down, his jaw clenching, rage shooting from his eyes like beams.

"You hated him. Wanted to *kill* him," he snarled, nodding at Croygen, then shook his head at me in disgust. "Guess we're all liars and thieves here."

"This has nothing to do with him," I tried hard to hold back the sob in my chest. "Let us leave, Killian, and no harm will come to you."

I might as well have sliced his artery right there, the hurt and pain I caused him over the centuries looping around my lungs like a noose.

"Too late for that, Kitty-Kat," he whispered. Broken. Cold.

And in that moment, I knew I'd lost him forever. The friendship and love we once had were now just cinders and ash.

"I don't want to hurt you." My chin quaked, my voice weak. "But we're leaving with the nectar—*no matter what.*"

Killian watched me; the threads of who we were to each other, centuries of being friends, had burned up in a blink.

Hate replaced love. Cynicism replaced hope. And disgust replaced me.

Then Killian's body jerked, and he fell to the ground, shuffling me back with a cry.

Cooper stood behind him, the end of his gun still up in the air, a smirk on his lips. "Thank me later, asshole!" He dropped his arm, nodding to where AB stood waiting for us. "Come on!"

My heart wrenched at seeing Killian lying there. This adventure led us back to each other, and I was not on the side I imagined I would be.

"Kill," I muttered his name to myself. Squatting down, I knew he was alive, but I still sighed when I felt his pulse strong under my fingers.

"He'll be fine." Croygen pulled me back up, his attention on Killian. He let out a heavy sigh, his throat bobbing. "You were meant to rule. You always were." Croygen spoke softly, but I could hear the pride and love in his tone for Killian before he huffed. "Still think you're a huge douche, though."

Snorting, I took a few steps and stopped, my heart rate spiking, the back of my neck prickling with fear. It was so fast I was sure my eyes were playing tricks on me, and I narrowed them on the dark corner.

"What's wrong?" Croygen picked up on my shift instantly, looking around.

"Thought I saw…" I swore I saw a woman with long dark hair standing against the wall like a ghost, watching us, but when I blinked again, she was gone. "Nothing."

Taking off toward Cooper and AB, Cooper yelled for Croygen to follow, turning me to the pirate.

Croygen stared into the darkness as if he also experienced something before he shook his head, jogging for us, the four of us running out of the tunnels.

I felt it happen. The door closed on my past, as if I had chosen my path without even knowing I had. My heart still broke at losing Killian because this time I knew it was for good.

It seemed I still preferred the devil.

Deep chills skated over my skin the moment we stepped outside, heading down the steps for the river. Commotion from the prison and castle soared down to us, a hawk squawking loudly over our heads as if calling out our location. But the noise wasn't what chilled me to the bone.

My fur prickled along my back, and my defenses rose as I picked up on a subtle whiff.

Death.

New death smelled of blood and rotting corpses, but old death was a dusty decay of bone and dirt.

Cooper pulled AB in close, his head whipping around, his teeth growing longer.

"You feel it too?"

He nodded, his nostrils flaring.

"So do I." Croygen yanked out his gun as we inched closer to the river. The boats meant freedom, and we had to escape before Killian's men got to us. Yet I could not move.

A panic I couldn't explain had me circling, feeling like I was surrounded in despair, absorbed in soundless darkness, robbing me of all my senses.

I was being swathed by doom… consumed by death.

Yells from guards from the roads leading down to us were getting closer.

We had to go. Now.

But the moment we moved, a hooded figure stepped in our path. Stringy dark hair extended out of the hood, as did a bony hand holding a sharp scythe blade. I sensed the absence of life. The deprivation of compassion and humanity. It devoured power, consumed life, and fed off your soul.

Over my long life, I had experienced a lot of fear and near-death situations, but this was on another plane of terror.

As more circled around us, I felt their attention directed solely at me.

The nectar pulsed inside my bag as if it was calling to them. Its heartbeat drawing them in like a siren pulling a seaman to his death.

Except they weren't beautiful women singing lullabies. These were Death's mercenaries.

Necromancers.

CHAPTER 19
Croygen

Death was something I'd flirted with most of my life, from the time I was six when I was the only survivor when the ship carrying my family sunk and I was too little to save them. Their screams still haunted me. But worse, I heard their silence. I lay on a piece of driftwood for three days until I was found, delirious and almost dead.

Many times, I had reached out to the other side and stood at the doorway of the in-between, wanting to join my family. To finally have peace.

Death rejected me every time. Spat me out and forced me to live in the guilt, the sins of my crimes.

Now Death's operatives were here, and for the first time, I was not inclined to bow to them. I'd finally found the serenity I had been searching for. And now I would beat Death at its own game.

Stepping in front of Kat with my gun ready, the seven necromancers circled us, coming for Katrina. Though the two closest to AB paused, as if they could smell the decay in her body, feel death was near. Her soul was being plated up for them like a buffet to devour.

Spikes tore through Cooper's shirt, his daggered spine

curving him over, his huge mass moving between AB and the necromancers, baring his teeth.

The lead necromancer in front of us swung her scythe down in warning, the other six gripping their deadly weapons, ready to fight.

"Kat." I swallowed, knowing my gun was useless against things already dead. "Might be a good time to shift."

"They want the nectar." She and I moved, putting our backs up to Cooper and AB.

"How do you know?"

"Because I can feel the nectar pulsing, like it's calling them."

"Well, fuck if Mr. and Mrs. Jolly Roger are going to take it from us." I snarled, pulling out my sword. My action was a declaration of war.

The necromancers moved faster than I was expecting; a bardiche weapon carving for me clanked against my blade. Its strength caused me to stumble to the side, unprepared for the power. Whirling around, I blocked the deadly bardiche weapon from slicing me in half, the razor edge cutting open my shirt, whispering against my skin.

Fuck, that was close.

Cooper roared, his claws clashing with their weapons, his Dark Dweller lashing out at three of them as the other three came for me and Katrina.

The problem was, even a Dark Dweller could be hurt. Could die.

Necromancers could not.

There was no fear if you *were* death.

"Ahhh!" Kat screamed as a lucerne hammer rammed down, flinging the sword from her hand, the metal skidding across the pavement. The necromancer lurched for her, its bony hands curling for her pack.

"Katrina!" I dove for her as a scythe came down on my

leg from another necromancer. Blinding pain erupted through my muscles, dropping me to the ground with a bellow. My nerves howled, and excruciating agony tore through me. Vomit pooled in the back of my throat, watering my eyes. Peering up, I saw Katrina's frame fall next to me on her back. The one with the Lucerne hammer stepped over her, pinning her to the cement with his weapon.

"Kat!" Her name was a hoarse whisper, and I tried to crawl across the ground to get to her, the scythe digging deeper into my leg. A pained howl echoed from Cooper, but my focus was hazy, completely locked on Kat.

I waited for them to kill us, to finish the job, but they just kept us both pinned down.

The leader of the necromancers was suddenly there. Its frame was petite, with long, desiccated hair, making me think it was a woman at one time. She stood over Katrina, awkwardly bent over with her warrior scythe.

"Noooo!" My nails dug into the asphalt, every ounce of me needing to protect Katrina. If they killed her, they'd better kill me right after because I would eradicate every one of them and burn them to ash in my vengeance, using their bones as kindling.

The blade sliced through Katrina's leather backpack's strap like paper; the leader clutched the bag with her skeleton hand, taking it from Kat.

Shouts and gunfire headed for us as Killian's men moved in. Ripping the blade from my leg, the necromancers backed away, slipping into the darkness like ghosts, taking the nectar of life with them. The only thing that might cure Annabeth and save Katrina from her oath was gone. But we had no time to think about it; Killian's guards were gaining ground.

"Kitten." Agony coursed through me as I tried to pull myself up, blood gushing down my leg, so I crawled to her. Grief crumbled Katrina's features when she heard me call to her, her body scrambling to me. Her emotions over losing the nectar pierced me like needles, and I felt her devastation.

"I'm so sorry," she muttered in my ear, anguish sobbing up her throat.

Cooper's half-naked frame, which had been covering AB, rose next to us, Annabeth lying limply under his protection. Her chest moved up and down to tell me she was still alive, but barely. The last of AB's energy had blinked out, like the necromancers had stolen it, feeding off her, robbing us of weeks we had with her, leaving us only hours, possibly.

Bullets zipped through the air.

"We have to go," I yelled through clenched teeth to Cooper and Katrina.

Kat propped her shoulder under me, getting me up to my feet as Cooper scooped up Annabeth's body, her head flopping over his arm.

"Ahhhhh!" I tried to walk, but my wounded leg folded under me, landing me on the ground. "Fuck!" Seething in pain, bile burned up the back of my throat and panic raced through my veins.

"Croygen, come on!" Katrina tried to get me up again, her head whipping to where the guards were approaching, desperation in her tone. "Please!"

Even if I did, I would slow them down. Get them all caught.

"Go!" I waved them on with a bark. "Get out of here!"

"No!" Katrina yanked on my arm, trying to get me to rise, but my leg was useless.

"I. Said. Go!" I growled, my nose flaring.

Cooper hesitated, his arms filled with his mate. My gaze met his, knowing he understood my look.

Get Annabeth the fuck out of here now.

Even if she was going to die, it should be at home with the family, with Cooper. Not here. And not now.

His head dipped in sorrow and regret, though I could tell it wasn't easy for him to leave me. Once the Dark Dwellers took you in as family, which somewhere along the way I became, they protected you. They didn't turn their backs on those they considered part of their pack.

But he had to protect his mate first.

"Kat, go!" I nodded after Cooper's fleeing form.

"No!"

"GOOO!" I roared, hearing the footfalls coming up on us.

"No." Katrina dropped down to me, her jaw set, stubbornness streaking her expression. "If we die, we die together."

"Kat…" Anger and emotion clogged my throat.

"What's that saying? A pirate will sink you with a kiss, steal your heart, and sail away with it. You already sailed away with it," she muttered to me as two guards stepped up, putting guns to our heads. I recognized both.

Connor and Vale.

"Get up," Connor ordered us.

"You know, why didn't I think of that earlier?" Sarcasm dripped off my tongue, along with beads of sweat. The wound hurt like nothing I had felt before, as if their blades were poisoned with death too. "Wish you told me that earlier. That would've been helpful."

Connor's lids tapered, peering at my slashed leg. It was trying to heal, but the muscle ached and throbbed, making me lightheaded.

Connor flicked his chin at Vale, telling him to get me up as he yanked Katrina to her feet. Vale hauled me up, getting another guard on the opposite side to take my sword, which felt like he had sliced off a piece of my body. It had only boeen separated from me a few times. And those people had come to regret it.

Vale and the other guard started to drag me toward their horses, nausea swimming in my head. "Sooo, Vale, ol' pal…

heard you get a little chatty with women you want to impress after a night at the pub."

"What?" His back went stiff. "How the fuck do you know my name?"

"Don't feel bad. Most get played by her."

Vale's shoulders tightened, his eyes shooting to the other guard, then back to me, understanding exactly who I was referring to.

"She's a devious one. I just wonder how your boss will feel when he learns it was because of you we knew how to get into the pri—"

I saw it coming, almost daring him to shut me up.

The handle of his gun hit the back of my head, spreading blackness through my vision like an ink spill, and I sank gladly into oblivion.

Escaping the pain.

Fleeing the truth.

Dodging the guilt.

We lost the only cure for Annabeth, and Katrina would suffer from a broken promise.

Once again, someone I loved was going to die… because I failed to keep them safe.

My lids blinked open, my brain taking several moments to process. I was slumped against a wall, my chin tucked into my chest, the cold stone aching every muscle as if it had been in this position for a while. My pants were still wet with blood, and my leg throbbed, the muscles knitting back together. Fuck, it hurt. I longed to shut my eyes again and sleep until I was fully healed, but I knew I couldn't let myself.

Trying to lift my head, pain shot up the back of my skull,

pushing bile up my throat with a groan. Flinching, I closed my eyes, trying to remember where the hell I was.

"Croygen?" A soft voice sank into my ears, filling my body with the need to open my eyes. To go to her. Katrina.

She was the lifeline pulling me out of the darkness, reminding me of every single detail of what happened. How the necromancers attacked us, the soldiers coming, and Vale knocking me out.

"Kat," I grunted, trying to move toward her voice before I even knew where she was, but my body wouldn't budge. The sound of metal clanging drew my lids fully open, my gaze going to the cuffs around my wrists, keeping me prisoner to the wall.

"You all right?" Her voice drew my attention across the room, seeing her outline against the opposite wall. "Your leg?"

"It's healing." Though it felt different, like the necromancer's blade marked me, like a wounded deer, so they could come back for me. Peering around at the space, shoving that chilling thought back, I noticed the stone walls, ceiling, and floor, the barred metal door locking us in. It was a cell, but somehow I knew it wasn't in that newer prison. It felt quieter, older, more part of an ancient castle. "You okay?"

My vision was sharpening, and the firebulbs in the passage were giving the room a little distinction. I recognized Kat's figure in the dim light. She had manacles around her wrists, which sat in her lap, legs folded, with her back pressed against the wall. Her bright cat eyes cut through the dark, spearing my chest.

"Fine." She tipped her head back into the wall, her regard going off to the side.

"When a woman says *fine…* that means she's not."

Cat eyes met mine; the connection buzzed between us, and I knew she felt as I did.

We failed. We had lost the nectar before, but there was something about this time that made it feel real.

Final.

Swallowing, I still spouted the lie we both needed to hear. "We won't give up. We'll find it."

"Yeah." She bobbed her head, yet it was not with hope. "It called to them. I could feel it."

"Have to admit, fighting necromancers was not on my bingo card."

Kat huffed at my joke, a tiny laugh which was half a cry, her head falling down, her loose hair curtaining her face.

"Hey?" I pushed the word out. As if I was right in front of her, lifting her chin, Kat's head raised up. "We will get your crew and your ship back. Okay?"

"What about Annabeth?" she whispered.

My teeth gritted, trying to hold back the despair building up like battery acid poured down my throat.

I gave no response, nothing that would be positive. AB wasn't long for this earth, and even if we went after the nectar, she would probably die before. The necromancers had already fed off her, stripping her of the soul that was already barely holding on.

I hoped Cooper and AB had gotten far from here. I hoped she would make it back to Zoey and Ryker in time. Be with her family at the end.

Tugging at my chains, I tried to adjust to the hard ground, needing a distraction from thoughts of AB.

"Do you know where we are?"

"We're in the palace," she responded. "They took us in a side entrance below the castle."

My head bounced, figuring that's where they put us.

"Has Killian—"

"Has Killian what?" The smooth, familiar voice jolted my muscles, causing me to stand up, my leg almost bowing under the pain of my healing wound. The chains kept my arms at my sides, my shoulders tightening in defense.

Katrina sprang up too, both our gazes going to the figure strolling up to the cell door.

With one hand in his pocket, Killian peered in with a smug superiority only wealthy and powerful people held. Like they were untouchable. The kid always had an arrogance about him, a front so no one would see he was just a scared, hurt little boy.

With time, his anger only grew—at me, at the world. He used it as a shield. Kat was the only person he let his guard down around. Except now, she was also his enemy.

"Have I been betrayed? Deceived?" He pinched his lips. "Yes, on both counts." His sharp eyes snapped from me to Kat, locking on her. "By someone I had trusted, loved, believed in…"

"Killian—"

"You don't get to speak," he barked at her, his hand coming out of his pocket, wrapping around the bars. "You conniving, backstabbing bitch."

"Hey!" I yanked on my manacles, anger narrowing my gaze. "Don't fucking talk to her like that."

"I can talk to her how I want!=," Killian snapped at me. "I was the one there for her, who didn't throw her off the ship like cargo, who was there through it *all*." Killian's glower moved over me with loathing.

"What? You deserve a medal for that? An award?" I seethed through my teeth. "You are *owed* her now?"

Killian's face flushed with fury, his hands yanking out a set of keys, ripping the door open.

"No!" Katrina screamed. "Killian, stop!" She tugged at her chains as Killian stalked up to me.

"Go ahead." I leaned closer to him. "I know you've been dreaming of this day forever. Well, here I am."

Killian's fist crunched across my jaw, slamming my body back into the wall. I was unable to defend myself or fight back. He had always been an amazing fighter. It wasn't just Master Yukimura who had taught him skills; I had as well, and now he had more muscle and strength behind him. Blood coated my teeth as he laid in another hit, his violet eyes igniting with bloodlust.

Katrina's cries became white noise, a soundtrack, while Killian worked out his hate on me. Falling to the ground, I let out a gurgled laugh, spitting out blood.

"This make you feel big and strong now?"

"Shut the fuck up!" he hissed, clutching my shirt, yanking me to him. "You may have gotten her to forgive you, but I was there. I saw what a betraying, lowlife piece of shit you are."

"It does say that on my business cards." I squinted up at him mockingly, one eye starting to swell.

"I will make sure you rot here before dancing with Jack Ketch," he snarled. An old pirate phrase for hanging. "The famous Silver Tongue Devil will have a pathetic end."

"Look at you." I grinned. "Can take the man out of piracy, but can't take the pirate out of the man."

"I am not a pirate." He shoved me back against the wall, his styled hair falling in his wild eyes, making the polished man appear more feral.

"Really?" I dipped my chin at him. For a beat, he glanced down at his sliced-up knuckles, his hair and suit in disarray. The polish was off, the *Kill*-ian I remembered coming out.

"Killian…" Kat's voice jerked his head, swinging him back to her.

"You…" He shook his head, inching over toward Kat. "How could you? After all he's done to you?" He motioned back to me. "He sent you away, practically leaving you to die on the streets."

"You don't understand…"

"No, I don't," he belted. "He murdered your father, Katrina! In cold blood. I watched him do it."

"You saw what you wanted to." I spat blood on the ground, pushing myself up to stand.

"I saw you stab her father, *your* first mate, in the heart with his own dagger. Tell me how I saw it wrong?" He shot back at me before facing Katrina again. "And how can you forget what he's done to you? The girl I knew wanted to hunt him down and kill him. Now what, you're fucking him instead or something?"

Pain and grief streaked over her face, giving credence to something I don't think he truly believed. Until now.

"Are you serious?" Killian stepped back, his head whipping between us. "You're *fucking* him?" He flung his arm in my direction. "Look at me!" He got in Kat's face, tears streaking down her cheeks. "This is how you avenge your father? Become the *whore* of your father's murderer?"

"Fuck you!" My anger, the need to stand in front of her and block her from his wrath, burned through my muscles.

"Kill, it's complicated," she cried. "I-I can't explain…"

"You know that's all you are to him, right?" Killian's temper was spiraling, years of pent-up emotion blasting out.

I normally was even-tempered, but everything in me vibrated with wrath, the need to protect, destroy anything that went after what was mine.

My mate.

The word rang through me again, settling into my gut with truth.

I had known it for a long time but didn't want to acknowledge it, thinking if I pretended it wasn't there, it would go away.

"He will fuck you over like he did all the rest." Killian got in her face, his body touching hers. "How can you be with him? How can you look at yourself? What would your father think? He betrayed your family. He took your father from you!"

A possessive roar scored my lungs, and I tugged on the chains. Fury consumed me.

"Get the fuck away from her!" My bellow shook the room.

"She doesn't belong to you!" Killian screamed back.

"Yes, she *fucking* does," I growled low in my throat. "And I wasn't the one to betray *him*. Rotty betrayed me. He is why I lost everything that night."

"Wh-what are you talking about?" Kat's head wagged with confusion, pain filling her eyes, needing answers. "That's not true. He would never do that."

"He did it for *you*." The memory spilled out; years of being locked away popped to the surface, whether I wanted it or not.

"I don't understand."

"You're the reason for it all."

"Go! Go!" I ordered what was left of my crew to abandon ship. The water washed the dead bodies back and forth across the deck, Master Yukimura's being one of them.

The pain of his death radiated so deeply, almost dropping me to the ground, wanting the sea to take me too. But I knew he'd berate me for not fighting to keep the rest of them alive. So many depended on me.

"No!" Scot bellowed over the stormy sea, the ship breaking apart with every crashing wave.

"That's an order!" I shouted, turning to retrieve Rotty. "From your captain."

The gold handle stuck from his chest, but he was half fae; he could survive if it didn't puncture his heart.

"Rotty!" I scrambled up to him, water splashing over, crashing down on us. "It probably just hit a lung. You'll be okay. Just hold on and let me get it out. You're going to be okay." My hand wrapped around the handle, ready to yank it out.

"No." His hand stopped mine. "It's too late."

"No, it's not. Come on, I can get you to the dinghy."

"I'm sorry." Something in his voice ran a chill down my spine.

"Don't be sorry. Get your ass up. The blade didn't hit your heart."

"Doesn't matter. This is the end for me."

"This is not the time to get all dramatic." I struggled to get him to sit up.

"I'm already dead."

"What are you talking about?"

"The blade…" He hacked, his hand squeezing mine around the blade. *"I had dipped it in goblin extract."*

"What?" My brain didn't want to understand what this meant. *"No."* I shook my head in denial.

"I am so sorry." His body jerked, the poison sinking deeper into his bloodstream. *"For everything…"* Grief lined his forehead, as if he was asking me for clemency.

"You have nothing to be sorry for." I felt helpless and scared. *"Don't give up."*

"Promise me you will keep Katrina safe."

"No need. You can do it yourself. I will get you off this ship. Just hold on, okay? Do it for Katrina."

"She is the reason for it all…"

It was his tone, his eyes, that coiled dread in my stomach. The storm howled around us, but it felt distant.

"What do you mean?"

"I'm so sorry, Croygen. I never meant this to happen." Hacking, a spittle of blood slipped over his lip, pain flinching his brow. *"She is my whole world. There isn't anything I wouldn't do for her."*

"I don't understand."

"Lowe…"

Dread dropped on me.

"A few months ago… at port." Rotty's spine jolted, and even being poured down with seawater, I saw sweat beading on his forehead. *"He told me he had her. Showed me letters she had been writing me. Told me if I said anything to anyone, he*

would kill her." I knew Rotty hadn't received anything in the last year from Katrina. He wanted to go find her, but business kept us far from that area.

"And you believed him?"

"I couldn't chance not to."

Swearing under my breath, I knew what was coming. Lowe had always been jealous of me, wanting the success I had. And if he couldn't have it, he wanted to make sure I didn't either.

"Katrina for my ship." My jaw tightened, realizing nothing today was happenstance. It had been planned. "Why didn't you tell me?"

"He said he'd do more than just kill her if I said anything. He'd force me to watch him with her... if I told you." He struggled to speak.

I wanted Lowe to burn in a fiery pit of hell.

A loud crack boomed as the main mast plunged into the sea, taking more of the ship down. My vessel was sinking into the deep blue sea with most of my crew because of Lowe's jealousy, because of Rotty's weakness, and because I forced her to leave.

"I betrayed you and failed her anyway." His back arched in agony, the poison working through him, though I had heard it could take a long time. It was the cruelest death—slow, excruciating agony. "Please, my friend. Promise me you won't tell her. I don't want her to hate me. To know what I did. What a fool I was."

"Gods dammit, Rotty!" I barked. Anger, sadness, and grief battled inside as I watched everything I loved vanish in front of me.

Because of Katrina.

The moment I had her disembark this ship, for the well-being of my crew and herself, I felt like she cursed me.

I still couldn't find my favorite jacket.

"Captain!" My name was called from the dinghies below. They needed to get the fuck away from here fast, otherwise they'd get pulled down with the ship.

"Go," Rotty ordered me.

"I'm not leaving you to die like this."

"Kill me," he pleaded, convulsing violently, more blood tricking out of his mouth.

"What?"

"There is no way to save me. I am already a dead man." He put my hands back on the dagger, his hand shaking, blood leaking from his lips. "Please. I need you to do it. I will continue to drown over and over as the poison slowly consumes me." He was right. I could do nothing to save him. The toxin was already in his blood. And if I didn't do anything, his end would be drawn out and utterly excruciating. Cruel. Horrific.

Liquid burned the back of my lids; my throat closed at the weight of his request.

"You ask a lot of me, friend." I bared my teeth.

"I know." Sorrow consumed his eyes, pleading for me to follow through on this final act. To see the friend, not the man who deceived me. "I don't deserve it, but I know you will do it anyway."

I would never allow him to wither and die a slow and painful death. I had to honor his years of service and dedication. Give him peace.

My world was turning black and ugly around me. I knew Rotty would tip me over, but I couldn't, wouldn't, let him suffer.

Nodding, I tugged the blade from his chest, my throat bobbing. I held it over him with quaking arms. A noise worked out of my throat, water almost blinding me, but his eyes stayed locked on mine. Willing me to do it.

"Please, watch over my girl," he whispered to me hoarsely, his body convulsing. "It has been an adventure, my friend." Dipping his head, he silently told me to go ahead.

I swung the blade down, going straight through his heart, burrowing it deep, slicing it in half. His spine arched, a small cry escaping him. I felt his heart take its final beat before he slumped back on the deck.

Rotty slipped away into peace while I sunk into hell.

Standing up, I yanked the dagger out, staring down at the only person I had trusted, and even he had betrayed me. Heaving in and out, anger and blackness clawed up over me like sludge.

Little did I know that night was the beginning of my end.

A long road leading me back to Katrina Roth.

My curse.

My blessing.

My mate.

CHAPTER 20
Katrina

As a very young child, I once fell into the wintery arctic sea. The cold was like a thousand razor blades slicing into my skin before everything went numb.

Anesthetized and disoriented, I literally froze up. And instead of swimming, I started to sink into the icy waters. Croygen had jumped in and saved me, pushed me up to where my father could reach down and pull me up.

The two men I adored more than life, had put on a pedestal, were now the ones pulling me under. Drowning me.

Shock once again stilled my body, my brain not comprehending the story he had just told.

My father had betrayed Croygen? Had he turned against his own captain, the crew, forsaken our home? For me?

"No." My head started to negate what he had said. "No. I don't believe you." Swallowing, I looked at Croygen, wanting it to be a lie. *Needing* it to be a lie.

Yet I felt the truth flow from him. That last barrier he had kept up now tumbled down, pouring in a flood of his emotions. The connection between us slammed into me like a wave, breaking me across the rocks.

"No..." My voice splintered, turning away, anger cracking through. "No! My father would never do that!"

"You are a fucking liar," Killian seethed, moving toward Croygen with fury, gripping his shirt. Killian had always been very smooth in fighting, a regalness in his form as if he was always destined to be a lord, but I saw it even more now. Killian the pirate was becoming the fae lord.

Croygen's bloody lip lifted, not flinching as Killian rammed him against the wall. Croygen smirked; his demeanor sang the song of authority, even if he was the one in chains. He didn't respond, dismissing Killian when his gaze came to mine.

The wave hit again, the deep pain and agony, the truth of the past, barren to see. And I felt it all. Raw and brutally real.

"No." Tears escaped my eyes, the last refusal barely making it off my lips as my body slumped back into the wall, a sob hiccupping up my throat. It was almost like I could see the event play out in Croygen's mind, taste the sea, hear the gunfire. See my father's dying figure on the deck.

"He never got my letters?" Though I had never told my father I had left school and was on the streets, I had begged him to come get me. I used to stand out on the port docks, waiting for the ship to come over the horizon, to see the familiar Jolly Roger flapping in the wind, ready to bring me home.

I had always thought my pleas fell on deaf ears.

He never knew. Though that didn't supersede what he did.

Mutiny happened a lot back in the day. It was upfront, an outright challenge to the captain. It was done with some kind of honor and forthrightness.

Though it never happened on our ship. Croygen was ruthless to others, but fair and democratic to his crew. And to the men on that ship, the worst, most abhorrent thing you could do was backstab and betray him.

What my father did, even if he thought he had to for me, was the gravest of sins. He relinquished our home, our family. Master Yukimura and so many others died that night because of my father. Croygen and Killian might have been killed as well. And he did it all because of me.

Guilt and awareness punched me in the stomach. A noise howled through my bones, sinking me down the wall, my legs no longer able to hold me. Everything I believed, everything I thought, felt upside down and twisted.

"You don't believe him, do you?" Killian stepped toward me, motioning back to Croygen.

My eyes lifted to Croygen, his dark eyes staring back into mine. For once, he wasn't guarded; he let me feel, let me see. My lids squeezed together, pushing out fat tears.

"Kat." Killian moved to me, crouching down. His hand gripped my chin up to look at him. "He's a liar. A thief. A killer." He cupped my face, his thumb sliding over my cheek.

"He's not."

"Yes, he is." Killian moved closer, his brow furrowing. "He can't be trusted. I know what I saw. Your father wouldn't have ever betrayed us. Ever. Deep down, you know the truth." I did. But it wasn't the truth he wanted it to be. "He's lying to make himself look better."

I tried to turn my head, emotion raining down on me, but Killian's hand curved me back to him. He stared down at me, his eyes once again resembling the boy I knew in the man before me. They were as violent as the sea, but I knew it was because he cared so much. Gazing up at him, more tears spilled down my face. I had missed him so much. More than I ever let myself feel. The ache was deep in my heart, like a missing piece of me was gone. Killian had been such a huge part of my life. My best friend.

"Have I ever lied to you?"

No. He hadn't, not intentionally, anyway. But Killian wanted Croygen to be the villain. He wanted me to hate him, tainting everything he said and did.

"Kitty-Kat," Killian spoke softly, intimately, drawing my face closer to his. I recognized it in his eyes. The want. The hope I would finally see him. Want to be his lover. "I've missed you." His mouth grazed mine. A low growl filled the cell, magic sparking against my skin, sensing Croygen coiling around me. "Stay with me."

"What?" I leaned back.

"All this." He nodded above. "I did it all for you."

Dread sank into my gut like lead. "Kill—"

"You want to sail around? Fine. I will build you the best ship, and you can be the fae lord's personal privateer. Protected under me. You will never know cold or hunger, and you will always be safe. Have money and riches beyond your wildest dreams." He twisted a thick ring off his finger, holding it out to me. "Stay with me, Kitty-Kat."

A gasp filled my lungs, seeing the gem set in the metal. It was the jade stone he had given me so long ago, that night he tried to kiss me in the crow's nest. When I departed the ship, I had left it behind in my jewelry box.

"I've *never* stopped loving you." He leaned over to kiss me.

A sonic boom exploded around and within me, Croygen's presence hitting so deep I felt the burns on my bones, forcing a cry from my lips. I had felt him before, but nothing like this. My spine bowed, pain and bliss scarring my tissue. It was like I had the deepest orgasm and the most painful trauma at once, sucking all the air from my lungs, my thighs pulsing as if I could feel him release inside me.

Marked and seared, he lashed through me with his tongue and whip. A punishment and a warning. For a moment, I swore Croygen was next to me, his face twisted in rage.

"I'll say this once." The chain rattled against the stone across the cell, a growl bouncing off the walls. "Get the fuck away from her."

Killian stood up, snarling at Croygen. "You don't get a say. We are done bowing to you. Think it's about time you met hiccupping the hangman's noose. But I'll leave it to Katrina how she wants you to die." Killian's attention was on me, but my eyes were locked on Croygen. And he only saw me.

The air crackled.

Heaving, my body shook. It was like his cock was still sheathed inside me. By his heavy glare, there was no doubt if he could fuck me in front of Killian right now, he would, punishing and cruel.

What was sick? I would let him. I craved it more than air.

"Katrina?" Killian's lids narrowed, noticing my focus was only on the man across from me, our tie pulsing the walls. I knew he felt it too, but the denial, the wish that I would choose him, had him ignoring it.

"Is that what you want to do, Katrina?" Croygen's voice was low and penetrating. "Want to tie me up?" His lip hitched in a sneer, his intense gaze never moving from mine. "Have me at your mercy?"

Fuck. Yes.

"Katrina?" Killian's tone hardened, his shoulders rolling back, his eyes bouncing between us. He was waiting for me to back him up, to finally exact my revenge on Croygen.

To the man he still wanted to believe murdered my father. But he hadn't.

The truth ran between us like water, clear and free. He was my father's clemency. Instead of letting him suffer, he gave my father peace. Years of believing something, of taking it as truth, were all a lie. My mind struggled to wrap around it, the devastation and need to deny still ripe on my tongue. Though it might have pardoned me from one prison, letting me love a man I thought I shouldn't, it put me in another cage. One of shame, guilt, and heartbreak. My father committed the worst of crimes. Against all those who died that day, the family who loved and trusted him. He thought he did it out of love, but he sacrificed them in fear.

My father was my world. My hero. And learning the truth felt like a burden I couldn't hold.

Why had Croygen kept it from me?

"Kat." Killian grabbed my wrists around the cuffs, bringing me up to my feet and crowding my body with his. "Stop letting him deceive you." He rumbled, gripping my face. "He's not a good man." No, he wasn't, but I wasn't a good person either. "He's a liar."

"No, you are."

"What?" Killian jerked back.

"You said you'd always be there for me." I swallowed. "But you lied, Killian. You forgot to tell me you'd only be there if I loved you back in the same way."

Killian retreated a few steps, his frame tight.

"Your love was conditional." I wasn't able to stop the heartache running down my cheeks. "I understand why you had to leave, but you broke my heart too. My best friend walked out on me that night. Abandoned me."

His jaw ticked. "You expected me to stay? To watch you fuck *every* man you met in a bar while I had to stand there silently and take it?"

"I thought my best friend would be there."

"And I thought mine would see the pain she caused me." His nose flared, his violet eyes sparking. He moved with stealth, his frame shoving mine against the wall, peering down at his nose at me. "Guess we were both mistaken." His entire air changed. "You are a fool, Katrina," he snipped. "But I guess you got what you wanted. You finally caught the man you desired, didn't you?" He clenched my chin. "I guess he's worth more than *any* friendship, more than me, more than your own crew." I sucked in at his claim. "Yes, I know exactly what you did to them. What happened to Polly and Dobbs. All because you wouldn't let him go. Nothing was more important to you, am I right?" He pinched my chin until a cry broke from my lips.

"Get the fuck away from her!" Croygen bellowed, manacles rattling loudly.

"Am I right, Katrina?" Killian pressed down harder, getting right in my face. "Answer me!"

"Yes!" The answer tore from my mouth without thought, the truth scraping like poisoned claws across my chest. I was despicable, but he was the reason for it all, as I was his cause. "He is—he's my mate."

"What?" Killian's eyes widened in horror, dropping away from me, his head wagging. "No."

"Yes." Croygen's heady gaze found me. No fear, not scrambling to find another excuse. It had been there for so long, waiting for us to accept it, to stop fighting. The moment he spoke, agreeing, I felt the bond sink into me, finally finding its home. A sly smile hinted on his mouth, and he craned his neck to Killian. "That's a twist in your plot, isn't it?"

"No." Killian shook his head more fervently. "Tell me you are joking, Katrina. There is no way that can be true."

I could say nothing in response. No lie in the world could cover what Croygen and I had between us now. It throbbed like a heartbeat, filling the room with energy.

And I knew the moment Killian experienced it too, when he read my expression. The most guttural pain carved through Killian, like the world he had built around himself had officially broken. The fantasy he had of becoming this leader, this man that I would finally take notice of… and love.

Instead, I fell in love with our enemy. The man he idolized, envied, and detested more than anything.

The cut was bottomless, striking Killian as if I had plunged my blade into his gut. In only a blink, I saw his heart shatter, his hope burn, and his soul shut down.

A wall stood before me. His expression went cold. Stoic. As if nothing in the world could ever touch him again. A completely different man stood before me. One that would watch life drain from my body without any emotion.

"Lord Killian?" A soldier poked his head into the room.

Killian continued to watch me, his expression stone. "Yes?" Slowly, he buttoned his jacket, becoming a fae lord, the last bit of the pirate vanishing. And I knew it was gone for good.

"You are needed upstairs, sir." The boy dipped quickly back into the passage. "There is a situation."

Killian glanced between us. Not one drop of emotion showed as he tugged at his cuffs, whipping around, sauntering out the door.

"Killian?" I called out his name.

He turned at the entrance of the cell. "You've made your choice, Katrina. You lived for him, now you will die *with* him." He seethed, turning to Croygen. "Live by the sword, now you will die by your *own* sword. Call it poetic justice."

The door slammed shut, echoing down the hall.

Cold, barren.

The passionate boy who dueled me on the ship's deck, the adoring man who battled by my side, who sat with me until the sun rose, talking and laughing.

He was no longer.

The meticulous, pitiless fae lord had risen in his place…

Becoming my enemy.

My heart thrashed in my chest. I let out the wail of a little girl who had forever lost her friend, not understanding all the adult complications. She didn't care how we got here; she just wanted her friend back. Killian had been such a core part of my life; after losing my father, he was who I had gone to. Had been my cornerstone.

Once again, he turned his back on me. And this time, he was going to make sure I paid for my crimes.

"Katrina?" My name called from somewhere outside of

me, my agony folding me in on myself, sobs racking through my body as I curled into a ball. It was all too much. My father, Killian, losing the nectar, Annabeth dying, and my crew would probably die because I failed.

And I couldn't even process what Croygen and I were.

"Kitten…" His voice wrapped around me, trying to keep me above water, when all I wanted to do was sink. "Don't give up on me now." His shackles jangled, trying to get as close to me as possible. "Look at me."

I didn't move.

"Look. At. Me. Kat." His demand was like fingers on my chin, turning my head to him. His dark eyes held mine. Fierce and soft at the same time. He allowed me in, the energy between us quieting my head and heart. "We're not dying here, you got me? I am *not* letting Killian touch you. And he doesn't have any say on how I go out—that right is yours now."

Oxygen caught my throat, his statement entrenching across my lungs. The meaning of it sparked through me. To Croygen, it meant more than I love you. He was trusting me with his life, his heart, his soul… and whatever I wanted to do, he would not stop me.

Trust for pirates weighed more than any treasure on Earth.

"Croy-gen?" My voice cracked, still wondering how he felt about all this. He put up a front for Killian, but did the fact I uttered the word *mate* out loud freak him out? Did he want this?

"We'll deal with it later." He shook his head, ending the conversation there, his arms tugging at the chains. "Right now we need to focus on a plan to get the fuck out of here."

"Say the magic word…" a muffled voice sang out from where Croygen was.

"What the fuck?" Croygen jerked, peering down at his jacket.

"No, that's not it, buttaneer." A fuzzy head popped out of

his jacket pocket, big brown eyes glittering from the dim firebulb light. "Try again… rhymes with honey and ends with super sprite the Monkey God King."

"Sprig!" I yelped, getting back to my feet, my heart bubbling at seeing his adorable face.

"Closer."

"You were there the whole fucking time?" Croygen exclaimed.

"You are really bad at this game, boothumper. That sounded nothing like the magic word." Sprig crawled out, climbing up Croygen's arm, noticing the manacles around his wrists. "Again? I know you're into some kinky stuff, but is this really the time?"

"Sprig." A low growl formed in Croygen's throat. "Get them off me now."

"I feel like we've been here before. You begging me to get you out of a bind. *Again.* Who's your savior?"

"Sprig."

"Who's your savior? Come on, big boy, you have to say it."

"I *have* to boil you in banana pudding."

"Guess someone wants to stay chained up." Sprig tipped his head at Croygen.

The pirate took a deep breath, staring at the ceiling. "You. Are. My. Savior." Every syllable sounded like glass being eaten. "Super Sprig, Monkey God…"

"King." Sprig chirped. "Don't forget the king."

A noise gurgled up Croygen's throat, spitting out the sentence slowly. "Super Sprig, Monkey God *King*."

"There." Sprig patted his arm. "Was that so hard?"

I had to cover my mouth to keep from laughing. Croygen leveled his gaze at me with a glower.

"Sprig, I'm getting you a bucket of honey." I grinned at Croygen with a wink.

"I like *Bhean chait.*" Sprig twisted to leap off Croygen, to head to me.

"No." Croygen grabbed him. "Just finish here first." His attention came back to me with liquid fire. "She will get what's coming to her *very soon.*"

It was a promise and threat, and every molecule in my body wanted it. I forced myself to look away; the air kindled with heavy magic, sucking the air out of the room.

How did I ignore this before? How was I able to push it away? Because now that it was said, the threads between us were palpable. Weaving and twining tighter, screaming out the bond there.

Metal clanked to the floor, snapping my head back to him. Sprig had worked quickly, getting both his handcuffs off. The moment Croygen was free, he darted to me. Sprig leaped to my arm, starting on my cuffs.

"You okay?" His hands slid up my jaw, his gaze dragging over me, seeing for himself I was fine.

"Yeah." I nodded, my lips pinching together. He saw right through me, understanding that physically, I was all right, but emotionally, I was far from it.

He watched me, his eyes tracking mine, not saying a word. We no longer needed to. The emotions were there to feel, to explore and taste. It scared the shit out of me, yet stilled something in me I never knew had been anxious and unsettled.

One shackle dropped, breaking our connection, peering down at the tiny monkey.

"Ugh, the tedious things us gods have to do. With eminent power comes so much responsibility. No one understands the sacrifice. What we do for others without asking anything in return." Sprig sighed dramatically, wiggling his fingers. "The power these hands hold is such a blessing and a curse."

"If you don't shut up and finish, I will cram those fingers up your blessing and out your curse-hole," Croygen grumbled.

"Someone's being a Viking-pirate."

"Sprig." Croygen ground his molars.

"Two buckets of honey if you hurry," I cut in.

Sprig smiled at me, working on my other cuff, sticking his tongue out at Croygen.

"You two." I shook my head. "You act—"

"If you say we act like brothers, I will leave you here." Croygen cocked his eyebrow, moving toward the cell door, peering out.

"Ta-da!" Sprig sang, the other manacle falling to the stone. My hands automatically rubbed where they had been.

"Thank you, super Sprite God King." I patted him on the head, smirking at Croygen.

Croygen snorted, his eyes rolling up as I traveled to where he was at the barred door, Sprig climbing up to my shoulder.

"You are very close to being voted off the island, pirate." Sprig stuck his finger out at Croygen.

"If I'm stuck on an island with you, I vote myself off."

"Too bad. Now you're stuck with me. Forever," Sprig volleyed back. "But you know how you can make it up to me?"

"Let me guess, it has something to do with honey," Croygen muttered, scanning down both ends of the hallway.

"I'm hungry. Actually, I'm past hungry. I think my insides are revolting. Screaming, *'Let him eat cake!'*"

"Get us out of this cell, and I will find you cake." Croygen motioned to the cell door. "And if you find my sword, I'll get you all the honey in the land."

My stomach sank, knowing Killian too well. Croygen's sword was too valuable to him to leave anywhere we could get at. It was a symbol, a power grab over his enemy.

So many times, Croygen let Killian play with it as a kid, pretending to defend the ship and save us from pirate hunters. He once adored his captain more than anything, then it turned to hate and vengeance. And like my father, I was the center of it.

"In allll the land?" An excited chirp came from Sprig, leaping to Croygen and down to the lock.

"You remember how we got down here?" Croygen turned to me. Since he was unconscious on the way in, I was the only one who sort of knew how to get out.

"Yes." I nodded. It was Croygen who trained me to be aware of my surroundings. To map it out in your mind, down to the smallest detail. Because that detail might be the difference between life and death.

"Okay, you lead, and I'll cover." Croygen touched his waist, realizing his sword was gone, his lip curling up. Killian having his sword, the one Blackbeard gave him, was an extra blow to him because Killian knew what that sword represented, what it meant to Croygen.

"Ohhh, sprite spit. This is a prickly one." Sprig's face scrunched up, his fingers working the lock. "Allll-most got it."

Far away, booms twitched my ears, jerking my head above us, wondering what they were.

"What?" Croygen asked. "You hear someone coming?"

"No. Not people." I held still, trying to hear it again, but was only met with silence. "Sounded like fireworks or something."

"Fireworks?" Croygen snorted. "Killian celebrating my demise already?"

"Allllll-moossstt therrree." Sprig stuck out his tongue.

"He'll probably plan a parade," I quipped.

"Alllllll moooosssttt—"

Clank. The door whined open.

"Who's your Monkey God King now?" Sprig held up his arms. "That's right, I am."

"Cork it, Marie-Antoinette." Croygen stuffed him in his pocket before creeping out of the cell, waving me on to take the lead.

My mind charted us down the hall, and my senses turned

up high, trying to smell or hear any threat before they saw us. With no weapons, I felt stripped and bare, trotting us up old winding stone steps, each one worn and different, slowing us down.

"I have to find my sword—"

Another boom echoed from a far distance, this time sounding more like cannon fire, halting us in our tracks. My head twisted back to Croygen, his spine stiff, his eyes darting around.

"Now, I heard that," he whispered, another blast resounding right after, telling us a fight was going on outside this palace. "Go!" He rushed me up the stairs, winding down another hall before my memory had us at a door that led outside.

"It's locked." Anxiety pumped at the back of my neck. Gunfire and yells slipped in through the cracks of the door. When I came through, they had guards on these doors too, but whatever was happening outside, they had left their post.

"Sprig?" Croygen grabbed the monkey from his pocket.

He sat in his palm, circling until his back faced the pirate.

"Sprig." Teeth clenched, Croygen's eye twitched. "Open the door."

"No," he huffed, glowering at the pirate. "I'm not talking to you."

"We don't have time for this," Croygen barked.

"*Bhean chait*, can you tell the scabby butthumper I am not talking to him?" He *hmphed*.

My gaze went to Croygen, not having to say a word but expressing everything he needed to hear.

Croygen breathed through his nose, his forehead lining like this was painful. "Please?"

"No."

"Sprig!" he barked.

"Say something nice." Sprig peered over his shoulder.

"I won't gut your girlfriend like a pig," he grumbled. I glared harder at him. "Fine. And I'll get you honey pancakes from Izel's… someday."

Sprig jumped up, twittering happily, leaping onto the knob and working his magic.

"See, was that so hard?" I poked at him.

"Kitten, you are walking a thin line right now."

"Only place I like to be." I winked at him.

"I could find other places—"

"Easy as honey pie!" The lock snapped, Sprig leaping back to Croygen. "Oh, honey pie sounds so—"

BOOOM!

The passage shook as an echo of a big gun thundered from a distance.

"That was definitely a cannon. Like a ship cannon." Croygen pushed past me, flinging the door open. The cool night air hit my face as we darted out the side of the palace, commotion pulling us around to the front, the river below us.

My feet came to a stuttering stop.

"Holy fuck." Croygen halted next to me. His gaze locked on the object firing from the Danube onto Killian's soldiers, who were fighting back from the riverbank.

A small ship floated close to the pier, and flying high in the mast, a familiar flag flapped in the wind.

The Silver Tongue Devil.

CHAPTER 21
Croygen

Disbelief rendered me speechless, my brain wanting to deny what my eyes were showing me. The skull and crossbones, the patch over the eye, the familiar font that waved at me like an old friend. It wasn't my ship, this one small enough to steer through the narrow, shallow river waters, but it was my symbol beckoning me home.

There was a jolt in my chest when I spotted the huge Cyclops and the Scotsman next to him, Vane, shooting from the crow's nest.

My crew. My refuge. My family.

The screeching of a hawk-shifter pierced the air, the bird circling the ship, something dropping from its talons.

Scot grappled for the object, chucking it back out, the cylinder exploding midair.

"Fuck!" I saw the hawk-shifter circle around again. It wouldn't be long until one of those actually went off on the ship, putting a nice hole in it. "Come on!" I yelled at Kat, my feet already racing down the hill toward the water.

Leaving my sword behind, knowing I had to walk away without it, cut deep. But Katrina's life was far more important. There wasn't even time to consider how the hell my crew was here. The only priority was getting the hell out.

Killian's men were completely focused on the ship, not noticing us sneaking our way to the river. The magic-infused fence around the palace was down to let them go in and out, which let us slip away easily.

We moved quickly, getting to the road at the bottom. Tension dribbled along my shoulders as I stopped us in an alley. Peering out, I saw most of the street was filled with guards. A barrier between us and the river.

We needed a way to let my crew know we were here and to start sailing south, picking us up down the way.

"Shit," I hissed, not seeing how the hell to get past all the soldiers without getting us killed.

"You trust me?" Katrina's voice jerked my head to her, my gaze searching hers.

It wasn't even a question. "You know I do."

"Then get yourself down to that bridge." She flicked her chin to a green metal bridge south of the palace.

"Why?" My throat tightened. "What are you doing?"

A smile hooked her mouth. Going on her toes, her lips took mine, kissing me hard before stepping away.

"Katrina." Her name was a warning.

"Oh, and don't lose my jacket or boots. They're special to me." In a blink, her body dropped, her clothes heaping up on the floor where she had stood. Her sleek black cat frame slipped out from under the pile, rubbing up against my leg. I could feel it, just as strongly in her cat form as human—the connection I tried to discount, pretend wasn't there. It was so fucking loud and vibrant, I had no idea how I ignored it for so long. Like a million vibrating threads connecting us, pounding against my chest like waves, washing through my soul like the sea. It was everything I didn't know I was missing. When I used to stand on the deck, the weight of the world on my shoulders, searching for something.

It was her.

With another *meow*, she slipped out of the alley, slinking quickly out of sight. Without question, I knew what she was doing—becoming a distraction. It was a strange sensation. I wasn't reading her thoughts, but I was just so tuned into her I felt like I was.

"Gods dammit, Katrina," I hissed, grabbing her clothes and boots. I tied her coat around my waist, gripping her boots under my arm. I trusted her more than anything in the world, which only made me more volatile. If something happened to her…

I never understood how mated couples said if one was killed, the other would follow behind. I thought it was pathetic. Now I fucking got it.

If someone just hurt her, I would rain my fury down on them and every last person who watched for centuries to come, torturing them painfully but keeping them alive to feel everything.

If someone killed her, this world was done. Me along with it.

Swearing under my breath again, I slipped out of the alley, keeping tight to the shadows. I was good at disappearing, a trick of the eye, but this was too many and too out in the open.

As I headed for the bridge, gunfire and yells dug in like spikes, wanting to draw my attention, but I kept on my mission, keeping her boots tight to my chest like I was holding onto her.

A loud *meow* pierced the air between shots. Katrina called them to her, directing all their attention away from me.

"What the hell? Did that cat just jump in the water?" a man spoke in Hungarian.

"That's the cat-shifter! Shoot it!"

My body whirled around, ready to fight, my anger blistering up my spine. The need to protect her overruled everything.

BOOOOM!

A cannonball hurled from the ship through a line of

soldiers, crashing into a wall, splintering stone into the air like raindrops. My body flew, rolling over the road along with Killian's men, tossing me like a doll. My bones crunched and my skin tore, the items in my hands scattering. I hit the ground, rolling over the concrete. For a moment or two, I was unable to move. My skin burned as my insides splintered, grappling for air.

Coughing, a man sat up next to me, his familiar features dropping my stomach.

Connor. His expression shifted as he took me in, realizing who was next to him.

"Hey!" He pointed at me, starting to get up.

It was now or never to make a break for it. I didn't even have time to check to see if Sprig was all right. My head spinning, blood dripping into my eyes, I clawed my way up, stumbling as my brain swirled with vertigo.

"Hey! Stop!" he belted at me. "Kill him!"

Bullets zipped by my head, my feet zigzagging me down the street, their bellows catching up with me.

Pop!

Grazing my temple, a bullet hummed in my ear, taunting me with its kiss of death. I pumped my legs and arms faster, ducking behind objects and tossing anything I could in the path behind me to slow them down.

Daring myself a moment, I curved my head back to the river, seeing the ship was moving, heading for the bridge. Sprinting onto it, I trailed along the railing, gauging where the best place to jump was. Climbing over the railing, every muscle locked down.

"Come on… come on," I chanted at the ship, noticing Killian's men getting closer. Their bullets would be here faster than the ship would.

The hawk-shifter screeched, diving down on me, her claws nicking at my head.

"Shit!" I bellowed as gunfire pinged off the railing, sparking the metal.

My time was up.

"Hold your breath, fuzzball," I muttered, taking in the ship's speed, seeing Scot and Vane at the bow. I sucked in and jumped.

My body plunged down, slicing through the cold water, the impact slamming into my chest like a bat.

There were so many times I had considered letting the sea take me after finding my family at the bottom of Davy Jones's locker. To find that peace I was always hunting.

But now my family was above, my peace was on that ship, and I no longer wanted the sea to take me. If she was alive, I would fight, kill, and demolish whatever it took to get back to her.

My arms pushed me through the murky water, swimming for the port side.

"Captain!" Scot's voice was the first to reach me, tossing down a rope ladder. My fingers caught it, and I struggled to pull myself up. My body was exhausted, injured, and fatigued. My leg still ached from where the necromancer cut into it, the binding muscles weak, forcing me to use more of my arms to pull myself up.

Shots volleyed back and forth, the soldiers' voices getting farther away as we slipped out the other side of the bridge, their rifles no longer able to reach us.

Thank the gods… we actually escaped.

"Here." Scot leaned over, clasping my hand to yank me up the last few rungs, my body dropping onto the deck with relief. The weight of my wet clothes, plus Katrina's jacket, was too heavy for me, my muscles shaking.

"Fuckfuckfuck." My hands tore at my jacket pocket, terror capturing my lungs, feeling his wet fur against my fingers, his body unmoving. "Nononono." I pulled Sprig out, his limp frame in a starfish position on the deck in a puddle of water. I watched his chest for movement, my pulse pounding in my ears. "Come on, gerbil..." Panic cut off my air, swallowing down the utter fear I felt.

His lips smacked, his tiny voice muttered sound asleep, curling on his side. "The honey bears want my brains."

A huge gust of air shredded my lungs, a hitch gurgling up my throat with a laugh-cry.

"You're safe..." I rubbed at his head, relief slumping me back into the railing. "You don't have any brains to give them."

Scot snorted, drawing my attention back to him. More of my men circled around me. Vane, Corb, Zidane, and shit, if I didn't want to break down.

"Fuck, it's good to see you all," I croaked.

"Aye, and you." Scot took my hand again, cupping it like a hug, his lids blinking rapidly, stuffing back his emotion.

"Kat?" I tried to turn my head, searching for her.

A grin hinted on Scot's face. "See for yourself."

"Croygen." Soaking wet and wearing someone's shirt, Katrina dove beside me, relief flooding her features. "Oh gods... you're alive." Her fingers slid over my wounds, making me flinch in pain, worry furrowing her brow. "What happened to you?"

Water and blood trailed down my face, my adrenaline waning, agony throbbing over my skin and bones. I was more hurt than I thought.

"My ass got tossed from that last cannon." I gripped her hands, my mouth brushing over her palm, needing to feel she was solid and real.

"Blame him for that." Scot thumbed over his shoulder.

"You're the stupid ass who got in front of it." A tall blond man strolled to the side of Scot, jerking my head to him.

"Cooper?" I stared at the Dark Dweller in surprise, not expecting to find him here with my crew. I assumed they were already out of the city, heading back for the States. "You're here." Another knot in my chest unwound, knowing they were safe. Alive. "Annabeth?"

"She's below. Resting."

"How?" I wagged my head, looking at Vane, Corb, and Zid, with Tsai up at the helm. Everything swirled in my brain, nothing computing, my body starting to shut down.

"I think you need to rest and heal before we get into that." Scot reached under my arm, tugging me up, Zidane getting on my other side.

"Fuck, I missed you guys," I whispered, still so confused how they were here. It was impossible to sail this far in such little time.

No matter how hard I tried to keep my lids up, they started to close. And as they deposited me on a bed down below, I swore I saw a small, familiar man standing in the doorway. Recognition almost reached me before sleep took me under.

A dull ache roused me from a deep sleep, my lids slowly blinking open to a room I didn't recognize, daylight streaming through the small window. Confusion filled my head with panic. I peered around, not knowing where I was or what happened.

Naked, my body still red in places from burn marks, I felt bare skin brush against me. My attention jumped to the figure lying beside me. For one second, I wondered whose bed I was in, which nameless woman I had fucked last night, what trouble I had gotten into. The sensation sizzled disgust and anger through me with nausea. And then my brain finally clicked on the figure. All the chaos going on in my head was instantly anchored and soothed.

Katrina.

Exhaling, my body calmed, relieved it was her next to me, not some other woman.

I took in her beautiful sleeping face, realizing how everything had flipped since she'd come back into my life. I never cared when I woke up in the bed of a woman I barely remembered. Shame or regret were never something I experienced. But from the second she stepped onto my ship, the thought of being with anyone else made me want to squirm out of my skin. I didn't comprehend that for a long time, but now I saw it so clearly.

When she declared to Killian I was her mate, I expected fear, claustrophobia, and the need to run. It did the exact opposite. Her declaration rooted my boots into the floor, made me feel like I could fully breathe—take on the world—and settled everything in place like the last piece of a puzzle.

It was everything I told myself I wasn't built for. So many amazing women had come into my life over the centuries, yet I felt nothing like this for any of them. It was what I wanted to feel for Lexie, what I hoped I might fake until it made it so. She deserved that kind of love more than anything. But it wasn't meant to be.

Little did I know it was another little badass from my past that would wreak havoc on my world.

Leaning over, I trailed my mouth over her lips, a soft purr coming from her as she stirred awake. I knew we had so much to talk about, so much to go over, but for a little while longer, I only wanted it to be us.

My lips grew hungry as I moved over her, settling between her legs, her naked body arching into me.

I knew we had a lot to talk about. Killian, the mate stuff, and her father… telling her the truth about Rotty and what happened that night was never something I'd planned to do. I wanted him to stay her hero, for her to always think the best of him. I thought it was better to keep her innocent and oblivious to his crimes.

But now I understood Katrina never needed to be sheltered. She was my equal, my partner, and truth was our foundation, whether we wanted it or not. Our connection was bone deep, cutting into us like DNA.

"I'm sorry," I whispered, my gaze zeroing in on hers, letting her feel my emotions. She knew exactly what I meant. A flicker of agony watered her eyes, her chin dipping in understanding. I was sorry for keeping it from her, but mostly I was sorry for the truth. For changing the view of her father she held all her life. "He did it because he loved you, Kitten," I muttered against her mouth. "And now I get why he did it. Just know, I would do so much worse." My cock slipped through her folds, stealing her breath. "I would sink every ship, slice every throat, and destroy everything in my way to keep you safe." My lips claimed hers, sealing my statement as a promise.

"Croygen," she groaned, her legs wrapping around me. I no longer felt any pain as I positioned myself at her entrance, her breath growing quicker, moving against me with desperation.

Biting down on her lip, I tugged on it as I sunk into her, filling her completely.

"Fuck," I growled, drowning in the sensations, my lungs struggling for air. There were so many ways I wanted to take her, some real kinky shit, and I would, but right now I wanted to fuck her so slow and deep she would never stop feeling me inside her. With deep, long strokes, my cock pushed inside her pussy. She was so tight around me my vision started to blur.

"Oh gods!" She bowed her head back into the pillow, her hips matching my need, our hands and mouths kissing, touching, and fully falling into ecstasy. The magic in the room crackled off us, enhancing the intensity. "Harder!"

Picking up my pace, I slammed into her, needing to be so

deep we had no space between us, our souls twining together. Something in my head snapped, a feral need gritting my teeth as I gripped her hips, holding her in place as I railed her harder.

A choked sob howled from Kat, her body shaking, her pussy throbbing around me.

"Croygen!" Her cat nails clawed into me as she climaxed, pumping around my cock, milking it.

"Holy fuck!" I bellowed, my hot cum filling her, making sure I marked every inch of her as mine as her brand marked through me violently.

There was no mistaking it—the bond between us knotted even tighter, plunging into my soul, inflicting overwhelming bliss that almost hurt. The sensation was so overpowering it took my sight, and I no longer seemed like I was in my body.

I was consumed. Fanatical. I continued to fuck her, so addicted I couldn't stop. Pushing through the need to collapse, I felt my cum coating us, squeezing out, rocking me even harder, my dick growing stiff again inside her.

"Oh gods…" she panted. I experienced everything she did—the wonder of what the hell was happening and how it could possibly feel this unbelievable. Her emotions only added to mine, spiraling us forward again, out of our minds.

"I can't stop fucking you." I pushed up her leg, hitting a spot that had her arching. Yowls came from her like a wild cat, her teeth and claws digging into my skin, the pain making me lose even more control. I was possessed.

An animal.

A devil.

Pulling out, I flipped her over, yanking her ass up and licking through her pussy. Kat choked on a cry before I slammed my cock back into her.

She screamed so loud, I felt it tattoo on my bones.

This was what I wanted. Forever. She and I, fucking, pirating, and finding our way through this world.

CROYGEN!

This time when she screamed, it wasn't out loud. Her cry pierced through every molecule in my body, charging up to my brain and down to my cock. I felt her clawing and screaming, rolling around in my soul like she owned it.

It was her house. She just let me live in it.

The walls shook, and the bed frame cracked as we climaxed together, suspending us in time and space before crashing us down to Earth.

My body fell on hers, covering her like a weighted blanket, both of us heaving and gasping.

"Fuck me," she whispered.

"I just did."

She huffed in amusement while sucking in gulps of air, sweat coating her skin, her chest vibrating with pleasure. "Seriously… what the hell?" She swallowed, her purr growing louder, no longer hiding it from me. "Is that normal?"

"I think it is for us." From my experience living with Ryker and Zoey, this would only get more intense. I'll admit, part of me always thought they had to be exaggerating a bit. I had experienced incredible sex before, *lots* of it. I mean, it couldn't be that much better, right? It was all the same mechanics.

I was *so* wrong.

Still inside her, I rolled her with me onto my side, wrapping my arms around her. I was so fucking satisfied, completely content and happy, it should have startled me. It was a new emotion for me. I always wanted more, always something to do, always moving.

It was painful to compare what I thought I'd felt for Amara to this. How much of my life I wasted, how superficial and toxic it had been. Though I guess going through it not only led me here, back to Katrina, it made me appreciate this so much more.

"Kitten," I muttered against her ear, kissing her neck.

"Do not think I haven't forgotten you lost my boots." She curved her head back to me. "You haven't made up for that."

"Oh? That wasn't enough?"

"Not even close." Her brow arched up. A challenge.

"Guess I should start working on that then." I nipped at her shoulder, my hands sliding down her figure, knowing where she was ticklish.

"No, stop!" She laughed, kicking her legs into me, trying to shake off my attack. I rolled over on her, pinning her to the mattress, floored by how ready I was to sink into her again.

I had an addictive personality, and Katrina Roth was going to be an uncontrollable obsession. One I would never recover from. And I didn't want to.

"Hey!" A pounding shook the door. "Can you two stop fuckin' for a moment?" Scot's voice boomed through the door. "We got shit to deal with."

Sighing, I let my head drop into her. Unfortunately, we did. Our secluded little moment was over. It was time to deal with reality.

And reality was a stone-cold bitch.

The sun was heading for the horizon, glowing off the steady line of trees and grass on either side of the riverbank as Kat and I stepped on the deck. My hand clasped around Kat's, and the late summer breeze tangling our wet hair. The shower was shit, but it was enough to clean off the sweat, blood, and cum.

I had slept over twelve hours, my body needing to heal, though the ache in my leg was still there, the wound taking slower than the rest to heal up. I was famished, but sleep and fucking Kat had me feeling even better than normal. No doubt it was all her who had me feeling like a rockstar, not the sleep.

"Captain." Zidane dipped his head when we approached, his brow lifting between us. "Looks like you are feeling better."

"Much." I clasped his hand in our shake, able to fully greet him. "Though I wouldn't turn down your jerk chicken or oxtail stew."

"How about pancakes? If any are left." Zid's expression flatlined.

"Let me guess." I chuckled.

"You tried to poison me." Sprig's voice came from behind, climbing up my leg to my shoulder, pointing at Zid. "Attempted assassination of the Monkey God King!"

"You were the one who ate all the cocoa powder," Zid clipped back.

"Good thing, it was clearly about to go bad," Sprig huffed, settling against my neck.

"It's *cocoa* powder, not chocolate."

"Well, your *cocoa* powder was bitter and going bad."

Zidane inhaled, pointing at the monkey. "That thing is a scalawag."

"And how dare you speak to me without addressing me by my proper title. Do you not know who I am?"

"Oh gods." Katrina palmed her face, holding back a laugh.

"See, she knows who she's in the presence of." Sprig motioned to Kat.

"Sprig, shut up." I wagged my head, heading to where I spotted Scot, Vane, Corb, Cooper, and Tsai on the deck, my heart surging with emotion at seeing them.

"Boy, even my deaf ears could hear you two." Tsai clicked her tongue, walking right up to me. The few teeth she had left peeked through her lips, a coy smile hinting. "But the magic between the pair of you. Thinking we officially have another captain on our ship?"

Heat slid up my neck, my gaze darting to Katrina for a moment. "Nothing's been discussed."

"Yeah, we *know*. Though we heard a lot of wailing to the gods." She cackled.

"You really are a menace," I muttered to her with a chuckle.

Reaching up, she cupped my face, dragging me down to her level. "I am so glad you are back. But now that you are safe, I want to kill you. Did I not warn you? The power that lay ahead?"

"And if I recall, you said if we went, not all of us would return. Well, we're all still here."

"With that tone, I'm about to make it one less." She patted my cheek hard, her voice going low. "Though physically we might all be here, not all of us fully returned." She stepped back as if it was choreographed, Annabeth standing a few feet behind her. Air evaporated in my chest, agony knotting my throat. The happy buzz I was on crashed down into dust.

Annabeth had always been thin and petite, getting more so as the disease grew. It had been less than two days since I'd seen her, but the difference in her was stark.

Her skin was so thin her bones protruded from them, and her face was gaunt, resembling the necromancers we crossed paths with. I felt it at the time, but now I saw the results of their power. They had felt her death so near, sucked vital energy from her, leaving her nothing more than the walking dead.

"Anna…" I barely got her name out. She struggled to walk to me, her bones jabbing me as I wrapped my arms around her. There was nothing there to hold, just a skeleton.

Sprig crawled onto her shoulder, curling up against her neck, his silence telling me how serious he knew this was, how devastated he was as well.

Tears burned in my eyes, sliding down my face as I held her, my hand running over her limp, dull hair. "I'm so sorry." A sob distorted my sentiment, and it took everything in me to not fall to the ground. "I'm so sorry." I couldn't stop apologizing, knowing I failed her too. And in that, I was failing Lexie all over again. The guilt over letting the nectar slip through our fingers gnawed at me, and now it was too late.

"It's not your fault." She tipped back, her blue eyes peering up at mine with a strength I could never fathom. "Please do not blame yourself. I will be so mad at you if you do. You are not to blame for my cancer, just as you are not to blame for Lexie's death. So please, for me, stop punishing yourself and let yourself be happy." She swallowed, struggling to talk for long. "I have learned more than anything to appreciate everything and live the fullest, happiest life… otherwise you're just wasting time. And time is the most precious thing we have that no magic can change." She took another halted breath, her fingers stroking through Sprig's fur, needing his warmth. "I do not regret one moment of my life. The ups and downs… finding a love I never imagined I would have in my wildest dreams." She looked back, smiling at Cooper, taking his hand. He appeared like he was going to lose his shit too, while she held us both together like a rock. "What I've experienced is more than some people get in their whole lives. I've been so lucky."

Her appreciation, gratitude, and outlook on all this were more daggers in my heart.

"I will get you home," I vowed. "I will get you to your family."

"You *are* my family, Croygen. Stop separating yourself like you don't belong. You do. That's not something time or space can ever change. No matter how long you are gone."

Yanking her back into me, I had to bite down on my molars, hearing them crack, to keep the sobs from wailing through me. I was terrified of what would happen when she finally passed—to me and especially to Cooper.

The only thing that took my attention was a man standing several yards away, his small statue almost a pillar along the masts. Pulling back from AB, I stared at the man, recalling seeing him last night before I passed out.

It was the guide who got us through the fae doors.

"You?" I stepped toward him, confusion wrinkling my forehead, glancing at Scot and back to the man.

"He delivered your message." Scot was next to me, explaining. "He is the entire reason we were able to get to you in such a short time."

Understanding cleared out my fuzzy head, putting it all together. "He brought you guys through the fae doors."

"He brought us to Budapest, where we *borrowed* this ship." Scot motioned to the small sloop we were on. "Cooper spotted the flag when we were sailing in. Was able to get our attention, told us where to find you guys."

My throat still tight, I bowed my head in gratitude at the man. "Thank you."

"Haoyu." He gave me his name.

"I thank you, Haoyu."

He returned the head bow, his face staying expressionless.

"Whatever we can pay you, I'm sure you want to get home when we reach our next port."

He dipped his head again.

"Where the hell are we, anyway?"

"Few hours from Belgrade," Scot answered.

"There is a fae door near there," Haoyu said.

"Can you take me to Singapore before you return home?" Katrina stepped up next to me, addressing the man. "I will pay you to take me."

"You have already paid." The man touched Rotty's dagger hanging from his waist.

"You mean take *both* of us." I twisted to her.

"No, just me." She shook her head. "Dealing with Batara and getting my crew back is my responsibility."

"I'm sorry, did you just miss the whole mate thing?" I turned to face her. "You aren't going without me."

"Yes, I am." She stepped right into me, her eyes filled with sorrow, darting to AB. "You can't leave. You know you can't... you won't forgive yourself."

"And if anything happens to you, you think I'll forgive myself then?"

"Croy." Her hands gripped my jaw, rubbing over my thick scruff. "You need to get her home. And you need to be with her. You know you do."

"Then wait."

"I can't." She bit down on her lip. "I've already waited too long." Her crew was probably being tortured every day—multiple times—if they weren't already dead. I understood, though I hated it. But nothing would stop me from getting to my crew too.

"Wait." I stepped back from her, my attention rolling down her. "The nectar is gone. We're walking away from it, but you aren't suffering."

She blinked at me as if she just realized that as well.

"What was your promise to Batara?" I asked. "I mean, the exact thing you made a promise to."

Words in the fae world were tricky; they held heavier weight than human words. And they were a lot different from my vow to Ryker after he saved my life.

"That I would find the nectar," she replied, her eyes drifting off like she was trying to recall the conversation.

"Did he ask you to bring it back?"

"Yes."

"But did you vow to do that? Think, Kat. What did he say right before you promised?"

Her attention snapped back to me, her eyes widening. "He said if I get what he wanted, everything will be returned to me."

"Well…" I tilted my head. "Technically, you did get what he wanted. You didn't promise to put it in his hands."

"You think—"

"Annabeth!" Cooper's cry cut Kat off, whipping us around. Cooper lunged toward AB as she dropped, her bag scattering stuff over the deck.

"AB!" I screamed, running to her. Cooper was already next to her, his hand running over her face, trying to wake her up.

"Baby, no!" He bent over her. "Please open your eyes. Please hold on for me, okay? Not yet. *Please…*" His pleading tone broke every fiber of my being, the pain so guttural I couldn't breathe. "Someone help!" he barked at us, but we all knew there was nothing we could do. Everyone stood helplessly watching.

"Anna!" Cooper held her, almost shaking her. "Don't. Leave. Me." Her lids fluttered open, but life was leaking fast from her. They stared at each other, and I could almost feel the last moments between them, the magnitude of their love. She reached up with a shaky hand, brushing his hair off his face.

"I love you." Her voice was a whisper, only meant for him. "So much."

A harsh sob heaved from him. "I love you too. More than I ever told you."

"You didn't need to. I felt it." Her eyes were dulling, her lungs slowing. She went still, and I couldn't tell if she was breathing.

"No." I sensed the agony building up, the struggle to siphon in air, breaking my soul.

"*Bebinn?*" Sprig whimpered, poking softly at her arm, looking at us for an explanation, his face crumbling. "*Bebinn!*" His eyes filled with grief and panic, his body moving frantically. Desperate. "Don't worry, *Bebinn!*" He spun around, searching for something, his voice going higher, filled with terror and grief. "Pam will comfort you. She will protect you wherever you go." He darted over to his tiny honey backpack, which had fallen out of AB's bag, the goat's head sticking out. Ripping his stuffed animal from it, black underwear flung out behind. A tiny pea-sized object stuck to the knickers dropped from it, plunking down on my boot.

I stared at it, my body freezing up, not wanting to blink in case this was all an illusion.

"Holy shit…" Katrina clasped her mouth. "Is that what I think it is?"

It was the nectar.

The barely bite-sized piece Dr. Novikov had cut back in the dragon caves. I hadn't even thought about it, convinced it was lost. Instead, it had been stuck at the bottom of Sprig's backpack the *whole* time, too small for us to feel its power, buried along with his cape I had shoved deep inside and forgotten about.

Holy. Shit.

Reaching down, my heart hammered with hope and desperation.

"Don't touch it!" Tsai yelled, her hands up. "I can feel it. It's too powerful."

Being blind made her far more sensitive than the rest of us, feeling things we could not. I never doubted or questioned her, but my brain was not operating on logic.

"I don't care! She's dying!" I screamed back, going for the item again.

Before I could grab it, Sprig zoomed in, snatching it from the top of my boot and scurrying back to AB, unfazed by the energy it contained. Sub-fae seemed like they were immuned to some fae magic.

"Open her mouth." Sprig dashed up to AB's face. Cooper tilted Annabeth's head back, opening her jaw, her chest no longer moving.

Sprig held up the piece over her, his head tilting. "This kind of looks like honey."

"Fucksake! Give it to her now!" I roared, crashing down next to the other side of AB's body.

Sprig let it go, the nectar dropping onto her tongue. Cooper closed her mouth, tilting her head back as I rubbed her throat, trying to get it down.

"Come on…" My focus was entirely on her, looking for any sign of life, any change. Every second that passed rose panic up my spine. Were we too late? Was she already gone? "Come on, come on, come on," I chanted.

Birds chirped and crickets buzzed with evening activities, but only silence came from Annabeth, her lungs not moving.

Cooper's breathing grew short and shallow, his eyes firing red, his shirt starting to tear, the beast taking over. "No!" He shook his head, not ready to accept the fact she was dead. "*Aaannnnna!*" He shook her again.

We were too late.

"Noooooooooooooooooo!" His bellow howled through the atmosphere, the sunset splashing across the sky in deep reds, oranges, and blues like his emotions were being painted. His anger, his love, his heartbreak, waiting for the darkness to set in because that was the color his soul was now.

That moment of hope would be his end. Cooper wouldn't come back… and a big part of me wouldn't either.

The heavy silence strangled me, my heart and head still at odds, staring down at my little sister. The only way I could continue to breathe was by imagining her and Lexie together. That at least they had each other.

"But *Bebinn,*" Sprig whimpered, his fingers caressing her cheek. "You said you'd stay."

I blinked. Why did her cheeks look so rosy? Wait… why didn't she look as gaunt and bony as before?

"Cooper," I puffed out his name, not daring to take my eyes off her. "Look."

His head jerked, following my focus, noticing the glow starting to emanate around her. "Anna?" Desperation had his eyes darting all over her, his hands touching her face.

Her body started to twitch violently, her limbs flailing as if she were being electrocuted, tossing Sprig off her chest and tumbling him to the floor.

"Anna!" Cooper's tone pitched in terror as her spine arched, her head slamming against the deck, convulsing brutally, foam pooling from her lips.

A cry broke from my mouth, my hands trying to protect her head, feeling like I was watching the last throes of death. I had witnessed many die—horribly violent deaths. But nothing felt so tortuous as helplessly observing someone you love perish—painfully—and not be able to do a thing. Kat squeezed my shoulder, undoubtedly knowing I felt broken.

Cooper tried to hold AB down, liquid from his eyes spattering across her cheek. His calls for her were white noise as her form seized, like it was being poisoned, tortured, and twisted. A guttural noise vibrated in her chest, and then her body went utterly still.

Deathly still.

"Ann…" Cooper whispered, his chest heaving, tears spilling down his face. I could see the moment coming. Darkness wouldn't take him. He would *become* the darkness. "Baby…" he croaked, his hand gripping her face, leaning over her.

Her lids flew open, her body lurching up, her head cracking into his as she sat up. A huge gasp filled her lungs with life. Coughing, her body shook, her eyes wide and scared, like she was just yanked from death's hands and was shoved back into life.

A few beats of shock suspended us in time. We paused in disbelief, not wanting to trust what our eyes were showing us for fear it was tricking us.

"Ow." She touched her head where it hit Cooper's, rubbing at it. "That hurt."

"Holy fuck!" Cooper bellowed. "Oh my gods!" He pulled her into his arms, holding her tight. "It worked." He kissed her sore head, drawing her closer, a sob cracking his chest in relief. "You're alive."

A noise huffed from my soul, my body sagging, tears burning my lids with relief and happiness. I felt Kat's hand still on my shoulder, and I gripped it so tight, needing her like an anchor. She was my world, my security, and my truth.

"Alive… and fae," Tsai spouted from behind us. "I can feel her. Her magic is *intense.*"

We watched Cooper and AB hold each other for a while as she caught her breath before she curved around to look at us. Her blue eyes were bright with tears, but also glowing now. She reached out to me, yanking me to her, picking up Sprig too, folding us all in a family hug.

I couldn't hold back anymore. The emotion of thinking we lost her took over. Sobs hacked at my throat. *We did it, Lex… we saved her,* I thought to myself. And I felt that where she was, she was smiling and cheering.

Good job, ol' man. I could hear her tease back, getting all sassy. *Now it's time to forgive yourself. Live your life and get into all sorts of trouble and adventures for me.*

Holding Annabeth, feeling the fae magic come off her, knowing she was safe… I exhaled again.

I let the guilt go.

"I will," I muttered to myself.

For the first time, I felt my life was just beginning. With Kat. There were so many adventures ahead, and I would always carry a piece of Lexie with me so she would experience them too.

Not out of remorse or obligation.

But out of love.

CHAPTER 22
Katrina

"Are you sure you don't need us?" Cooper asked again, peering down the gangway toward Haoyu, who waited for us on an abandoned dock. We were a few miles outside Belgrade, where nature was moving back in and taking over.

"No." I was so tempted to say yes, to have more people to help me get my crew, but I knew I couldn't risk any of them. I had already gotten my own killed. "You need to get home. Even if she's better." I nodded at Annabeth with a smile. "She still might have some fae growing pains."

"I feel great." Her blonde hair glowed like the moonlight shining down on her. Her skin was bright, her cheeks rosy. Annabeth had looked fae before with her delicately stunning features, but now she really was.

It was like she always was meant to be one of us.

Cooper had not let her go for a moment, his arm tight around her, kissing and touching her with no reservation. They looked like a newlywed couple—so deeply in that giddy love, unable to keep their hands off each other. I had a feeling it wouldn't be long until they couldn't, and this time when they had sex, it would be on such a different, deeper level than they ever had before. Her being fae was going to change their relationship for the better. He would be able to really let go with her now.

"I need to do this," I reassured them. "And the more of us, the more chances of someone getting hurt. I have to face Batara on my own."

Neither Cooper nor Scot looked pleased, their eyes darting to Croygen as if he was going to give them an opposite order.

Don't you even think about it. My thoughts shot to him.

He snorted, raising his hands enough to tell me he got my message. Or at least felt my warning.

We hadn't discussed how things would work, but neither of us would be first mate or crew. We were both captains, which might be a problem.

"Get back to our ship," Croygen ordered Scot. "Make sure Cooper and Annabeth get to Seattle safely. And then head for Singapore." He turned to Cooper and AB.

Annabeth swallowed roughly, her eyes teary. "The moment you can, come home to us." She stretched on her toes, hugging Croygen. He held her tightly, his throat bobbing and head nodding, not able to answer.

"Stay safe," she whispered to him. "I love you."

"Love you too." He could barely reply.

Croygen broke away, clasping Cooper's hand, saying goodbye while AB and I embraced. Her strength had tripled from when I first met her, and I sensed the magic billowing off her, probably exploding emotion and energy through her.

"You are our family now, Katrina. So I need both of you to come home safe. Okay?" She squeezed my hand in sincerity, including me as one of their own without hesitation. I knew Lexie would always be here, a part of both AB and Croygen, but I no longer saw her as a threat. She was a comrade. Someone else who fell in love with Croygen, most likely wanting to kill and love him at the same time. And that I could relate to.

"Sprig?" Croygen peered around.

"Probably passed out somewhere." Cooper shrugged. "Face down, letting himself drown in an inch of honey."

"Wouldn't be the first time," Croygen scoffed.

Saying goodbye to the rest of the crew, Croygen grabbed my hand, pulling me down the ramp toward Haoyu. I glanced back one more time to see everyone lined up at the railing, my heart squeezing before we cut through the foliage growing up rampantly.

I hoped I would see them all again. Somewhere along the way, all of those people had become my family.

"Right up here." Haoyu motioned in the dark. Once again, I saw the wavy air, popping and fizzing with magic.

"Don't let go, Kitty-Kat." Croygen's hand gripped mine harder, clutching onto our leader as we stepped in.

Twisting. Turning. Darting through a rainforest, farmland, going out in a smelly alley with people having sex on a dumpster. Faster than I could blink, my stomach knotted, my lids closing, letting Croygen pull me through. Fuck, I hated fae doors.

Ramming through another one, we came to a halt, stepping out into humid air, dawn just a breath on the horizon. My head swam as I gripped Croygen's hand and took in the scenery, realizing I was high above, overlooking Singapore.

"Holy shit," I gasped, taking in how high up we were. We were close to the now closed Skypark observation deck, the one famously resembling a ship on three towers sailing through the air. A sky pirate ship. "I've never been up here before." I went to the railing, looking down at the boat dock across the bay. Croygen came up beside me, both of us taking a moment.

It was too dark to see the cracks of the crumbling city, too far up to see the poor and hungry. Up here, the elites would drink their champagne and eat their appetizers while those below suffered. It had always been like this, but now it was magnified by a thousand.

"I think Pam might have vomited in your coat again." A voice jerked both me and Croygen to his pocket.

Sprig popped out, his nose wrinkling. "No, she *definitely* did."

"No." Croygen shook his head, staring at the sprite. "Nononono."

"I know you hear that a lot from ladies, pirate."

"You can't be here." He yanked Sprig out of his pocket. "You should be with AB. Heading home to Zoey and Ryker."

"Think you would make it without me, boothumper?" Sprig let out a hearty, forced laugh. "You wouldn't survive a day without me." He jumped on Croygen's arm. "I am the feared and magical Monkey-Sprite God King!" He raised his hands up. "With mystic hands and a beautiful and stunning Goat God Queen at his side!" He motioned to Pam in his backpack. "Though she smells a little like puke right now."

"Sprig." Croygen pinched his brow. "Annabeth is going to be freaking out."

"Yeah." He sighed, his voice going softer. "But you need me more."

I went still. For once, there was nothing but sincerity in Sprig's expression, his enormous eyes wide, staring at his "big brother." Then in a flash, he swished his hand, rolling his eyes. "You would die without me, butt-raider, admit it."

"Actually, we do need you, Sprig." I grinned at him, causing Croygen to groan. He had gotten us out of a lot of tight spots, and I had no idea what was ahead of us. Probably a lot of locks and chains. "We need our magnificent Monkey God King." I feigned a bow, smirking at Croygen.

"She is the *only* reason anyone can tolerate you." Sprig spoke to Croygen, gesturing at me.

"You are so gonna pay for that, Kitten," Croygen muttered to me, turning to Haoyu with a resolved exhale. "Please let Annabeth know we have him when you return."

He dipped his head.

"Thank you, Haoyu." I stepped closer to him. "For all you've done. I hope our paths will cross again someday."

Tugging out my father's dagger, he placed it in his palms, offering it back to me.

"No." I wagged my head. "It's yours."

"*No*. It is *yours*," he replied. "I may be human, but I can feel its power. Who it calls for. It *belongs* to you."

My lashes fluttered with emotion as he laid it back in my hands. The dagger felt different this time. Instead of being my father's demise, it was my father's serenity. The blade carried a piece of him, his life, his story, but I hadn't forgiven him. I still didn't understand how he could do what he did. But I loved my father. Any part of him I could still have, I wanted.

"Thank. You." My throat thick, I accepted back my father's dagger.

"I know we will see each other again." Haoyu stepped back, and in a blink, he was gone, disappearing within the fae door.

"Wait, did that asshole just leave us fifty-plus stories up with no way down but the stairs?" Croygen stopped dead.

Fuck.

"Oh yeah, who's the pony now?" Sprig pretended to ride Croygen's shoulder. "Go, horsey. And on the way, can we stop for breakfast?"

"Sprig, I'm gonna chuck you off this building."

"Is that a yes or no to breakfast first?"

My legs still shook as we made our way across the Helix Bridge, heading toward Batara's palace. After fifty-seven stories down from the Skydeck, my muscles trembled like mini earthquakes.

Our feet pounded in sync as a thin band of yellowish-orange glowed from the east, putting sharper shapes to buildings and objects and coloring the shadows dark blue.

I couldn't help but look over at the boat dock, my heart both longing and dreading to see if my ship was still there, waiting for me to rescue it.

A gasp filled my throat, my borrowed shoes coming to a dead stop. My attention was locked on the place that used to be called *The Float.* It once held concerts and entertainment, but it had been ripped out and made into a shipping/trading dock for Batara.

A rope seemed to lasso around my lungs, squeezing out all the air.

"What?" Croygen's head whipped back, sensing I was no longer beside him. He glanced around, trying to find what caused my reaction. "Katrina, what's wrong?"

"Look." I pointed. He followed my hand, his eyes squinting, trying to see what I could through the shadows.

My ship.

It wasn't the tug of my heart feeling like I found my old friend, a connection tying a pirate to their ship. No, it was the commotion going on around it. Batara's flag flapped from the mast as dozens of men wheeled on crates, loading it for a journey.

It felt like coming home to a stranger in your bed, violating your home. Probably thinking I was long dead, Batara was using it as his own, preparing for a grand voyage.

"Come on. Let's get a closer look." Croygen flicked his head, leading us off the bridge and down toward the dock. Pulling up our hoods, we weaved through the loud stalls, dodging the horses and buggies carrying barrels and chests, the early morning hours a bustle at the docks while the rest of the city slept.

Creeping closer, we hid behind a stack of crates, peering around to my ship, watching the people moving on and off it.

My teeth drove into my bottom lip, forgetting how beautiful my ship was. I had worked so hard for it. The people and things I sacrificed. I had fucked up a lot of things, but that ship was still my pride and joy. The need to run to my baby, to claim it back, curled my nails into my skin.

Yells and orders came from the deck, but I couldn't see by whom. "I want to get a little closer."

"Are you kidding?" Croygen's head wagged. "No. We are already too close. If just *one* person recognizes you *or* me, it's all over."

I knew that, yet I was unable to stop. Something twitched every muscle, pulling me toward my ship, as if my gut knew something I didn't.

"Kat!" Croygen hissed behind me as I slinked around, moving closer to the ship.

I didn't get far before two massive men strolled up the plank with huge trunks on their shoulders.

Oh. My. Gods.

The twins. Typhoon and Hurricane. They were alive.

I felt a cry burn up my throat when a hand clasped over my mouth, yanking me behind a wagon.

"Gods dammit, Katrina," Croygen muttered in my ear. "Take a breath." He commanded my body to listen. "Calm down, or you're gonna get yourself killed. And me with you... and I am too sexy to die." He held me tight, getting me to breathe with him, and my heart slowed a bit. He took his hand off my mouth. "I'm figuring those two men are part of your crew?"

"Yes." I nodded, swallowing. "Ty and Cane." Guilt knotted up in my esophagus as I watched the twins reach the deck. Dressed in lightweight dark clothes, I could see their cheeks were sunken in, thinner and paler than they used to be, but other than that, they appeared fine. At least from here. The most important thing was they were alive. "Batara must be using them as labor."

"Makes sense. They know your ship and how to sail it."
He held me against his chest for another beat. "You going to behave?"

I nodded.

"Such a liar." He nipped at my ear, letting me go.

"Hey, was that the last of it?" a familiar woman's voice yelled from the bottom of the plank at the twins.

It was as if another arrow shot through my ribs, penetrating my lungs. Zuri. She strolled up the gangplank, conversing with Ty. Her usually thin frame was smaller, her curly hair tied up with fabric, and she carried maps and folders in her arms.

Seeing her billowed emotion in my chest. Were they the only ones, or were the rest alive too? I hadn't seen Gage or Moses, but Zuri and the twins were okay. They were who I had to save before my ship departed and I lost them on the sea.

It wasn't a choice for me.

"Fuck, Kitten, I really wish I didn't know you so well." Croygen peered at the ship, then back at me.

"I have to. They're my crew."

"I know." He blew out, pulling a gun from his belt. Scot supplied us with weapons before we took off, though I knew Croygen still was hung up on losing his sword. Especially knowing Killian had it. "This isn't going to be easy."

"Nothing ever is with us." I cocked my gun, holding it to my side.

"This is a fun circle back. This is the pier you boarded my ship from almost two months ago, flipping my world upside down."

"What goes around, comes around."

He huffed, patting his jacket pocket, making sure Sprig was safe in there. He had fallen asleep about two steps down from the observation deck.

"Come on." I rolled back my shoulders and snuck toward my ship. The morning light was inching higher every moment, stealing away our shield. As we crept up, my ears were tuned in, listening for any movement near the gangplank. All the voices were strewn together, sounding further on the ship as they loaded the galley below.

Keeping low, we slunk up the plank almost on our bellies, my body twitching with the need to shift to become almost invisible. Croygen was right beside me. I felt his presence not just physically, but coiling through me, the bond between us sharp and evident.

Peeking over to the deck, my senses absorbed everything, not seeing many moving around, most probably below stocking the hull.

Click. Click. A gun cocked into the back of my head, another at the back of Croygen's from behind us.

"Get up," a man's voice snarled behind me. His voice made me recall him as one of Batara's men, one who had sailed out with me on that fateful night. He pushed the barrel harder into my skull. "Now!"

"You too," the other man ordered Croygen.

Do what he says, Kitten. I sensed more than heard Croygen, his worry for me pumping into my chest.

We stood slowly, our hands up, and they urged us farther onto the deck while one man stripped us of our weapons. Everything in me wanted to fight, to slam my elbow back into his face, but the thought of Croygen getting shot and killed kept me obedient.

I was twisted around, the guard's dark, beady eyes rolling over me, recognition sinking in. I could see deep scars and burn marks marring his face and arms, almost disfiguring him.

"Well, well." He curled his lip. "Look what the cat dragged in. A dead body." Anger sparked through his eyes, as if I was to blame for the explosion on the ship. "This is going to be fun." Slamming the gun into my head, he shoved me forward, my feet stumbling to stay upright.

Croygen's aura coiled around me protectively, wanting to lash out at that man like a snake.

"Chief?" the man called out. It was the title many used for the first mate. Chief master. "Look what crawled up to shore."

A few men on deck stepped out of the way, directing my attention to a figure behind, the one they all focused on.

My legs almost bowed, confusion poking at my reality.

What the hell?

Zuri stood there, her muscles tightening.

What was going on? She was chief master? How?

Zuri's jaw twitched, the only thing on her that betrayed her recognition of me. Her looks fooled people. As an earth fairy, she was stunning and angelic, but the girl was tough as nails. Her hair was loose and natural, but that was where she stopped being a typical earth fairy. She was excellent at hiding all emotion. She was who I sent in when I didn't just want a physical threat like the twins, but a cold, chilling warning.

"I guess I shouldn't be surprised you'd show back up sooner or later." She strolled up, her orange-brown eyes jumping from me to Croygen, a frown crinkling her brow. "Guess you finally got what you wanted. Though for all your claims about revenge and hating him, he's still alive."

Zuri was a tough girl, but I knew her. I helped her out of poverty. She was putting on this act, pretending I was the enemy, for Batara's men.

She had to be.

"Weapons?" She spoke over my head to the guards.

"Just two pistols and a dagger." The man behind me handed them over to her, my eye catching on my father's dagger glinting in the morning sun.

She nodded, taking them.

Smart girl. I thought. She now could give them back to us when the moment was right.

"Captain will be interested in seeing you." Her gaze drew

back to me, her expression still emotionless. "I'm sure he will be *thrilled* to see you're still alive." She whipped around, heading for the helm. The men shoved us forward, pushing us through a throng of crew that had gathered on the deck. To the side up near the quarterdeck, I saw the twins, their blond hair and height making them stand out like neon signs. They stood still, but their eyes widened, meeting mine in a moment of true shock.

"Captain?" Zuri called ahead. "Thought you might want to see the scurvy dogs we found trying to stow away onboard." Zuri addressed a man in a captain's hat, his back to me.

He twisted around.

Like a boat capsizing on a stormy sea, I felt my entire world flip over, sinking me under it.

The crooked, wicked smile I knew so well, one usually meant for our enemy, pulled on his mouth. "Kitty-Kat."

I barely breathed, nothing feeling stable under my feet.

"Gage…" I whispered.

My gaze darted between him and Zuri, trying to make sense of this. Batara had made him captain? This had to be under duress, right? They were the ones who could sail this ship. Batara had to be using them as slaves.

Yet why give them titles? Hand them such freedom if they are prisoners?

"Wow." Gage strode closer to me, his gaze rolling down my figure salaciously. He did that all the time, but this time, something about it itched my skin. "You look stunning for a dead person." His eyes met mine, his friendliness dropping away. "But you have to be a ghost. That's the only explanation for why you would abandon your crew. Leave them to be tortured, starved, and locked in a rat-infested cell to rot."

"I had to." My heart pounded. "He told me if I didn't get this nectar for his son, he would kill all of you."

"So where is this nectar?" He opened his arms. "Did you

come back offering it to him, finally here to save us?" The ridicule was thick in his tone.

"It's more complicated…"

"No. It's simple." He stepped up to me, snarling. "You left us here to rot."

"I'm sor—"

"I don't want to hear your excuses." He shook his head, his attention rolling over me again. "We were told you were dead, yet here you are *months* later. And I don't recall you ever trying to rescue us in that time. What do you think, Zuri? Think she's coming to *save* us now?"

My head whipped to her, my breath starting to clip, waiting for a sign, a glance from her that told me she was on my side. That this was all a ruse. I grasped onto the idea because it was the only thing that made sense. Except… that was not what I got. Rage and hate stabbed through Zuri's eyes to mine before she turned back to Gage, her chin rising.

"No, Captain." She shook her head, gripping the handle of my father's dagger she took from me. It was in her tone, her demeanor. I knew. My crew had turned their backs on me.

Declared mutiny.

Betrayal and guilt, anger and grief, all slammed together like a storm, my legs quivering.

"We *know* your true priorities." Gage's attention slid to Croygen with a pointed look. "I probably should feel giddy being in the presence of such a legend. The reason Katrina made every decision she did for centuries. Should I bow to the great Silver Tongue Devil?"

"A parade would have been nice," Croygen replied dryly.

Gage chuckled, though he was anything but amused. He stepped closer to Croygen, looking him up and down, sizing him up.

"Funny, Kitty-Kat." Gage stared at him, speaking to me, trying to subtly challenge the man who stood inches above him.

A small growl came from Croygen, who didn't like him using that nickname. "I thought he would be dead by now. I mean, wasn't that your whole plan. Revenge? Killing the man who murdered your father?" He peered over at me. "Or was that all bullshit too?"

"Things have changed—"

"Yes, they have." Gage cut me off. Tearing off his hat, he barreled up to me. "See this, Katrina?" He pointed at his half-sawed-off ear. The stump had healed over, but was gnarly and jarring. "This is what you let happen. Your command and decisions led us that night. Polly, Dobbs, and Ruby trusted you, and you got them killed." He spat. "And now Moses is dead too."

"What?" I gasped, acid running down the back of my throat. Moses was dead?

"Tortured to death in the middle of the square for all to see," he fumed. "He kept telling us he believed you were alive and you'd come back for us. Look where it got him. He's dead."

I glanced over at Zuri, needing confirmation, wanting to see her response, to comfort her. They had been like brother and sister. First to fight with each other, but first to defend the other to outsiders.

Anger tightened her jaw, seething hatred burning in her gaze. At me.

"I'm sure you can still visit what's left of his skull hanging on a spike at the palace." Gage drew my attention back to him.

I wanted to cry, to curl into a ball. Ruby, Dobbs, Polly, and now Moses were all gone. And it all led back to me.

"I'd think you'd blame the man who did it to you." Croygen gritted through his teeth. "Not turn your back on your captain, who went through hell to get back to you."

Gage didn't respond to him, his focus locked on me. For a moment, I saw hurt before he boarded himself up again.

"I realized I was the one who should have been in charge the whole time. To save *my* crew." He shook his head, baring his teeth. Somewhere in my gut, I felt a tug, Croygen calling my name, but I couldn't break away from Gage, disbelief making everything feel far away. "I should've known when even *Killian* couldn't take your bullshit anymore. He ran far away from you; you were that toxic. You know there was talk of mutiny then. Did you know that? But we all still believed in you. Trusted you would lead us when all you cared about was *him*." He flicked his chin to Croygen. "We're fools no more."

I couldn't find the words to speak or fight back. His anger and betrayal knocked me on my ass, but a huge part of me felt I might deserve it. That he was right. I had been so tunnel-visioned on Croygen, to being better, richer, more powerful. Though none of them complained when riches and fame rained down on us because of it.

"I was your trained lap dog for centuries." Gage got in my face. "Not anymore."

He stepped back with a smug grin.

"This is now *The Bloody Hangman*." He swung out his arms over my ship. Batara's symbol was on it, declaring who it flew under, but now I saw the name below. Something Gage always wanted. To be captain.

"This is *my* ship. And you are *trespassing*." He stared at me as his voice sang over the deck. "And you know what happens to those who trespass on my ship… we *kill* them."

CHAPTER 23
Katrina

Gage's words blasted over the ship like a cannon, knocking everyone into action, crying out for our blood.

Katrina! I heard my name bellow through me as Croygen slammed his elbow into the guard behind him, whipping around and grabbing his gun, shooting him dead in a blink. A shot rang right by my ear, and the man behind me dropped to the ground, snapping me out of my bewildered trance. Croygen pointed a weapon at where he had been. His eyes caught mine for a moment. A thousand words and lifetimes were spoken, a connection saying everything we didn't have to utter out loud.

Swiping up the discarded gun and sword from the guard, Croygen and I moved together, knowing our odds weren't great, but we'd go down fighting side-by-side.

Pandemonium roared down in a fury of chaos. The sounds of blades and howls of bullets crooned like a bad opera. Dramatic and shrilling, we pranced over the stage, fighting and killing those in our path.

Stay the fuck alive, Kitten. I felt Croygen growl through me, our movements in sync, our skill keeping us living in a sea of our enemy.

You too, pirate.

Clank! Clank! Pop! Our weapons sang loudly as we battered the circle forming around us, reducing the dozens of crew Gage had attack us. Yet it wasn't enough. We were outnumbered.

Out of the corner of my eye, I spotted a small, brown, furry object racing across the deck.

"Sprig!" I bellowed his name as a bullet pierced the wood where he just was, tossing his tiny body forward. "Nooooo!"

I reacted without thought. When I ran for him, a body rammed into mine, crashing us to the floor with a crunch. A fist slammed into my face, cracking across my cheek. "You deserve to die a horrible, slow death," Zuri snarled, her fury bubbling up. She always had a temper, a bad one, but it had never been turned on me. "You should feel all they did to us."

"Then go ahead," I snapped back, blood trickling down my face. "You want to kill me, Zuri? I got you out of poverty, helped your family. Now I'm your enemy?" I felt like they had been brainwashed. How long before torture broke you? Where they built you back in their image. What level of hell had they suffered when I was gone?

"I watched them slowly, so *inhumanely,* brutalize and butcher Moses. And he never stopped calling your name… like you were some god coming to save him." She spat on me. "I used to believe in you too, but now I see we were both fools. You should be the one in his place." She yanked out the dagger she took from me. My father's. How apropos to be killed by the very same dagger on the deck of a ship like he was. "You should die for what you did to us."

With a cry, the blade headed for my heart.

This was it. My end. And the only thing I thought of wasn't Moses or Zuri… it was Croygen.

Her body suddenly flew off mine, her head hitting the deck with a crack, her body going limp, the dagger falling onto the floor.

A huge blond man stood over me, his chest heaving, his expression stone, but his brown eyes were soft.

"Cane?" I gulped, sitting up and blinking at my savior.

He leaned over, offering his hand. I grabbed my father's dagger as he yanked me back to my feet. He was the quieter one compared to Ty, but his silence made me feel safe.

"You-you saved me." I blinked up at him.

"Of course. You are my captain."

"I am?"

"Always." He dipped his head, his voice low and deep. "Zuri and Gage let their minds be seduced. Let him poison them with words." His eyes darted around, looking for any threat. "Ty and I are faithful to you. Moses never forgot that either."

"Do you have her?" Ty ran up, his gaze taking me in, his shoulders lowering at seeing I was okay. He glanced down at Zuri's unconscious form, frowning. "We have to get out of here."

My gaze went back to searching for Croygen, finding him in the center. Just one shot, and he could be killed.

"Croygen!" I lurched for him.

"No!" Ty grabbed me. "You'll be killed!"

"I won't leave him to die!"

Pop! Pop!

Like fireworks, small explosions started to crackle and spurt from a group of barrels near the main mast. Dread sunk in my belly. Someone lit the gunpowder barrels. And I knew exactly who that someone was.

"I'd move it, *bhean chait*!" Sprig yelped, sprinting up my leg to my shoulder. "That thing is about to explode... like now."

"Not *again*..." I whined, spinning around. "Croygen!" I cried his name, feeling the twins on either side of me, taking their posts like they always did. "Croygen!" I bellowed, trying to find him through the throng of people. Everyone was running around the deck trying to get off the ship, causing bedlam, no longer caring who was friend or foe.

"Katrina!" Croygen's body rammed into mine, his arm going around me, his hand grabbing Sprig, tucking him into his chest right as the fuse hit the powder.

Boooooooom!

Our bodies flew in the air, catapulting into the bay like debris. Crashing into the salty water, I spun around like laundry. It took me a few moments to find which way was up, pushing for the surface. Sputtering, I broke through, gulping for air.

"Kat!" Croygen heaved in relief, swimming over to me. "You okay?"

"Yeah." I nodded. "You? Where's Sprig?"

"Did you see me flying through the air? Superman can kiss my furry butt!" Sprig sat on Croygen's shoulder. "I don't even need a cape! I am truly a God King!" He held up his arms. "It's a bird, it's a plane… noooo, it's Super Sprig! The incredible and divine Monkey God King Sprite!"

"Does his title keep getting longer?"

"Shush, peon! You only speak when Sprig, the *extraordinary* Monkey God King *Super* Sprite, tells you so!"

"There's definitely no living with him now." Croygen snorted.

"Ahhhhhhh!" He zoomed around Croygen's shoulder in fast circles. "I am a goooooooodddddddd!"

"No. Don't you dare pass out now," Croygen warned. "Not here."

"Ahhhh—" The monkey face planted in the water, Croygen instantly scooping him up, the sprite limp in his hands, snoring.

"And he did it anyway." Croygen rolled his eyes, treading closer to me, his eyes going up to the fire billowing from the mast. It wasn't destroyed completely, but the blast had certainly crippled *Revenge* for a few weeks. "We have to go."

My head dipped in agreement, seeing people rushing back on to put out the fire, my throat balling into a knot.

"I don't want to leave it," I whispered. It was my ship, my dream, my world at one time. And now it was in my enemies' hands, being captained by one of my ex-crew.

I felt betrayed. Assaulted. It tore me in half, like I lost everything I had worked for.

My home.

My friends.

Recalling Zuri and Gage's expression, their disgust and hatred, the pain sunk deeper. Knowing Moses died still believing I would come back for them. I was too late. For all of it.

"Kat," Croygen spoke firmly, but I felt his sympathy through the link. The understanding. He too had lost his ship to a friend who betrayed him.

Maybe I was having to pay for my father's crime.

A whistle speared by my head, splashing the water, jerking my head up to see a few of Batara's men lining up at the railing, shooting at us.

"Shit! Come on!" Croygen started swimming with one arm, keeping Sprig above water with the other. Both of us moved quickly to get out of firing range. Guards were probably already on foot, coming around the bay for us.

"Captain," a deep, familiar man's voice called, jerking my head. Cane and Ty were soaking wet and bleeding as they climbed up on a pier, motioning us over. We swam toward them, gunfire raining down on us as they pulled us out.

"We have to get out of here." Ty moved me in front, rushing us forward. "Find a hideout for a bit."

That was the problem. Zuri and Gage would know all our hideouts and safe places.

Croygen placed Sprig's sleeping body in his coat pocket, brushing back his wet locks. "It's been a while, but I know of a safe house in Chinatown." He motioned us to follow.

I glanced back at my ship a final time, grief flooding my chest. *I will come back for you.*

Without another word, the four of us darted into the alleys of Singapore, running for our lives.

The best way to get lost was to hide among the densest, most poverty-stricken parts of a city, which was most of it now. People didn't have time to care or take notice. They were just trying to survive. So, in the heart of bustling Chinatown in a cramped alley above a basic market, we disappeared.

"How do you know about this place?" I peered around the bare-bones one-bedroom apartment, which had four cots but only two mattresses. Along with a minuscule bathroom I wasn't sure any of the three huge guys would even fit in, and a living room/kitchenette, which contained a small table and chairs. The positive was it looked clean enough and had an escape ladder out the back window.

"Ummm." Croygen busied himself, checking out the sightline from the living room. "Long story."

"Ah." I dipped my head, hating that I felt a pang of jealousy. "A place to meet up with your *paramours*." I tried to sound flippant.

"In this dump?" He swung back to me, feigning being aghast. "Who do you take me for?" A cocky smile crept up his face, strolling toward me, his dark eyes sizzling over my skin. "No, *Katze*," he muttered, his body looming over me. "It was a safehouse for those who needed to hide out for a bit."

"From what?" My fingers curled into his damp shirt, unable to stop touching him.

"Opium trade." His throat bobbed, his gaze going down. I saw Ty and Cane moving around in my peripheral, sniffing and investigating every square inch. "Back in a very dark time, late eighteen hundreds, I got really heavy into trafficking it." He shifted on his feet. I felt the torment worming through him. "It's one of my only regrets."

"Why?" I asked because I sensed far more to the story than just getting into the drug trade.

"Because my daughter, Rez, ended up being one of the many victims of it. She was sex trafficked. Drugged, raped, and beaten in the club by a very sick man, by keeping her high and dependent. So out of her mind, she didn't care about anything except her next hit. Who knows, I might have been the one who helped the drug get to that club."

He hadn't talked about Rez much on our journey, but I could feel his love for her, the guilt he bore not being there for her.

"They would've gotten it no matter what."

"I know." His lips thinned. "Doesn't make it any easier."

"Captain?" Ty stepped back into the main room, Cane beside him, turning us to them. "All clear."

"Thank you." I stepped away from Croygen, peering at the three men. My head still tried to compute all that happened today.

"We all need to talk." I took one of the chairs at the table, my legs about ready to collapse on me. "I know this will be hard, but can you tell me what happened after you were captured?"

Cane's hands rolled up, a vein in his arm popping.

"Not in detail," Ty spoke strongly. "But Batara's torture was thorough—asphyxiation, electric shocks, beatings, mock executions…" He drifted off, seeing Cane stir on his feet. "The whole time he used you as the reason, the blame for our suffering, had us repeat it on a loop. And slowly, I spotted Gage accepting it. Zuri fought it longer, but after Moses was killed, she cracked too. Anything to stop the pain. It went from telling Batara what he wanted to hear to them starting to believe it. The more you agreed with him, the better things would be. Food, freedoms, a bed, a shower."

"The reward and punishment system." Croygen dipped his head up and down in understanding.

"Except the punishment wasn't necessarily on us if we did wrong." Ty glanced over at Cane, coming back to me. "Moses was killed because Zuri tried to fight back."

"What?"

"I think Batara suspected she was at a breaking point." Ty gulped. "Moses was murdered the next morning. And she was forced to watch every second of it."

I bowed over my legs, wanting to throw up. I knew awful stuff was happening, but to hear about it was different.

What Zuri must have gone through psychologically... The pain and grief so deep it had to be pointed at someone else. Her heart, soul, and mind broke all at once, her hurt twisting and morphing into something she could handle. And all she saw was I was the cause of it.

"Fuck." I stood up, tears sliding down my face, feeling the pain I caused all of them, the weight of my actions. One slipup, one wrong decision, changed everything that night.

Good and bad.

I never regretted that it had brought Croygen into my life, yet it didn't take away the regret, the guilt, over letting my crew down. Of getting half of them killed.

"Hey." Croygen tugged me to him, though I didn't want to be comforted. I didn't deserve it. "Kat."

"No." I pushed him away.

"Listen to me." He grabbed me again, and I felt his soul wrapping around me, easing my grief.

"No!" I thrashed against him, a sob working up. "I don't want you to make it better."

Warning growls sunk into the air, my two guardians stepping toward Croygen, their teeth growing into canines they bared at him.

"She said to back off," Cane muttered in a threat, their natural response to protect me.

"And I'm telling you to fuck off." Croygen faced the twins, his shoulders rolling back.

"And I'm telling you to get your hands off her." Ty puffed up his chest, his snout and teeth morphing.

"O-kay. Whoa!" I jumped between them. "Stop."

"Tell your pooches here—"

"Croygen." My palm pushed against his chest, my lids lowering on him. *Back off.*

His glare matched mine, and he exhaled at my order. His jaw locked tight. He shook his head and stepped back, but looked ready to lurch forward and fight if he needed to.

Turning to my men. "Guys, things are a little different." I went into a quick summary of what had happened since I left them, what Batara made me promise, and how Croygen fit in now. "You don't need to protect me with him. Ever. He's part of the pack." Pack was family to them. They'd kill and die for them. "You understand what that means?"

Ty and Cane glowered at Croygen, but nodded their heads.

"How did Gage get to be captain of my ship?" I turned the conversation back to them.

Ty licked at his lip. "After Batara felt he successfully broke him. He started to offer more freedom. Incentives. When Batara had trouble getting men who could successfully sail *The Revenge*, Gage told him he could do it with Zuri as his first mate." Ty swallowed. "Cane and I knew we could no longer trust them. Batara had bent and formed them to be his soldiers. They were now spies for him. We had to pretend we were with them."

"How do we know you're not pretending now?" Croygen confronted.

Cane's nose wrinkled with indignation, a growl humming in the back of his throat.

"Because." Ty stepped up in front of his brother. "We are

faithful to *our* captain. She saved us from a life of slavery. And…" He leaned into Croygen, the tension still thick between them. "We are excellent at sensing people's true character. If they are a good person or not."

Croygen crossed his arms, staring boldly at Ty, a challenge to dog-shifters, daring them.

The boys responded. Hearing their low growls, I stepped between them again. The situation needed to be defused.

"Guys, please." I held up my hands. "We are on the same team, and we need to trust each other. We already have too many enemies."

All three men huffed, looking away.

"Would you give us a moment?" I asked the twins.

"We'll go make a loop around. Look out for any threat." Ty stepped back for the door.

"Maybe get some food and supplies," Cane added, following his brother out, clicking the door shut behind them.

"Do we have to keep them?" Croygen grumbled. "Can't we have them rehomed?"

"Croy…" I sighed with a laugh, feeling disgusted that I found humor right now.

"What?" He shoved his hands in his jacket, pulling out a sleeping monkey. "We already have enough pets." He grabbed a cloth from the kitchen, bundling it up under Sprig and placing him on the table. "It's like a fucking zoo here. A cat, a gerbil, and two guard dogs that don't look housebroken to me."

Staring at Sprig's peaceful frame, I let my shoulders roll forward, the burden pulling them down. A sob hurtled up my throat, choking me.

"Shit." Croygen's arms went around me, holding me as I cried. For Moses, Ruby, Polly, Dobbs, for the pain Ty and Cane went through. And I cried for Zuri and Gage, the loss of my family, and knowing I was partly to blame for their betrayal. I couldn't say I wouldn't have broken either, taking the opportunity to be free, to sail as a captain, even if it was under someone else's flag. And I grieved for my ship. My dreams were being taken from me. I deserved to feel the burden. To feel this grief.

Croygen held me tight, giving me everything I needed without saying a word, pulling back when my sobs waned.

"You can't take on all the blame, Kitten." His thumbs wiped the tears from my face. "We are pirates. This is what we signed up for. It's the dice we roll every day. Good or bad. Riches and fame, or imprisonment and torture. Or death. It's what makes our blood sing, walking that line." His dark eyes stayed firmly on mine. "You made the decision you had to in that moment. And that is the responsibility of being a captain. Sometimes our choices don't have a right or wrong. We do our best with the circumstances we are given. And like you, Zuri and Gage made a choice too."

"But—"

"No, buts." He cupped my face. "Don't do what I did. I punished and hated myself for so long. Blaming myself for everything. Living in rage and hate." His nose touched mine. "I know what it's like to carry all that guilt. I didn't know Moses, but it doesn't sound like he would want you to punish yourself for something you can't change."

No, he wouldn't. Moses believed everything was connected and things happened for a reason. He wouldn't blame me at all. Which made it worse.

"I finally found you again. Live with me in the now." His mouth dragged over mine. "And take your pain and grief out on me, *Katze*."

Desire surged up my vertebrae when his mouth claimed mine hungrily, giving me no option but to follow him over.

Digging his hands into my hair, he walked me backward toward the bathroom, ripping the damp jacket and top from my body and dropping them in a trail across the floor. Pushing his coat off his shoulders, the heavy material smacked the tile, our need clawing through us, kicking us out of our shoes and pants.

Shuffling me into the compact space, he tore my bralette off my frame, then reached over and turned on the shower, his mouth never leaving mine.

"I'm gonna fuck you hard, Kitten," he rumbled in my ear, setting fire to my blood. "I want to feel every ounce of your anger, your pain. Use my cock as your confession booth. Let me feel every one of your sins. Feel the blood of your kills and the souls of your prey."

My mouth took his, my tongue ready to confess, to extradite my offenses. My hand unbuttoned his pants, shoving them down. I gripped his thick cock, causing him to moan, my pussy throbbing to feel him.

Stripping the rest of our clothes, he walked me under the water, washing away the film of salt, blood, and sweat. His mouth devoured, his tongue curling around mine, heating me up as cool water cascaded down on us. We weren't gentle or sweet.

This was an all-out war. To save my soul.

His body flattened me against the tile wall, his hands in my hair, his thigh parting my legs. Naked, I still needed to claw in deeper, to take everything from him. To find peace, feel anything other than pain.

"You can't hurt me, Katrina." He sucked on my bottom lip, biting it. "So let go."

His permission was a trigger, breaking my hesitancy and flooding me with the euphoria of giving over entirely.

Biting, hitting, and clawing, I let him experience my rage, encounter my guilt.

Croygen took it, only riling him up more, his dick throbbing against my stomach. My nails tore down his chest, my teeth nipping at his V-line, my lips sucking over the tip of his cock, both of us groaning as his taste slid down my throat. Taking him in farther, I sucked so hard his legs bowed. Croygen placed his hands against the wall with a loud moan, swearing under his breath.

"Kat…" There was a warning, but I didn't listen. I wanted to break every rule, tear down every wall, and burn everything to the ground. I wanted to make him bend. Have him completely in my power.

With a snarl, he pulled away, his breath ragged. "I know what you want." He grabbed me, pulling me up to my feet, twisting me around and pressing my breasts into the wall. Wrapping my hair around his palm, he tugged it, pushing my ass into him. "But I know what you *need*," he growled into my ear, sliding his cock between my ass cheeks.

With his free hand, he grabbed the shower head, moving it down and rubbing it over my clit.

I shuddered a noise when the pressure hit me, my fingers digging into the tiles as his cock threaded through my folds, getting so close before sliding close to my ass.

"Croygen…"

"I can feel you," he muttered. "Feel what you really need." His fingers parted me further before I felt the tip of him hinting at my entrance, making me feral with need.

Pinning me harder into the wall, he pushed in more before he pulled out again.

"Croygen, please."

"Hold this here." He moved my hand to hold the shower head, the water stream filling me. "Hold it tight, Kitten." His fingers pushed into my ass as the pelt of water rubbed at my clit.

"Oh gods!" I cried out.

"You better cry out my name instead." He took his hand away, his cock replacing his fingers, pushing into me. I jerked, my teeth biting down on my lip until I tasted blood, but soon the pain morphed into overwhelming sensations, his cock hitting every nerve.

"Oh fuck… Kitten…" He groaned, sinking in deeper. "Fuck. Fuck," he hissed, my ass curving into him until something snapped. I felt no pain. Nothing but need.

I became feral and wild. Losing all decorum. There was only primal and depraved.

I screamed, I yowled, I clawed at the walls and snarled as he fucked me. My legs spread more, riding the shower head as he drove in from behind, my pussy already spasming. I never wanted this to end, but at the same time, I couldn't stop the race to the climax.

"No," he grunted, yanking out of me, forcing a cry from me. He grabbed the shower head, placing it back. "Not fucking yet."

He flipped me back around and lifted me up, my legs wrapping around him. He shoved me against the wall, spreading me wide, plunging his cock into my pussy.

A sharp gasp howled from me, my body trembling with pleasure, so much it burned through my veins. Croygen bellowed, pushing to the hilt, fucking me so hard I lost air flowing into my lungs.

He felt so fucking good inside me. This was what I wanted even as I watched him fuck that woman against the wall. I knew how incredible it would be. Knew eventually it would be me in her place.

"Croygen!" My heels dug into his ass, my nails tearing into his skin, my sharp, elongated teeth biting down on his shoulder, flooding him with my rage and desire. I took it all out on him, letting him have full control, hammering into me as I let go.

"FUCK!" Croygen bellowed, his muscles jolting as my pussy clamped down on him with as much teeth and vengeance, buckling his legs, slamming him deeper into me as we crumbled to the floor of the shower, hitting a spot that had me jerking as if I had been electrocuted.

My body continued to ride him as wave after wave of his cum filled me, our hips bruising each other as we consumed each other's souls. Feeling everything the other did.

Overwhelming desire raged like a firestorm, ripping all my senses away, shutting down against the barrage of pain and pleasure. An entity floating through, understanding even in death, Croygen and I would find each other. There was no end or beginning. We fucked, lived, and died with the same breath.

I fell into his chest, the water raining down on us, our lungs desperate for air. My muscles shook violently, feeling how deep he still was inside me, how easily he could make me come again, though my body felt raw and exposed, my nerves too close to the surface.

"Fuck, Kitten," he rumbled hoarsely in my ear. His hands cupped my face, pulling it back enough to kiss me. Slow. Soft. His meaning in it struck my heart.

I love you.

Pulling back, I peered at him, a smirk dancing over his mouth, knowing I fully heard him.

"This." His hands moved down to where we were still connected, his seed gushing over his abdomen. "Needs to stay in here where it belongs." His fingers scooped up his cum, pushing it back inside me, rubbing it over my clit.

"Croy-en." I stuttered over his name, my eyes squeezing shut as another small orgasm brutally quaked through me, feeling him harden inside me. "Think I'm done with you?" His hips pushed up. Slow and deep, he moved inside me, his cock thickening and growing with every pump. "I will never be done with you."

A groan tipped my head back, and my body started to respond, already feeling the burn of pleasure clench through my thighs.

"Where we live or what we do?" He gripped my hips, controlling the methodical speed, compelling me to feel every inch of him, every vein and muscle. To experience this without the haze and frantic need we usually were consumed with. "I don't give a fuck. You want to be captain? Make all the rules? Fine." He stroked deeper, his eyes intent on me. "Want to sail around the rest of days tracking down your ship and avenging your enemies? I am by your side, Kitten."

"Croygen…" I tried to ride him faster, pleasure burning up my spine, my lids closing at the onslaught, sensing this orgasm might destroy me.

"No." He held me firmer, keeping his deep, penetrating strokes even. "Look at me, Kat."

Biting on my lip, I forced my eyes open.

"Keep them on me," he ordered. "Watch me fucking you, feel me invading your pussy." He picked up his tempo, making me whine with need. "Because it is mine. And when that door shuts for the day, I'm the one to make the rules."

"Co-Captain." I grunted, hearing my voice hitching, my climax crackling at my skin.

"Co-Captain?" He huffed, his hips moving faster. "That should be interesting."

"Until I get my ship back, then we sail them together as a fleet."

"Fleet? I like the way you think, Kitten." His palms slid over my breasts, pinching at my nipples. I moaned, my eyes rolling back. "But whichever ship, I'm still in charge in the bedroom." He wound his fist in my hair. "Got it?"

I nodded. Everywhere else was up for grabs.

"Now fuck the shit out of me, Katrina." He yanked on my strands, pulling me down as he slammed up into me.

I let out a scream. Punishing, cruel, and bruising, we challenged, we matched, we sank deeper into each other, feeling our bond knot with unbreakable certainty. There was no way to ever undo it. And I never wanted to.

I rode him, and he took my nipple into his mouth, nipping

down as he rubbed my clit. Blackness dotted my vision, a cry tearing from my soul as my orgasm ferociously overtook me.

And I went with the security my mate would protect me. Keep me safe. I had someone I could fully trust.

And to pirates, that meant everything.

CHAPTER 24
Croygen

My lids fluttered open, the late afternoon sunlight filtering through the curtains suggesting I had at least slept a few hours. My muscles were sore, and my bones ached, but a grin tugged at my lips, instantly seeking Katrina on the small cot, pulling her tighter against me, nuzzling into the back of her neck. My cock was ready to push back inside her, waking her up the same way I put her to sleep.

From the shower, I carried her limp body to the mattress, where I passed out right next to her, my body giving out the instant I set her down.

Sex with her? Fuck… I had no words, except *I want some more, please.*

Taking a deep breath of her smell, every muscle relaxed in a peace I never knew could be felt.

I could so get used to this. Seeing her next to me, feeling her naked body against mine. I never thought I'd want just one woman for the rest of my life, but there wasn't an ounce of me that wasn't completely hers. Was this what it was like having a mate? Even the idea of anyone else made you feel sick? Like you wanted to crawl out of your own skin.

I thought of all the times I had made fun of Ryker after he met Zoey. Now he was going to rub my face in it… and I was just fine with that.

Suddenly, I felt homesick. The reason I'd left, ran away, had completely vanished, and now I felt the hole in my chest they had filled. I missed them. So much of Wyatt's life I had lost because I couldn't face the void Lexie had left.

Lexie no longer felt like something I needed to run from. Let's be honest, she had followed me anyway. If anything, she was pulling me back, telling me it was time to go home.

Katrina stirred, putting my attention back on her. Brushing the hair off her face, I stared down in wonder. In such a short time, she had changed everything. I wasn't someone who believed in fate. I thought we made our own destiny, but I couldn't deny the choices and incidents that led to us sailing in at that exact moment and her climbing up onto my ship.

My hand slid over her hip, and she let out a small moan as my fingers parted her, my mouth craving the taste of her. I started to slide down her frame, wanting to wake her up with my tongue.

The front door swung open, hitting the wall.

Pirates lived and slept on guard, ready to pop up and handle attacks from all types of enemies (most of mine were scorned lovers or husbands of scored lovers), and we were tuned into the slightest shift in the air. Danger held a lot of weight in the atmosphere, a tangible energy.

Tension blasted through the apartment, boots hitting the tile.

Katrina jerked up as the door to our room swung open, my hand already gripping the gun I put under the pillow, ready to shoot.

Cane and Ty burst in, their expressions hard, their muscles constricted.

"What?" Katrina breathed out in fear, grabbing the sheet to cover herself, reading their demeanor.

"Batara's men are coming," Ty barked as Cane tossed the clothes we left in the hallway and bathroom at us. "We have to go now!"

Leaping up, Katrina snatched up her clothes, both of us getting dressed in a hurry.

"Are you sure they are coming *here*? Or just out looking for us?" Katrina followed them to the main room, shoving her shoes on.

"We overheard them." Ty reloaded his weapon as Cane packed the supplies they bought into a bag. "They know where we are."

"How?" I pulled on my boots. "This place is magic guarded. No one saw us come in here."

Ty loaded his gun with more bullets. "I don't know."

"We didn't stop and ask." Cane finished his brother's thought.

"Can I ask if any of you brought food?" Sprig climbed to the edge of a table. "Like a little snack before. Or maybe a full meal? I mean, I need nutrients first. It has to be lunch or dinner time, right? Supper? I'll take dessert first too."

"Spri—"

A crash banged downstairs in the hallway leading up, scrambling us into action.

"Go! Go!" I pushed Katrina toward the back window. "Sprig!" I screamed, seeing the monkey leap from the table to the stove. "We're not cooking you dinner."

"I got this pirate," he chattered. "They will be dazzled by the great, the super-duper, high Monkey-Sprite God King! They will fall to their knees!"

Boots clomped up the stairs, and a bang hit the door, making it wobble on its hinges.

"Sprig, come on!" I raced to the window, the twins already pulling Katrina through.

"Ty!" Kat's tone jerked my head toward her, seeing the figures climbing the ladder behind Ty. He whirled around, shooting down at them.

They were circling around us, cutting off our escape. And my mind kept rolling around with how the fuck did they know about this place?

Wood cracked as men broke through the front door, my mind racing in a panic.

"Roof!" I belted, lifting Katrina to jump up on the roof while Ty and Cane shot at the soldiers coming at us both from below and through the apartment. "Shift!" I yelled at her, sensing how badly Katrina wanted to become a cat. How easy it would be for her to escape.

"No!" She got up on the roof, shooting past the twins at the endless stream of men coming for us. Her desire to fight by my side overruled her instinct.

Scrambling up next to her, it took everything in me to not force her to get her safe. But I felt her, her stubbornness, her claim as my equal. She was by no means a damsel in distress and would always stand by my side and fight, as I would her.

"Sprig!" I yelled again, desperate to see him climbing from the flat's window. The twins scaled up to the roof as we covered them. The moment their boots hit the roof, I grabbed Kat's arm, pulling her as I ran over the uneven terracotta tiles, firing back at our assailants.

Bang! Bang! Bullets whizzed by us, forcing us to duck and weave, slowing us down as they gained on us.

In the distance, the bay sparkled with the final hour of daylight, a beacon of hope. Of freedom.

Water equaled sovereignty. Get a few miles off the coast, and Batara was no longer in his domain. He was in ours.

BOOOOOM!

The roofline shook as an explosion thundered behind us, throwing us forward, debris showering down around us. Covering my head, I peered back. Smoke billowed up from where the safehouse once was, now a chasm of rubble and dead bodies.

Acid poured into my gut, my chest clenching as I stared back in horror.

"Sprig…" I muttered, my head shaking. "No." I pushed

up, despair raking at my airways, a terror so deep I couldn't process anything. Though I knew Sprig was the one to do it. He took out more than half the men coming at us, but in doing so…

No, my head shook, not able to say the rest, not able to even think the rest. Did he sacrifice himself for us?

Popopopopop!

Gunfire skated by my face, grazing my chin and bolting me out of my trance. My stomach sank at the sound of yells from below. Batara's men filled the street, some on horseback, shoving people out of their way, a few holding black market automatic rifles pointed right at us.

"Kat!" I grabbed her, yanking her up, right as a spray of bullets dug into the clay tiles where she had been.

Survival instincts kicked me to act, to keep her safe. My legs pumped, my gaze noticing a gap between apartment buildings up ahead.

"Faster!" I bellowed, sprinting. My legs stretched, leaping onto the flat roofline with a crunch, rolling over it. Katrina easily leaped it, her body landing near mine.

Bullets shot out, and Hurricane hit the roof with a cry.

"Cane!" Kat moved for him, but the bullets ducked her back into me.

Ty landed by his brother.

"Brother!" His gaze went over Cane in worry, seeing where he had been shot.

"Fuck," Cane huffed, holding his side, blood leaking through his fingers. "Keep going. I'll catch up." He waved us to go, sweat pouring down his face, pain turning his skin pale.

"I'm not leaving you," Ty clipped in anger. "We stay together. Always."

Voices from below were moving in closer, trying to find ways to get up to us, while there were still more coming after us who didn't get blown up.

"You two go," Ty ordered us.

"No." Katrina shook her head.

"As long as we're alive, our duty is to keep you safe, Captain. You must go *now*," Ty gritted through his teeth, practically giving her an order.

It was the only way for us to all survive. To split up. I may not have liked the twins, but one thing we all had in common— keeping Katrina safe.

"No—"

"Meet us at the dock." I cut her off, clutching her arm, looking directly into Typhoon's eyes. "*Whatever* it takes." I wouldn't let Katrina lose any more people she cared about.

He bowed his head.

I sprang up, moving away from the twins, firing my gun at the guards about to leap over to us. Katrina discharged a flurry of bullets with me, tearing into the group, dropping the numbers to only a handful before our guns clicked empty.

"We have to go." I turned, pulling her with me, darting across the roof as the guards below yelled at us. Leaping from roofline to roofline, we raced down the spine of the buildings, heading for the water.

"We need to get down." I darted for an escape ladder, knowing we were too visible up here. Chinatown was busy, and Katrina and I were good at getting lost in a crowd.

Scaling down, my feet hit the pavement, my hands going to her waist, helping her jump down. Creeping to the end of the alley, I peeked out, only seeing shoppers and people going on about their day.

"Clear." I threaded her hand in mine, my head swiveling around as I pulled us out into the lane. We moved quickly and quietly but tried to appear as nothing more than a couple out walking, enjoying the impending evening and cooler breeze.

"Move out of the way!" a man's voice boomed in Mandarin, horse hooves clipping the road.

Glancing over my shoulder, people parted for Batara's men, the group leader spotting me. "Get them!"

"Kitten. Run!" I yelped, both of us taking off down the street, shoving and pushing through the crowds. Twisting, I yanked down food stall signs and pushed over crates, trying to put up any roadblocks between us.

Not caring about innocent civilians, the guards fired on us, darting us down alleys and through shops, trying to lose them.

Katrina's feet hit the ground fanatically, trying to keep up with mine. We wound through the streets, no longer hearing the yells after us.

"Did we lose them?" she panted, glancing over her shoulder.

"I think so." I motioned her to follow me, feeling the salty air from the bay drifting over my face. We were so close. We just needed to find a boat to "borrow" and get out of Batara's reach.

"This way." I retook Kat's hand. A persistent need to feel her, to know she was right beside me, had me wanting to touch her constantly.

We turned a corner, taking us right along the bay where restaurants and shops had resided before the Fae War. It now felt vacant and abandoned, used only for fishermen and tradesmen to hook up their ships.

Kat came to a dead stop beside me, a sharp gasp hitching her lungs. My eyes took a moment longer to see what she did.

A line of Batara's human guards waited for us, but the one in front, a stocky man holding a curved katana, was fae. Deep, old magic circled him, itching my skin.

"Gou," she whispered.

A choked cough came up my throat. "Gou?" I had heard of him. He was a proficient, twelfth-century samurai warrior. Ruthless, with no moral compass or loyalty to anyone. Including fae.

"He murdered Ruby," she whispered, more to herself than me. "Sliced her throat right in front of me."

Her fingers went to her father's dagger, mine to the blade I took off the dead guard on the ship. They were the only weapons we had between us, our guns out of ammo and my real sword back in Budapest.

"Kat." I swallowed as Gou stepped toward us, the line of guards following him, their guns pointed at us. "I don't think that's going to help us very much."

The thought of fleeing turned my stomach, but I was also a pragmatist. And I didn't like our chances of survival.

"On three, we run," I muttered to her. "One. Two. Thr—"

Her feet stayed rooted, her glare still on Gou. I realized she had cut me off, not letting me experience the blinding rage she felt, the overwhelming need to destroy him, to avenge Ruby. She gripped her blade.

"Dammit, Katrina. We can't win this." I wrapped my fingers around her wrist, yanking her with me. I got two steps before more guards came around the corner, blocking our escape.

"Fuck." I stepped back, my eyes going around, trying to find anything to use as a weapon. In the past, we might have had a chance, but nowadays with guns, we were shit out of luck.

Gou came for us, drawing up his sword. He didn't speak or waste his time. He didn't get off on prolonging it or torturing his victim.

He just killed.

"Kat!" I grabbed her, putting my body between them. My sword clanked against his katana, the power vibrating through me, rattling my teeth.

Grunting, he twisted around, his blade grazing my side. I barely got out of his way before it came back for me.

I was good, even fantastic with a blade, but he was better.

Batara's men moved in on Katrina, pulling me back to guard her.

"Croygen!" she screamed in warning as Gou's blade came down for me like a guillotine.

Bang!

I froze, trying to locate where the bullet hit me, when I saw Gou's eyes widen. A hole through his brain. Blood gurgled out of his mouth, and his body fell to the ground, revealing his killer behind him.

Ty stood there, his gun still pointed, his features more dog-like than human. Cane was only a few feet away, barely standing, shooting at anyone near Katrina, his side still leaking blood, his brow dripping with perspiration.

"Thanks," I breathed out.

"I did it for her," he snarled, shooting at others as the four of us clustered together. I pilfered the weapon off Gou, his katana solid in my hand, and picked up a gun from another dead body, firing at the guards.

"Come on!" I motioned them to follow, slipping us up the plank of an old wooden fishing boat with a small wheelhouse. Helping his brother, Ty plunked Cane down at the bow next to Katrina, both firing at the enemy as Ty untethered us. He pushed us out as the tiny, motorized engine, the same ones the Somalia pirates used, tried to turn over.

"Come on, come on." I tried to encourage it, the men only steps away from jumping on, their bullets splintering the wood of the boat.

The engine sputtered to life. "Go!" Ramming into reverse, the boat jerked back, struggling to keep up with my demand. Gunfire cracked along the tempered glass, forcing me to push harder on the throttle as I swung the wheel, curving us around, before slamming it into drive. The boat kicked forward with a sputter and cough.

"That would've been a lot fucking cooler if I was in a car," I muttered, my adrenaline pounding in my veins.

Kat and Ty moved to the starboard side, shooting back. A strange sensation tickled at the back of my neck, pulling my focus as if my intuition just knew.

She stood behind the men in the dusk-lit alley, the shadows painting her hair a deep purple.

Amara.

Sucking in, I blinked, and when I looked again, the alley was empty.

I wanted to believe the murky darkness was playing with my mind, making me see her. That there was no way she would be here, but my gut knew better.

"Fuck." I berated myself for being so stupid.

She knew about the safehouse. Amara was with me many times when a drug trade went bad and we had to hide there. We used the back exit before. She would know exactly where we were. Where I'd be hiding. How to trap us.

"Hurry!" Ty pounded on the window, breaking me out of my thoughts, noticing Batara's men getting on fancier boats they had at the dock.

We weren't safe until we got out to sea, to international waters.

The handful of boats with much better engines roared behind us, gaining speed quickly.

"Faster!" Ty yelled again.

"I can't!" I snapped back. "This thing isn't made for a boat race. Unless you and your brother want to jump out and lighten our load."

Ty glowered back at me through the window.

"It's an option." I shrugged.

Bullets tore at the old rotting wood, the engine sputtering in strain.

"No, no, come on, baby." Sweat dripped down my spine, and I pushed the throttle more. "Just a little more." Passing some of Singapore's old icons, I saw the open ocean past the Marina Bay. Two hundred nautical miles beyond that, we were free.

Hitting slightly rougher water, the boat's engine crackled, dying out.

"Fuck!" I bellowed, trying to turn the engine over, only hearing it snort and gasp. "Please, please…"

Crack!

The window by my head splintered, the safety glass not breaking, but it would only take one more shot before it would give way.

"We're almost out of bullets!" Ty banged on the window again. "They're gaining on us!"

"I know!" I tried again to get the engine started. It rolled over and then died a horrific, gasping death. "Fuck. Fuck. Fuck!" The buzz of the other motors felt like nails in the back of my brain, their boats parting, ready to circle us.

"Croygen!" Katrina's voice popped my head up, her arm pointed forward. My gaze jerked to follow her gesture, my eyes widening at the sight before me. Like the sea goddess Calypso was offering up a gift, bequeathing help to her faithful sailors.

And I've been a very good boy.

The majestic black beauty glided over the water like a dream and nightmare all at once, the skull moniker flapping proudly in the breeze, giving no mistake to who it was or the power it bore.

The death that would rain down.

"Yesssss!" I screamed, coming out of the wheelhouse, my heart exploding at seeing my ship sailing for us, dwarfing all the tiny boats, including us. "Oh, baby, how I've missed you," I spoke to my ship, my heart feeling like my family was truly together.

Gunfire poured down on the boats around us, circling us in a bubble, like being in the middle of the eye of the storm. My ship had to stop where it was, the water getting too shallow for it to proceed. There really wasn't any way they could reach us. Our boat was nothing but a bobbing buoy.

"We have to swim."

"What?" Cane's already pallid face bleached. "I'm not

crazy about open water. Plus, I'm bleeding. It's like an invitation to sharks."

"Yeah, and they love the taste of dog."

"Croy." Kat sighed, climbing over the railing with me and looking at the twins. "You'll be okay."

"Yeah." I nodded sardonically. "Just swim really fast." I dove into the water, feeling more than hearing Katrina scold me, making my lips part in a smile as I swam for my ship.

Reaching the port side, I clung to the rope ladder, waiting for Katrina to start up first.

"You really are an asshole," she teased, pulling herself up.

"You know who you fell in love with." I winked.

She paused for a moment, her mouth parting. It took me a moment to realize what I said. It wasn't a shocking claim. We were mated, but we hadn't said that word yet. Not out loud.

"Yeah." Her gaze met mine. "I do." She swallowed, her cheeks pink. "I lo—"

The twins swam up, ending our moment. She turned away, climbing up to the deck.

"Sharks didn't eat you?" I grumbled. "Of course. My luck." Following Kat, I scaled up, Scot grabbing my arm and tugging me in.

"You guys have impeccable timing." I clapped him on the back.

"Thank Haoyu." He motioned to the man standing near the helm.

"You're still here?" I pulled off my drenched jacket.

"Yes." He bowed.

"He's not the only one." Scot nodded to the people still shooting at Batara's men. Zidane, Vane, Corb, and…

Cooper and Annabeth.

"What the hell?" I shook my head. "I thought you guys were heading back to Seattle."

"We don't walk away when family needs us." Annabeth

lowered her gun, walking over to me with a smile. She glowed even more than she did before. The fae magic worked through her system, turning her into some fae goddess. She was illuminated from the inside out, appearing happier and stronger than I had ever seen her.

Pulling her into a hug, I squeezed her tight.

"Ugh, you're soaking, and you smell like brine." She pushed me away with a smile, then looked around. "Where's Sprig?"

Her question popped every protective bubble I had put around myself, not daring to even think of him since the explosion. I gave him a lot of shit, but that was what we did. He did feel like my little brother. And the love I felt for him… I sensed the hole burrowing into my chest, exactly in the outline of the sprite who stole everyone's heart.

"Croygen, where's Sprig?" Annabeth stepped back, intuition bristling her shoulders.

I wasn't able to breathe, the agony almost crumpling me over.

"Anna…" I could barely get out her name, my words evaporating on my tongue. Everything felt in slow motion, seeing Ty and Cane climb onto the deck, the flag snapping in the air like a whip. "He-he didn't make—"

"How DARE you peons treat the high lord, super Monkey-Sprite God King in this manner." The voice speared through my chest, whirling me around to a drenched monkey on top of Cane's shoulder, his face furrowed. "I smell like wet dog now."

"Sprig?" My cry bottomed out, my head and heart still not wanting to fully believe what my eyes saw. "I-I thought…"

"That might be your problem, butt-muncher. You tried to think."

"Sprig!" I couldn't stop. Barreling over to him, I swiped up his tiny, wet body from Cane, holding him tight against my chest. A sob squeezed out, turning into a wheeze.

He was alive. He was here. He was safe.

"I can't breathe, pirate." He tried to push his head out of my hands. "You're trying to kill me. Again! I mean, you didn't even get me lunch before. Or was it dinner? Ohhhh, is it too late for pancakes? Do you smell dog too? Oh, but a honey-dipped hotdog would be satisfactory. I mean, until you got me a proper meal."

"Shut up, gerbil." I kissed his head. My lids squeezed for a moment, taking a huge exhale, needing a moment. Katrina didn't touch me, but I felt her there, her body calming mine though she was feet away. "How? How did you escape?"

"Please." Sprig rolled his eyes, squirming from my hands and sitting in my palm. "Who do you think I am?" He motioned to himself, taking my notice of his singed tail. "I am a god! Fire does not dare touch me. Death flees in my presence. Danger is in awe of my power."

"Really?" I tried to hide my smile. "And what happened here?" I picked up his overcooked tail.

"It dared for a moment, but then I put it in its place."

"You ran for it." I chuckled.

"Whatever. I caught up with those two mutts on the roof after."

"Then he passed out." Cane rumbled, holding his side. "I stuffed him in my pocket."

"And you didn't tell me?"

"Between which time were we being shot at did you want us to chat?" Cane glowered.

Fair enough.

"Thank you." I held Cane's gaze. He dipped his head, both of us looking away quickly, not liking having to be nice to each other.

"Zid, can you look at his injury?" I asked my crew member, nodding at his still bleeding wound.

"Sure." Zidane motioned for him to follow, both brothers going down into the galley.

"Wait, that man makes the food, right?" Sprig already jumped off my shoulder, darting after Zid. "Do you have honey knots? Honey churros? Honey meatballs? Honey chicken nuggets in honey dipping sauce? Honey vanilla pound cake…" His voice disappeared under the ship after the men.

Fuck, I loved that little sprite.

"Ummm, Captain?" Vane called from the railing. "I think it's time to go."

Glancing past him, I saw a Chinese junk ship sailing out of the port, Batara's flag waving from it, heading for us.

"Tsai!" I yelled out her name. "It's time for your magic."

"Boy, my magic has been dropping men to their knees since my first husband."

"That one dropped from death."

"Not his adopted son." She cackled, wiggling her barely there eyebrows. "Wow, that man knew what to do with his tongue. And his sword."

"Wait." Katrina whipped around, her mouth parting. A smile grew on my face, knowing her schooling on my ship as a kid was telling her exactly who this woman was. "Are you… are you Ching Shih? One of the most famous women pirates in the world?"

"Shhh." I winked at Kat. "We don't use that name anymore. *That* woman died a long time ago."

"Retired!" Tsai cranked the wheel. "Though I thought when you said I'd be surrounded by men all the time, there'd be a lot more sex."

"Oh my gods… I knew it!" Katrina stared at Tsai in disbelief as the old woman steered the ship away from the coast, turning us out to the open sea with grace and swiftness. "But why change it to Tsai's name?"

"Because he had me screaming it out so much." She hooted. "His father was an asshole, but Tsai… now I really enjoyed him. You know he died while I was having sex with him. Just couldn't handle it. Rode him too hard." Tsai's white eyes stared up at the sky like she could still read the stars, dictating the exact direction we needed to go. "Thought I'd honor him."

"I can't believe this," Kat muttered to me. "She's a legend."

"So are you, Kitten." I brushed my shoulder into her, drawing her attention to me. "And if I die, I hope to go out with you riding me too." Her eyes flickered with heat, telling me I might get my wish later. I turned to her, the breeze blowing her hair, the sunset glowing over her face. "Until then, you ready for more adventures? Make our own legends? The tales of Puss in Boots and the Silver Tongue Devil."

Her hands slid up my face. "I want forever with us pirating and sailing all over the world."

"Okay to make a stop in Seattle first?" I drew her closer, wrapping my arms around her waist.

She smiled, her head turning to the coastline, the last bit of light reflecting off the buildings. But I knew where her thoughts were, the pain of what she left behind here.

"We will come back for it." I nuzzled into her. "Someday we will get the *Revenge* back." I knew what the ship meant, the loss of her crew, their betrayal. "Until then, I hope you will make this your home, Co-Captain."

"Things will get interesting."

"How we like it." I tipped my head into hers.

"I see a lot of fights ahead."

"Guess we'll have to battle it out in bed."

"You know I'll win."

"I told you I was in charge there." I knew she would probably win in there too. There wasn't anything I wouldn't do for her, though I would put up a fight just to see her get riled up.

"If we are to do this, we have to change the name." She nodded up at the Jolly Roger.

"What were you thinking?" Swallowing, knots wound up my gut. That had always been my moniker. My signature.

A seductive smile turned up her lips as they brushed up against mine hungrily.

"Puss and the Pirate."

"Sold." My mouth claimed hers, the ocean air wrapping around us. Her lips tasted of salt, sea, and home.

"Please, watch over my girl." Rotty's voice replayed in my head.

It might not be the way he imagined, but I would keep a very close watch over her until I was no longer of this earth. And I would make sure she was always safe, happy, and loved.

And thoroughly fucked. Multiple times a day.

What can I say… Yo ho… It's the pirate's life for me.

EPILOGUE
Croygen

The sun sparkled off the bay water. The cool air had this part of the country deep in autumn, with a hint of winter on the horizon.

My knuckles curled into the wood railing, and I kept my gaze steady on the coastline, feeling a bundle of excitement and fear at once. I couldn't see them yet, but I knew they were there. Waiting. Watching me sail in like I sailed out of their lives years ago.

"Hey." I felt Katrina long before her body settled beside me at the taffrail. It seemed there wasn't a place she went where I couldn't pinpoint her or reach out and have her come to me instantly.

Like she did me. And I seemed to know when she consciously and unconsciously wanted me to find her.

There wasn't much of this ship we hadn't fucked on. And it seemed to be an unspoken competition with Cooper and Annabeth, which I'm not sure I wanted to think about. AB was like a pubescent fae, coming into the fae magic. It hit her hard, which all of us could testify made you horny as fuck. Let's say she wasn't so sweet and demure when it came to Cooper anymore, and he was no longer afraid to let his Dark Dweller

330

out with her. It got loud, and there was some property damage between us all.

Scot, Vane, and Zid had to stop a few times at ports to get *our* energy out of *their* systems. I actually think Tsai went to shore last time. That was *definitely* not something I wanted to think about.

Hoayu departed us not long after Singapore with triple the payment that would have been customary and a promise of more.

"Thank you, my friend." I bowed to him. "You don't know the honor we bestow on you for all you have done."

"The honor is mine." He bent his head in return, peering at all of us. "There is a Chinese proverb: *An invisible red thread connects those who are destined to meet, regardless of time, place, or circumstance. The thread may stretch or tangle, but will never break.*" His gaze met mine. "We will meet again."

And I believed that. Hoayu's life was threaded through ours now, and I had no doubt we would see each other again. Probably sooner than later. Plus, he was a handy person to have around. Just wished he could drag my whole ship through one of those portals.

"You okay?" Katrina's hand rubbed down my arm, drawing my attention to her.

"Yeah." I nodded.

"Liar."

"Not sure why you bother asking, then." I winked at her. We had yet to really learn barriers with each other, to give each other a little privacy, which would come in time. I kept expecting to freak out at not being able to hide my emotions from her. That she would sense the buzzing of my thoughts and feelings. But it didn't bother me like I thought it would.

"They love you." She nodded toward the coastline. "They just want you happy."

I knew that, but I still couldn't hide the weight I felt

creeping back on my shoulders the closer we got. The guilt and heartache of Lexie.

Curving to Kat, I realized a lot of my nerves were coming from her. "Are *you* okay?"

"Oh, sure." She leaned on the railing. "Meeting the family, who, no matter what, will look at me, thinking Lexie should be here next to you, not me."

"Hey." I grasped her arms, swinging her fully to me. "That's not what they will think at all." My palm cupped her face. "Lexie or not, you were always my future, Kitten." Her stunning eyes flicked up to mine. "I was always meant to find my way back to you." I kissed her nose. "Plus, you already know half the family. And they love you." I nodded back to AB and Cooper.

I still felt her nervous energy, knowing it was Zoey she was most anxious over. She wanted Zoey's acceptance, knowing how important she was to me and how much her approval meant.

"Is the badass ruthless pirate, Puss in Boots, actually scared?" I muttered against her mouth, my lips grazing hers. "She can drop brutal men to their knees, slice them in half, but is terrified of meeting my family?"

"Give me someone to stab anytime over this." She folded her arms, pretending not to be affected as my teeth nipped at her lip. "And I can't cut anyone in half anymore. You lost my boots, remember?"

Scoffing, I grinned against her skin. "I will get you new ones."

"Promise?"

I lifted my head, sparks dancing in her eyes with the challenge.

Grabbing her face, I kissed her deeply, my tongue curling around hers. "I *promise*," I rumbled into her ear, her body shivering with desire, feeling my vow settle in right between her legs, where I wanted to claim it later.

"Land a-hoe!" Sprig jumped onto my shoulder, his voice yelling in my ear.

Kat leaned back, laughing.

"It's land *ahoy*—never mind." I palmed my face, shaking my head.

"Oh, I get it! You land-a-hoe. That's your reward when you get there?"

"Yep." I nodded, taking Kat's hand and smiling down at her. "That's exactly what it means."

"Pam does not approve of being called a hoe."

"Land a-farm animal doesn't have the same ring to it." I fought back my laugh.

"No, but she's okay with land-a-goat-goddess-queen." Sprig patted Pam's head from his backpack. "Right, baby?"

"Good for you, Pam. Demand respect." Kat spoke back to her like she was real, winking at me.

Groaning under my breath, I darted my gaze to her. "Were you demanding respect when I was spanking you last night?"

"As long as you call me your pussy-goddess-queen while you do it."

My molars clenched together, my cock responding instantly to her, making her smile smugly at me. "So gonna pay for that later, Kitty-Kat."

"That better be another promise."

Fuck.

"Look! Look!" Sprig started hopping up and down on my shoulder, cutting through the heated moment. I turned my gaze to the shore, pulling AB and Cooper to the railing with us. "*Bhean! Bhean!*" he cried out, going in circles over my shoulder, jumping from me to Katrina, to AB and Cooper and back again. "Viking! *Buachaillín!*" That was his name for Wyatt, meaning boy. "MATTY!"

Like an arrow, I inhaled sharply as the figures became clearer and larger the closer we sailed.

It was as if they had been waiting since they watched me sail away, the vacancy still apparent, but it no longer hurt as much to see them.

Zoey's brown hair was pulled back in a ponytail, and she was even more beautiful than I remembered. A watery smile appeared on her face, her green eyes bursting with excitement and love. She stood on the dock, Matty tapping his paws excitedly while the intimidating blond-haired Viking towered next to her. Ryker held Wyatt with one arm, the toddler squirming and waving excitedly as my crew prepared for berthing.

"Oh my gods!" Annabeth squealed next to me, her hand on her mouth, tears flowing down her face, hopping up and down, ready to explode off this ship. "Wyatt! He's grown so much, I swear."

Tsai sailed us smoothly in while Vane, Ty, and Zid pulled down sails. Cane and Corb tied us up as Scot pulled the gangway.

It was barely down before Annabeth and Sprig were tearing off, running toward our family so freely and happily. Cooper jogged right behind.

Nervous energy fluttered in my chest. The sudden need to run, to avoid the emotions attacking me had me staring at the exit, my feet stuck.

Katrina's fingers laced through mine, her hand squeezing tight. She didn't need to say anything. She was there by my side. Whatever I needed.

My anchor.

Swallowing, I rolled back my shoulders, laying up a wall as I strode off the ship, Katrina right next to me.

Zoey was gushing over Annabeth, her expression in complete shock and joy at seeing Annabeth's transformation to fae.

Then she stopped, her head swinging to me.

I thought I was prepared. I thought I could smile, shake hands, and hug without much fanfare. We were excited to see each other, all the hard stuff behind us.

As her green eyes met mine, everything I held as defense dropped away.

Being so young when my family died, I never had a real home. I jumped around, never putting down roots. Never having people, I was able to completely be myself. Where I wasn't captain, where I wasn't ruthless or charming. Katrina had changed that, but now it made me realize what home really meant.

It wasn't a place.

It was these people.

A cry broke from Zoey, her magic jumping her right to me, crashing into me, her arms going around me while her sobs filled my ears.

At that moment, everything broke.

The guilt, heartache, denial, grief, anger—it all flowed out like an infection, needing to be let out, exorcising all the poison and pain.

As I held Zoey, I no longer had a choice to barricade myself. It all came crashing in, forcing me to feel everything. And I let it. We expelled our loss and heartache together, filling the space with love, forgiveness, and understanding.

I should have been there for her instead of leaving. She, most of all, was devastated by her foster sister's death. But all I saw was me. My pain.

"I'm so sorry," I croaked, tucking her tighter into me. "I'm so sorry."

"No." She shook her head and pulled back, her face dripping with tears. "There is nothing to be sorry for. Not here. Not with us."

My eyes filled up with more tears. "I shouldn't have left you guys."

"You came home. That's all we need." She embraced me again. Glancing over her shoulder, I caught Ryker's white eyes. He dipped his chin, and I pulled back from Zoey, walking straight to him. We had never hugged or even admitted we liked each other, but Ryker had been part of my life longer than anyone. Our bond strung us together over centuries. He was my brother. Good and bad.

His beefy arms embraced me, turning enough to not squeeze Wyatt. "Glad you're home." Ryker pounded my back. "But did you have to bring the furball back? It was so peaceful here."

A short laugh hitched my throat. "Sorry, my babysitting duty is done." I leaned down to Wyatt. "Hey, little man, do you remember me?"

Wyatt cooed, lifting his arms to me. "Unfle Mofen."

Laughing, I picked him up, his chubby arms hugging me.

"Sorry, man, closest we could get." Ryker shrugged with a half-smile.

"Answered to worse." I tickled his tummy, hating all the time I had missed with him.

Turning to Katrina, I ran my hand through her hair, pulling her to me and putting Wyatt on my hip.

"Everyone, I want you to meet Katrina. She's…" I took a breath. "My mate."

There was no shocked gasp or exclamation like I was prepared for.

"No, shit," Ryker scoffed. "We sensed that shit before you even made port."

"Nice to meet you, Katrina." Zoey stepped closer.

"Kat," Kitten replied. "Kat's fine."

"Welcome to the family, Kat." Zoey pulled her in and hugged her, shoving past all the awkwardness, making Katrina part of the family.

Lexie would always be here, a missing piece we would

have to acknowledge every day because we'd never stop missing her. Loving her. But instead of a vacant spot, I felt her there. And she was smiling.

We had all been through so much together, the absence only showing me the binds that tied me to this group. No matter where I was in the world, these people were my family.

And wherever they were, I called home.

Katrina

Six months later

The wind flapped at the tied-down sails, the ship creaking as if slowly waking up after a cold winter, stretching its back like a cat.

The breeze on the sunny day was still chilly, winter still trying to cling to the air. But every day spring crept in, the flowers blooming and turning everything lush and green here.

I had never lived this far north in America, and though there were times I had enough of the rain, longing for the warm beaches, the beauty here was breathtaking.

Scot, Corb, Ty, and Cane were loading the ship below me, carrying hundreds of crates into the storage, sinking the ship down a few feet under the weight of merchandise—items from the Unified Nations people would pay in abundance to get their hands on in the Eastern Bloc. All directly from King Lars himself.

The demon king was not at all what I expected. He was *more*. Intense, powerful, sultry, scary, and dominant, but also gracious and kind, especially when he was around the family.

And though that man was one of the best-looking guys I had ever seen, his mate, Fionna, was as equally stunning.

338

Everyone I had grown to love here was—Rez, Ember, Zoey, Queen Kennedy and her two adorable hellion twins, Nic, Torin, Ryker, and *every one* of the Dark Dwellers… holy shit. I kept teasing Croygen that if I wasn't mated to him, I'd be making a home at the dweller ranch.

Every time I told him that, the harder and kinkier he would fuck me that night. You'd think he'd put two and two together by now… I was doing it purposely for that outcome.

"You don't think I know." His deep voice growled in the back of my ear, his arms coming around me at the rail, locking me in.

Sucking in, desire shivered through me, capturing my breath. My body's response to him wasn't letting up like you'd think after six months of being together nonstop. It cranked up higher and hotter. I was so fucking addicted to him, so in love with him, I almost didn't recognize myself.

It excited me that this mated connection always made us feel vibrant and new, like I couldn't think of anything else until he was inside me. The need was so intense it blurred my vision.

"I know you, Kitty-Kat." He leaned in, nipping at my ear, his cock pressing against my ass. "But I'm fine playing your game." His nose dragged down the curve of my neck.

"Croygen…" I moaned, between a whimper and a warning.

"The moment we're out to sea, I'm tying you to the helm and fucking you against it."

Sucking in sharply, I felt him kiss my neck before stepping back, favoring his one leg. He didn't talk about it much, but I knew the wound from the necromancer's blade still ached. A permanent scar from their poisoned weapon of death. As if the kiss of the steel had branded him, marked him as theirs later. They would have to deal with me if they ever wanted to claim the rest. It would be a fight to the death. And I'd use every one of the necromancers to protect him.

"Captain… I mean Captain*s*." Scot emphasized the last part, twisting me around to see him. It was going to be a work in progress to figure out how this would operate between us. Two stubborn hot-heads in control. This might be a disaster.

"Everything is loaded, and Tsai is set to sail," Scot reported.

"Thanks." Croygen's head turned back to the dock. Rez, Zoey, Ryker, Wyatt, AB, Cooper, and Matty were all there to say goodbye. My throat thickened, already missing the family I had grown to love. Rez, Zoey, and I probably bonded the most, all of us clicking like we had known each other for years. And the shit we gave Croygen together was always fun. His daughter and he had a unique relationship, more friends than anything, but I saw the deep love and respect between them. One night at Christmas, the two of them sat away from everyone else and talked. Really talked. Still trying to figure out what role they played in each other's lives. It wasn't roses and rainbows, but I think they both walked away feeling in a much better place. I know there wasn't anything Croygen wouldn't do for her.

With me, there were also some bumps along the way, the slip of Lexie's name instead of mine, a memory of Lexie and Croygen together. But I knew they cared about me. And Lexie became more like a family member I never got to meet but thought I would have adored. She sounded feisty as hell and gave it back to Croygen.

Waving at them, I bit down on my lip, trying not to cry.

"We'll be back." Croygen kissed my head, his hand rubbing my back. "Roots and sails."

"Roots and sails." I repeated our new mantra. We made a pact that every five to six months, no matter what, we'd return. I doubted we'd make it that long. Wyatt was growing too fast, and honestly, I loved having a big, crazy family.

Christmas was so much fun; Sprig passed out in the

mashed potatoes doing snow angels while singing about saint honey tits. One drunk and naked pixie named Cal tried to swim in the butter while the serious pixie, Simmons, kept skidding off the table every time he tried to land using his mechanical wings. It was chaotic, crazy, and I think I was drunk for three days. Don't play *I never* with Dark Dwellers and demons.

It reminded me of the time on the ship when I was young, before everything got twisted up. The family I had been aching for, I had—and more.

Ty and Cane untied us, pushing us out as Tsai reversed us into the bay, Zid and Vane pulling up a few of our sails.

"Look up." Croygen nudged me to peer up high up the mast where the Jolly Roger snapped and waved.

"Oh my gods." A smile took over my face, seeing the new skull with a pirate hat and patch over its eye. Below it was a pair of tall boots and the moniker *Puss and the Pirate* scrolled across. "Croygen…" My eyes watered up again. Seeing that hit hard. He was making sure I knew this was our ship, our home.

We were in this together.

"And as I promised." He waved Vane over, who held up a pair of tall, heeled boots, almost an exact replica of what I had before. But these were even sexier than the other ones.

"Got these specially made for you in Spain." Vane winked at me, handing them over. "The best craftsmanship and leather you will find anywhere."

"These are gorgeous." I gasped over them, petting the leather like it was sacred.

"Of course they are. He put me in charge of getting them." Vane flipped them over in my palm, showcasing the bottom of the boots. "Specifically crafted for our captain." Two daggers were embedded in the heels.

"Oh my gods… thank you so much." I almost choked over my words, my gratitude overwhelming me. Croygen's crew had accepted me with no pushback. That wasn't easy, I know.

And they adjusted to Cane and Ty being part of the crew with more ease than I was expecting.

Though I knew both these gifts were all Croygen. Looking up at him, I hugged the boots to me, letting him feel my emotions.

"Don't think you won't be wearing *only* those later, when I bend you over the wheel," he growled into my ear, hardening my nipples instantly.

I would make sure he felt every ounce of my appreciation.

A noise worked up his throat; he probably felt exactly what I wanted to do. He went to the railing, staring back to the dock at the people lined up at it, tapping his chest for each one of them.

"Wait…" He paused, his eyes going big. "Where's Sprig?"

"Get out! That honey hollandaise sauce is for the chicken. Get out of the bowl!" Zidane's voice bellowed from below.

"Oh, fuck." Croygen's head dropped.

"Now your fur is in the sauce, monkey."

"How dare you address me by a common name. You refer to me as your Superior Highness, Super-Mega-Sprite, the Divine Deity, Monkey God King!"

"The mega is new." I grinned at Croygen, elbowing him.

"Not too late to turn back." He nodded at the shore. "Toss him overboard."

"What would be the fun in that?" I shrugged one shoulder.

We both knew Zoey or Ryker could use their Wanderer power and jump and get him anytime.

Croygen's fingers wrapped around my arm, pulling me into him with intensity. "Under this flag, we will sail together, *Katze*." He held my face. "The sea is our empire… take what you can."

"Give nothing back," I whispered hoarsely, finishing the sentence before our mouths crashed together hungrily, sealing our declaration with desire, an unvoiced promise.

There was a ship and a sword out there we needed to get back. We were not the people who forgot. Who let bygones be bygones. No. We sought revenge, battled with vengeance, killed with cruelty, and fucked in their blood.

Together, we would ride the seas and seek those who had betrayed us.

A crew, a ship, and a sword in a fae lord's hands.

Our adventures were just beginning. And those who crossed us were going to learn.

Dead men tell no tales…

The End

Thank you to all my readers. Your opinion really matters to me and helps others decide if they want to purchase my book. If you enjoyed this book, please consider leaving a review on the site where you purchased it. It would mean a lot. Thank you.

ABOUT THE AUTHOR

USA Today Best-Selling Author Stacey Marie Brown is a lover of hot fictional bad boys and sarcastic heroines who kick butt. She also enjoys books, travel, TV shows, hiking, writing, design, and archery. Stacey is lucky enough to live and travel all over the world.

She grew up in Northern California, where she ran around on her family's farm, raising animals, riding horses, playing flashlight tag, and turning hay bales into cool forts.

When she's not writing, she's out hiking, spending time with friends, and traveling. She also volunteers helping animals and is eco-friendly. She feels all animals, people, and the environment should be treated kindly.

To learn more about Stacey
or her books, visit her at:

Author website & Newsletter: www.staceymariebrown.com

Facebook Author page:
www.facebook.com/SMBauthorpage

Pinterest: www.pinterest.com/s.mariebrown

TikTok: @authorstaceymariebrown

Instagram: www.instagram.com/staceymariebrown/

Goodreads:
www.goodreads.com/author/show/6938728.StaceyMarie_Bro
wn

Stacey's Facebook group:
www.facebook.com/groups/164836894537 6239/

Bookbub: www.bookbub.com/authors/stacey-marie-brown

ACKNOWLEDGEMENTS

Kiki & Colleen at Next Step P.R. - Thank you for all your hard work! I love you ladies so much.

Mo &Wendy - Thank you for making it readable! So lucky to have you both to make me sound intelligent!

Jay Aheer - So much beauty. I am in love with your work!

Judi Fennell - Always fast and always spot on!

To all the readers who have supported me - My gratitude is for all you do and how much you help indie authors out of the pure love of reading.

To all the indie/hybrid authors out there who inspire, challenge, support, and push me to be better: I love you!

And to anyone who has picked up an indie book and given an unknown author a chance.

THANK YOU!

FOREIGN TRANSLATIONS

Italian Editions

L'oscurita Della Luce Serie (Darkness Vol. 1) (Darkness of Light)
Il fuoco nell'oscurità: serie (Darkness Vol. 2)
Gli abitanti dell'oscurità (Darkness Vol. 3)
Il sangue oltre le tenebre (Darkness Vol. 4)
Blood Beyond Darkness (Darkness Vol 5)
West (Darkness Vol 6
City in Embers (Collectors Vol 1)
The Barrier Between (Collectors Vol 2)
Across the Divide (Collectors Vol 3)
From Burning Ashes (Collectors Vol 4)
The Crown of Light (Lightness Saga #1)
Lightness Falls (Lightness Saga #2)
The Fall of the King (Lightness Saga #3)
Rise from the Embers (Lightness Saga #4)
Savage Lands (Savage Lands Series #1)
Pezzi di me (Shattered Love) (Blinded Love Series #1)
Broken Love (Blinded Love Series #2)
Twisted Love (Blinded Love Series #3)
Descending into Madness (Winterland Series #1)
Ascending from Madness (Winterland Series #2)
Royal Watch (Royal Watch Series #1)
Royal Command (Royal Watch Series #2)
The Unlucky Ones
Buried Alive

Portuguese Editions

Savage Lands (Savage Lands Series #1)
Wild Lands (Savage Lands Series #2)
Dead Lands (Savage Lands Series #3)
Bad Lands (Savage Lands Series #4)
Blood Lands (Savage Lands Series #5)
Shadow Lands (Savage Lands Series #6)
Silver Tongue Devil (Croygen Duet #1)
Devil in Boots (Croygen Duet #2)
Caindo na Loucura (Ascending into Madness) (Winterland
Tales Livro 1)
Saindo da Loucura (Ascending into Madness)(Winterland
Tales Livro 2)
Beauty in Her Madness (Winterland Tales #3)
Beast in His Madness (Winterland Tales #4)
Má Sorte (The Unlucky Ones)
Sob a Guarda da Realeza (Royal Watch #1)
Royal Command (Royal Watch #2)

Polish Editions

The Boy She Hates (Shattered Love)
(Broken Love)
(Twisted Love)

Czech Republic Editions

Divoká říše (Savage Lands #1)
Wild Lands #2)
Dead Lands #3)
Shattered Love #1

French Editions

Savage Lands #1
Wild Lands #2

Israel (Modern Hebrew) Editions

Savage Lands #1
Wild Lands #2
Dead Lands #3
Bad Lands #4
Blood Lands #5
Shadow Lands #6
How the Heart Breaks

Turkish Editions

Savage Lands #1
Wild Lands #2
Dead Lands #3

Russian Editions

Savage Lands #1
Wild Lands #2
Dead Lands #3
Bad Lands #4
Blood Lands #5
Shadow Lands #6